"Few writers blend mystery and the supernatural as well as Sarah Pinborough, but there are none who do it better. Quite, quite brilliant."

—John Connolly, author of *The Wrath of Angels*

PRAISE FOR
A MATTER OF BLOOD

"Those who like their fantasy dark should grab Sarah Pinborough's *A Matter of Blood*."

—*The Times* (London)

"Pinborough's fiction moves at a breakneck pace. Once you start, you can't stop. More importantly, her stories have resonance. She understands how people tick. I always trust the ride, because I know I'll wind up someplace good."

—Sarah Langan, author of *The Keeper*

"*A Matter of Blood* is one of the more successful blends of police procedural, horror and fantasy I've encountered, with an engaging and damaged main character I'd be pleased to follow further. If there's any justice, [this] will be her breakout book."

—*Locus*

"A gnarly, involving and atmospheric mystery that explores some very dark territory. It's uncomfortably timely, exceptionally well written, and shows that whatever genre she's working in, Pinborough is . . . well worth keeping an eye on."

—*SFX*

"Pinborough's characterization is extremely strong, creating believable characters that are simultaneously distinctive whilst integrated into a dynamic network of relations . . . As the first part of a trilogy, *A Matter of Blood* is extremely effective; I eagerly await the publication of the sequel, *The Shadow of the Soul* . . . If Pinborough can build upon the intensity of feeling on display at the end of this volume, the series promises to be a real treat for fans of horror and crime alike."

—*Strange Horizons*

A MATTER OF BLOOD

THE FORGOTTEN GODS: BOOK ONE

SARAH PINBOROUGH

ACE BOOKS, NEW YORK

THE BERKLEY PUBLISHING GROUP
Published by the Penguin Group
Penguin Group (USA) Inc.
375 Hudson Street, New York, New York 10014, USA

USA / Canada / UK / Ireland / Australia / New Zealand / India / South Africa / China

Penguin Books Ltd., Registered Offices: 80 Strand, London WC2R 0RL, England
For more information about the Penguin Group, visit penguin.com.

A MATTER OF BLOOD

Published by arrangement with the Orion Publishing Group.

Copyright © 2010 by Sarah Pinborough.
Ace Books are published by The Berkley Publishing Group.
ACE and the "A" design are trademarks of Penguin Group (USA) Inc.

Ace trade paperback ISBN: 978-0-425-25846-0

An application to register this book for cataloging has been submitted to the Library of Congress.

PUBLISHING HISTORY
Gollancz hardcover edition / March 2010
Ace trade paperback edition / April 2013

PRINTED IN THE UNITED STATES OF AMERICA

10 9 8 7 6 5 4 3 2 1

Cover art by Neil Holden / Arcangel.
Cover design by Lesley Worrell.

For Stephen Jones, without whose words these words
would have had a harder journey to the page.
Thanks for everything, Jonesy. x

A thoroughly good person is as
unbalanced as a thoroughly bad one.
—UNKNOWN

PROLOGUE

The orchestra of flies buzzed above the mutilated corpse. To the man watching from the doorway they looked like an unruly audience in the gallery cheering on their support. More scuttered across the macabre stage below, flitting their way amidst the heaving mass of maggots, giving the very dead individual that was their theatre pretence of movement, life. The large window against the far wall was open, but still the room stank of decay. The man in the doorway sighed and for a second the flies stopped their dreadful whine and the shiny white pupae paused in their writhing.

The body was lying on the antique wooden desk, one arm hanging limply over the side. Where the steady trickle of blood dripped silently the thick red carpet was now a much deeper crimson. There was nothing elegant in the rips across the torso tearing apart the dead man's skin and exposing organs and entrails. It must have happened fast though, the man in the doorway thought. Otherwise he'd have heard screaming.

The buzzing started again and he gritted his teeth.

"This has to stop."

The noise got louder.

He stared at the body, and the heavy workman's boots that pro-truded from the tan chinos that John MacBrayne wore whenever he was speaking on television or leading one of his ridiculously ineffec-

tive protest meetings, as if by not buying a decent suit he was making a statement against The Bank and its more controversial interests. Its alleged more controversial interests, he silently corrected himself. Still, it was clear that Mr. MacBrayne, for all his irritating tenacity, would be leading no more marches.

"I don't know what you think you're achieving," he said, "or what point you're trying to make." For the first time irritation crept into his voice. This wasn't like the last two. This was going to take some effort to clear up; John MacBrayne had become something of an unlikely public figure. He looked at the mutilated body. The deep tan from years spent in the African sun had faded now into a drained pallor. Death had taken hold and he had to admit its effects were mildly fascinating, even after all this time. He drew his attention back to the hovering insects.

"We need to meet with the others. They can help you."

For a moment the room was still again, and then the flies and maggots rose as one from the body with such force that the corpse shivered visibly before falling still. The air was alive as the swarm twisted and turned, flecks of black filling each corner of the vast room before pulling into a shape that was almost human, and for the briefest of moments, a flicker of sharp eyes and blond hair peered out from within the rippling body.

The man in the doorway smiled. That was a mistake. The unnatural figure exploded, sending flies like splinters shooting across the room. The man flinched despite himself, one arm rising slightly to protect his eyes. He lowered it slowly.

"This has to stop," he repeated against the bitter hiss of the swarm. The dark shadow didn't answer but twisted away from him and, in a cloud of tiny beating wings, escaped out through the window and into the cool afternoon air.

The man in the doorway remained where he was for a moment, thoughtfully watching it disappear, before turning his attention back to the dead man on the desk. He sighed again. He had so much to deal with, though this would be manageable, if tiresome. He looked again at the open window. First, he had a phone call to make. The room and the dead man stayed silent as he turned and quietly closed the door on them.

CHAPTER ONE

It's the little things that count.

Carla Rae's cooling body was testament to that. Her wide eyes no longer shone as the drying surfaces became sticky. With no further call to pump through the lifeless veins, her blood settled heavily in her limbs. The cheap electric clock on the bedside table ticked the minutes away, moving on from the moment of her death without even a hitching breath of hesitation. The world continued. Twenty-five-year-old Carla Rae didn't. There would be no twenty-sixth birthday. The inner mechanics of her body were accepting that, even if in the dying moments her mind had raged against the inevitability.

Tick tock. Silent body-clock stopped.

Gases began to accumulate where stomach acids were no longer working to digest the Chinese take-away she'd eaten not that many hours before. Soon, if left untouched, her flat belly would rise into a swollen ball of foul-smelling air before it escaped loudly in a last and woefully late warcry against the silence of death—but it wouldn't come to that for Carla Rae. The small pinprick in her arm, the life now growing in her eyes and the words scrawled in crimson across her naked chest would ensure a neat and clinical autopsy on a metal bed less soft than that on which she currently lay. Not that she would notice. The soft flesh that had been Carla Rae's home was beyond feeling anything at all.

* * *

The real matter of life isn't about decisions, it's about choices. Decisions are the big things; they're thought out, weighed and evaluated. Each brings a unique set of consequences, maybe good, maybe otherwise, but they're of our own making, and that is a comfort in itself. Even the bad ones we'll take on the chin, albeit quietly railing against our own stupidity. Decisions make us think we're in control.

It's the little things that count: the choices.

It's enough to drive you crazy if you let it: we don't think about choices; we just *make* them. And yet those fleeting moments are dependent on the moment or mood, and all entwined with an endless series of other choices made by people unknown. It's almost funny—if you've got that black kind of sense of humour. Little choices stories are everywhere, but they're blaming luck, or fate—they scream out from the pages of grubby tabloid newspapers and cheap TV channels. But those stories are wrong.

There is no luck. Or fate. It's your own choices that will fuck you up.

Or at least that's what DI Cass Jones was thinking as he stood in the doorway looking at the naked body face up on the untidy bed. What God-awful mistake did she make that she died here, on these stained sheets, in this shithole estate? Did she decide to walk instead of getting a cab? Did she accept a drink from the wrong almost-handsome stranger? Five minutes earlier, five minutes later—who knew where she'd be? Maybe still lying here, maybe breathing in ignorance somewhere else. It always came down to choices.

He sighed, his brown eyes bleary from a day that had already been too long. Whichever it was, the game was all over for her; now she was just one more statistic in a world that was rapidly caring less about statistics.

Outside, night was only just beginning to crack the sky, fracturing the deep blue of the dying day with streaks of orange and red, filling the small bedroom with an eerie gloom. It had been a hot day and the stale air was rank as stagnant pond water. Cass found himself breathing shallowly through his mouth.

"Can someone open a window or is that too much to ask?"

The poised camera flashed brightly over the body before the unfamiliar photographer turned, his green plastic suit rustling. "Too much to ask." He grinned, his face young and free of lines, which was enough in itself to make the detective inspector want to punch him.

"Say cheese." Before Cass could react, the bed and the figures around it became black voids haloed in white as in the gloom a haze of buzzing flies darted to safety in the corners.

"Jesus Christ!" The backs of his eyes had the scene imprinted in reverse lights and shadows before it started to fade.

"Sorry." The cameraman shrugged, still smiling. "I sometimes get this overwhelming urge to photograph someone that's living. Call me twisted."

From beside the bed, a crouched figure rose. "And if you carry on like that, it'll be only the living you're working with—if you're lucky to be working at all." The voice was acid-sharp and the young man visibly shrivelled into his plastic coating as he gurgled a muted apology.

"Now piss off and take those cameras back to the van." He was still unimpressed.

DI Jones stared at the junior examiner as he squeezed awkwardly past, two cameras in one hand, the heavy protective case in the other. When he was trapped somewhere between Cass's shoulder and the doorframe, the DI leaned forward.

"If I ever hear that picture's been developed, I'll be looking for you." For a brief moment, Cass was sure he could hear the boy's heart pause. "Do you understand?"

The assistant nodded vigorously and Cass shifted half an inch to his left and let him go.

He watched him wearily, for a moment overwhelmed by the sheer stupidity of youth, as the boy rapidly disappeared into the mêlée of SOCOs filling the rest of the flat. He needed to learn his place, and he also needed to learn that DI Cass Jones wasn't known for his perky sense of humour. And, more importantly for the assistant, neither was

Dr. Mark Farmer. In the current lack-of-jobs market there was no room for stupid mistakes, and one day, when he was older and wiser, he might realise that Cass had done him a favour.

"New assistant?"

"My penance for training the last one up so well." The ME pulled his hood back, thick silver curls springing free across his head and down to his shoulders, turning him from coroner to ageing rock star in one swift movement. He frowned. "What are you doing here, Jones? This isn't your case."

"It is now." The air trapped by the nailed-down window seemed denser, almost clinging to the body like a mourning relative. It felt like day-old cigarette smoke against the roof of Cass's mouth as he said, "Bowman was rushed to hospital this morning with a suspected burst appendix. Looks like he could be out of action for weeks, so his case-load's been passed on to me. No extra pay, of course."

"Of course." The ME shrugged. "Although peritonitis is nasty. He's lucky to be alive."

"No luck involved: the stupid bastard's been complaining about feeling like shit for a couple of weeks. He should have gone and got it sorted ages ago. It's not like the police don't still get NHS."

"Ah yes, the perks of being a civil servant." The coroner looked ready to launch into his usual bitter commentary on the state of Britain, the world and life-everlasting should he be given even the slightest hint of encouragement, but Cass, with little interest in politics and even less in Farmer's particular viewpoint, refused to be drawn, forcing the ME to fall silent. Cass was too tired and pissed off to be a willing sounding board, and the stench in the room was such that surely they all wanted to be free of it as soon as possible.

He peered at the girl's naked body. The poor cow's ribs jutted upwards over her concave stomach in a way that suggested either poverty or an advanced eating disorder. Given the cheap dye job on her almost-ginger hair, perhaps an attempt at blonde, Cass figured the former. Her large nipples were now simply islands of pink on the tiny curves that were almost breasts. Would she be any less flat-chested standing upright? He doubted it.

"What is this? Number four?"

The ME stood alongside him. "Yes—at least we can presume so. I'll confirm when I get the toxicology results back after the PM. You're going to have some catching up to do if you want half a chance of solving this one. I'll send all my notes over to you. I presume your sergeant's still getting *debriefed* by Bowman's sergeant? So she should have a good idea of what's going on. Or is that over now?"

Cass was surprised. Farmer wasn't normally one for loaded remarks, at least outside of those that served to support his delicate left-wing sensibilities. For once, Cass would have preferred that; Claire May's private life was none of Farmer's business. He ignored the question, saying, "May's staying on the Jackson and Miller case and I'm keeping Blackmore on this one. Stupid to switch them over as I'm working both. If I change them we'll all be confused rather than just me."

His fingers itched for the feel of a cigarette and a quiet space to just empty his mind and breathe. It had been a bitch of a day, and he figured Farmer's hadn't been much better. Resources were tight and everyone was overworked. The image of the smiling bobby on the beat had been murdered long ago. His unsmiling eyes scanned the bed's contents.

The young woman's skin was pale, with no hint of tan lines, either fresh, or the final fading memories of a holiday long gone. An empty ache touched the pit of his stomach. It wasn't quite pity, but it was close enough. Neither he nor the doc had had as bad a day as the dead girl in front of them.

NOTHING IS SACRED was daubed across the top of her chest, below her angular collarbones and above her poor excuse for breasts. Somehow that thick crimson splatter made her death even more pathetic than the dingy flat ever could. *Nothing is sacred.*

"You're telling me, mate," he muttered under his breath, directing the words at the ghost of the stranger who'd stood where he was standing now, intently painting the letters onto the dead woman's cooling flesh, no doubt thinking he was doing something profound. Cass Jones knew better. There was no message in murder; this was just some sick bastard making excuses for his choices.

"How long's she been dead?"

"A few hours. He may have had her here longer, but I'd say he killed her around about midday or one o'clock."

"Who found her?" Cass was surprised anyone had found her at all. Most of the flats in this block were either condemned, with squatters in, or inhabited by the kind of people that had no concern for their neighbours.

"He wanted her found. There was a boombox on, playing some kind of thrash metal music; he must have put it on just as he left. It was loud enough to piss off the people on either side. They kicked the door in around four and then called the police. And here we are."

"And here we are," Cass repeated softly. A thin bracelet that probably wasn't real gold hung from the wrist that flopped over the side of the bed, a miniature horse hanging from it. Her lucky charm? "What about her eyes?" he asked. They looked normal enough, but he wasn't the expert.

"I'll let you know once I've taken a look under the microscope. I can't see properly in this light. She's not been dead long enough for them to develop, but I'm presuming she's the same as the others."

Cass figured the doctor was right. "Who was she?"

"Her name's Carla Rae. Your lot have her purse and bag. Her ID card was in it. She's twenty-five, unemployed, unmarried. She was a nothing. A nobody." On the other side of the bed, the ME gathered the tools of his trade together. "I'm done here. I'll get the body-baggers in and get her back to the lab. Should have an initial report for you by end of play tomorrow."

Crouched by the bed, Cass nodded slightly. *A nobody. A nothing.* For the first time in their long association, the DI realised that perhaps he didn't like the ME all that much. He doubted Carla Rae would have either. A small bruise had bloomed around the tiny pinprick in her arm and he froze for a moment, wondering whether he could feel her calling out for answers.

Outside, street lamps flickered into humming existence. Cass sucked in a lungful of the woman's death before standing up and stepping back so the paramedics could roll her into the black zip-up. He glanced at his watch, the numbers glowing naggingly back at him, and his heart speeded up; shit. He needed to kick his lethargy back into touch. It was just gone five-thirty and he had to be in Soho in thirty minutes' time. It was his day to collect.

The dying embers of the day clung to the skyline, and peering blearily out through the windscreen Cass wondered if maybe the world might truly be in the grip of some insanity that was slowly hugging it closer and refusing to let go. *Things were going to get better.* That's what the newspapers and perfectly presented newsreaders kept repeating. Cass couldn't see it though. As far as he could tell, they were all sinking deeper and deeper into the shit, and no one had a rope to cling to, let alone a shovel big enough to dig them out. And as the world got crazier, so did the rules, leading to situations like this one, which had him heading into Soho for a transaction all the bosses over at Scotland Yard must know about but obviously preferred to ignore. Maybe they liked to pretend their shit didn't stink the same as everyone else's.

But then, he figured, lighting a cigarette as the traffic crawled towards the inevitable central London almost-gridlock, what did he know? He'd been wallowing in the brown stuff for longer than he cared to remember. Smoke filled the confined space and he grinned, enjoying it more because it was illegal to be smoking inside the car. Understanding the thrill of breaking rules was what made Cass Jones such a good policeman. Despite his disgruntled colleagues' assertions that Cass was just lucky when it came to solving his cases, he knew luck had nothing to do with it. Cass was a good copper because he thought like a criminal, and that was all there was to it. He took another long drag before winding down the window, letting the smoke escape to join the other poisonous fumes belching out from the vehicles shuffling their way through the centre of town. The air reeked of life.

The heaviness he'd felt watching the dead woman's body being bagged up finally lifted as the car filled with the earthy noises of the city. There wasn't a place in the world to beat London Town. It was grimy and gritty and cold and damp, but it was a tough old place that had survived for centuries; the ghosts of the past lurked on every street in the shape of the buildings and the plaques that proudly declared their long-gone residents, bolstering the living with the solid anchor of their heritage. It would take a lot to bring London and her Londoners to their knees. They might be buckling under the recession, but the city would find a way to bring them all through. It always did.

He flicked the butt out of the window and thought of Carla Rae again. London's residents now at least had the prospect of a serial killer to look forward to. There had been four dead women found in the same circumstances in the space of two months, and in these straitened times, where bad news of some sort or another filled the papers every day, the press wouldn't pass up a juicy story like this once they'd joined the dots. At least once this was splattered across the pages of the tabloids it might distract the masses from their own misery for a while. Once they'd devoured the details of the deaths—the *murders*—of those less fortunate, then out of the woodwork would come everyone who'd ever known them, or dated them, or been in the same bar, or who'd just always had the feeling that fate would not be kind. Everyone loved the thrill of *it could have been me*. It made them feel lucky, when of course there was no luck. There were only choices.

Cass didn't care that people would get a thrill from the death of Carla Rae; that was only human nature. What he cared about was that the press didn't get hold of too much information. The words scrawled across the women's chests, *that* they could have. But the eyes were different. They needed to hold back those details if they were ever going to weed out the crazies who would be lining up to confess as soon as the papers hit the stands.

It was nearly an hour after leaving the tower block in Newham that he finally edged the Audi out past a bus and pulled into Denman Street. The narrow street just off the Piccadilly end of Shaftesbury Avenue was a tiny vein almost lost in the heart of the city, but as with most things, appearances were deceptive. He left his car in the cramped and ridiculously overpriced NCP car park and walked the few steps in the cooling air to the discreet entrance to Moneypenny's, one of Artie Mullins' nightclubs, and checked his watch again. He was still late.

Cass pushed the button by the door and then looked up at the small camera attached almost invisibly at the corner of the building. A moment later the buzzer sounded and he was inside, jogging down the stairs to the basement club. Below the street it could be any time of day or night, and there was something about that which appealed to Cass. Time stood still away from the hustle and bustle of the city and the rise and fall of the sun, and that allowed a sense of freedom, even if it was only a short-lived flight of the imagination.

"You're late." Arthur—Artie to his friends—Mullins sat at the long bar, sipping beer from a tall glass. "If it was any other fucker I might think they weren't coming." He grinned, one gold cap flashing against the tarred brown of the rest of his teeth. "Not you though, Jones. I think you'd collect even if some bastard had taken your kneecaps out." He stood up and pulled out a second stool. "Beer?"

Cass nodded and sat down. "Sorry. It's been one of those days."

"Aren't they all?" Like most of London's hard men, Artie had spent a lot of time body-building in gyms in the past and his thickset frame looked out of place behind the slick modern bar. As he bent over, Cass could make out the start of a paunch under his polo shirt. Cass wasn't fooled by it. Artie might be pushing sixty, with his gym days well behind him, but he was still one of the most dangerous men in the criminal underworld. Cass liked him, though. He couldn't help himself.

Artie pulled a bottle of Beck's from the row of illuminated fridges beneath the mirrored back bar and popped the lid off before handing it across. "Here you go. Same as normal."

"Thanks." Cass left the thick brown manila envelope on the marble surface. He wouldn't bother counting it—Artie Mullins was no mug. He wouldn't rip off the police.

"It's a funny old world we're in, isn't it?" Artie's face cracked into a grin that sent a shockwave of wrinkles across his leathered face. It was the same comment he always made on pick-up days, and as usual Cass couldn't think of an answer. He clinked his bottle with Artie's and took a long swallow. It *was* a funny world. There was no denying that.

Back in 2011, as the government realised that there was no way the country could financially sustain itself, the real no-holds-barred cutbacks began. They didn't even bother trying to dress them up. The

NHS virtually disappeared for all except the chosen few sectors of society. No state pensions for anyone over forty-five—and those that were already paying out were to be cut back to the minimum. Police pay became performance-related: the more arrests that led to convictions, the more you got paid. Although still running in principle, in reality that initiative worked for about a week, because the gap between arrest and conviction was often months, even years, and the paperwork took forever to fill in and keep track of.

They all still claimed it when they could, because of course arrests and convictions were still being made, but then someone came up with a more reliable way of getting paid. The police chiefs sitting in their ivory towers and dreaming up these half-arsed schemes chose to ignore the fact that it was much easier for the rank and file to take their performance-related pay in cash from men like Arthur "Artie" Mullins, a tax-free cash bonus for simply not arresting certain people; in effect, for leaving the firms alone. Cass always thought of it as a non-performance-related pay scheme.

In the main, most coppers—Cass among them—were happy to take it. No one wanted to spend their days chasing low-life scum just so they could earn a decent wage. There would always be people out there selling drugs, and even more that wanted to buy them, and yes, they could drive themselves into early graves chasing them all endlessly, but what would be the point? There was always someone else more than happy to take over, and as far as Cass was concerned, they could carry right on with their business, as long as they didn't start making things dangerous for mainstream society.

The world wasn't fair. Instead, like Cass, it was just tired—but when those firms stepped across the line and let their business affect the ordinary world of the nine-to-fivers, then he felt his blood rise and the policeman in him came to life. And as long as that didn't happen, the system worked just fine and everyone was happy.

"Today's been in a league of its own." The beer was cool and it left a refreshingly bitter after-taste at the back of his throat.

"Yeah?" On the other side of the bar, Artie watched him. "They still got you coming after me for the murder of those two boys?" His eyes were hard. "Not that I have to ask. I've developed a case of permanent plainclothes shadow. It's a right pain in the arse when I'm trying to do business. I should sue you lot for loss of income."

Cass shrugged and Artie smiled. Beneath the surface warmth, there was something of the shark in it.

"Funny how my money buys safety for my employers, but not for me, isn't it?"

"You know the bonus doesn't cover that kind of shit. They might have been aiming for Macintyre, but whoever shot those kids broke the rules. All bets are off in this case."

There was a pause and Artie sipped his beer, then looked at Cass thoughtfully over the rim of the glass. For his own part, Cass lit a cigarette and then met the man's gaze. He was tired and all he wanted to do was go and shower Carla Rae's death away, but he'd known this conversation was on the cards. The boys had been gunned down the week before, and all fingers pointed to Artie Mullins. For those screaming for a quick arrest, Artie was the obvious choice. Sam Macintyre was becoming quite a force among the firms, and he was a clear rival to Artie's rule. It was pretty obvious that he had been the drive-by shooter's target, even though it was the two kids, who just happened to be passing by, who ended up bleeding to death on the pavement. The whole thing was a fuck-up and everyone was screaming for a name, the press, the commissioner, even the rival firms. Both sides of the law wanted it sorted quickly so they could get a swift return to the status quo.

"What's *your* view though, Detective Inspector?" Artie put his glass down. "You think I did it?"

"No." Cass met his gaze. "Not your style." He meant it too. Artie Mullins had been around a long time. If he'd wanted Sam Macintyre taken out, he wouldn't have done it Hollywood Mafia style. "Not that my opinion counts for much," he added. "I'm only the officer in charge. My job is just to do as I'm told and take the shit if we don't catch someone."

"It counts to me." The cold glint had left Artie's sunken eyes and Cass felt a small knot untie in his stomach. He wasn't ashamed of being slightly afraid of Arthur Mullins. It was probably a healthy response.

"I don't want Macintyre dead." Artie sniffed. "Not yet anyway.

He's ambitious, but that's not always a bad thing. And the Irish are better than the Yardies. That lot don't have any code. And if I *did* want him sorted, then I wouldn't have done it so fucking loudly. I'd have taken him out somewhere private—somewhere he wouldn't be found."

Cass nodded. "That's what I figured. But you're the top dog, Artie. They all think it's you. You're the one who's potentially got the most to lose by Macintyre's rise."

"Then you're going to have to convince them otherwise." Artie winked. "Although they've got no evidence it was me, so they can hang off my arse and follow me around for as long as they want. Suits me fine—saves me sorting myself out some extra protection while persuading the Irish this was nothing to do with me."

"But if it wasn't you, it was still someone. Those two kids are still dead."

Artie nodded. He leaned forward, keeping his voice low so that his drawn-out north London mumble was almost a growl. "I'm no grass, Jonesy, everyone knows that, but if I had something on this one, trust me, I'd give it to you. We've had a nice little balance since we started the arrangement between you lot and us lot. We get on with our business and you get on with yours." He shook his head.

"I'd never have gone for a hit like that. Not in a public place with schoolkids around. The way I see it is you'd have to be one of three things to take a pop at someone like that: plain stupid, a lunatic, or too powerful to care about the consequences."

Cass wasn't sure if it was the dim lighting or whether a dark shadow passed across Artie's face. It was almost like a flash of fear, but Cass found that hard to believe. Who was there for Artie Mullins to be afraid of in the London underworld? The moment passed and the old gangster smiled. "And I may be a bit of all three, but not enough of any one of them to make this my doing." He paused. "I rest my case, your honour."

"I'll tell them that back at the station. I'm sure they'll take your word for it."

Artie laughed, and then coughed, the rattle in his chest declaring a lifetime of too many cigarettes and not enough fresh air. "You do that." He waited till the small fit had passed. "So if you haven't been trying to nick my arse today what's been keeping you so busy?"

"They think Bowman's bloody appendix has burst. I've got to cover his cases until he gets back, but fuck knows when that will be." He shook his head. "So now I'm working two murder cases and all because that bloody jobsworth didn't want to take a couple of days away from his desk."

He drained his beer and picked up the brown envelope before getting up from his stool. "I'd better go. It's going to be an early start in the morning and I'm not designed for dawn." He tucked the money inside his jacket. The plainclothes officers who were no doubt watching the club would know what he was doing here, but there was no point in making it too obvious. Appearances were everything.

"I'll do my best to get them off your back, Artie, but all I can advise is sit tight. We've got no evidence leading back to you, so you know how it goes. Keep up the 'no comment' line if we pull you in and they'll have to back off in the end."

"I know the drill. Done it often enough over the years." He grinned. "Now fuck off before the girls start turning up or you'll never leave."

Cass smiled, although he could feel it was slightly sheepish. He knew his own weaknesses, but he wasn't sure how much he liked other people spotting them that easily. It sometimes felt to Cass that he'd spent his life trying to mould himself into a good man, and in most ways he'd managed, but when it came to the opposite sex, the leopard couldn't quite get rid of those spots. He'd almost given up trying.

"We all have our sins, Artie. I've learned to live with mine."

"That's what I like about you, Jonesy. You know your shit smells the same as mine." Cass headed back towards the stairs and the pavement, where time had been slowly ticking by.

"You know, if you ever get bored paying taxes and fancy a change of sides you've always got a job working with me."

Cass laughed and waved, but didn't answer. He took the stairs two at a time and was happy to get out into the cool night air. In some ways, Artie wasn't that different from the police commissioner. What neither understood was that he just couldn't see things in terms of sides any more. It was just everyone doing their thing, and the way Cass saw it, he sat somewhere in the middle. If he ever had been on the good side, he'd lost that place ten years ago when he was undercover. Everyone knew that. There was no going back, no matter how much they all pretended. All things considered, he was pretty happy that he'd learned to live with it.

CHAPTER TWO

The envelope pressed uncomfortably against his chest as he slid behind the wheel of the Audi and he tossed it onto the seat beside him before letting out a long sigh and shutting his aching eyes for a brief second. It was finally time to go home. He wished the thought raised more joy in his heart. He briefly considered stopping somewhere for a drink on the way back to Muswell Hill, but decided against it. There were only so many more disappointed looks he could take from Kate, and only so much guilt he could stomach. On top of that, he now had two high-profile murder cases to solve, with not a single lead for one, and a lot of catching up to do on the other; drink wasn't the answer, not right now.

He drove out of the small street and navigated through Soho. Although rush hour was virtually over, central London was still a mesh of traffic and people weaving in and out of each other; pedestrians and vehicles moving at an almost identical speed in their haste to reach their destinations. No one looked happy; most just looked drained. Lights dazzled from the shop fronts of the Georgian buildings on either side of Regent Street and streaked across his windscreen, vying for attention with the headlights of the oncoming traffic. They blurred the people hurrying around his unmoving car, needing to get home so the same routine could start again tomorrow.

No wonder crime was rising. There were no thrills to be found in simple pleasures any more. The passers-by were all filled with a grim determination that few journeys home warranted, and none of them took a moment to look up at the strange wonder of the city that glittered around them. They had no time to marvel at the magnitude of the task the builders had set themselves, or the beauty that had been wrought without a single piece of machinery, just imagination and determination. DI Cass Jones knew that in the main he was a miserable bastard, but he always looked up. Funny that it had been a gangster not dissimilar to Artie Mullins who'd taught him that—and just in time for when he really needed it.

As he shook the memory away, the picture of Carla Rae's lifeless body rose up in his mind to fill the space. Her last night had slipped by and she'd probably not even taken a moment to enjoy it. It was unlikely she'd paused to see the beauty of the bright lights competing with the stars to keep the world safe. She wouldn't have savoured the cold air in her lungs, or the goosebumps dancing on her arms as she did whatever she did that led her to that filthy Newham flat. He doubted she had ever realised just how wonderful being alive really was. Maybe she did, just before the darkness claimed her.

His phone vibrated and he tugged it free. It was Claire May, his sergeant. His eyes ached looking at the glowing name. She rarely called him just for a chat any more. Maybe it wasn't time to go home after all. He pressed the green answer key and held it to his ear.

"Yep."

"Hey, boss. Are you home yet?"

"I should be so lucky. I'm on my way though. Why?"

"Something's arrived at the station for you. I think you should see it straight away. I've been trying to ring you for half an hour, but your phone's been going straight to answer phone."

"I had someone to meet."

There was the slightest hesitation before Claire spoke again. "Oh yeah. Of course."

"What is it?" Cass didn't have time for Claire's discomfort with the pick-up. She took her money like the rest because she was bright enough to not rock the boat. They'd had a brief relationship, when he and Kate had split up briefly, and he'd tried to get her to see that the world wasn't black and white but a multitude of glittering greys. He hadn't quite succeeded. She was too young. A few more years of policing would wisen her up.

"It was delivered by hand. It's a DVD. The picture's pretty bad, but it's a film of the Jackson and Miller shootings."

The city lights brightened in a surge of adrenalin and his tiredness was gone in a snap. "I'll be there in ten. And get the envelope and whatever else came with it down to forensics. See if we can get some prints or DNA or something."

He dropped his phone on the passenger seat and put his foot down, weaving through the traffic past Oxford Circus and onto the Marylebone Road back to Paddington Green Police Station, ignoring the men in bright jackets setting up the kerbside barriers for the protest march the next morning. Cass wasn't even sure what this one was supposed to be about, and since that bastard MacBrayne had gone missing a few months back, the various protest groups seemed to have lost their way. Maybe they had a point, and maybe they didn't. Cass was too busy fighting person-on-person crimes to start worrying about corporate ones.

The phone rang again and he pushed the answer button as he held it to his ear, not pausing to check the screen.

"What else, Claire?"

"Cass?" A heavy breath filled his ear, as if the person on the other end hadn't expected him to answer it. "Is that you? I've been trying to reach you for days."

Cass gritted his teeth. Christian. This he really didn't need. He should have checked the caller ID.

"Sorry, mate. Things are more insane than normal round here at the moment. I'm heading back to the station. I can't talk now, something big's come up on one of the cases I'm working."

"Look, we really need to talk, Cass. I mean it."

His brother sounded funny. He was always softly spoken, but tonight his voice had a sharp edge to it. What was it? Fear? Cass felt his heart tighten. Whatever it was, it didn't change the fact that he had no desire to talk to Christian. Not now. If he were honest with himself, he'd happily go the rest of his life without speaking to his younger brother again. Their parents had died five years ago and he'd managed to pretty much avoid him since then, other than the occasional birthday or family lunch he hadn't been able to wriggle out of. And then a few months ago Christian's son Luke had collapsed at school, and his little brother had needed more support. They'd spoken occasionally since then, but Cass knew he hadn't really given Christian much in the way of a shoulder to lean on. That wasn't in him, not now.

"Is this to do with Luke?" he asked finally. "Kate said he was okay now? Isn't he?"

There was another pause. "No, it's not Luke. Not as such. I don't want to talk about it like this. Not while you're driving."

He knows. The thought peeled strips of Cass's heart away in serrated chunks. *After all this time, she's finally told him.*

"Well, I can't talk now." He heard the snap in his own words. "Why don't you call me at home later. Give it an hour or so?"

A sigh of relief rushed through the handset. "Thanks, Cass. Thanks. I didn't know who else to talk to. You will be there, won't you? This . . . I don't think this can wait."

"Just give me an hour. Call around eight."

"It's . . ." Christian hesitated. "It's about redemption. That's the key." He was talking softly, as if someone might be listening. "Redemption and corruption."

"Call me at home. I've got to go." Cass ended the call before his brother had finished his sentence, aware of his own lie. There was no way he was going to be home by eight. He'd ring him back tomorrow. Maybe. If Luke was fine then he didn't feel so bad. Whatever else was going on in Christian's life, or head, he was a big enough boy now to deal with it by himself. They hadn't been like brothers in a long time. Lights glared at him as they passed. Redemption? As far as Cass could tell he was beyond that. Maybe Christian was starting to live up to his name and their father's expectation. Maybe he'd found God. Cass's eyes burned with the grit of exhaustion. Well, good luck to him, but he could leave Cass well and truly out of it.

The inside of Paddington Green Police Station was just as austere as its ugly 1960s exterior. Although it was no longer the national base for interrogating high-profile terrorist suspects, it was still the most secure police station in London, and was occasionally used as an overflow unit for when the Anti-Terror Division, normally based at the new Centre for National Security, needed a second location (generally for reasons they chose not to share).

Cass could live with that, however much it pissed off the bosses. Even though they'd lost a great deal of their forensic equipment to the CNS when it opened, Paddington Green still had more technology available than the rest of the city. If the chief super and those above him couldn't see past their dented egos to recognise that fact, then more fool them.

The brightly lit corridors had emptied somewhat, the admin staff and constables having signed off and become part of that mêlée of faceless people filling the streets outside, but as Cass headed upstairs to the open-plan Murder Squad floor there were plenty of plainclothes detectives milling around the building. They were like him: the career policemen.

He found Claire May in his office at the back of the area that was now his Incident Room, for four women's deaths as well as two boys. Tomorrow he'd get the teams to divide the space up and bring in the boards from the serial killer case—they couldn't pretend it wasn't a serial killer any more, not now—and set them up at the other end of the room from the Jackson and Miller ones. Moving the boards from Bowman's domain would help—he was fucked if he was going to keep running backwards and forwards between the two units like a headless chicken. He wanted everything right where he could see it. His brain worked better that way. He smiled at the pretty brunette who was concentrating so hard she hadn't even seen him come in.

"How are you liking the boss's chair? Comfy?"

Claire looked up from the computer screen and smiled. It was a warm, open expression, and Cass hoped no one would ever take it away from her. No doubt someone eventually would, but he was glad that he hadn't been that man. What had happened between them had been short and sweet, but it hadn't been about love. Not romantic love, at any rate.

"The seat's a bit big for me, but I guess that would be your middle-aged spread."

For the first time that day, Cass laughed. "Let's hope you're still this gorgeous at my age. Now shift and show me what we've got."

She'd been right. The picture was grainy and the absence of sound gave the black and white film an eerie quality. He watched it in silence through to the end, then said softly, "Play it again."

Claire clicked the mouse and the frozen scene once again burst into life. Formosa Street was part of Little Venice, not far from Paddington Green Station itself, and although a number of shops and restaurants were now closed, it was in a wealthy enough part of town that many of the bistro-style cafés and boutiques were still in business. There was no timeline on the film, but Cass didn't need it. The shootings had taken place at 3:45 p.m. on Monday, 9 March. Whoever was filming must have started not long before that. The cameraman had positioned himself—or herself—on the other side of the road, at street level. Maybe he was in a car with the window wound down, or just standing in a shop doorway; it was hard to tell. The tech boys could figure that out.

Cass peered at the moving image, trying to absorb as much as possible. In the background the colour of the maroon awning of the Café de la Seine seeped away to dark grey. Through the glass he could make out customers at the front tables, a waitress in a white blouse moving between them, the only clearly defined shape in the gloom. A man's hand rose as he sipped his coffee, his cufflinks glinting against the window. Cass switched his attention to the pavement. Pedestrians strolled along the narrow path, pausing to peer into the shops on either side. The range of the camera was limited and Cass fought his frustration; this was the best lead they'd had so far. He needed to make the most of it.

A heavyset middle-aged woman paused in front of the café and pointed at the cake display. She spoke to her friend for a moment, they both laughed and the thinner one dragged her away. Cass's heartbeat quickened. There were only seconds to go now. A black cab passed, slowing, and Cass figured that was the one Macintyre had arrived in. Somewhere out of shot he was paying the driver and getting out. At least now they had a chance of getting the licence plate, since no one had come forward yet. The case was thin on witnesses, despite so many on the screen in front of him. It wasn't any surprise to anyone on the investigative team. The firms weren't to be messed with. Even ordinary citizens understood that enough not to get themselves involved.

Macintyre strolled into view. He paused at the right-hand side of the café and lit a cigarette. At six foot four, the thirty-eight-year-old Belfast man was an imposing figure, but for the briefest second there Cass hadn't recognised him. His trademark gingery-blond hair was hidden under a trendy black hat and he wore dark glasses. Cass couldn't remember if it had been sunny on the ninth. He needed that checked. It looked like whatever Macintyre was doing in Little Venice that day, he hadn't wanted to be recognised. His leather jacket looked soft and expensive. He took two long pulls on the cigarette cupped in his right hand before glancing around and taking a couple of steps forward.

On the left-hand side of the screen the two boys appeared. Justin Jackson and John Miller, both twelve years old, had left Our Lady Catholic Secondary School on Senior Street at three-thirty to walk home to their houses on Warrington Crescent, off Clifton Gardens. Cutting through Formosa Street was part of their usual route.

Cass watched as Miller swung his PE bag against the back of Jackson's knees and the other boy returned the favour. They both looked at each other and laughed, their mouths moving quickly. Cass figured he could get the speech boys to look at what they were saying, but it was probably just teenage jokes and insults. They were private words. They were the boys' last words.

A car drew up in the middle of the road and even with no sound on the film Cass was sure he could hear the screech of those tyres. From within the car, the tip of a semi-automatic rifle emerged from the open window on the far side. Nothing of the person holding it was revealed. Macintyre threw his cigarette down and then visibly started as he stared at the car. His mouth opened and he was already dropping to the ground as the boys passed by in front of him, still laughing as they blocked his body.

After that, everything happened fast. Jackson, the black one, was standing on the right, on the road side of the pavement. He fell first. Cass watched the laughter fade from John Miller's face as his friend fell into him, propelled by the power of the bullets hitting his body. Though Miller was trying to hold him up, Jackson fell to the ground. Cass could see the blood staining Miller's hands. The boy didn't move, frozen in shock, as shapes inside the gloomy coffee shop darted madly about. Customers ran to the back, many probably scurrying out of the rear exit. They must have done. There were far more cups and plates left on the tables than witnesses who stayed to give their statements to the police.

Macintyre was no longer visible. He'd crawled under a car to wait the shooting out. The car was already pulling off when the final round of bullets hit John Miller, standing stupefied over his best friend's crumpled body. He was thrown backwards into the Café de la Seine, landing on the remains of the shattered glass door, looking almost as if he was trying to climb in.

The car had sped away, its number plate covered, as Cass expected it would be. Somewhere not very far away from the chaos they'd left behind in Formosa Street, the failed assassins would be swiftly dealing with the vehicle. It was probably destroyed by now. Not that it would stop Cass's team from looking for it. There were few enough leads without giving up on the car. Who knew? They might even find it. Stranger things had happened.

Formosa Street was silent. Shoppers were emerging from wherever they'd hidden themselves when the attack started, moving slowly, all focused on the two dead boys. One woman dropped her shopping bags and turned and screamed, her mouth forming a large O. Macintyre reappeared onscreen, dusting himself down as he got to his feet, his hat now in his hand. And then the one small piece of good news in this case came into frame.

A local beat copper, Jack Charter, had been patrolling the streets around the schools because shopkeepers had reported thefts of sweets and magazines by groups of kids; some of the shopkeepers had even claimed Miller and Jackson were among the culprits, but no newspaper would touch that. The boys were angels with the Angels, according to the tabloids. Cass thought they were probably just ordinary boys who weren't above nicking the odd Mars Bar, and he thought that made their deaths even more tragic. An old ache stabbed at his soul and he pushed it away. This wasn't the time.

On the screen, Charter ran into the shot and grabbed Macintyre's arm. Before he knew it, the boss of west London was handcuffed to a local uniform. He wouldn't be going anywhere without taking the policeman with him. Cass liked that constable. He'd go a long way, thinking like that. The fight visibly went out of Macintyre and his shoulders slumped. Cass recognised the sigh of a man who knew he had a good few uncomfortable hours of "no comment" ahead of him.

A small crowd had gathered around the dead bodies and all Cass could see was a sports kit bag lying in the road, its drawstring done up tight. The picture cut abruptly to a fuzzy haze. Whoever had been filming had obviously decided they'd seen enough.

Cass sighed and leaned back in his chair. "That's not one we want the parents seeing. I think they can probably live without that." The families had obviously taken the deaths of their sons badly, and now, probably tomorrow, he was going to have to go see them again. At least he could tell them that there'd been some developments. He couldn't send anyone else to do it; the families were his responsibility and they needed to see the person in charge, but he wasn't looking forward to seeing their pain, still red-raw and bleeding.

Claire perched on the edge of the desk. She crossed one leg over the other and as she leaned back on one arm, Cass couldn't help but watch her. At twenty-seven, she was an undeniably good-looking woman, but he thought that by the time she hit thirty-five, she'd probably be beautiful. Her brunette curls were pulled back in what had probably started the morning as her usual sensible tight bun. He wondered if she realised how attractive she really was.

She tucked a loose curl behind her ear. "Who do you think filmed it?"

"God knows. Maybe someone who wanted evidence of the hit? Maybe someone set Macintyre up and wanted to film it for posterity."

"But why then send it to us?"

Cass shrugged and stared at the silently crackling screen. "Well, the quality's not good. It's maybe a copy of a copy. Anyone who wanted the truth to out could have sent it. Let's face it, it's not as if the firms are ever short of people willing to double-cross them for the right money." He looked up at her. "I'm going to make a copy, then this one can go down to forensics. I take it you didn't stick your prints all over it when you took it out?"

"There may be one or two partials at the edges, but nothing the lab can't work around. I was careful, but I thought it was more important we see what was on it."

"Good. But now I want every tiny scrap of evidence we can get off the surface. There must something in there to tell us who sent it. You've sent the envelope down?"

"Yes, straight away. They were just heading home. It's logged for testing and printing first thing tomorrow."

"Okay. I've got to get up to speed on these murders of Bowman's first thing in the morning. By the time I've done that we should know something about how this got to us. And then I can go and see the parents again. At least this time I'll have something vaguely positive to tell them."

For a moment the image of the dead boys blurred into Carla Rae's body, still lingering at the back of his eyes. The shootings had happened a week before, and Cass had seen the ruined bodies on the slab, and plenty of pictures of the boys when they were alive and smiling. Seeing the transition from one to the other played out onscreen in front of him was a different matter. The sudden change from life to death, wrought in an instant, was something he'd never get used to—which was ironic, really, given the number of times he saw it happening behind his eyes. An event from a different time and a different place, maybe, but the transition from living to dead was just the same. Maybe it was something no one ever got used to. His head ached. A beer, a shower and then sleep. That was what he needed: to lose himself for a few hours.

He looked up at Claire's open face. He too had heard the rumour that she was dating Blackmore, but he could see the torch she still carried for him shining in her eyes from time to time. She'd not reproached him when he'd told her he was getting back together with Kate. She'd said it was the right thing to do, after all they'd been through together. There was something beautiful about Claire May's goodness, even if she was a little naïve. It would be so good to dip into that, to take comfort from the feel of her living warmth wrapped around him, just for a few moments. Claire was young enough to believe that love could cure all your ills. He didn't agree. He'd long ago learned that it was far more likely that your ills would kill your love—but the power of Claire's belief was enough to make the world a better place, if only for a short while.

He leaned back in his chair and let the moment pass. It was just a small fantasy, nothing more. Their brief relationship was long in the past, and they were finally getting back onto some kind of less-awkward footing with each other. And then of course there was Blackmore. The last thing he needed was a moment of self-indulgence fucking up the relationship between the two teams that, for now at least, had to work together.

He smiled at her. "You've done good, Sergeant. Now get yourself home. Your overtime's in for today."

"So's yours, just in case you've forgotten. What time did you get in this morning? Six?"

Cass nodded. It had actually been before five-thirty, but he had no intention of letting his sergeant know that. "I couldn't sleep. And anyway, I'm a DI. The force gets to own your soul when you get up the ladder. Haven't you figured that out yet?"

She laughed lightly. "I sometimes wonder if you still have one, Cass Jones."

Her words were only a joke, but they echoed inside him. "And now you know." He forced a grin. "They keep them all locked away down in Evidence. I just hope when I retire they don't give me bloody Bowman's soul back by mistake."

"Oh, he's not so bad."

"And you're too nice. He's an arrogant prick. But you'll figure that out one day, trust me."

They paused, divided by his cynicism and her belief in the best in people. It worked well when they were on a case, one often seeing something the other had missed, but in personal discussions it inevitably ended in stalemate.

Cass slapped the desk. "Off you go. I'll take another look through this and copy it before taking it down to Evidence to hold until morning."

"If you're sure." She gave him a smile.

"I'm sure. Get some rest. I'll see you here at seven sharp. We've got a busy day ahead of us."

"Slave driver!" She gave him a playful wink before disappearing down the corridor. He watched her switch the lights off in the empty Incident Room and vanish into the darkness before he returned his attention to the screen.

He'd saved the footage to his USB pen and was watching it through for the third time when there was a light knock on the door and Mat Blackmore peered in.

"Sorry to disturb, sir. Is Sergeant May still around?"

"She's gone home. About twenty minutes ago. How's Bowman?"

"Okay, I think. They were doing some exploratory stuff last time I called. Haven't had an update since."

"Sounds painful." Cass waved the younger man in. Even though it was the end of a long day, the sergeant's suit was crease-free and his pink shirt remained tucked in perfectly. Was that a Bowman regulation, or was he ridiculously keen to climb the greasy pole? He hoped it wasn't just the way Blackmore chose to dress. Uptight dressers usually made for uptight people. Time would surely tell. For now he'd give the detective the benefit of the doubt.

"You may as well see this now that you're on the case. It was sent in anonymously." He clicked on play and Blackmore leaned in to watch.

After a few moments, Blackmore frowned, and then his eyes widened. "Is this the Jackson and Miller killings?" He paused. "Someone *filmed* it?"

"And for some reason thought we should see it."

They remained silent as the boys died violently and quietly on screen.

"Do you know who sent it in?" Blackmore ran his fingers over the short strip of beard that ran from just under his bottom lip to the curve of his chin. "Fashionable" beards left Cass cold. He couldn't see the point of them, unless of course the sergeant, who was a year or two younger than Claire May, wanted to look older. In which case, he'd failed miserably.

"Nope. I doubt it was a concerned citizen, though. Someone wanted this caught on camera, and someone, either the cameraman or someone else, wanted me to see it."

Blackmore stared at the screen a little longer and then smiled. "A mystery in a mystery. At least we won't be short of work in the morning."

"You're not wrong. I'll see you at seven. In fact, I want the boards from the serial killer case in here *by* seven. Can you organise that?"

"No problem. See you then, sir."

Cass carefully picked up the original disc and slid it into an evidence bag. In the gloom of the corridor he saw the blue flash of a mobile phone screen lighting up before the doors leading to the stairs creaked and Blackmore disappeared. He couldn't fight the small grin that twitched the corners of his mouth. He was probably ringing Claire May. Couldn't even wait until he'd got out of the building. Cass wondered if he'd ever been like that; full of the optimism of youth. Maybe, a long time ago. But it had been well and truly knocked out of him by the time he was Blackmore's age, that much was for sure. His time in SO10 had taken care of that.

Even though it's been hours since he left the heavy metal track playing loudly in the high-rise, it still echoes in his head. It's starting to irritate. He lets it run on in the background of his mind as he watches the street. It will fade soon enough. Everything does. He knows this because he's fading.

He doesn't have to wait long. The homeless shelters fill up quickly in London. Hard times have fallen, and among the drunk and the mad are the dazed and ordinary, who shuffle inside in the hope of a bed, wondering how on earth this could have happened to them. Tonight, though, it's not the people he's watching. The people are, as they have always been, irrelevant. Flies buzz under his collar. He blinks them quiet. There is enough noise in his head and he's tired.

The boy, aged about seventeen, comes out of the shelter and takes a few steps before shouting an obscenity back at the door. There is no real menace or energy in it. His shoulders slump and he lights a cigarette, then crouches down to stroke the puppy that bounds and bumbles beside him, looking up at him with adoration.

"No space tonight?"

The boy is surprised to see the man in front of him. His emotions are clear too: suspicion, fear, and then wary curiosity. The man has that effect. His face is rugged, but handsome and open. Kindness and gentle humour live there.

"They won't take Sam," the boy says eventually. Hearing his name, the puppy's tail wags faster and he pulls at the string lead to get closer to the man.

"That's a shame. He looks like he's got the makings of a good dog." He pats the soft, warm head, and the small creature nips and licks at his fingers, the chubby body wriggling with excitement.

"He's great." The boy grins. His fears have disappeared in a moment of pride. "He's only eight weeks old and he already knows his name, and he'll sit when you tell him."

"You can't leave him somewhere and get a good night's sleep and then find him in the morning?" The man keeps his tone light. He doesn't need to ask the question. It's the puppy he needs, just to make sure everything goes as planned. He doesn't need to do this, but the habit of testing them dies hard.

The boy's eyes darken with imagined hurt. "Nah, no way. He'd be shit-scared all night." He shakes his head hard. "I couldn't do it. If those bastards won't let Sam in, then I'm not staying."

The man smiles. "Together or not at all?"

"Yeah, that's right." The kid grins again. His teeth haven't started to rot yet and there's no sign of drug abuse in his clear eyes and skin. The man thinks that given time and a different set of chances and choices this boy could have grown into a good man. He is kind. The man knows that. He can see it. But he can also see exactly how this boy will end.

The man looks down at the mongrel puppy again. The dog yaps for a moment and then looks up at the boy. For a second the boy forgets the man is even there. He loves the dog. He thinks he and the dog love each other unconditionally. It strikes the man that the boy knows very little about the nature of love.

"I was going to take a walk down by the river," the man says. "Feel free to tag along." He smiles. "Sam looks like he needs to shake some energy off."

There is only the briefest moment of hesitation and then the boy smiles. "Sure, fuck it."

The boy is not smiling a short while later in the minutes before he dies. Neither does he care about the puppy that is tied up to the lamppost, whining, scared and confused. In fact, his last snotty words are, "Take the fucking puppy if you want it. Just don't kill me. Please." There is no hope in his words though, and the man finishes him quickly after that before letting the body roll into the water. The man smiles sadly as he unties the puppy, who jumps and licks and wags his tail for reassurance. As they walk away, the puppy doesn't look back. So much for love, the man thinks. One day, he'd like to be proved wrong.

CHAPTER THREE

Kate was just putting the phone back in its holder when Cass came through the door and for a second he thought she had jumped slightly when she saw him. Had things really got that bad between them?

"Who was that?"

"Christian." She didn't look at him but stared at the wall, one hand still resting on the handset.

"Shit." Cass looked at his watch. It was nearly nine. An itch of guilt roiled in his stomach.

"Don't worry. I told him you'd call him tomorrow. He said that was fine because he had stuff to do tonight." She sounded vague.

He glanced down the corridor to the kitchen and spotted the half-empty bottle of wine. "Thanks." He paused. "How was he?"

She lifted one shoulder in a shrug and he saw her bones shift under her smooth skin. If she dieted much more she'd disappear. "He seemed okay. Why do you ask?"

"I spoke to him briefly earlier and he seemed agitated by something."

"Did he say what?"

"No." Cass tossed his keys on the side, along with the brown envelope of cash Artie Mullins had given him. He could feel her eyes watching it from over his shoulder. She knew what it was. She'd long ago come to terms with the necessity of the bonuses. "I was driving, and something had come up in the Jackson and Miller case. I had to get back to the office."

"Of course you did." She smiled, but it did little to hide the acid in her voice. She shook her head, thick strands of hair loose around her shoulders. "I don't know why you work so hard." She picked up her wine glass. "It's not as if they're ever going to promote you."

"Thanks." He stared at her. She wasn't wearing a bra and her flat belly showed in the gap between the shoestring-strap T-shirt and her low-slung jeans as she leaned against the wall, one hip thrust outwards. Kate, unlike Claire, was an undisguised beauty. Even now, with the atmosphere taut between them, he could feel himself drawn to her.

"I'm sorry." She spoke so softly that he barely heard her. "That was uncalled for."

Cass said nothing. Her blue eyes looked almost black as she watched him. "I mean it. I'm sorry."

"Forget it. We both know it's true."

"I shouldn't have said it though." She pushed herself away from the wall. "Are you hungry?"

He thought about it. "No. No, I don't think so."

"A drink then." She sauntered towards the kitchen and he watched the movement of her slim hips. "Help me finish this wine." She rolled the glass loosely in her hand.

"Okay." He didn't say any more, not wanting to break this unexpected—if uneasy—truce in the stalemate of their marriage.

"Unless you've got something else to do rather than entertain your wife for a few hours?"

Her voice was almost flirtatious, and Cass felt his tiredness ebb away slightly. Why did he find his wife's unpredictability so attractive? The times she hated him, he could almost respect. Even if she didn't *know* about his drunken (and not-so-drunken) one-night stands and ragged affairs, he was sure she must still have her suspicions. Their brief split nearly two years ago hadn't mended anything. He sometimes wondered why they still clung together in the face of all their failings. Was it just the sex?

In the kitchen she picked up the bottle and a second glass. "Is straight to the bedroom okay, or would you prefer polite conversation in the lounge first?"

He looked at the stranger he loved, his eyes tracing the familiar curves of her body. Her nipples were hard, straining the thin fabric of her T-shirt, and for an instant Carla Rae's dead body flashed before him like a photograph. He blinked, and drowned it in the darkness of his mind. Life, that was what he needed now.

"No." He grinned. "The bedroom's fine with me."

Even as their sweat cooled the awkwardness re-emerged from the shadowy corners of the room and squeezed between their entwined bodies, a cold, deadly thing intent on pushing them apart. Cass pulled Kate's slim body closer, but he could feel her arms begin to stiffen, as if now their blind lust was spent, she didn't know where to put her hands.

She pulled away, leaving only cold air to mark her skin on his. "Let me get rid of this."

Cass watched her pull on her thin robe as she padded to the en-suite bathroom, the used condom carefully pinched between two fingers. She held it with something like disdain, and Cass thought that pretty much summed up their marriage. There were bits of it she liked, but she didn't like herself for it.

He pushed himself up on one arm and took a long gulp of his untouched glass of wine. The now-warm Chardonnay had an acid bite that didn't suit his taste, but he swallowed some more. The bed felt huge around him. From the bathroom came the sound of brushing teeth, swift and efficient. So the rare romantic moment was over. He turned his pillow over to the cool side and lay back. The toilet flushed. In some ways she wasn't so different from him. Although the closeness in their marriage had slowly faded since the abrupt end of his SO10 undercover operation back in 2005, they rarely went more than a week without seeking each other out physically. That chemistry that had flown like an electric current between them when they'd first met hadn't died out, like it did in so many marriages. In those relationships people sank into some kind of faux-happy platonic companionship and drifted through years of life together, hiding the cracks behind the business of raising children and buying bigger houses. He wasn't sure if either was ideal, but he'd take what he and Kate had over the other any day. At least it was honest.

The bathroom door opened. Her hair was pulled back in a neat ponytail and she kept her robe tightly closed as she returned to her side of the bed. For a while they lay there in silence. Although Cass's eyes ached with tiredness, the clock was only just ticking round to half-past nine. It was too early to sleep, and too late to get up again. The awkwardness that was the only child of their strange marriage embraced Cass and he felt tension knot in his shoulders. His breathing sounded irregular in his chest, and he could barely hear hers.

"Why did you do it, Cass?"

He rubbed his tired eyes and then rested his arm across them. He didn't need to ask what she meant. It was the same question, always. It was the only question. It was the cause of the rot in their marriage, hidden deep. It was like a corpse dumped and left to bloat on a river-bed, but it was there all the same.

"I don't want to talk about it, Kate." He tried not to let a long sigh escape with his words, but he failed.

"I do."

The mattress creaked. In the darkness behind his closed, covered eyes, he thought perhaps she'd sat up.

"Well, I don't. It's been a shit day in the middle of a shit week."

"You never want to talk about it."

Her tone had hardened and his skin prickled. Great. Just what they needed. A post-sex argument. Echoes of colour swirled behind his closed lids and he thought he saw the outline of wide, dark eyes in them. He opened his own before those from the memory could take shape completely. She was right. He never did want to talk about it.

"Just not tonight, Kate. Okay?"

"It's never any night." The words were hot and angry. "I need to understand it."

"Kate, you know there's nothing more I can say." He stared at the ceiling. "And I don't see why you need to discuss it tonight. Just let it go."

"If only we could." She rolled onto her back, mirroring his position. The invisible divide down the middle of the bed had never felt more pronounced to Cass, as if the mattress itself were straining to tear itself in two and make the break definite.

"I've had to live with it too, you know. All these years," she said, "the looks at parties. The whispers among the other wives. The way they left me out of everything as if I was *tainted* by what you'd done." She swallowed hard. "I stood by you, Cass, when they said it was over for you. That even if you kept your job, you'd never be promoted. And then even after . . . after *the thing* that happened with us . . . I stood by you."

You didn't really have anywhere else to go. He bit the retort back. This was an old argument that refused to die and there was nothing new to throw at each other in the ring, primarily because he rarely joined in. He wasn't going to make matters worse by starting now.

"But I did get promoted. And now the wives would speak to you, if you'd let them. Although God only knows why you'd want to hang around with the tennis club brigade."

She let out a derisive snort. "You should be a DCI by now. They were only forced to promote you this far because you're so bloody good at your job." She made it sound like an insult, and the words stung like one. "You might as well live at the station, and for what? You think they don't still all talk about it? Talk about you?" She barely paused for breath. "I hate the way they look down on us. And I hate that you don't care."

She'd run out of steam. Cass sat up, swinging his legs over the side of the bed. He didn't turn to look at her; he knew her face pinched tight when she was angry, her delicate features pulling in on themselves and making her look mean and bitter. He didn't need to see that.

"That's not *living with it*, Kate. That's just living with the consequences of it. It's a different thing entirely." He searched in the gloom for his underwear and pulled it on. "Trust me."

"Why can't you just tell me why you did it? Why can't you just tell me that?"

He tugged his jeans on and a sweatshirt. "I'm going for a drive."

She stared at him and her shoulders slumped forward. He'd seen Macintyre do just that movement on the grainy film of the boys' shooting. The fight had gone out of her. The argument was over, for today at least.

He left her sitting silently in the gloom, but when he reached the bedroom door he turned. She looked tiny and fragile on the vast bed, and he thought for a moment that her eyes were shining with the hint of tears. He hadn't seen her cry for a long time.

"I'm sorry, Kate," he said. "I can't tell you, because I can't remember. You know that. I don't *know* why I did it, and that's all there is to it. Some days I don't know what were my reasons and what were those they told me to say, or what I thought I should say. It's all a mixed-up mess in my head. It was a long time ago. I was a different man." *And I really don't want to think about it.*

Downstairs, the lights were still on, and the brightness felt almost judgemental as Cass passed by. He picked up his car keys and Artie Mullins' envelope. He shook out the bunches of notes that would be dished out to the team on Friday night in the car park at the back of The Swan on Kilburn High Road. He rummaged through until finally he saw a small folded wrap of shiny paper probably cut from some trashy porn magazine. Inside it would be a gram of cocaine, maybe two.

Right at that moment he was grateful to Artie for his occasional gifts. He didn't have a habit, but he'd be lying if he said he didn't have an occasional hobby. He listened for sounds of movement from upstairs before quickly chopping a line on the back of the envelope. The house remained silent.

He pulled a note from its batch and rolled it before quickly snorting the white powder up through his right nostril. By the time he'd replaced the note and resealed the envelope, his front tooth was going numb and the powder was trickling pleasantly down the back of his throat, dispelling his tiredness as it powered its way into his system. Cass smiled. It was strong stuff, cleanly cut.

He looked upwards, seeing through the bland plasterwork to the memory of the tiny figure on the bed upstairs. Would she ask him to stay? He lingered for a moment, almost willing her to scream at him, but Kate stayed silent. The door clicked shut behind him. As the buzz reached his head, he found it easier not to care.

"You've got to look up, Charlie."

It's raining and they're standing under the awning of the betting shop. Birmingham unravels around them in a network of littered streets that darken under the constant muddy downpour from the steel-grey sky. The chips are hot in their paper wrapping and the older man grabs a handful and his lips smack together as he eats them. This afternoon is all about learning to make the most of simple pleasures, and despite the dirty water that's blown into their shelter on the wind and soaked the bottom of his jeans, Cass feels happy. He likes this man. He can't help it. He smiles.

Brian Freeman grins back, the expression making a Picasso portrait of his face. Brian "the brain" Freeman had had his nose broken four times by the time he was seventeen. His jaw is slightly misaligned on the left side, shattered during a fight with three Chelsea football fans, back in the day when he was a young man and football hooliganism was how a respectable bloke spent his weekends. Brian had once said that the fighting gave blokes purpose, *whatever that was. A grin cracking his wrecked face, he'd said there was nothing like the buzz of kicking a few heads in on a Saturday afternoon to get you ready for a night on the town. He is fond of the memories, even the painful ones, the simple pleasures to be had in the thrill of a kick-in.*

The Chelsea fans, two trainee bus drivers and a train engineer, left Brian and his mashed-up face for dead. It wasn't a clever move, not finishing the job. Brian and his brothers, George and Bill, tracked them down. They didn't kill them, but gave them such a beating that the train engineer would forever after struggle with words of more than two syllables. One of the bus drivers spent two months in hospital not only drinking through a straw but pissing through one too. The last anyone heard of the third one, he wasn't leaving his wheelchair in a hurry. No one ever saw them at a game again.

Brian Freeman gave up fighting not long after that. Not because he didn't like it—he fucking loved it (he grins whenever he says this too—wide, like an excited child)—but because he discovered he had other talents. He'd left the fighting to Bill and George because he'd realised, he told "Charlie" while tapping the side of his weatherbeaten head, that he had what most of the muscle didn't. He could think. He had the smarts.

"You've got to look up, Charlie."

Cass is so absorbed in the hot chips, the chill in his toes and the sheer freedom of the afternoon, that for a moment he's almost forgotten he is "Charlie." This is strange, because most of the time he finds it hard to remember he's Cass. A bus stops in front of them and Cass sees his face reflected in a filthy window. He wonders if that's his face or Charlie's, but then sees his eyes. The eyes are the same. His eyes, whoever he is.

"Oi, you muppet! I'm talking to you."

Brian nudges him, and he turns. The old man repeats himself. "You've got to look up, Charlie. Wherever you are, make time to look up." He points a thick finger, and Cass follows it above the top of the bus. He swallows his chips.

"You see, Charlie? How about that, then?"

Even through the grey rain, the skyline is extraordinary. From where he is standing Cass can see the glass elegance that is the new Regency Tower, standing like a shard of diamond amidst the grit of the sixties and seventies buildings surrounding it. His eyes move up to the peak, one hundred and twenty feet above the ground. There's no grime on it; the steel and stylish green glass somehow maintain their shine, despite the lack of sunshine, or perhaps in defiance.

"Don't just look at the obvious, mate. Look around it." Brian's voice has dropped into gruff softness, the tone reserved for a favoured grandson. Cass smiles and thinks that if Santa had a brother who hadn't lived up to family expectations, then maybe he'd have a voice like Brian Freeman's: cruel and kind, rolled into one.

He does as he's told. As his eyes narrow and focus he takes in the curves and shapes, finally starting to appreciate each unique building. He spies a clock embedded high up in the face of what he will later *learn is a Georgian building. His smile breaks into a small hiccough of surprised laughter. The clock is too far up the wall to serve any useful purpose, apart from anyone happening to look out of the opposite building at the same level. Whichever long-dead man designed that feature had placed it there purely for his own pleasure: a secret thing, only for those who bothered to look up.*

His eyes drift. Gargoyles that have been completely invisible during the year he's spent in Birmingham suddenly reveal themselves, rising proud from their arches. Even from so far away Cass thinks he can see tiny details like grimaces and wrinkles on their monster brows.

He stands like that for several minutes, drinking it all in.

"You see, Charlie," Brian smiles, still chewing on the cooling chips, "simple pleasures can be had in just looking up."

"You're not wrong," Cass agrees. His London accent is thicker than it is naturally, because Charlie is supposed to be the nephew of Andy Sutton, a player in one of the north London firms. Sutton is legendary across the country, but he is also on the police payroll. The kiddie porn charge is dropped, and Cass is suddenly Sutton's newly invented nephew Charlie. Everyone's happy.

Cass has been using this accent so long he wonders if he'll ever find his own accent again. "It's fucking amazing," he says.

"When things seem like shite around you, just look up. It'll give you a whole new perspective." The old man takes his own advice. On that dank autumn afternoon Cass thinks Brian Freeman looks every one of his sixty-three years. The humour fades from his eyes as he looks around him. The skin of his neck doesn't tighten when he lifts his chin but hangs like a wattle. The lines carved around his eyes deepen as he frowns. "Sometimes you've got to look at things from all the angles, you know?"

Cass nods. He's twenty-five years old. He's clever, but the man beside him is like a dinosaur of knowledge and experience. He has existed in times Cass can only imagine, and has done things Cass has read in files that are endless in their documentation of crime and violence, but that sometimes he can't reconcile with the person he has come to know. He likes Brian Freeman. He can understand how he came to this life.

It's all a mess, of course. Even back then, when his own skin is smooth and his consciousness is merely an empty space in his head, he knows that.

"To get the clearer picture," Brian continues.

Cass nods again.

"And aside from that"—Brian screws up the rest of the chips inside the paper and tosses it into the pavement bin—"buildings are fucking beautiful." He sniffs. "Here endeth the lesson. Now, come on. Let's go to the pub and investigate some other simple pleasures."

He laughs, loud and gruff, and Cass laughs with him. They laugh like men that rule the world but the world just hasn't figured it out yet. As he climbs into the waiting taxi, a fat roll of notes stiff in his pocket and without a care in the world, Cass almost believes he is Charlie, and there is no Kate waiting for him patiently in London, who doesn't know the things he's doing—and enjoying—in the name of his job. His heart heavy for a moment, he looks at Brian beside him and wonders where the dividing lines are. He's not sure he can see them any more.

"Home, James," Freeman says to the cabbie, and then laughs at his own poor imitation of a posh accent.

Cass peers out of the window. The world blurs, and mixed in with the streets of Birmingham he sees London's streets. He frowns. His head hurts. The rain outside is changing colour. It's not grey any more. It's thick red. Something warm hits his hand and he looks down, confused. The crimson stands out against his pale skin. Another drop joins it and he feels its heaviness as it thuds into the back of his hand. His nose is running. He turns to Freeman and tries to say—have I got a nose bleed?—but the words stop in his throat as Freeman's eyes widen, his mouth falling open in horror.

Cass raises his hand, his fingers seeking out the familiar shapes of his nose and mouth. There is nothing there. He reaches further, his hands sinking into a sticky warm mess. He turns for help, but Free-

man has vanished. The seat is empty. Cass leans forward and taps on the plastic division between him and the driver. His heart pounds and his skin suddenly feels terribly cold.

The cabbie turns round. He has no face either, just the torn fleshy remains where one has once been, sitting in a concave half of his head. He raises a hand and slowly wiggles his forefinger from side to side, as if Cass were a naughty child. There is something cold and heavy in Cass's lap and he finds he doesn't need to look down or feel it to know what it is.

Finally, he screams.

Cass awoke with a start and his confused eyes focused on the curve of the steering wheel and the grey sleeve of his sweatshirt. They were both very close up. His arm was tucked between the wheel and his head, and it was numb. His car. He was in his car.

He sat up slowly, every joint in his stiff body screaming at the movement, and looked down at his arm. A blossom of blood stood out in the gloom of the dawn. He peered into the rear-view mirror and saw the crust of red that circled his right nostril. Great.

Outside, the delivery truck that had woken him completed its manoeuvre, the screeching wheels thankfully falling silent, the brakes hissing in relief. Cass leaned his thumping head back against the seat. His mouth was dry and the inside of his nose burned as he breathed in the cold morning air. The jigsaw pieces of the evening came together in his mind. The picture they formed wasn't pretty.

One line had turned into two and then three, and on until he'd done at least a gram and a half; he remembered that. He'd driven; for how long he wasn't sure. The street lights and the people who wandered in the night had glowed and he'd been entranced by them, he remembered that. He sighed with the memory, and forced a dry swallow. He must have tripped out on the gear. Finally, he'd pulled into the twenty-four-hour Tesco car park not far from the estate in Newham where Carla Rae had died. He was going to get cigarettes and then petrol. *That* he remembered. He yawned and peered around at the cup holders and side pockets. There were no cigarettes in the car that he could see. He must have just parked up and passed out. The day was not starting well.

He was frozen. He turned the key that was still in the ignition and set the heater to blast. He shivered as the vents and what was left of the drugs in his system blew any last cobwebs away. The clock glared at him. It was five a.m. He groaned and put the car into gear. No rest for the wicked.

In the morning light that glared through the slatted gaps in the blinds, he stripped off and stuffed his clothes in the washing machine, turning it on before heading up to the shower. He didn't use the en-suite bathroom. In the bedroom he pulled fresh clothes from the cupboards as quietly as he could, although he was sure Kate was awake. She lay on her side facing away from him, and there was a stiffness in the slim line of her back that betrayed consciousness. He wondered how she would react if he ran a finger down that line and whispered how sorry he was for everything. For a moment he thought he might do it, but instead he found his legs carrying him to the spare room to get dressed. There wasn't enough time for that kind of apology, and anyway, it would be like sticking a plaster over a bullet wound.

In the end, he left the house without speaking. Their marriage worked better that way.

CHAPTER FOUR

"You'll be pleased to hear that this is definitely number four." The ME pulled the sheet back from the body on the metal table with brisk efficiency. Cass peered into Carla Rae's face and felt nothing. Displayed on the slab like this she was simply evidence. The dead woman in his memory, trapped in the crime scene photographs, she was the victim, not this cut-open, soulless corpse.

"Oh yeah, that's cheered me up no end." Blackmore stayed slightly behind Cass and he wondered if it was just that he didn't want to get any trace of death on his crisp apple-green shirt. He was warming to the sergeant's ironic tongue, though. He'd give him that.

"It should do." Cass didn't look up. "It means that at least we don't have to worry about a copycat as well as a serial."

"Remember," Farmer said, "serial is a taboo word on this case. We don't want the press hearing a whisper of it."

"Like we can stop that! They have better informers than we do." Cass folded his arms across his chest. "So, what have we got?"

"Cause of death is the same as the other three. A lethal injection of pentabarbitone, delivered intravenously into the arm here." He highlighted the small bruise on the inside of her elbow.

"Were they all injected in the right arm?"

"Yes—and pretty much in the same spot."

"Would it be painful?"

"No, not at all. Quite the opposite in fact. Pentabarbitone is a barbiturate—a tranquilliser. It's called Nembutal in the U.S." Farmer smiled, grimly. "It's the euthanasia drug of choice."

"And currently the drug of choice in Hollywood," Blackmore added. "Often the cause of accidental suicide when taken with alcohol."

"You've been doing your homework," Farmer said approvingly before turning his attention back to Cass. "Your sergeant's right—although our killer isn't actually using Nembutal. He's using veterinary pentabarbitone. It's what they use to put animals down."

"What's the difference?"

"Very little really. Nembutal also contains propylene glycol, and there are no traces of that in any of the victims." He paused. "The drug works by slowing down the body's respiration until breathing stops altogether. The woman died quickly and painlessly. They all did."

Cass frowned. "How hard is it to get hold of this drug?"

"Not that easy. Veterinary surgeries and their suppliers will all stock it. Any pharmaceutical company that makes drugs for vets will also have it." He shrugged. "But sales and usage will all have to be recorded."

The feel of the morgue's cool air on Cass's skin was keeping his brain firing, and he was grateful. He was going to need as much help as he could get today. His bones ached, from sleeping in the car and the cocaine comedown. "Is it difficult to administer?"

"Not overly. If it's injected too quickly then the sudden cessation of respiratory functions can cause a heart attack. But that wasn't the case with any of our victims."

"So he knows what he's doing."

"It looks that way, yes."

Cass logged the information in his brain to mull over later. Why hadn't the killer just used coke or crack or H—something that would be much easier to come by and much harder to trace? All of those would be equally lethal if injected in the right quantities.

The profiler was coming in later. Maybe he'd be able to shed some light on that. Cass looked up. Farmer looked tired. Blackmore looked slightly bored. Cass didn't care. Maybe he could have read all this in the files, but if they wanted him up to speed he preferred to see for himself, and to actually hear the information. That was how he worked best; that way he could ferret out all sorts of nuances he might miss just reading the report.

"What else?"

"As with the others, there's no evidence of any recent sexual activity."

"And yet he strips them naked?"

"And why he does that is your job to find out," Farmer pointed out. "Maybe it's a kinky thing, or maybe it's just practical. He doesn't want to leave any evidence."

"Maybe." Cass looked at the corpse and for a moment saw Carla Rae reanimated, her weighed and analysed organs back in her torso, all functioning perfectly. He could see her in that grimy Newham flat, terrified, slowly peeling off her clothes with trembling fingers and hoping that whoever it was standing watching in the shadows would just get it over with, do what they wanted with her and leave. Unfortunately, he did.

"And her eyes?"

"Ah. Here is the very interesting bit."

Blackmore suddenly stood upright, his attention engaged.

"I found the eggs, right in the corners of her eyes. The tricky little bastards were slipping round to the back . . . although if I'd left them another couple of hours they'd have come wriggling out all by themselves." He waved Cass over to his microscope.

"Musca domestica eggs. The common housefly. The eggs are like tiny grains of rice when they're laid, one and a half to two millimetres in length at most. They normally hatch within six to eight hours—that's when they turn into the maggoty larvae we all know and love. In two or three days they begin the transition to pupae, developing a harder, browner shell, and then they finally hatch into flies. Obviously all this is weather-dependent. The hotter it is, the quicker the process."

The doctor stopped, looked at Cass and smiled wryly. "Trust me, I already knew quite a bit about the common or garden maggot before this bastard showed up, but over the past two months I've become a world-class expert. Once you've had time to take a good look at the other three case files you'll see this vic is the first one we've found so early. Jade Palmer had been dead approximately one week, Amanda Carlisle six days, and Emma Loines three days—some of the larvae were turning into pupae when she was found. Have you seen the photos?"

"Only in passing. I'll take a proper look after them when we're done here. Carla Rae's the freshest—that makes her the most important if I want to catch this fucker." Cass couldn't help feel a twitch of disgust as he pulled away from the lens. He wasn't keen on flies, but maggots revolted him, and knowing that these little white grains would soon be wiggling around in the poor woman's eyeball was enough to turn his fragile stomach. "So what was the interesting bit?" he asked once he'd gathered himself.

"The eggs I found in her eyes were perfect. Any damage done to them was by me, I'm afraid to say."

"And?" Cass wasn't sure what the doctor was driving at. "Spit it out, man."

"It looks as if they were laid there. I have absolutely no idea how someone could have placed them so perfectly without damaging a single one." The ME frowned. "I'm going to have a go at it this afternoon, when my irritating little shit of an assistant gets his act together and brings me some eggs, but I wouldn't lay bets on me to succeed."

"Maybe he *did* get a fly to lay them there," Blackmore said.

Both Cass and Farmer turned to look at him.

"I've heard of flea circuses too, Mat, but they're like Santa. They don't exist. It's all just a trick." Cass looked over at the ME. "Figuring out how he did that is down to you. Maybe get that assistant of yours—"

"—Eagleton. Josh Eagleton," Farmer interrupted. "I suppose we can't go on referring to him as 'that little shit' forever. And I fear he'll probably be around for a while. Under that thick layer of stupidity he's surprisingly clever. He's started to use his initiative too. Had the swabs done on this one before I'd even got my scrubs on."

"Then maybe get Eagleton to pick you up a few flies to play with too. See if you can find a way to get them to drop the eggs so precisely."

"You make it sound so easy."

"I'm sure for a man of your capabilities it's child's play."

Farmer's perma-tanned skin was like worn leather, and with his long grey curls he looked like an ageing hippy, but Cass reckoned he could see the ME's colour fading as they spoke, as if his body knew it wasn't going to be going near a sunbed or swanning off on a quick weekend to the Costa del Crap any time in the near future.

He sighed and returned to the subject at hand. "And the writing on her chest? That was done in blood, yes?"

"Ah, 'Nothing is Sacred,'" Farmer said, "although I can't see what was possibly sacred about this girl to begin with."

Cass's irritation with the doctor rose again, but he bit it back and let the man continue.

"Yes, it's written in blood and it's a DNA match with the others. It doesn't belong to any of the victims—not the ones we've found thus far at least." Farmer shrugged. "It could be his own, of course, but it's not on file so I can't give you anything from that. We're still running a comparison against trace evidence found at the scenes, but he's not exactly leaving these girls in clean environments. There are hairs and body fluid residues all over the squat this one was found in, from dozens of people. But we'll do our best."

"Maybe next time he'll fuck up and leave us something. In the meantime, do what you can with what you've got and stay in touch."

"You think there'll be a next time?"

"That's why they call them serial," Cass said, dryly. "Because they just keep on coming."

By the time they got back to Paddington Green the profiler was waiting for them. Cass took the case files and sent Sergeant Blackmore to make copies for the profiler to keep. He grabbed two coffees from the machine and strode along the corridor towards the far end stairs up to the third floor, where there were a number of small conference rooms.

As he passed the Incident Room—*his* Incident Room, now—it looked like everyone was working. Officers at both ends of the room were on the phones, and bits of paper and files were being passed around. He hadn't expected anything less. Murder Squad officers were not known to be slackers—aside from the passion for the job most of them shared, the official bonuses were too good if they actually scored a conviction. And it wasn't as if the two units didn't have enough to be working on.

The Miller and Jackson team were using the new information in the grainy film to build a more accurate timeline of events. That would help them piece together Macintyre's movements, as well as the two boys'. They still desperately needed to find out how the shooter had known Sam Macintyre would be in Formosa Street at that precise time. Someone must have grassed him up, but getting any information from anyone Macintyre associated with would be like getting blood out of the proverbial. No one wanted to look like they were in on the hit, but nor were they wanting to be seen talking to the filth. Sorting that timeline was going to be a long and painfully slow process.

On the far side of the room he spotted Claire, hunched over a phone by the window. He'd told her to find the cabbie who'd dropped Macintyre off outside the Café de la Seine, and he imagined that was what she was doing. She probably had a name for him by now. He was most likely a daytime driver, so he could be anywhere in the city right now. By the time she got the man in, she'd have a file an inch thick on him, his life, his family, and whatever bad habits he might have imagined hidden from view. If he was in any way associated with Sam Macintyre's firm, then his sergeant would know before the driver even realised he was getting pulled.

Cass gritted his teeth as coffee slopped over and burned his hand. Bowman's lot had plenty to be getting on with too. First they had to dig around in Carla Rae's life, get an idea of who she was and how she lived, and track her last movements as precisely as possible. After that, they'd have to cross-reference all the new information with what they had for the three prior victims. What they needed were links between the four. So far, all they had in common was that they were all female, relatively poor, and now dead. Hopefully, Carla Rae's death would give them a new piece of the jigsaw puzzle. Time would tell. Unfortunately, in any murder case, time was the killer of conviction.

Blackmore spotted him and came over, pushing the heavy swing door from the other side. "Let me take that, sir," he said, reaching for the thick file that was wedged under Cass's armpit. He added it to his own pile. "I'll bring these up. Do you need me in with you, sir?"

"In an ideal world, yes, but in this one I need you in the Incident Room more," said Cass. He transferred one coffee cup to his other hand and led the way up the stairs. "I'll tape what he says and give you a copy before we brief the team. I want you on that pentabarbitone. I want to know where our killer scored it."

"I'm on it, boss."

The first body had been found two months ago, and Bowman had already had the team on the phone to just about every vet, hospital and pharmacy in London chasing reports of stolen or missing barbiturates, but so far they'd come up blank. Now Cass wanted the search widened, starting with the greater London region, but going further if necessary. They knew fuck all about their killer—he could be a pharmaceutical rep or travelling salesman, or maybe a relief vet, stealing what he needed as he went. But it was more likely he'd have gone for one big steal, rather than risk getting arrested for something as ordinary as theft. Somewhere, someone was missing a substantial quantity of the drug. They just needed to find out who.

"And keep on Forensics for anything the CSTs might have found in trace that links with any of the other crime scenes. You know how slack some of these techies can be—they're not police, they're paid by the bloody hour. Make sure they're working."

"You got it, sir."

As they passed under the bright strip lighting, Cass noticed the dark shadows under the sergeant's eyes. Maybe Blackmore wasn't sleeping so well either. Changing to a new DI in the middle of a case like this couldn't be easy, especially when you were sleeping with—or at least intending to sleep with—the boss's sergeant—and not just his sergeant, but someone the DI had history with. What a bloody nightmare that must be.

"And thanks for the file," Cass added, "I'll be up to speed by the end of the day."

"You seem pretty on the ball to me, sir."

Cass silently wished he were. He could feel the fingers of the dead women and the two boys tugging at his clothes, demanding justice. Their touch brought a cold chill to his soul. Common as murder had become in these times when tempers were frayed and money was tight, Criminal Murders, as these they were now classified, were rare. Most killings were committed by civilians, ordinary people caught in a moment of madness, taking their frustrations out on those they loved or had grown to hate. Both these cases were different. These were calculated, beyond a quick fix. And somehow he'd ended up with both of them.

It didn't come as a surprise. God, if he existed, had long ago stopped being a friend to Cass Jones.

He lifted one cup and sipped. He needed to concentrate on the here and now. His nose itched at the scent of cheap coffee. At least the dry soreness left by the strong powder was fading.

Although what was left in the wrap was too light to feel, Cass was suddenly aware of it, lying hot and heavy in his pocket as if it were truly the weight of his shame, all his guilt folded carefully into the shiny piece of magazine. As soon as he could, he'd get to the bathroom and tip it away. Enough was enough. *Until the next time*, a small voice in the back of his head whispered. Cass ignored it. Maybe there would be a next time, but it wouldn't be until after these cases were done. The grip of those dead fingers was far too strong. They'd drown him in blood if he let them.

"So you've got a serial on your hands," said Dr. Tim Hask, the sentence a statement rather than a question. His green eyes twinkled out of his heavy face as he smiled and a network of fine veins crackled across his full cheeks to a kind of a purple peak on his nose. If the profiler's body and face had been criminal evidence, Cass thought, they would reveal the sin of gluttony: a love for good food and good wine, and plenty of it. Cass wondered if his own face betrayed his sins in the same way. He hoped not.

"How can you tell?"

Hask got to his feet with surprising energy for a man of his proportions. He was a few inches shorter than Cass's six foot, and oval, his body expanding massively at the waistline and tapering down through almost womanly hips to his neatly shod feet. His full head of light brown hair was brushed to one side in an untidy parting, and there were no hints of grey in it. Cass reckoned Tim Hask to be no more than forty, but he didn't believe that he was likely to see fifty. Morbid obesity was on a sharp rise in England and this man could easily be its poster boy.

"Nothing clever, I'm afraid." He grinned warmly, causing his jowls to wobble alarmingly. "My services are rather expensive. It's rare for the police to be able to afford me."

"I'm afraid we can't afford decent coffee either." Cass passed him the cup. "So I apologise in advance to your taste buds."

Blackmore had told Cass that Bowman had wanted to call in a profiler after the third body had turned up two weeks previously, but it took the fourth death, Carla Rae, to get the headshed to authorise the expense. Hask was considered top of his field in Britain, and was well respected across Europe and the United States; he didn't come cheap.

He looked at Cass. "I occasionally help out the Feds, but much of my time recently has been spent psychologically evaluating employees for big companies, and being an expert witness in cases of fraud or industrial espionage. While I obviously deplore the need, it will be nice to get my teeth into something meaty again."

"The original pictures are in that folder." Cass passed it over. "There's a copy here for you to take with you."

The profiler shook his head, his eyes growing serious as he pulled the photos out. "Thank you, but that won't be necessary. I've already had the file faxed over to me." His fat hands carefully arranged each set of photos on the table in the order of the vics' demise, and then placed the secondary shots of the crime scenes above each pile.

"Maybe we should have done this over the phone, then," Cass said, feeling a little put out.

"Absolutely not." Hask moved the picture of Carla Rae's abused body an inch to the left. "I so rarely get to work on something that actually means anything these days." A small shard of a smile twitched at his cheek. "And this is as much about your brain as mine, DI Jones."

"Call me Cass."

"Cass, then. My point is: *I* can't catch the person who did this. I can only give you suggestions about the person and their motivations. If you get any hunches, then I will probably be able to tell you if you're headed in the right direction." He spread his hands wide across the pictures. "These girls need your brain as much as mine—more so, in fact. We have the best chance of catching him if our minds work in some kind of synthesis." He paused. "Plus, I've been hankering after some time in London. I haven't been back for a while, and all the better if it's on someone else's dime." He chuckled.

"Well, any help you can give us will be greatly appreciated."

The two men examined the pictures in silence. Cass had seen them before, briefly, when the case was still Bowman's, and then in a hurried flick through of the file before heading home the previous evening, but this was the first time he'd really *looked* at them. Hask might already be seeking out clues, and evidence of method and similarities, but Cass wanted to see the people these bodies had been before their lives had been stopped so unexpectedly. He wanted to know them a little, to recognise them. He shivered, as if he felt the cold touch of their fingers on his.

Jade Palmer, twenty-two, was the first to die, a week before her body was found in a boarded-up repossession two streets away from her family home just off St. John's Wood Road. The derelict house was only a mile or so from where Cass was standing now, and part of him was wishing the killer had struck in Newham first, and made all this someone else's problem.

Jade smiled up at him from the photo on the desk. Her thick shoulder-length hair was braided in cornrows, and the stud in her tongue glinted in the reflected shine of the camera flash. It was a healthy smile, full of life, but Cass thought he could see a hint of wary shadows creeping into the corner of her eyes where only a few months later a crazy man would plant fly eggs. Until her body turned up, found by some council housing officer inspecting just how much—or more probably how little—work needed to be done to make it habitable, no one had reported her missing. Apparently, she had a habit of just taking off, so none had been worried by her absence.

With no permanent job and few qualifications that meant anything, it appeared that pretty Jade Palmer's life consisted of taking up with one unsuitable man after another, drawn, like so many others, to danger and excitement without realising that there was always some kind of price to pay. Even though she would now be forever twenty-two, Cass thought echoes of those exciting, dangerous men had already made tracks on her soul. Downstairs some unfortunate constable was trawling through lists and hunting all those men down. Maybe one of her boyfriends had suddenly turned psycho—but Cass doubted it. He knew how those gangsta-boys liked to work, and it wasn't like this.

The photographs showed her decomposing body examined from all angles, her dignity stripped away by the flash of a camera. A close-up highlighted swollen eyelids, lips and tongue, not a result of any injury or beating but simply the efficient progression of nature. As soon as death had occurred, Jade's silent body, already a busy little ecosystem, had gone into overdrive, the myriad tiny organisms working furiously inside her to recycle the nutrients contained within her carcass.

The silver stud in Jade Palmer's tongue stuck out in ironic mockery: a final "fuck you" to a world that had finally fucked her. It was the only thing really recognisable on a body that had lost both shape and colour. He looked back at the smiling face captured in the first photo. This would be the image that would haunt him, not the dead thing below.

Next to Jade was twenty-eight-year-old Amanda Carlisle. She was a curvy brunette with an unhealthy sheen to her skin. The photo had been taken in a pub and she had a cigarette in one hand and a drink in the other—some variety of lager or cider. Unlike Jade Palmer, she had a steady boyfriend, a truck driver, and a job as a waitress in an Islington café. She'd been there for the past two years and was known to be polite, friendly and punctual. Maybe it was the regular diet of fried eggs and chips that was responsible for the pale, greasy skin. Amanda and her boyfriend rented a small terraced house a street away from where she was found, naked and scrawled on and left to rot in forgotten dust just like the others. This time the empty building was not abandoned but up for sale, one of many around there. The estate agent had been making his rounds. He went to check everything was okay and found Amanda Carlisle lying on the sitting room floor.

In the period between her death and her discovery, the fly eggs inserted into her eyes had hatched successfully. One close-up focused on several well-developed maggots, in the third stage of their development, according to the fact sheet someone had thoughtfully inserted into the file. Cass grimaced and looked away.

At least Amanda Carlisle had been reported missing, by both her boyfriend and the café owner. She'd worked the late shift, closing up at ten, but had never made it home, a ten-minute walk at best. Cass didn't have to meet her boss to know that he'd probably had a few sleepless nights over the past month since her decaying body had been found, even if there was nothing he could have done.

The third victim stared up at him. The picture looked to have been taken outside a pub on a summer's afternoon. Emma Loines wasn't smiling, but watching the camera thoughtfully, as if whoever had taken the photograph had caught her in the middle of a private dilemma that she hadn't been able to resolve before the shutter released, capturing her like that forever. Unlike the other three, Emma Loines wasn't in her twenties; she'd died just two weeks before her thirty-second birthday. She was an office temp who had moved down to London from Manchester two months previously to take a full-time job. She had been living in a bedsit in King's Cross. Cass thought it was no wonder she didn't look happy. King's Cross was a dodgy area at the best of times, all street prostitution and low-level crime, but as the country—and the rest of the world—took an economic nosedive, the streets of King's Cross got even busier.

Emma Loines had been found two weeks ago, in a small flat almost as dingy as the one in Newham where Carla Rae had died. It was a rented property a couple of streets back from the station, vacant after the forcible eviction of the last tenants. The landlord found the body when he went to meet a John Smith, who'd called about the flat but never showed. Surprise, surprise. The number on the landlord's mobile turned out to be a payphone in King's Cross Station. Cass thought the landlord must have been pretty desperate to let the flat if he'd bothered to turn up for someone who called himself John Smith—or maybe he was used to having anonymous tenants. It was the right area for it.

When she was found, Emma Loines had been dead for approximately three days. She'd failed to turn up for a meeting with her new employer, and after trying her mobile and getting no response, he'd given the job to someone else. That was the way of this brave new world, after all. As soon as the body was ID'd the nationwide computer revealed that her parents had contacted their local station with concerns over their daughter's silence a day and a half after her arrival in the capital but they'd been politely ignored. No one cared about missing adults, that was the cold hard truth. The only missing people who would get police attention these days were the kind who turned up murdered. Cass was glad he hadn't had to be the officer to explain to Mr. and Mrs. Loines that their daughter now fell into that category.

And then there was Carla Rae. The crime scene pictures were pretty familiar now, all variations on the same theme. Cass looked at the sadness in Carla Rae's eyes. The photo wasn't new; he thought it had been taken a year or more ago. Carla, tatty blonde hair hanging lank over her shoulders, was standing next to another woman with similar features: a sister, perhaps. Neither woman looked over-happy to be there, and Cass felt a twinge of sorrow for this poor, dead stranger whose family couldn't even come up with a current picture of her. The night before she was killed, Carla had been in her local pub. She'd had two halves of lager, then gone to the Chinese take-away that was on her route home. An uneaten bag of prawn crackers—*Free with Every Takeaway!*, according to the menu—and a dirty plate were found in the kitchen, so he reckoned it was safe to assume she'd got home safely. But what happened to her after that; what she did and who she saw— all that was just a black hole. Cass's men were working hard to fill in the missing pieces of Carla Rae's last night on this planet. It was her fingers that were digging so painfully into him. *She* was his case; just like the schoolboys. The others could go and haunt Bowman. He sighed. If only it worked like that.

He looked up to find the profiler watching him. "Sorry. I haven't had much time to check these over myself."

"Interesting that you focus so much on the pictures of the victims while they were alive."

Cass smiled. "We're not here to analyse me, and I couldn't afford your rates even if I wanted to, so let's stick to the bodies at hand. What can you tell me?" He reached over and clicked on the Dictaphone at the end of the table.

Hask lowered himself down into a chair, ignoring the fact that he was spilling uncomfortably over the sides. "Well, let's start with the general stuff, not forgetting that despite my extortionate fees I can't give you any absolutes. Law of averages suggest that you're looking for a white male. Female serial killers are extremely rare, and that, combined with the choice of female victims who are left naked, points definitely towards a male."

"We think so too," Cass agreed. "The call from 'John Smith' confirmed our suspicions."

Hask shuffled through some of the photographs. "His crime scenes are organised." He looked up. "But you don't need me to tell you that these aren't crimes of passion. He's treated each victim in exactly the same manner, which would imply that they're targeted strangers rather than people he actively knows, or who have overtly offended him in any way."

"If this is what he does to people who haven't offended him, then I'd hate to be the one to piss him off," Cass commented.

Hask smiled. "I take your point." He looked back at the pictures. "Where are their clothes? Does he take them away with him?"

Cass nodded.

"These crime scenes are very controlled," Hask continued. "Normally in a case like this I'd suggest that he's keeping personal items like clothing as a keepsake—a kind of memento. He relives his various crimes by touching or looking at something he's taken from the victims." He shook his head. "But I'm not so sure with this one. Keepsakes are normally one particular item of clothing; perhaps underwear, or shoes. If he's taking everything it could just be removal of evidence. That would fit in with his need to control the scene."

He frowned and Cass stayed silent. He could almost hear that very expensive expert brain ticking over as he pieced things together, and he didn't want to do anything that might break that concentration.

"It's important to him that they're naked," Hask said finally, almost to himself. "That much is obvious. And they were all found in empty buildings, not their own homes. Maybe it's important to him that they're stripped of all identity. He's taken them out of their clothes and their homes."

"But he didn't take Carla Rae's bag with her purse and ID in it," Cass said. "Unless that was a mistake."

"I don't think this guy makes mistakes. Not yet, anyway."

"Me neither," Cass agreed. "And he wasn't rushed at the scene, not the last one, at any rate. He left a boombox with some God-awful heavy metal music playing just to make sure the body was found quickly."

"What was playing?"

Cass shook his head. "I'm not sure. I'll find out."

"Do that. I doubt this one would have chosen music at random. There may be something we can use in his choice, as I'm presuming he didn't leave anything as useful as fingerprints behind?"

"You'd be presuming right."

Hask turned his attention back to the pictures of the naked dead women and sighed. "Okay, it's not about making them anonymous. It is about making them vulnerable and exposed. We're at our weakest when we're naked, not only physically, but emotionally too. Years of conditioning have hard-wired us to feel shame at our own nudity." He grimaced. "You could call it the Adam and Eve complex—although that's not a technical term."

"He feels power over them by leaving them naked?"

"The power trip is clear, yes. I'll come back to that." Hask tapped two fingers on his bottom lip for a few seconds.

"Right. It's not about taking their identity. These places he leaves them are all disused homes of some sort, aren't they?"

"Yes. The last was a squat. One was an empty rental, one was a boarded-up house and another was a repossessed house up for sale."

"All abandoned homes. So it's important for him to displace these women: to leave them in their most honest state, in a place they don't belong."

"Why would he want to do that?"

The profiler shrugged. "Your guess is as good as mine at the moment."

"And the clothes?"

"Possessions would create a sense of belonging. We fill our homes with our things. He wants them out of place, so he takes the clothes with him. I doubt he keeps them. Maybe they'll turn up dumped somewhere, or perhaps he'll burn them. Either way, it doesn't really matter. Despite the nudity, these crimes aren't sexual. He won't have ripped their clothes off, and I sincerely doubt he's left anything in the way of DNA or trace evidence behind."

Cass was studying the photographs again. "I think he makes them strip themselves," he said, "and then makes them put their clothes in a bag. That's how I see it playing out in my head."

The profiler looked at him thoughtfully. "Exactly how I see it too." He smiled. "You don't get a refund, though."

"It's not my money"—Cass smiled back—"so enjoy it."

"I shall, believe me—and perhaps we should go to the Ivy? We must eat, after all."

Cass definitely approved of the profiler; he recognised that same disregard for authority that he himself had struggled with all his life. "Make it the pub and you're on," he said, then added, "But if it's not sexual, what's his motive?"

"I should imagine he has more than one, some conscious; others less so. He's making a point of some kind—or sending a message. Each victim has 'Nothing is Sacred' painted on them in blood, but the meaning isn't obvious to me. Could be a religious thing, perhaps someone who has lost their faith. But sacred can also mean 'respected,' or valued in a non-sectarian way. Given that he writes this on a dead body in blood—a key element of life—I believe it's more likely to be the concept of life he thinks lacking in value rather than the women themselves. He might have picked women rather than men purely because they're physically weaker."

"Although if he is making a religious point, then perhaps he's picked women because it was Eve who fell to temptation, and was therefore the first sinner," Cass added.

"Could well be." Hask looked at him. "You don't strike me as a religious man."

"I'm not. But my father was." Cass paused. "For what it was worth."

"Something you want to share?"

"Not really." Cass was grinding his teeth again. It was a bad habit; one he couldn't shake. In his mind's eye he could see the flames, even though he'd been miles away when the accident happened. Sometimes he was sure he could feel them burning him in his sleep. "I'll just say his faith was sorely tested at the end."

"Sorry to hear that."

Cass was surprised to find that he believed Hask to be sincere. "Well, shit happens, doesn't it?" He looked down at the pictures. "There's no escaping it."

"Yes." Hask spoke more softly. "We have enough of Heaven and Hell in this life without worrying about what might happen in the next." After a moment, he rubbed his hands together and focused once again on the task at hand. "The method of death is interesting too. Precise injection of pentabarbitone in every case."

Cass was glad to be back on sure, gritty ground. This was his world, and he was safe here. "Why didn't he use cocaine, or heroin, or some other street drug? There's enough of the stuff out there, and people die of overdoses every day. There'd be no risk of it being traced either."

"Those drugs wouldn't suit his purpose. Pentabarbitone is used to put animals down—cats, dogs, our beloved family pets." He smiled sadly. "That's what he's doing to these women. He's putting them down as if they were animals. He sees himself as more powerful— maybe he pities them, perhaps he's even fond of them, in an abstract, distanced way. If he'd used another drug, it wouldn't send the same message, and it certainly wouldn't have the same effect. A heroin or cocaine overdose would kill the victim by inducing a sudden, violent high, followed shortly thereafter by a massive heart attack. This drug is far more clinical. He's injected them with exact amounts to slow their breathing until it stops. There's no euphoria involved. He basically sends them to sleep and switches them off."

"You make them sound like machines."

"On the physical level, that's exactly what we all are. Maybe that's part of his point."

"What about the fly eggs?"

Hask's whole face wobbled as he let out a small laugh. "Ah, the best saved until last. I have to say I was surprised by those. This killer is a bit of a contradiction in some ways. He kills so clinically, and then adds the gruesome flourishes with the written message and the flies. Fascinating."

"Less so for the officers on the scene, I should imagine."

"Fair point—but fascinating all the same. Again, the eggs—and the eventual flies—could symbolise the cycle of life. By placing the flies on the body he's emphasising that decay feeds new life. Flies have a relatively short life cycle, so he could be using that to make a point about the lives of humans. Here and gone in an instant."

"Which backs up the idea of him seeing his victims as a less-important life form."

"And what do we do to flies, Inspector? All of us, regardless of our personal ethics?"

Cass paused and thought of Kate in the summer, rolled newspaper in hand and a disgusted expression marring the beauty of her face. "We swat them," he said, finally. "We kill them without even thinking about it."

Hask smiled. "He's thinking of us like flies: unimportant and easy to kill. Something has happened to this man to make him see life, people, maybe even society as valueless. Perhaps he picked these women because their lives were dull, wasted. None of them had achieved a great deal in terms of education or career. None of them have children, which might be important: these women have all failed to use what you might call the female body's main function: to carry the next generation."

"And if there is any sort of religious undercurrent, then surely the act of marriage and procreation would be considered sacred," Cass said.

"True. None of them are virgins." Hask finally reached for his coffee. "Although I don't think he's judging them on their morals. They're alive, but they're not living, not in his eyes anyway."

"Their lives are humdrum? But whose isn't?" Cass asked. "The whole world's broke and depressed. There must be a link other than that. Why these four women out of a million other Londoners?" Cass stared at the frozen faces spread out on the table. "He must watch them. To know a little bit about their lives he must watch them for a while."

"I agree. And finding the link is your department. I can't see anything obvious, but there will be something, so it's up to your team to find it, hopefully before too many more women—or men—die."

"There's no doubt that this man will kill again?" Cass knew the answer in his gut. He'd said as much to the ME.

"Of course not. He's getting better. And more confident. He *wanted* this last body found quickly. He's proud of his handiwork. He wants *you*"—he spread his hands—"us, *society*, to be impressed by him."

"Oh, I'm impressed," Cass growled. "Maybe if I go on the news and tell him so, then he'll just turn himself in."

"God, this coffee is truly bad." Hask snorted into his cup. "This killer may well turn himself in one day, but not until you understand his message." He sighed. "And we're a long way from that."

"Any ideas on who we might be looking for?"

"A quiet man. Controlled. Someone who works nine to five but who has maybe changed jobs a few times—not too often; perhaps every couple of years or so. From the evidence we have so far, I'd say our killer is torn between belief in the physical and the spiritual, and he can't reconcile them. That divide probably runs right through him, and his job choices will vary to reflect it. Perhaps he's done manual labour and then switched to an office job. I'd say that he's also neat and careful. The way he lays them out and takes their clothes shows us that."

He paused for a moment, then, steepling his fingers, continued, "He's above-average intelligence. I think whatever he's trying to work out through these murders is a philosophical issue for him. He's not a passionate man. I doubt he has a wife or a long-term partner, although I'd put him at over thirty-five. I don't think he has any sexual hang-ups, but the concept of love maybe eludes him, so his sexual relationships will likely have been short-lived. Physically, I imagine he won't be un-attractive. He might even be charismatic. You've got no sign of any struggle and no reports of these women being dragged kicking and screaming to their final destinations. He is likely to have persuaded them to go with him willingly, maybe for sexual reasons, but not nec-essarily. He's probably average height, maybe taller, and relatively strong. Physical fitness would tie in with his feelings of superiority."

"He sounds like a model citizen," Cass commented, "the murdering of innocents aside."

"That's likely just how he appears on a day-to-day level—but there will be glitches, flaws jittering under the surface. He brings to mind Harold Shipman a little. Do you remember him? Suspected of killing two hundred and fifty pensioners? It was nearly twenty years ago now. He committed suicide back in 2004 while serving life for fifteen murders."

"I remember him. The GP who injected his patients, right?"

"That's the one. On the surface he was a mild-mannered, very calm man, but underneath there was this huge ego at work. He was treated for an addiction to prescription drugs early on in his career, and there was evidence that he was using again later on. If you look closely, there'll always be signs of things that aren't well."

"How did he get caught?"

"Some relatives and an undertaker became suspicious—but ulti-mately he was caught because he changed his MO. He forged the will of one of his victims so that she left everything to him." He shrugged. "There are those who say he did it in order to get caught, but I don't go along with that. I think he wanted the money so he could retire abroad and his ego convinced him he could get away with it." His shrewd eyes met Cass's. "It's nearly always the ego that gives them away. That sense of self-importance that grows with each life taken often leads to some kind of slip-up. Or what your killer is doing will lead to his arrest."

Cass looked quizzical. "What's our killer doing?"

"He's speeding up, of course. The gap between murders is getting shorter. Whatever satisfaction he's getting from watching these women die isn't lasting so long. On some level, even if he doesn't realise it himself yet, he's losing control, and as he keeps on killing, he'll make a mistake. He's bound to."

"But in the meantime I've got more bodies to look forward to?"

The profiler nodded. "You can't make an omelette without breaking a few eggs."

Neither man smiled.

CHAPTER FIVE

Cass took a note of the hotel where Dr. Hask was staying and left a constable to find him a ride into the West End. He headed down to the Incident Room and tossed the tape onto Blackmore's desk. The young sergeant was talking into a phone and was about to end the call but Cass shook his head. It wasn't as if he had much to tell him.

A light hand touched his shoulder.

"How did it go with the profiler?" He caught the scent of vanilla perfume. At some point in the past year, Claire May had shed the last traces of girlishness and become all woman. It suited her.

Cass shrugged. "The only time-saver is that we can stop looking at the boyfriends. Neither Jade Palmer's collection of one-night-stands nor Amanda Carlisle's bloke fit Hask's profile." He nodded at Blackmore's desk. "It's all on the tape. You'll get a copy when it's typed up. See what you think."

"So he didn't tell us the killer's an albino dwarf with one leg?" she asked. "That's a real pity. Can't be many of them in London." She kept her face deadpan.

"Unfortunately not." Cass let the seriousness drain out of his own face and winked. "But that would stop all our fun."

When she smiled, Cass noticed her skin was still fresh, wrinkle-free.

"Well, I may not be Dr. Hask, Profiler Extraordinaire, but I do have something positive to tell you."

"Go on."

"The lab rats got something from that envelope."

Cass felt his heart pick up. He didn't need cocaine to get it going this time. This was the thrill of the chase kicking into his system.

"It's a print," she continued, "but don't get too excited; it's pretty smeared. They're going to do what they can with it and then run it through the system to try and find a match."

"It's a whole lot better than nothing." Cass grinned.

He checked his watch. He felt like he'd done a day's work already but it was only half-ten. It had barely started. "What time are we expected at the Jacksons'?"

"I told them eleven. The Millers will be there too."

"Then let's go. Blackmore can hold the fort here. I need to pick up a decent coffee on the way."

"You look like you need one."

Although she delivered the line with a teasing smile, Cass felt his neck burn a little under his collar. He caught sight of his ghostly reflection in the glass and knew she was right. His eyes were like dark pebbles at the bottom of a muddy pond, and the lines that patterned his rough skin seemed to be sinking in even further. He tore his eyes away from the shadowy outline of the man he had become. For a moment he considered diving into the toilets and flushing away the coke, but Claire was too far ahead of him, her car keys already in hand. It would have to wait.

As he followed his sergeant, his ex-lover, into the stairwell, he tried to ignore the small flutter of relief in the pit of his stomach.

In the ten days since the two boys had been gunned down, the media had started taking liberties with the truth. Since the turn of the century, knife and gun crime had risen steeply as more and more teenagers found themselves out of place in the world around them. Instead, they sought some sense of belonging in the gangs that ruled the poverty-ridden estates across the city, like the one where Carla Rae had died the previous day. Young black kids growing up on the estates had little choice but to join one of the gangs; those few who tried to keep their heads down rarely lasted long. The gangs had become training grounds for the criminals of the future and they were efficient at it. Those who survived childhood graduated to the firms, where they discovered colour was no longer an issue. They'd become part of a new breed, their skills honed and their hearts hardened, where the divisions had nothing to do with race or colour and everything to do with them and us, "them" being normal society. Cass hated the new-style crims taking over London's streets. They had none of the honour of those old dogs like Artie Mullins. Artie was a bastard, right enough, and he'd done some evil things to keep his grip on the top, but he never involved civilians.

When Justin Jackson and John Miller died, the media held them up as an example of how things could be: two children who had maintained their friendship despite their different skin colours. Difference was, Justin Jackson didn't live on a bleak housing estate. In fact, Cass thought, as he followed his sergeant into the Jacksons' elegant lounge, if anything had kept Jackson and Miller's friendship firm, it was probably that they still had beautiful lives in a world where everyone else was busy tightening their belts. But the press didn't focus on that. Perhaps they felt people would have less sympathy for rich children than they did for poor. Cass didn't get why there had to be more to the tragedy than two children being accidentally gunned down. What exactly did the readers need in order to actually feel something?

"Take a seat, please." Clara Jackson's clipped English accent cut off Cass's internal rant and he moved across to one of the two large cream sofas that faced each other across a glass coffee table. It looked as if no one had ever sullied it with anything as common as a coffee cup. She returned to her own place beside Eleanor Miller as Cass sat opposite. It seemed to him that the two women, although both still holding onto the kind of beauty money definitely could buy, had diminished somewhat since he'd first met them. The early lines they'd obviously pampered and massaged out of existence had crept back, sinking into the hollows under their eyes. The clothes they wore were still expensive, but they no longer looked as if each garment had been carefully chosen, more as if they had just donned whatever came to hand. Both faces were bare of make-up, though their highlighted and styled hair still hung perfectly despite being mostly ignored other than a quick, distracted shampoo in the shower. That was the kind of cut that cost money.

But Clara Jackson and Eleanor Miller had suffered a reality check. They were both facing the appalling prospect of having to continue with life in the face of death.

As Clara took her seat, the women's hands automatically joined, thin, knotted fingers grabbing each other. Cass thought the papers should run a picture of those hands. Maybe then they'd see that sometimes elaboration wasn't necessary. The two women sat in silence, their pain filling the room.

"Have you got something to tell us?" Paul Miller stood behind his wife. He was thirty-eight, but over the past ten days all the years that his son would never see had etched themselves into his flesh. Where the women clung together, their grief gripped tight in those manicured hands, the men stood stiff, side by side, but a world apart. Clara and Eleanor's eyes flickered to each other, a tight ghost of a smile passing between them, as sharp as a sliver of glass. Paul Miller and Isaac Jackson kept their dead eyes focused entirely on Cass. The foot between them was like an ocean; cold and endlessly deep. What would happen if they touched? Cass wondered. Would their terrible controlled heartache finally flow free?

Cass pitied them. Despite their big salaries, another world had crossed paths with theirs. Choices had been made by people they would never meet, and they needed to find some meaning in it, not just that their children's deaths were merely the outcome of someone else's bad choices. These were men used to making decisions and calling the shots, and the fact that this random event had been so completely out of their control must surely be tearing Paul Miller and Isaac Jackson to shreds. They could call it bad luck, or fate, but naming it would not ease their pain. They'd realise that soon enough.

"There has been a development," he said, trying, in the presence of ladies, to gentle his rough accent. "We've been sent a film of the shooting." Eleanor Miller flinched slightly as if the word itself were a gunshot.

"A film?" Isaac Jackson's eyes widened in his grey face. Like Paul Miller, his usual veneer of success had abandoned him. "Someone filmed it? But why—?" For the first time, the two men glanced at each other, for the briefest moment.

"We're not sure yet. But hopefully it'll give us some fresh leads."

"Fresh leads?" Eleanor Miller snorted, a mockery of a laugh. "You haven't *got* any leads." Tears filled her bloodshot eyes and Cass saw her knuckles whiten as she gripped Clara Jackson's hand. They were a contradiction, these two, locked into each other's pain and yet completely alone. It didn't look like their men were giving them much in the way of comfort. Cass thought of John Miller, still fixated on his broken friend's body as the bullets ripped through him, and then Carla Rae, dead in the rotting flat. Everyone was alone in the end.

"I appreciate your pain and frustration, Mrs. Miller." He chose his words carefully. He hadn't ever experienced their pain, and he wouldn't insult them by suggesting he had. "But you have to believe that I really want to get the bastards who did this." Behind him, a mobile rang and Claire moved out into the hall to answer it.

The tension in the room was threatening to swallow him. "And I just wanted to let you know that we do now have some more information to go on." He watched her eyes as the anger was replaced by a fragile and terrible hope. "I wanted you to know that first."

Both women nodded, slowly and carefully, as if the action might snap their necks like autumn twigs.

"But I can't tell you what those leads are," he continued, talking slowly now, as if to a child. "It's important they stay confidential. But I promise you that I will do everything that I can to find out who was responsible for killing your boys." He couldn't tell them that the leads were minimal; that the best they had was a licence plate for a taxi-cab, a partial print and a few minutes of grainy image. They had leads now, for the first time, and that was all that mattered.

"Cass." Claire stood in the doorway, chewing her bottom lip. She looked very young.

"Cass, we have to go."

Cass frowned. She never called him by his first name; not in front of other people. He stared at the slight flush in her cheeks and the way her eyes bored into his. His stomach froze.

"What's happened?" He hadn't realised he'd already got to his feet. For a brief moment he saw his father, screaming as the flames raged, and then the image was gone. The sickly feeling in the pit of his stomach remained.

"We have to go. Kate's at home waiting for you." She couldn't look at him, but her own eyes were reddening, like Eleanor Miller's had only seconds ago.

There was a roaring in Cass's ears, drowning out any other sound. He stood in the doorway now, examining the cream-coloured walls. He could almost smell the paint. Behind Claire, a painting hung unevenly. It looked expensive, and Cass thought it was a shame no one could be bothered to straighten it. His heartbeat quickened. Behind him, the Millers and Jacksons watched from where they stood, enveloped in their own bubble of grief.

"Just tell me what's happened." His voice was low, and every hair on his body trembled. Something in his world had changed beyond recognition, beyond fixing.

"It's Christian," she said after a long pause. "He's dead. And his wife. And son." She paused. "It looks like murder-suicide. I'm so sorry."

And then the world collapsed.

On the way home Cass saw the world around him too clearly, every image over-bright, with too much colour. His feet moved like lead through the house as Claire burbled apologetic goodbyes. Cass heard her as if they were both underwater. The cream walls were too clean, and he flinched away from them. Lilies in a vase on the table by the door yawned towards him, leering from their open mouths. Beneath them, tucked under a large conch shell, a pile of letters was stacked, white envelopes against the red mahogany table, and he felt like he was choking in blood.

"How?" he asked finally as they drove through the central London streets teeming with thousands of small lives, all going about their daily business as if there would never be a *last* day.

"Cass, I can't . . . Let's wait until you're home."

"I'm not a fucking child, Claire," he exploded. "Just fucking tell me!"

"I don't know the exact details," she said at last. "Blackmore just said there was a gun."

"A gun?"

"A shotgun."

"That can't be right." Cass stared through the windscreen and shook his head. Bile rose in his throat and he swallowed it back down. Somewhere up ahead the lights turned green, but he didn't really see them. Beneath the numbness, his brain twisted, trying to make some sense of it, but this was all wrong. That Christian was dead was wrong; that Jessica and Luke were dead was wrong. That Christian had killed them? And with a shotgun? He couldn't find a place for that to sit in his head. He tried to picture his baby brother, the shy, clever youngest son, loading cartridges into a weapon and then quietly blowing the life out of his wife and child. It played like a badly acted movie behind his eyes. The role was miscast. It wasn't Christian.

"Where the hell would Christian get a shotgun from? Christian wouldn't know what to do with a gun. He wouldn't know how to load it, let alone fire it." He shook his head fiercely. "This is not right. Christian couldn't do a thing like that."

I maybe could, he almost added. *I could, but not Christian.*

Claire said nothing and even though he was immersed in the first flood of his grief, Cass could understand why. She wasn't going to point out the obvious to him. In this world they lived in anyone could get a gun if they had the money for it—and not even a lot of money, not these days. Everyone knew someone who operated on either side of the law, or in the grey area between the two. Christian might have been naïve but he could have gone into any one of a hundred pubs and got himself a shotgun, for no more than a couple of hundred quid. Even if he had no connections himself, all it would have taken was a few weeks of sitting and drinking quietly in the same gaff, making sure his face was familiar before approaching someone. Anything was possible . . . Anything but the idea that Christian would kill his family. Kill himself, maybe. But never his family.

The car moved into Muswell Hill, taking Cass on his normal route home, but the trees lining the roads were making unfamiliar shapes against the sky. The cars looked too wide. Everything was an inch out of place. The world was an inch out of place.

"He's been trying to speak to me." He spoke into the window and condensation formed against the glass. He couldn't look at Claire. "He's been calling my phone for days. Work and home." He paused. "I didn't speak to him. Even last night I said I'd be home when I knew I wouldn't be."

"We've had a lot on." Claire pulled over in front of his house. "It's not your fault."

Cass made no move to get out. "Isn't it?" He lit a cigarette and felt the hot smoke burn against his dry mouth. "He had something on his mind. I wasn't listening."

"Did he say what it was?"

"No." The short conversation of the night before played over in Cass's head. "Nothing that made any sense. I cut him off."

Pain caught the back of his throat and for an awful moment he thought he was going to break down and start crying like a child, sitting there in Claire's car, Claire, whose heart he'd once broken in a quiet way. And his wife was probably sitting in their lounge doing some crying of her own. Nothing changed. He swallowed the well of emotion. *Christian was dead.* He heard the words in his head, but still they refused to take root.

A warm hand rested on his knee. "You couldn't have known, Cass. These things . . ." She shrugged. "They're unpredictable. You can't tell when someone's going to snap."

"Christian wasn't the snapping kind." He pulled hard on the cigarette, creating a barrier of stinging smoke between them.

She ignored it.

"Cass," she said, softly, "this isn't your fault. Don't try and make everything your fault because you made one difficult call ten years ago. Isn't it time you started to forgive yourself?"

"This *really* isn't the time for that, Claire."

Cass didn't look at her, and eventually she sighed in defeat. "You want me to come in with you?"

He laughed dryly. "I don't think so. Kate doesn't know what happened while we were split, but you know what women are like. I think she *knows*. There's only so much I can take in one day."

The hand slid away from his leg, leaving only an echo of its warmth. "Well, if you need me, just call."

"I'll see you in the morning. I'll be in by half-seven."

"You don't have—"

"What else am I going to do? Sit around and look at old pictures and cry?"

"That's what most people would do, Cass, yes. It's what you do when you lose someone."

Cass pushed the door open and flicked the butt into the gutter. The cigarette smoke was making his nausea worse, and he had this awful feeling that if he sat there long enough, flames would start to lick at his feet and neither of them would ever get out.

He gave her an awkward smile. "I know you're probably right, Claire. But I'd go mad." He sighed. "I can't let these cases slide, either. We owe those boys, and those poor dead women. Time won't wait for me to deal with my own shit."

"I'll pick you up in the morning, then."

He frowned.

"Your car's still at the station, remember?" She smiled. "If you change your mind about coming in, just let me know. Even if I'm already outside, okay?"

"Thanks." He got out of the car. "But I won't change my mind."

"I don't expect you will."

The look of gentle pity on Claire's face, probably not that different from the one he'd given to Clara Jackson and Eleanor Miller barely forty minutes previously, was enough to make him shut the car door and walk away. Cass knew he, of all people, did not deserve pity. Christian, Luke and Jessica deserved the pity. For a second he felt surrounded by dead children, all pointing accusingly at him. Forgive himself? How the hell was he ever supposed to do that? Claire kept the car running behind him but he didn't turn back. As he got to the front steps she pulled away and he let his shoulders slump.

There was too much weight on them.

Kate sat on the sofa, rocking backwards and forwards, her pale skin blotchy with tears. Sergeant Blackmore stood at the fireplace beside a man Cass didn't recognise. They nodded awkwardly at Cass and he returned the gesture. Kate didn't look up but pulled the cushion she was hugging closer to her chest. He flinched at the thought that she'd probably gain more comfort from an inanimate object than she did from him. Maybe it was time he stopped fighting it. He let people down. It's what he did.

"It's true, then?"

Blackmore nodded. "Sorry, sir."

"Don't be. You didn't shoot them." From the corner of his eye he saw Kate flinch. She never could stand his roughness, but he didn't know any other way to deal with pain.

The unknown man, thickset, in his fifties, stepped forward. "Detective Inspector Jones, I'm DI Ramsey. From Chelsea nick."

An American accent, and phrasing slightly odd. "Not originally, I take it."

"No. I guess home is really Eerie, Pennsylvania, but I left twenty years or more ago. Wouldn't recognise the place if I saw it now—and it certainly wouldn't recognise me."

"Were you on the scene?"

Ramsey nodded. "Yeah, I'm Murder Squad, like you. Responding car called us out. You know how the drill goes. I got there at about two this morning."

"How were they found?" Cass's voice sounded like a stranger's in his head. Was he really talking about his little brother and his family? The world glimmered as his breath hitched and stuck in his lungs as shock took a brief hold of him. For a moment it was as if a watery glow, like early autumn sunshine, coated Ramsey, shining out from the corners of his eyes. Cass blinked and it was gone.

"Your nephew was shot in his bed. Died instantly. He wouldn't have known anything about it."

"And Jessica?"

"The shot must have woken her up. She was found in the doorway of the main bedroom. He shot her once in the chest at point-blank range. She would have died instantly too." Ramsey kept his voice level. "It looks as if your brother then went downstairs. He shot himself in the lounge."

"Christian would never do something like that."

Ramsey shrugged and Blackmore looked down at his feet.

Cass felt his frustration rising. "I know it's the normal response from a relative, to disbelieve. I fucking *know* that." He swallowed hard and lowered his voice. "I'm just saying that Christian *really* wasn't the type."

"According to your wife he'd been trying to reach you for a few days? Is that right?"

"Yes. But I spoke to him briefly yesterday. He didn't sound suicidal."

"He was agitated." Kate's voice cut in, a monotone. She followed it with a loud phlegm-riddled sniff. "When he rang here last night he didn't sound right."

"I thought you said he sounded fine?" Cass stared at his wife, aware of the sharpness in his voice but unable to stop it. Kate met his eyes and for the first time, after everything they'd gone through in their marriage, he was sure he saw hate burning there. He winced.

"I said what you wanted to hear." A tight smile twisted on her lips as more tears spilled from her red eyes. "You weren't going to ring him anyway. You never do."

The truth stung him, and although his immediate reflex was to deny it, he bit the words back. It was a pointless argument. She was right. If she'd told him, it probably wouldn't have made any difference. He looked back at Ramsey. "Something was bothering him, yes."

His fellow DI's hooded eyes were thoughtful. "I sense there's more."

Cass shook his head a little. "It's just the way he sounded. He wanted to talk to me. I mean, *really* wanted to." He looked at Kate. "And my wife's right; I haven't been good at staying in touch. Ever since our parents died I've let our relationship slide. We're both grown-ups, with jobs that take up a lot of time. We spoke more frequently when Luke got ill, but even that wasn't that often. But the past few days, he's rung a lot, trying to catch up with me. He had something he wanted to tell me. It just doesn't make sense that he'd do this *without* having spoken to me first." Suddenly exhaustion seeped into his shoulders and he felt himself sag. "It doesn't feel right."

"There often isn't a lot of sense in suicide, boss," Blackmore said.

Cass glared at him, and was pleased to see Ramsey send him a sharp look too. The young man shrank back slightly against the wall.

"I understand where you're coming from," Ramsey said, stepping forward, "but you've got to let me run this and see how it plays out. And although we're treating this as murder-suicide, with no current outside suspects, there are two murders, and so the process is the same as always. Mark Farmer's the ME on the case, and you know he's the best. And if there's evidence of any outside interference at the scene, then trust me, the lab boys will find it." He paused. "That's the best I can tell you."

Cass nodded. Bile rose in his throat again, burning the soft tissue that was already sore from the cocaine he'd taken the previous night. This was too surreal, a bad trip. He still hadn't thrown the wrap away, and he caught himself wondering if maybe one small line—just a small one—would make the world a little better. It wouldn't help the pain, but it might just ease the huge tumour of guilt that was growing inside him. He squeezed the thought away.

"Thanks," he said. "You'll let me know when I can start arranging things?" *Things: caskets, flowers, cold graves.* None of the words fit with Christian in his head.

"Will do."

"If you need me I'm normally on my mobile. I've got two heavy cases on the go, so that's the best way to reach me."

The other DI didn't look surprised, nor did he try to persuade Cass to stay at home, and Cass liked him for that. Ramsey led the way out into the hallway, and after saying goodbyes, and telling Blackmore he'd be in tomorrow morning, Cass closed the door. The house felt like a tomb around him.

Now Kate's sobs echoed out from the lounge. She was taking it hard, he thought, and considered going to her, maybe putting his arm around her—but instead he ran to the downstairs bathroom and vomited loudly.

When he was done, he sat there with his head resting against the cool tiles until the heat left him and he started shivering. It felt surprisingly good. Eventually Kate peered through the door and handed him a glass of water.

"Are you okay?" The words were awkward. Her voice was thick with snot and the remnants of tears, and she didn't sound like herself. She stayed in the doorway, on the other side of the threshold.

"Do you think Christian did it?" he asked.

His throat was dry and he drained the water, fighting his stomach as it immediately tried to reject it. He didn't answer her question. Given the situation, and the fact that he was curled up against the wall of the toilet, he figured the answer was clear.

Eventually Kate shrugged. "I don't know." Her eyes focused on the hand basin, clearly not wanting to look at him. He watched her pick absently at the skin around her fingernails.

"What do you mean, you don't know?"

She chewed her bottom lip and Cass thought he saw the water in her eyes turn to ice for a moment. "There was a time when I thought *you* couldn't do something like that."

Cass recoiled, his skin cooling further. "How can you equate what I did with this? Jesus, Kate."

Finally, her eyes met his. "I can because you *do*. That's why you don't talk about it." Her tears rolled again, spilling in large drops from her chin. "I don't know whether Christian did it or not. But do I believe he *could*? Of course I do. I think we're all capable of terrible things if we're pushed, or if we're put into situations out of our control. And sometimes it's not our fault." Her breath hitched in her chest. "It was only you that ever thought you were beyond redemption, Cass, no one else. And now look where you are. Look at everything around you. It's all turned to shit."

One word cut through the sting of the rest: redemption. *It's about redemption. That's the key.* That was what Christian had said to him just before Cass had cut him off. Was that what Christian wanted to talk to him about? Forgiving himself? Even if Jessica had told him about their long-ago affair, why would he forgive Cass and then shoot her? And if it was for anything else, then why would it be so important to Christian now? There had to be more to what he wanted to talk to Cass about. Maybe Christian had done something and it was redemption for himself he was after . . . but by suicide? There had to be more to it. He banged his head slowly against the cold tiles. Or maybe he was just *wanting* there to be more so he could go on thinking that this wasn't a crazy gene taking his baby brother over the edge and he hadn't even noticed.

"Are you even listening to me?" Her voice was cold again, all emotion leached out.

"This isn't about me."

"No." She smiled, but there was no warmth in it. "No, it isn't. You're just making it that way."

"What the hell is that supposed to mean?"

"You figure it out."

Cass put the glass down carefully on the floor, determined not to throw it. "My brother just died, Kate. Why are we fighting?"

They stared at each other for a long time across the abyss that separated them.

"Because it's all we know what to do any more." She crouched beside him. Close up, even under the bright lights and with her face streaked and blotchy, she was still beautiful. "Apart from one thing." Her fingers ran gently through his hair and her body heat reached for him. "I'm sorry. I'm so sorry." Her voice was barely a whisper. "Come upstairs, Cass. Please."

She kissed his head before getting up and walking away. After a while Cass got up and followed her. He needed warmth, and God help him, whatever love she had for him was all he had left.

This time, however, they were both saved the awkwardness of the quiet time afterwards by the quiet buzz of his mobile ringing. Cass stared at the ceiling for a minute before sitting up to take the call. He knew who it would be. Ramsey. And he knew what he'd want. Some-

one had to do it and Cass was the only one left. He listened and muttered a quiet "yes," before reaching for his discarded clothes. The car
would be coming for him in twenty minutes.

The morgue was cold, and even out in the corridor, Claire shivered.
She didn't have to be here. She could be on her way home, or at the pub
with Mat, or even still at the station, but there was no way she'd let
Cass Jones do this alone. Mat hadn't understood why Cass had wanted
to go through this procedure at all when photos would have sufficed.
But then, she thought, wrapping her arms round her slim body in an
effort to fight the chill, Mat would never see how deeply Cass's still
waters ran. Of course, he'd want to identify the bodies himself. It was
as close to paying them some respect as he could get straight away.
Shoes tapped their way along the corridor and she looked up.

"Sir," she nodded at Ramsey.

"What are you doing here, Claire?" Cass said. "The fewer dead bodies you see in your life the better for your soul and your sleep, trust me."

"This is different."

"No it isn't. Not for you."

"I would want a friend with me," she answered softly. "I'd want
you with me."

Inspector Ramsey had stepped ahead and she was glad. Although
their relationship was over and done a long time before, she knew it
wouldn't take a genius to see the strength of feeling she still had for the
tall, dark detective. She might fool herself at times, but she wouldn't
fool anyone with half an eye for these things.

"You ready?" The DI looked back at them, one hand already pushing the door open. "Let's get this done quickly."

Claire followed the two men inside. Her mouth dried as she drew
level with Cass. She'd done this before; it wasn't the presence of death
that disturbed her, it was these particular deaths which made her
stomach flip. *Cass's family.* A brother he'd rarely spoken about, a wife
and a child.

"You know how this works, Jones." Dr. Farmer was gripping the
handle of the first metal drawer. "I'm sorry."

"Get on with it," Cass growled.

Claire wasn't fooled. She saw the twitch in his jaw as he clenched his teeth. She'd seen that before in the heat of a very different kind of emotion.

The drawer slid open. Even from where she was standing, slightly behind Cass, Claire could see that the space was woefully too large for the small figure inside. Dr. Farmer reached in and carefully folded down the sheet from over the boy's face.

"Is this your nephew Luke Jones?" Inspector Ramsey asked.

The child was perfectly still against the metal, his blond hair combed backwards away from his face. Claire wasn't sure that's how he would have worn it to school. There would have been gel and spikes by this age, or at least the semblance of a style emerging. His skin was pale and smooth and his eyes shut. He had long eyelashes, she noted, and they were dark. Her heart squeezed tight. This was the third dead boy she'd seen in a month, all blasted by bullets. Somewhere under the sheet would be the cleaned-out mess, all that was left of the slight boy's torso.

"Yes." Cass didn't take his eyes from the boy's face. Even knowing him as she did—or thought she did—Claire wondered how he could stay so self-contained. She watched him as Dr. Farmer closed the drawer and opened the second. Another sandy head was revealed, closed eyes, closed mouth. Calm after the storm. Claire tried to imagine the woman animated, maybe calling to the child now lying so still in the darkness on the other side of the metal wall. She shivered again, this time not from the cold, but at the speed at which death could come. Jessica Jones had gone to bed fully expecting to get up and feed her son, ready to send him off to school, to face another ordinary London day. Instead, one blast to the body and she was gone. Claire's own mortality clung to her for a moment, time and place unknown but there all the same, just waiting for her arrival.

"That's my sister-in-law, Jessica Jones." Cass's words were hard but fast. At his side, one hand was clenched. Claire wanted to prise those fingers open and take his hand, for her own comfort as much as his. Maybe he'd been right. Maybe the dead were to be avoided when possible. This wasn't like seeing the Jackson and Miller boys dead, or any of the other corpses she'd had to deal with in her time on the force. This was something different. These were personal deaths: parts of Cass Jones' life gone, forever.

"You may prefer to provide photographic identification for Christian," Dr. Farmer said. "I've done what I can, but given the nature of his—"

"Is his face recognisable?" Cass said. "If so, then just open the bloody drawer."

The ME tilted his head in an almost nod. Claire could see he thought Cass was crazy, and now that they were here, so did she. Why would he want to cause himself that extra pain? Surely it would be better to remember his brother whole? It was almost as if he wanted to add to his own suffering.

After the drawer opened there was a moment of silence. Claire glanced only briefly inside. She'd seen this kind of death before, car crash victims and suicides. Despite Dr. Farmer's best efforts to pull Christian's face back into place, it didn't quite sit right on what was left of the bones of his skull. The shotgun had destroyed the top of his head, and no doubt taken the back out completely. Someone, either the ME or his assistant, had folded a sheet and placed it beneath the destroyed head, attempting to make it lie at least close to where it should. There was very little left for Christian's skin to cling to, and even with whatever tricks of his trade Dr. Farmer had used, it was clear that this was just a mockery of how the man had looked in life.

Inspector Ramsey turned away, and Claire knew it wasn't from the sight of the body. It was from the man standing beside it. Did Cass even realise how terrible the expression on his face was? Claire had expected to see pain; but what she was looking at was something else, a whole whirlwind of feelings trapped in brown eyes and clenched fists. He looked haunted. As if there were too many demons fighting to control him.

"That's Christian."

As soon as he'd spoken, Cass turned and walked from the room. Inspector Ramsey went to follow him, but Claire grabbed his arm. "Let him go, sir."

The DI stared at her and almost pulled his arm away, but then he stopped. He must have read the look on Cass's face too. "Maybe you're right."

"I know him. He just needs some time on his own."

They walked down the corridor side by side, but quietly. Neither was interested in small talk. Cass's pace had been fast and angry and he was long gone by the time she walked out into the evening air. Her heart suddenly felt heavy. Despite what she'd just said to Inspector Ramsey, she really wasn't very sure she knew Cass well at all.

It was raining when Cass paid the cab driver and stepped out onto the pavement a street away from where Christian lived in the chic end of Notting Hill. It was gone midnight, and other than the rhythmic on-slaught of the falling water the roads were quiet. He'd gone to the pub and then home briefly, relieved to find Kate sleeping, her passion spent. Arguing and sex, the two went hand in hand down the aisle of their marriage. They were now in the lull before the next fight, a period when they moved around each other like strangers, both wondering what it was about the other that could inspire such negative passion. It wasn't a good place to be, but at least she'd stopped crying. She'd done enough of that for both of them.

Rain beat at his face as he turned away from the main road and down towards the house where Christian and Jessica had lived for the last decade. Even as a much younger man, Christian had always been so reliable. He'd worked hard all his life, crunching numbers for people who were too busy being out there actually living, spending the money they'd made, to do it for themselves.

When The Bank was formed back in 2010, the one company that had a chance of bringing the world back from the brink of disaster, Christian had been head-hunted, and almost as soon as he'd arrived he'd thrived, with promotion following bonus following promotion. He must have earned three times Cass's salary, maybe more, but he and Jessica had never wanted to move. They'd had Luke there. It was their home.

It didn't look much like a home now. It was dark and cold, and the thick yellow ribbon wrapped around it declared it out of bounds. The bodies were out and most of the plastic-suited plod had gone. One van further along the road had its engine running, and Cass presumed some poor sod—either freelance or the new boy—had been left there to see if anything else developed over the course of the night. Looked like most of the press thought they'd got all they could from the scene of this crime; they'd already started the hatchet job on the monster who'd so brutally murdered his wife and son. Between the ongoing story of Jackson and Miller, the murder of yet another young woman and this, even in a city where violent death was becoming more and more frequent, the editors of the red tops would doubtless be rubbing their filthy hands in glee.

A uniformed officer stood in front of the crime scene tape, his reflective yellow jacket shining clearly, even through the rain. There would be another at the back, and perhaps two more in a nearby car. The team had had nearly twenty-four hours inside so the scene had pretty much been processed by now, but there was no shortage of ghouls and freaks who would love to get inside the house before the blood had dried. The police guard would be present until the cleaning team had been in and returned the walls and carpets to some semblance of normality.

Cass crossed the street at the corner and kept in the shadows. Lights shone from several of the houses around him. City crime didn't normally touch these people. The recession might have forced their children out of the private schools and chichi nurseries that once littered these middle-class streets, but the residents here were not yet touched by the social effects of the global slide. They might know neighbours, friends, even, who had had to move away, selling up cheap if they could, having their houses repossessed if they'd acted too late. Cass wondered if any of this had shocked the good burghers of Notting Hill, if any of them had been quietly peering out from behind their curtains as a bailiff's van removed someone's last goods and chattels and wondering what on earth could have happened to cause this tragedy, and how they didn't spot the signs.

As he pulled his badge out from his back pocket, Cass thought how little he knew about his brother's life—not just the day-to-day minutiae, but who his friends were, what his dreams were, his ambitions . . . These were just empty spaces in Cass's memory. He bit back his guilt, but it raked at his insides. It shouldn't have surprised him; he'd made this situation. He just hadn't expected Christian to change it. Not like this.

The constable couldn't look Cass in the eye, and he wondered if maybe they'd met before in the canteen, or perhaps over paperwork processing. It was possible. They walked in silence from the gate to the path, and when they reached the front door, Cass ducked under the tape.

"Thanks for this."

The constable nodded. He looked very young. "There are gloves in a box just inside the door. If you could put some on . . ."

Cass nodded.

"The SOCOs are done here now. The case being, well—" His voice stumbled. "I don't think they're looking for anyone else. But it's best to be careful."

"I won't be long." He pushed open the broken door and stepped inside.

It was cold—that was the first thing he noticed, and the air inside already smelled damp. When the team arrived on the scene they would have turned off the central heating as a matter of course. For most of the day the front door would have been left open as people trudged in and out, bagging and photographing and scraping. It hadn't taken long for the March weather to chase out any hint of human scent and replace it with this chill emptiness.

He flicked the light on. At the bottom of the stairs a pair of scruffy trainers sat beside some polished brogues, black lace-ups, looking as if they'd been kicked off in haste. They were all small: Luke's shoes. A knife ran its serrated edge through his heart and he forced his feet forward. He needed to *see*. The stairwell rose upwards into blackness. Cass didn't turn the hall light on. Christian wouldn't have done. The light might have woken Jessica or Luke, and that would have made things messy. As he climbed, Cass imagined the weight of the gun in his hand, primed and ready to fire. Did Christian have spare shells tucked into a pocket, just in case he didn't kill his family cleanly? His mouth dried as the darkness of the landing reached out for him. Had his brother's mouth felt the same? Had the weapon slid about in sweaty hands?

Luke's bedroom was at the end of the corridor. He'd go there first, just as Christian had. The floorboards creaked as he walked. Ahead, the door was wide open and the lights were off. Cass saw it differently. The door would have been a little ajar, revealing the small glow of a plug-in night-light. That was probably enough for Christian to aim properly. He wondered if Christian had made sure Luke had left it on last night so that he would make no mistakes. *When had Christian learned to shoot?*

Cass reached the doorway and took two steps inside. Even in the dark, the black stain across the bed shone out, as if the child's unreleased scream had been trapped in his warm blood and soaked into the shredded soft flesh of the mattress. He tried to imagine Christian standing over the sleeping form of his sick eight-year-old son and blasting a hole into him. His breathing quickened. He couldn't look at the football posters on the wall and the school books scattered over the small desk that would never be written in again. Luke was dead. Killed by his father. It was true.

He turned and almost stumbled, gripping the door to keep his balance, half-expecting to feel Luke's small bloody fingers pulling him back, squeezing in alongside those others that already tugged at him . . .

There was nothing. In the hallway he took three long breaths. He wanted to run. He wanted to stay. The conflicting urges waged silent war as he leaned against the wall. Somewhere downstairs a clock ticked loudly and he concentrated on the sound until he'd regained his equilibrium before slowly taking the two extra stairs up to the next landing, where the master bedroom was.

It was pitch-black away from the glow of light at the bottom of the house, but it wouldn't have been by the time Christian reached it the previous night. Jessica had woken up at the sound of the first gunshot. She'd have turned on the bedside light straight away. Cass flicked the switch at his side, illuminating the short passageway, and stared into the open bedroom. He could almost see Jessica sitting on the edge of the bed, her eyes widening as she realised that the sound hadn't just been in her dream. Maybe maternal instinct had told her that something was terribly, terribly wrong. Perhaps she called out Christian's name as she finally got her legs to move so she could run to check on her child.

She'd died in the doorway. Her blood had soaked into the cream carpet, a foot or more on either side of the door. Christian must have shot her from the first step, otherwise the blast would have flung her backwards. What was running through her head in those last moments between seeing the gun and the shell hitting her chest? Did she see the madness in her husband's eyes? Did she wonder, after all these years, if somehow he *knew*? Or would there have just been blind terror?

His head filled with the half-forgotten scent of oatmeal shampoo, and he remembered how he'd wrapped his hands in that thick, blonde hair and buried his face in that clean smell. He remembered how she'd hated herself for it, and then hated him. Blood smeared the skirting boards, as if perhaps she'd tried to hold on to life by grabbing at them. He hoped she hadn't died hating herself. She didn't deserve any of it.

He turned the light out and went downstairs. The large living/dining room was open plan, with an occasional step up or down to ring the changes. The reclaimed hardwood floorboards shone, and he could see the indentions in the two huge sofas where his brother's family had sat in front of the plasma TV the previous evening. The *TV Times* was open on the coffee table, next to a small ring on the surface where a mug had recently sat and was now probably bagged and tagged and removed. Was that Christian's last cup of coffee? Had he sat there and drunk it before heading upstairs?

Cass moved up to the dining area. He swallowed hard as heat flushed through his system. One chair was turned out from the table, and behind it the wall was tie-dye-splattered with blood. There was more than blood there, even if his blurring eyes didn't want to see it. There would be skull fragments and grey clumps of his brother's brain clinging to the paint and plaster. The knife that had been toying with his heart made its final incision and cut deep, tearing the organ in two. His baby brother had died here. He'd killed his family, come downstairs and carefully tucked the shotgun under his chin and pulled the trigger.

Water trickled over Cass's own chin and as he wiped it away he was surprised to find it tasted salty. It wasn't rainwater dripping down from his hair but tears. He gritted his teeth, trying to contain his grief, because he needed to *see*. There was more blood around the chair itself, but it had none of the angry energy of the spray on the wall. This blood had dripped slowly, like his tears, ticking away the minutes until the neighbours had called the police and outside life had invaded the house. He couldn't picture his baby brother here. Why hadn't he shot himself upstairs, where he could lie with Jessica or Luke? What could possibly have made him want to do this—and this way? *Look, we really need to talk, Cass. I mean it.* Cass remembered his own impatient reaction to Christian's words and the way he'd shaken him off like an irritating puppy. His baby brother had needed him, and once again, Cass hadn't been there. Emotion pressed into his chest like a rock, suffocating him.

The chair fell out of focus and as grief, anger and guilt raged through him Cass let his head hang and the tears come. Heaving sobs racked his body; his shoulders shook and, oblivious to the blood, he sank to his knees as if he were praying. For a while the world around him was lost.

When Cass finally came to, his legs were numb and he felt cried out. He was about to pull himself to his feet when the clear sound of footsteps on the wooden floor cut through his pain and dragged him back to the here and now. The footsteps stopped behind him. He sniffed hard and wiped his eyes, dragging the back of his hand across his face like a child. This was all he needed: to be found curled up on the floor sobbing his eyes out by some constable barely out of Hendon. It would be all round the nick by the morning. He hated that it mattered to him, but it did. Reputation was everything. He'd learned that the hard way.

"I said I'd be out in a minute."

The figure behind him stayed silent. Cass frowned and lifted his head. His eyes widened. Below the seat in front of him, the pulled-out seat on which Christian had died, was a shiny pair of black lace-ups under dark trouser hems. Fresh blood dripped beside them. He watched a solid crimson drop tumble and break against the wood. A tiny particle landed on the highly polished expensive leather of the left shoe. *Christian's shoes.*

His breath trapped in his chest, Cass scuttled backwards and blinked. The feet were gone. He spun onto his knees to face the intruder behind him, but the room was empty. Trying not to panic, he forced himself upwards, his joints stiff, complaining, and started turning this way and that, looking for whichever bastard was stupid enough to play games with him, here, at this time.

His body trembled. The house was empty. There was no dying brother in the dining room chair. He let out a laugh that was almost a cough and a sob. Of course there wasn't. Christian was on a slab in the morgue; dead and gone. His lace-up shoes and black suit trousers would be in an evidence locker somewhere until the case was formally closed, when they'd be burned in the incinerator. It was just his mind playing tricks. That was all. Too much cocaine and too little sleep and too much death, all catching up with him.

His legs felt unsteady and he reached clumsily for the chair at Christian's desk. It had been built neatly into the alcove under the stairs so he could be part of the family while he worked. The family that he'd one day murder as they slept.

Cass slumped into the chair and let out a low moan. Fucking drugs. He hadn't taken any that night, despite the almost overwhelming temptation, but whatever was still in his system from the night before had obviously kicked in again, taking him on a little bonus trip. His eyes felt like they were burning in the corners. He ran one hand through his thick dark hair, then rubbed his face. He was cold.

His heart thudded back to something resembling a normal pace and he finally turned back to the dining room chair. It was empty. Of course it was. What he'd seen had just been a figment of his imagination. It had been a moment of madness, that was all. It wasn't real. For one thing, why would Christian still be wearing his office clothes at midnight? He came home and got changed, just like every other nine-to-fiver in the city. Two uniforms: suited and booted for work, smartly creased chinos and Lauren polo shirts for play.

He looked at the desk and frowned again. Christian was nothing if not anal; it was part of what made him so good with numbers. So what was his laptop bag doing sitting on the desk with the tiny, top-of-the-range computer sitting on top of it, unopened? He tilted his head. It looked like Christian had been about to start work, or was putting it away, and neither scenario made sense. He wouldn't have got it out for a suicide note; those were virtually always handwritten.

He lifted the machine carefully and peered into the bag. The lead was still inside, tucked into one of the holders. The strange vision temporarily forgotten, he looked back at the mug ring on the table and the discarded magazine. Those didn't make sense either. Christian would have tidied up. It was his nature. Even if doing something as terrible as this, he would have made sure everything was in its place first. He would need to feel ordered. Cass chewed his bottom lip. Something wasn't right. He could feel it in the pulse of his blood. Working entirely on instinct, he slid the laptop carefully into its case and tucked the slim bag into his jacket. He folded his arms across his chest, holding it in place. It was dark outside and the constable was young. If he hunched over and looked upset enough, he might just get away with it.

Luckily, the rain was coming down heavier than ever and the duty policeman had to squint in the downpour to see him as he nodded his thanks. As he headed towards the main road and the hope of a taxi, Cass guessed that was the last time that copper would come out on night duty without an umbrella. That was the thing with policing; the only way you really learned anything was the hard way.

Kate was still asleep when he got in, breathing in long, exhausted sighs as she twitched restlessly, the sheets snarled up around her legs. Cass watched her for a moment and then pulled the door quietly shut before going downstairs. After a moment of thought he squeezed the black case into the tiny gap behind the TV where it was fixed to the wall. It held steadily. That would do for now. He wasn't really sure why he'd taken the laptop. He doubted it even belonged to his brother; it was probably the property of The Bank—but if it came down to it, so was pretty much everything else in the world. It just felt right to take it. If he hadn't thought he'd seen those feet, he probably wouldn't even have spotted it. Maybe his mind was trying to tell him something—or maybe, he thought as he headed to the kitchen, subconsciously he just wanted to have something personal of his brother's. And he knew Christian well enough to know his laptop was probably the most personal item in the house.

After grabbing a beer from the fridge he called the station, then the mobile number the duty sergeant gave him. It rang out several times before a sleepy voice answered, "Ramsey!"

"It's Jones."

There was a pause as the other DI came to slightly. Sheets rustled, then he said, "Do you know what time it is?" He groaned and then answered his own question. "God, half-past two."

"Sorry. I just wanted to ask you a question about my brother."

"Go on."

"What was he wearing when he was found?"

"Why do you want to know that?" Despite being obviously sleepy, Ramsey sounded curious.

"I just need to know. For my head." It was the best he could come up with, and it was the truth, in its own way.

Ramsey sighed. "Okay. He was wearing a pale blue shirt and black Armani suit trousers. His jacket wasn't on and his tie was loosened."

"And his shoes?" Cass gripped the phone and the beer bottle tight.

"Brogues. Polished black lace-ups."

Cass couldn't speak. The world shifted again.

"Can I go back to sleep now?"

"Yes, sorry," Cass mumbled, already flipping his phone shut. "Thanks."

He sat still, staring at nothing for a long while, before draining his beer and going up to the spare room. He had to be up early in the morning and Kate deserved a lie-in. The crisp sheets smelled fresh, of soap powder, and felt comfortingly anonymous under him. There was something soothing in that. He let his tired eyes shut. From the other room he heard his wife let out an anxious whimper and he wondered what plagued her sleep. For his own part, when the cold fingers finally dragged him down to the darkness, he dreamed of shoes that left no bloody footprints.

CHAPTER SIX

Claire rang him four times before he finally woke up, disoriented by the unfamiliar surroundings. For a moment he wasn't sure where he'd expected to be: his own bed, or curled up on the floor in his dead brother's house. He swung his legs over the side and yawned. He looked at his watch. It was eight o'clock, and that took him by surprise. He'd expected her here by seven-fifteen. Trust her to take it on herself to give him a lie-in. He stretched. To be fair, it was probably a good thing. It might have been only a few hours' sleep, but it had been deep, and for the first time in God knew how long he felt refreshed and alert, despite the hollow ache in every bone and fibre of his body.

He wrapped the sheet around him and let Claire in, then showered and dressed while she made coffee and toast. He paused as he pulled on his trousers, staring at the darkness of the fabric, reminded of that strange moment in the gloom at Christian's house. He felt vaguely unsettled by the experience, and in the bright light of the morning the idea that he'd seen or heard anything supernatural in the house was ridiculous. He regretted his call to Ramsey too; he'd just been overwrought.

He reached for his jacket and headed back down the stairs. There was nothing more to it. Christian had done a terrible thing and now they were all dead. There was nothing he could do about it apart from add more guilt to the load his soul was already bearing. He should have spoken to his brother and he hadn't. It was done. He had to live with it. He'd learned to live with worse.

He sat on the second-bottom step to pull on his shoes—black lace-ups, although not expensive, highly polished hand-tooled brogues like Christian's, just scuffed chain-store shoes. Space felt empty around him. They were all gone now, all his blood relatives: his parents, and now Christian and Luke. Maybe he'd always been the outsider, or maybe he'd just made himself that way, it was hard to tell, but his heart ached as he realised there was now no hope of ever going back, even if he knew how.

Claire pushed a mug and a plate over to him as she finished a call on her mobile. He took the coffee, but ignored the toast. She looked at him, but didn't ask the question aloud. They understood each other too well for that.

"I had a call from the lab on my way in." Excitement warred with pity in her clear eyes.

"And?"

"They got an ID on that partial print. It belongs to an Adam Bradley. He's a twenty-two-year-old known junkie with four petty theft convictions."

"No shit."

"And there's more. You're going to love this bit."

Cass watched her over his mug. Claire was many things, but over-excitable wasn't one of them. His unease and grief slid sideways, not disappearing, but sinking into the corners of his mind where it could wait until a quiet moment to catch him again. Claire had something good to tell him. His heart thumped. "Get on with it then."

"They've rechecked it several times, just to make sure. Adam Bradley is also on the long list of people whose DNA was found in the squat where Carla Rae died."

"What?" Coffee slopped over the side as Cass almost dropped the mug.

"One of the empty junkie syringes was his. Mat—Sergeant Blackmore—took a car to pick him up. His known address is that block two floors down from the murder scene." She held up her phone. "That was Mat. Bradley was fast asleep when they got there. No resistance. They're taking him back to the station now."

Cass grinned. "We'd better make sure we're there to meet him then."

Adam Bradley was twitchy. He picked at the scabs on his skinny white arms with nails bitten down to the quick. His face was gaunt, framed by black hair that hung almost to his shoulders and was thick with grease and full of dandruff. Cass reckoned that as junkies went, Adam Bradley was pretty well on his way to being a veteran. His bloodshot blue eyes flickered nervously around the room, going everywhere but to Cass. He licked his lips frequently, but ignored the plastic cup of tea on the table in front of him. Tea wasn't going to help Adam Bradley feel better.

Cass slid a cigarette across and watched as Bradley's trembling fingers took it. He sucked the smoke in gratefully; any high in a rock-bottom low. Cass lit one of his own. He could sympathise with that feeling, not that Adam Bradley would ever realise that. Through the glass he was pretty sure he could feel DCI Neil Morgan's disapproval, but he ignored it. The one place in the country where people could smoke indoors was the interview room of a police station or a prison . . . but only if you were on the wrong side of the bars. Well, fuck that, Cass thought, if the little fucker in front of him got to smoke, then he couldn't see why he had to go without.

Tim Hask had arrived at the station just after them. He was watching the interview from the other side of the glass, but Cass figured he could go home, save himself the effort. It didn't take an internationally renowned profiler to know that Adam Bradley didn't kill those girls. He couldn't keep his hands steady enough to plant those fly eggs for one thing. And for another, it was obvious from the state of him that the only person Adam Bradley was intent on killing was himself. It was the DVD Cass was interested in, and that case had nothing to do with Hask.

"You need a shower," Cass said finally.

Bradley snorted, a nervous laugh he hid behind the hand curled across his face. The cigarette was never more than an inch or two from his mouth. As he hunched over, the bones of his shoulders were clearly visible, poking through the grubby, out-of-shape T-shirt.

"No, really. You stink."

The young man shrugged. "No hot water."

As he spoke Cass saw gaps where his side teeth were missing. He had a year, two at best, before the lab boys would be scraping him off the floor of some doss house or other. Cass didn't feel any sympathy. Life was hard and everyone had to learn to live with the choices they made. Bradley made a choice every time he cooked up some H. He looked like he'd long ago accepted the lows with the highs.

"Tell me about the envelope."

Bradley's eyes narrowed with junkie meanness. "What envelope?"

"Listen," Cass growled, leaning forward, "I don't know how you think this is going to play out, but I will tell you right now, it won't be with me sticking twenty quid in your pocket and sending you on your way with a 'thanks for the information, come back soon' kiss."

He snorted again. Cass figured it was a nervous reaction. It looked like that was *exactly* how Adam Bradley saw the interview going. Addicts were invisible people, and there were plenty of them—and not just in the rougher parts of town, either. As the economy crumbled, so drug usage rose, dragging many traditional middle-class areas of town into squalor. From their street corners and squats, junkies saw and heard things, and many policemen would slip them a twenty out of their own pocket for anonymous information. A quick arrest and conviction would earn much more than that. Cass thought it was interesting that Bradley obviously had no idea how deep the shit was around him.

"We have your fingerprint on an envelope that was delivered here for me last night. Do you know what was in that envelope?"

Bradley replied with silence and an insolent stare, but Cass recognised a twitch of fear in it.

"It was a DVD. A film of two boys getting gunned down in central London last week," Cass said, producing a couple of stills from his pocket and laying them on the table between them.

Adam Bradley's eyes widened. "That was nothing—"

"And on top of that, we can link you to another murder scene."

This time the junkie's swallow was audible. "I don't know what you're talking about, man," he whispered, his voice trembling. "I don't know what's going on"—his eyes flickered over to Claire, looking for some support—"but this is some kind of crazy set-up. I don't know nothing about no one dying."

"A woman was found murdered in a flat two floors above yours two days ago. We found a used syringe with your blood in it in the same flat. That was the same day the envelope arrived containing a film of two more murders. The envelope had your fingerprint on it." He paused. "Can you see how things might be looking very bad for you?"

For the first time since they'd brought him in, Adam Bradley showed some energy. He leaned forward, his elbows on the table. "I don't know nothing about them things." His foot twitched under the table. "I don't know nothing."

Cass watched his eyes watering up. In the bright light his tears shone pale yellow for a moment, and something about that disturbed him. He stared, but it was gone. Bradley was just crying, that was all, which didn't come as any surprise. It didn't take much to make a junkie cry. They spent most of the time thinking the world had done them wrong, so tears were never that far back.

"Prove it." He ground his cigarette out in the tin ashtray and blew the last lungful of hot smoke into the sallow, pockmarked face in front of him. "It was you who brought the envelope here, yes?"

"Yeah, but that was all I did. That was—"

"Stop whining," Cass barked. "If it was nothing to do with you, then who gave it to you? And where?" He slid the cigarettes across the table and his voice softened. "Take your time. Tell me everything. I want every detail. It would be easy for me to get a quick conviction on you with the DNA evidence we've got already. If you leave anything out, getting your next fix will be the least of your worries."

He meant it too. He needed every little detail. Witnesses never knew what was important and what wasn't, and too many cases got fucked up because of a detail left out of a statement because *the witness* didn't think it was relevant.

"Where did you meet this person?"

Bradley lit a fresh cigarette from the burning filter of the first. There was no tobacco wasted. "I saw him on Wednesday morning. I couldn't sleep. I needed a hit. I'd waited till about seven-thirty before going out to see if I could score something on tick till I'd sorted some cash. There was this bloke—he was just wandering round the blocks." He sniffed, regaining what little composure he had. "I thought he was lost or something 'cos he was well out of place. I thought I might have a go at tapping his wallet. I used to be good at that shit when I was a kid."

"What did he look like?"

Bradley looked around the room, then focused on Cass again. "Old—I reckon he was about fifty, maybe even older—but old in a way like people are that have money. He had grey hair—well, more silver, you know what I mean? And a tan. He was wearing a dark suit and a long overcoat. Wool, maybe, but something expensive. And he had very white teeth. They was perfect."

Cass detected a touch of envy lurking in Bradley's voice.

He was surprised to find himself impressed—and a little sad. Hidden within that ruined exterior was the wreckage of a good mind, the ghost of a man who could have been something.

Bradley went on, "And he was carrying a briefcase kind of thing, but soft. I thought maybe he worked for the council or something."

"You've got a good memory for detail."

A soft smile brushed across the man's lips. "Not really. He was one of those blokes you don't forget in a hurry."

"So what happened?"

"I stumbled, and bumped him, to get my hand in his coat. I was good too, given how shaky I felt. Anyone else and I think I'd have got away with it." He drew on the cigarette. "Most people like that, they sort of, you know, pull away if someone like me goes near them. Like they're going to get the bug just by looking at us." The bug: the street name for Strain II, the new variant of AIDS that was proving impossible to treat. As with the original virus, it preyed on the junkies first, finding an easy way into society through shared needles. The addicts had always been ostracised, but once the bug came along, *no one* would touch them.

"In case you were wondering," Claire looked up from the file she'd opened, "you're clean. You don't have the bug."

The man's eyes widened and he started to smile for the first time since they'd picked him up.

"Well, that was on Wednesday," Cass added. "That's two days ago. This is a whole new world."

Bradley shook his head. His eyes were gleaming. "I haven't shared nothing since then."

"Hooray. You live to infect yourself another day." Cass leaned forward. "Back to Wednesday. You tried to rob this man, and then what?"

"He grabbed my arm. He had gloves on, leather maybe—they were soft, but he had a real firm grip. I thought he might break my wrist." He flinched at the memory. "I think I shouted at him, called him a perv or something. I tried yanking myself free." He paused. "And then he smiled. And I don't know why, but I just stopped struggling."

"What happened next?"

"He said he had a job for someone like me. Wouldn't take long, and paid well. I thought he meant something"—he looked up awkwardly at Claire, a little embarrassed—"you know, to do with sex, and I told him I didn't do that. And I don't. He just laughed at that."

Cass thought he could see the stranger's point. Even without the bug, he figured Adam Bradley's body was probably host to myriad other unpleasant infections.

"I told him I needed to sort myself out and that I couldn't think. He must have seen I meant it 'cos he let my arm go. I was sweating bad, and the cramps were coming on. He asked me where I normally went to shoot up and I told him—well, I gave him the address of the squat two floors up." He looked at Cass. "Where you lot found that woman. A mate of mine was dealing out of it before he got nicked a couple of weeks back. He gave me the key, told me to keep an eye on it while he was away. Anyway, I told this bloke to meet me there in ten, fifteen minutes, to give me time to sort myself out."

"Did you ask him for money?"

Bradley nodded. "Yeah, but he said not till after. He said I looked 'resourceful enough' to get what I needed without his help." He shook his head. "I knew he was laughing at me, but I didn't care. I could feel him watching me when I went off, all the way."

"Did you think about not meeting him at the flat?"

"No." He shrugged. "Not just 'cos he was offering me dough; there was something about him that freaked me out—still does, if I think on it. It was his smile, and the way he gripped my wrist so tightly, with his eyes shining and just smiling the whole time like I was his oldest mate in the world. I wouldn't have wanted to not do what he wanted, even though he hadn't threatened me or nothing. You ever meet anyone like that?"

Cass tried not to glance at the two-way wall. "My boss has his moments. Go on."

Bradley smiled nervously, before refocusing on his memory. "So he was there waiting for me when I got back. He opened his bag—his briefcase—and took out some things. There was this big envelope. It had a typed label on it already: Detective Inspector Cass Jones—that's you, I guess."

Cass nodded, and waited for the rest of the story.

"I was sitting in the armchair, sorting out my shit, and he put it on the arm of the chair and then chucked a pair of gloves on my lap. Nice leather ones, expensive, I reckon. He said I was to deliver his envelope to Paddington nick, right after he'd gone, and to make sure I wore the gloves when I did it, and to bin them after. And not to give my name."

"Did he give you his?" Cass asked, almost flippantly, and found himself almost shocked into silence at Bradley's reply.

"Yeah, he did, as it goes. He gave me the hundred quid, and I thought he was leaving so I shot meself up. But he didn't go; he was peering out through the curtains and going on and on about how everything was planned and there were no coincidences. He kept saying everything happened for a reason, and asking if I believed that. I wasn't really listening, I'd got the dosh and I just wanted him to go. He gave me the creeps. When the smack hit me I said something like, 'Who are you, anyway?' He smiled that creepy smile again and said, 'My name is Mr. Bright.' It was a real smug smile, as if I'd done just what he'd expected."

"Mr. Bright? No first name?"

"I don't think he's the sort of bloke that uses one." Bradley had nearly finished the second cigarette and the trembling in his hands was getting stronger. "I don't remember much after that. I zoned out a bit, and when I came to he was gone. I went down to my mum's place for a while and when I was a bit straighter I brought the envelope here."

"How did the print get on it?"

Bradley shrugged. "I knocked it off the arm of the chair. I started to pick it up when I remembered about the gloves. My finger just touched it once. Didn't think it would matter." He smiled a little. "I guess I was wrong."

Cass leaned back in the chair. Something was bugging him, tickling away at the back of his brain. "How did you get here and back?" he asked.

"Bus and then tube."

"Did you go straight home?"

"No way, man." Bradley shook his head vehemently. "I went to pay the bloke I owed and pick up some more H and he told me there was cop cars all over my block, and to maybe go and see some friends or something till they were gone. It's what I did."

Cass suddenly realised what was bugging him. They'd had to break into the flat where Carla was lying dead, serenaded by heavy metal music. "Did you leave the squat unlocked?"

"No, I always shut it properly." Bradley looked awkward. "Thing is, when I finally got home and straightened out, well, I realised the key wasn't in my jeans."

"Was that the first time you noticed it was gone?"

"Yeah. I didn't think to check before. I was too busy thinking about getting that envelope delivered. I thought it was in my pocket."

Cass frowned. "Could this Mr. Bright have taken it?"

Bradley shrugged, his face a little embarrassed. "I don't know, man—I was out of it for a little while. He could've, I guess, before he left."

"Think hard." Cass felt his patience begin to wear thin. He was still sick with his own grief that he was trying hard to ignore.

"Is there anywhere you could have left it? Or could someone else have stolen it from you?"

The boy sat silent for a minute. "He could have taken it from me in the flat. I told you, I was well out of it. But there was this bloke who fell into me on the Tube too, so maybe it slipped out of my jacket then. I was just thinking about keeping the envelope safe." He shrugged. "I don't know where it went. I just know that I don't have it any more." His eyes were almost puppy-dog in their desperation. "I had nothing to do with anyone dying, honest, man."

Cass found himself nodding. "I believe you."

A constable took Bradley back to the cells and Cass sent down a consent for methadone. He wasn't ready to let the kid go yet, and he obviously needed something to get him out of his own personal hell. Maybe if they kept him in long enough he'd leave the H and the needles alone and stick to the substitute. It wasn't likely. No one on the streets really wanted anyone else to get out; if one was drowning, he would cling on to those around him so they could all go down together. As soon as Adam Bradley was back on the estate, someone would be quick enough to lead him back into temptation.

"So, what do you make of all that?" Claire asked. She looked at the huge bulk of the profiler, who'd joined them, and then back at her boss. "Are the two lots of killings linked? How is that possible?"

Cass tucked the chair under the interview desk and leaned on the back of it. "What was it our mysterious Mr. Bright said—there are no coincidences? Everything happens for a reason? So we've just got to find the reasons, that's all." He looked around, thinking, then continued, "Let's work it through one thing at a time. This Mr. Bright has a film of the boys being shot. How or why we don't know, he just has. He wants to get that to me, the investigating officer, but he doesn't bring it to me directly. So why not?"

"The man's got something to hide," Hask said. "The fact that we find a woman dead in the same flat on the same day he's been there would indicate that he's potentially our serial killer."

"Exactly. And that ties in neatly with his 'no coincidences' statement."

"But why would he want to help you if he's doing something criminal himself?" Claire rested against the corner of the desk.

"Good question. Dr. Hask?"

"Power trip. He wants to give you a gift."

"Are you saying he feels sorry for me?"

"I think this one sees himself as above everyone else, regardless of who they are. I think maybe it's his God complex coming into play. But yes, on one level he's taking pity on you."

"But he gives me a clue to a *different* case. That doesn't make sense."

"Maybe he is proving his omnipotence to you. He's doing one set of murders, but he also has more information on other deaths than you do. He wants you to be in awe of him."

Claire frowned. "But if it had all gone the way he'd planned it, and Bradley had worn the gloves, then we wouldn't have ever known it came from him."

The *click* of the lighter was loud in the silence as Cass lit another cigarette. "Then it must have gone as planned."

"You've lost me."

"Don't you think, Doc?"

"I agree." Hask smiled. "Everything about this man says organisation, precision. If he really wanted the envelope delivered anonymously, he could easily have posted it, or actually walked in with it himself. If he'd worn a hat and a normal suit, then the cameras wouldn't get much for an ID, would they? Middle-aged man of average height—London's full of them. And I would say that he's certainly confident enough to do something like that without turning a hair."

"I think you're right," Cass said. "He picked Adam Bradley on purpose. No one in their right mind would give a junkie from the estates a job to do and expect them to carry it out perfectly. He wanted us to track it back to him . . . but he didn't want to make it that easy. Maybe he asks around, finds Bradley had some form so he knows we'll have his prints on record. He makes sure Bradley knows his name—"

"—although Bradley says he asked him for that," Claire interjected.

"Yeah, but he'd have told him one way or another. He wanted us to have that name."

"I agree." Hask folded his hands across his vast belly. "He also put the envelope on the arm of the chair and threw the gloves into Bradley's lap. If he'd wanted the boy to remember to put them on before touching it then he'd have put the gloves on top of the envelope." He shrugged. "I wouldn't be surprised if he'd even gone so far as to smear the fingerprint onto the envelope himself when Bradley was out of it. Just to make sure we got a usable one."

"I'd go along with that." Cass sighed. "So he thinks he can play games with us."

"He was testing you."

"Oh, nice. Did I pass?"

The profiler snorted. "Looks that way. At least he's made some contact. Now the next move is his."

"How does he fit with your profile for the serial killer?" Claire asked.

"Well, he's certainly self-controlled. Calm and collected. Smart. Over thirty-five. And from the way our messenger boy described him, he's also charismatic. This elaborate trail he's leading to himself ties in with the flamboyant gesture of the flies. And it shows intelligence. He certainly appears to be a man with an office job—the expensive coat, the suit, the briefcase—and he's urbane, well spoken, so fits in to normal society. To then kill someone in the same location seems slightly off to me; almost too obvious . . . but given everything else, I'd agree this could well be our man."

"Which means there must be a link between these cases. There has to be. And there's something on that film we're missing, something he wants us to see." Cass rubbed his face. "I need to look at that film again. And so do you, Claire. We need to find whatever it is we've missed."

The sergeant pulled a tiny USB pen from her pocket. It was the one Cass had saved the film onto the night before last.

"I grabbed this from your desk for you. I presume you meant to take it home."

Cass smiled. "Thanks." He slipped it into his pocket. "Okay, so now let's think about that film. What did you find out about the cabbie?"

"Not much to help us there. He says it was an ordinary pick-up, and we can't find anything on file to the contrary. He's been a driver for twenty years and never had any problems. He saw what happened on the news and realised straight away that it was him dropping Macintyre off. He said he thought about coming forward but his wife persuaded him against it." Her eyes drifted over his shoulder as she added, "I can't see how he's in the firm's pay though. He doesn't seem the type." She frowned. "Sir?"

For a moment Cass thought she was talking to him until shadows shifted in the corner of his eyes. He turned. The room was filling up with bodies. The DCI had come into the interview room, followed by Blackmore, who moved to stand along the back wall. Ramsey positioned himself beside him. Cass frowned. What the hell was Ramsey doing here? These cases weren't in his remit.

"Something we can do for you, sir?" Blackmore seemed to be very intent on staring into the stained floor. Cass's stomach tightened.

Detective Chief Inspector Morgan kept his hands in his pockets as he stepped forward. His face was grim.

"We need to have a chat, Cass."

"Tell me this isn't because I was smoking in the interview room?"

The DCI didn't smile. Over his broad shoulder Cass saw Bowman leaning into the doorway. He didn't look so great—what was he doing out of the hospital so soon? He looked at each of them, but only Ramsey met his eyes. His expression was unreadable.

"What the fuck is going on?" Cass broke the silence.

"We need to speak to you in connection with your brother's death," said DCI Morgan, his voice sounding official. "We've found some evidence at the scene."

The air heated up around him, burning his face. "Yeah, I was there last night. I should have said. The constable let me in. He told me to wear gloves, but—"

"It's not that kind of evidence."

Cass felt his throat tighten. "Well, we'd better go and talk, then," he said finally. "And we can straighten this out. Because I don't have a fucking clue what you're on about." His voice was calm, but his body was raging, adrenalin pumping hard. What the hell did *we've found some evidence* mean? He hadn't been to Christian's house for months, maybe longer. He looked at Claire as he followed the DCI out of the room, then at Ramsey. For a moment he could have sworn that he saw a flash of something gold glowing from the corners of his eyes, and then it was gone.

CHAPTER SEVEN

The sun shines on London now, but the rain that poured down the previous night has soaked the earth's skin. The air smells of wet dirt. The bench beneath him is still wet, and will leave his clothes damp, but he doesn't mind. His arms ache from polishing the pews, ready for the lunchtime crowds that will gather the next day to let music soothe their souls for a brief half an hour.

Everything is brief, he thinks, as he watches the flowers that are contemplating an early bloom. He stands and stretches, the muscles across his back rippling, and he remembers his own strength from so very long ago. He had been glorious. Sometimes it's hard to remember how things were, before. Beyond the small garden around him, the city laughs and cries. It is busy here; it practically screeches life. He sighs. He knows better. There is no life; there are only the various stages of dying. He knows this—since the first sign that things were changing among his kind, he's felt it: the empty loneliness, the quiet fear in his stomach, the sink into humanity . . . the constant buzzing under his skin and in his head. A rustle as an old man turns the pages of his newspaper. Two boys' faces stare out at him. It's purely imagination, a flight of fancy, but it feels as if their eyes are accusing him, even from within the flat confines of the printed surface. He stares back. *Their deaths aren't his guilt. He merely provided the test. It was others who were found wanting.*

A couple stand up from the bench opposite, where they've eaten sandwiches together. They are dressed smartly. They smile and are happy. They are lucky enough to have good jobs, and now they have found love. They think the world is their oyster, and that life will go on and on like this, as if living under some blissful rainbow.

He sighs as he watches them go, and the flowers tremble. There is not even a hint of the Glow about them. They are nothing. They are no one. The woman laughs as they pass through the gates and back into the mêlée of Covent Garden. He wonders at the irony of that joy, which will be so fleeting. She will be dead within three years from the tumour quietly growing inside her. She will delay seeking medical help for the pain she gets when she bends over because she isn't eligible for the NHS—what's left of it—and she hasn't kept up to date with her health insurance. She'll think it's not worth paying for all those tedious tests; it'll turn out to be fibroids, everyone knows that it generally is. They will be married by then, and he'll stay with her out of duty, but within a month or two of her final diagnosis he will be sleeping with her best friend and telling himself it's for comfort and not because he's always wanted to fuck her. They stay together even after that heat of first lust is as dead as his first wife and when their second child has arrived he will spend hours looking at her and then at himself and wondering what happened to them.

He knows all this from the trace of their scent as they pass, and he knows that this is the nature of mankind's love and always has been, from the very first. The couple are still laughing as they round the corner, completely intent on each other, and he gives them no more thought, other than adding their drop of futility to the growing ocean that resides inside him. They are nothing, and he has a bigger game to think about before the rot within takes hold. The conspiracies never stop in their world that is built on lies.

He smiles, his mood lifting, and a solitary fly creeps out from beneath the collar of his sweater and tests the air for a moment before taking off. He thinks of Mr. Bright and his need for order in chaos;

forever the architect he once was, constantly planning and watching and preparing for the future. He wonders, as he walks towards the church door, if his own interference has been noticed yet. The others have underestimated him. His powers are drained, but not yet lost. He'd watched the architect. He'd seen the meeting and then followed the boy. He remembers the frailty of the young man's wasted body under him as he stumbled across him in the train and carefully slid the key out of his pocket and into his own hand.

His smile stretches into a grin. Bright was looking for him, and now he'd made it so the precious policeman was looking for Bright. The architect believes that nothing is coincidence; he will have given the boy his pompous lecture. And now those words will have trapped him and the hunter becomes the hunted, at least for a while. Touché.

The inside of the church is quiet and he's glad to be away from the hubbub of the outside world. He doesn't care how the game will eventually play out. He won't be there. He can feel his bones desiccating as he still breathes. Everything is dying. Nothing is sacred. Inside there is just machinery. And their souls are impure. He has tested people and found them wanting. There is no real love.

He sits in a pew and breathes in the heady scent of polish. It will have faded by the time the vicar starts the evening service, and by the concert the next lunchtime it will have disappeared as if it never existed. He thinks of the vicar of this actors' church, and of a pretend religion whose house celebrates the art of pretence. He is a good man, and kind, but he is dying, just like all the rest.

Outside, the rush of lunchtime fades into the calm of the afternoon and he pulls off his baseball cap while he waits. This isn't an act of respect, it is just that his scalp itches. He feels nothing for the beliefs this building holds. His hair is still thick and sandy-blond, in contrast with the lines that have started to dig into his skin. It is artlessly messy, a style so many models and actors strive to emulate. He is handsome. He always has been. He stares up at the decorated walls above the altar and wonders how it is that he can find a kind of peace here, among these misguided beliefs, but he does.

Time ticks silently by and he watches those that come and go. An old woman dressed in black prays in the pew two in front of him. She's on her knees and her eyes are squeezed tightly shut. There is a faint glimmer around her. Her husband is long dead, but she has at least another ten years ahead before she joins him. She prays for fifteen minutes and then lights a candle before scurrying back out, eyes cast down in shame for her own continued existence.

A few moments later and heels click slowly down the central aisle. The scent of polish is forgotten. He knows these heels. They're not high, and the walk is hesitant, the weight on the toe rather than the heel, an apologetic step. He doesn't pretend to pray; he just sits as he is, staring at the altar.

She takes the pew alongside his, on the other side of the aisle. Like him, she simply stares at the altar. He doesn't need to look at her to know that she's the one he's been waiting for. Hannah West. She comes twice a week, sometimes three, not when the concerts are on, but in the quiet times, when the rest of the world is too busy for the peaceful space of the church.

Her sigh is soft, but he hears it. Her head is tilted as she sits with her sensible overcoat undone and her nurse's uniform visible. He's watched her emotional exhaustion grow over the weeks, as her shoulders slump forward a fraction of an inch more with every visit. He wonders if she's even noticed that her walk home from the hospital now takes her four minutes longer than it used to. Her pace has shortened, her steps slowed, even though she has a family waiting for her. He thinks perhaps that she's finding it harder and harder to raise her own energy levels in order to pretend to share in their joy at each other and the world. She is lost. She can feel it, but she doesn't know how to change it.

He watches the tiny signs as her body tenses, ready to get up, and he rises before her, moving towards the bank of candles. He is a few steps ahead and this is good. He doesn't want her to feel as if she's being followed. Her eyes follow him though, drawn by his golden hair and furrowed brow. He has tried hard to be invisible over the past months, to be just like one of them, but it's difficult. Even though they can't see the Glow, he knows they feel it. People are drawn to him,

*even those without a trace of the Glow in themselves—a genetic mem-
ory of the truth, perhaps. It's been a long time since he's walked freely
among them without being bound by the shackles of the Network.*

*He feels her come alongside him, but it's only when she speaks that
he visibly registers her presence.*

*"I've seen you here before." Her voice is gentle, and there is a hint
of an accent. Somewhere north. Somewhere she once belonged, before
the capital lured her.*

"I work here." He smiles a little. "Well, I'm a volunteer."

"No job?"

*"Is it that obvious?" He feels her eyes take in his casual clothes. It's
been a while since he's worn a suit. His soft olive corduroys and sweatshirt are all he needs now.*

*She shrugs. Her shoulders are strong. She's not skinny like the last
one. "It seems to be a safe bet these days."*

*They are speaking softly, although the church is empty. The vicar
is in his office at the back, preparing a sermon for the handful of people who will gather here on their way home after yet another long day
of pointless work. He will try to give them hope, but he will fail. They'll
take his words anyway, and he'll hope they'll make a difference.*

*She rummages in her bag and pulls out her purse. It's small. She
has to be careful about how much she spends. Nurses don't earn
much, and her husband works in a small supermarket. Still she slips a
few coins into the box at the front before taking a candle. She lights it
from one behind and then places it in a holder. They both watch it
flicker.*

"Who do you light it for?" he asks at last.

*Her eyes don't waver from the flame. "Everyone." Her voice is like
satin, and in the flickering light her skin looks almost beautiful.*

*He takes a coin from his pocket, avoiding the key that still sits there,
and slides it into the box himself. It clinks briefly and then hits wood.
Not many people are paying for their candles these days. Everyone is
looking out for themselves. Everyone always does in the end.*

*"Do you think things will get better? Do you think there is hope
for us? The world?" She pauses. "I work with Strain II cases. It's*

hard . . ." She glances back towards the altar. "It's hard to keep my faith."

He tilts the white wax stick, which starts to melt before the wick bursts alight. "Maybe things will get better, for a while. But I don't have faith."

She looks at him, trying to see into his soul. He wonders what she would say if she could.

"So why light the candle?"

He smiles at her. "Because the Glow is beautiful."

He is standing so close that her warm natural scent overpowers the acrid polish that clings to his own clothes. She is so alive. He wonders how it will feel when he switches her off.

CHAPTER EIGHT

"You've got to give us something." Ramsey was starting to sound as tired as Cass felt. "We've got your DNA, indicating you had sex with Jessica Jones in the hours prior to her death, and your fingerprints are on the shotgun. There must be something you can tell us."

They'd been sitting in the over-warm interview room for almost two hours and they were just going round in circles. Cass wanted to bang his head against the solid table and scream. Instead, he lit another cigarette and gritted his teeth. There were only four left in the packet. *Your DNA and your fingerprints.* Even though the list of the evidence they'd found had been repeated over and over, it still sounded surreal.

"I keep telling you, I don't understand it. It's got to be a mistake." He looked up at Ramsey and shrugged. "I don't have any answers."

"Your brother's dead wife had your sperm inside her." Bowman snorted derisively. He was seated next to Ramsey on the other side of the grey desk, and Cass was pleased to see him flinch slightly when he moved. His appendix might have turned out to be fine, but he was obviously still in pain from whatever was making him ill. "There's one obvious answer that I can see. You were fucking her."

Cass glared. And so the trip round the circle began again. "I've already told you that I haven't seen my brother or his wife in months. I was not there that night."

"But you admit you were fucking her?"

Cass wanted to reach across and punch the smug bastard in the stomach, right through his stitches. He wanted to rip out his heart, just so Bowman could know what it felt like.

"I was not sleeping with her, but—as I have already told you, eight times—we had a very brief affair five years ago." The words were like razor blades, slashing his guilt into his flesh. He had wanted what Christian had, and so he had taken the only part of his life that he could. His throat tightened as his brother's open, smiling face rose up, unwanted, in his memory. Christian had always been happy to see Cass. He'd never lost that puppy-dog adoration he'd had for his elder brother when they were kids. For a moment, Cass's vision blurred and he sucked hard on the cigarette. Bowman would love to see him break down, but that wasn't going to happen.

"What is it with you? Do you have to fuck every woman you meet, Cass?" Bowman shook his head. "You're fucking unbelievable."

"Enough."

Cass was too angry to pay any attention to Ramsey's interjection. He glared at Bowman's pale face. "I met your ex-wife, remember? But even I wouldn't have touched that ugly bitch."

"I said *enough*!" Ramsey snarled. "Leave your problems outside and let's run this interview like the professionals we are supposed to be." He turned to look at Bowman. "And if you can't manage that, then you can go and wait outside. This is my case. You're just in here out of courtesy to your DCI. Do you understand that?"

Bowman reluctantly nodded and Ramsey turned back to Cass. "And I know this isn't easy for you, but try not to make it any harder on us all." He paused and took a deep breath. "So when did the affair end?"

"Almost immediately after it started. Neither of us liked ourselves for it. From start to finish it can't have been more than three months. It finished when my parents died." Cass met Ramsey's gaze. If it had just been Ramsey in the room and no tape recorder, then perhaps he would have opened up, told him the details. There was something about the man that he liked. He felt a connection with him. He figured that Ramsey might just understand without judging . . . but there was no way in hell he was going to reveal his sordid little secrets in front of Bowman, knowing that every dirty little fact would be clinically typed up and put in a file for anyone to read. Some things were supposed to live only in a man's soul.

"It was wrong. We both knew that," he repeated quietly, "and it was not something either of us were wanting to start up again, ever. They got on with their lives, and raising Luke. I stayed out of the way as much as possible. Me and Kate—"

"—your wife," Ramsey interjected, clarifying for the recording.

"Kate, my wife, and I would visit for Luke's birthday, or Christmas sometimes. I saw them maybe three or four times a year. Kate saw them more often, but not exactly regularly."

"And as far as you're aware, your brother never found out about the affair."

"No, I'm sure he didn't know. When he rang me the other night he didn't sound angry—maybe anxious and wound up about something, but not angry."

"Although we only have your word for that," Bowman added.

"I guess you do." Cass refused to rise to the bait. "But Kate spoke to him briefly. I'm sure if he'd told her that I'd been screwing his wife she would have mentioned that when I got home."

"You can never tell how women will react."

"I think I probably know my own wife. We've been together a long time. She's not the sort to take that sort of thing quietly."

Bowman smirked, making Cass want to rip his heart out all over again.

"Okay," Ramsey said, ignoring the DI, "let's get back to the gun."

"Christian didn't own a gun."

"Well, whether he'd owned it for long, had only just bought it or had borrowed it from someone, there it was, found next to his dead body, and your fingerprints were on the barrels."

Cass stared. "The barrels? Not the trigger? Look, I've said this before and I'm going to keep repeating it until the cows come home, *because it's the bloody truth*: as far as I was aware, Christian didn't own a gun. I wasn't there that night. I don't know what happened, other than what's in the report. Until Claire told me they were dead, I had had no bloody idea."

He leaned forward, looked at Ramsey. "Look, I wish I did know more. I wish I could understand what my brother did. But I don't. *And I wasn't there.*"

"Which brings us back to where you were." Bowman made a pretence of flicking through papers. "You drove around London and then fell asleep in a Tesco car park down in Newham? It's not exactly the most watertight of alibis, is it? You're not even clear on where you went before deciding that Tesco was the best place to lay your head for the night—when you're in charge of two serious cases."

Ramsey sent the DI a sharp glare. "Stay on the point."

"With all due respect, I am on the point. The Tesco security camera has his car parking up at gone three in the morning. He could have been anywhere between the time he rowed with his wife and stormed out of the house and when he ended up there. And he can't tell us where he was."

"I did tell you where I was," Cass said, trying to keep hold of his exasperation. "I was driving. And I can tell you where I wasn't. I wasn't at my brother's house."

"Again, we only have your word for that." Bowman's voice rose slightly. "So you go out and get drunk, or whatever you did, and then, after sleeping it off in a car park, you go home and stick your clothes straight in the washing machine. Nothing else, just your clothes. And we're just supposed to take you at your word?"

"Like I said, I stank," he sighed. "And I had some blood on my sleeve."

The room fell silent.

"Oh for fuck's sake, you moron, it was *my* fucking blood! I'd woken up with a nosebleed."

Both pairs of eyes stared at him. He stared back. "Go and check my fucking car. If I'd been at the scene, then we all know I'd have been covered in it. I just had a nosebleed. I went home and stuck my clothes straight in the machine. I didn't think to go upstairs and get the rest of the fucking laundry. I just wanted to get showered and get to work." He turned to Ramsey. "It's a set-up. It's got to be. I can't see how it can be anything else."

"How about this: you'd seen your brother's wife earlier in the day. She'd told you he was going to be working late—we've got him on security camera leaving his office at The Bank at 11:30 p.m. Maybe you decided to go back to your lover's house for a while. Have a quickie."

"And what?" Cass almost laughed, it was so ridiculous. "Get caught and then sit there on the edge of the bed, waiting while he shot his wife and child? Don't be so fucking stupid. That's just fucking crazy." He stubbed his cigarette out. "It doesn't fucking work and you know it."

"Well, what about this, then? Your brother's acting funny. He calls you and your wife. Maybe Jessica is worried that he's found out about your dirty little secret. You're out driving around and you decide to call round there, check everything's okay. But when you get there it isn't. Your brother opens the door, gun in hand and covered in blood." Bowman leaned forward, his voice low, almost conversational.

"You're a policeman. You know what you're doing, so you talk him down a bit. You go inside and into the dining room. At some point he tells you what he's done. Maybe he starts to lose it again. He points the gun at you and you wrestle. He falls back into the seat and somehow he pulls the trigger. Completely shocked, you find somewhere to park up and calm down for a couple of hours. When you know your wife will definitely be asleep you go home, wash your clothes and then go to work as if nothing has happened."

Cass stared at him. "How many times do I have to say this? It didn't happen. I didn't have sex with my brother's wife. I wasn't there."

Ramsey rubbed his face. "But you can see how it could look that way."

"Or maybe it was you that snapped," Bowman cut in, "you that blew them all away."

Cass gripped the edge of the table to stop himself lunging forward.

"Enough, Bowman," Ramsey barked. "Right, let's look at the facts again—just the facts. For a start the only prints on the trigger belong to Christian. And although there is a fingerprint of yours on the gun, I have to be honest with you, I don't see you leaving it there. You're not that careless. On top of that," he looked up, "Hask is pretty convinced you're not the murdering type."

"That shows what *he's* worth." Bowman pushed his chair back and stood up. "Every fucker on the force knows that Cass Jones is a killer. The worst kind. It's all in the files."

Cass's blood boiled. "I did what I did, Bowman. You weren't there. And do you ever wonder what you would have done in my position?"

"Get out, Bowman." Ramsey's voice was low but deadly. "Get the fuck out of here before I do something that I might not regret." Even with the hint of molasses in his accent, the words were sharp.

The DI glared at Cass as he paused at the door. "You think you're above everything, Jones. You always have. But you're not. You got away with murder once and still kept your job. It's not going to happen again."

Ramsey stood. "That's not your call, Bowman. Now why don't you go and cool your head somewhere else. You've got plenty out there with your own caseload to keep you busy."

"My pleasure."

Cass figured it was taking all Bowman's reserve not to spit in his face. He contented himself with slamming the door.

"I always knew that bastard didn't like me, but I never realised just how much until now," he said quietly. Despite the foul taste in his mouth he lit another cigarette. His lungs felt cold from smoking too much, but he sucked in hard regardless.

"It's true he doesn't seem too keen on you." Ramsey waved away the offered Marlboro. "But he made some valid points. The way he suggested things went down could play out in court, you know." He held his hands up as Cass opened his mouth to protest again. "For what it's worth, Jones, I believe you. But if someone is trying to set you up, then they've done a pretty good job."

"Someone isn't *trying*, he *has* set me up."

"Then give me suggestions. Who and why?"

"Maybe whoever tried to kill Macintyre wants me out of the way. Maybe they think I've got something."

"Killing your brother's whole family is perhaps a little far out, don't you think? Just to get you off a case?"

"They shot two schoolkids in broad daylight. They didn't seem to feel too guilty about that."

Ramsey shook his head. "It's still extreme—especially when from what I can gather you didn't really have a lot to go on."

Cass knew his fellow DI was right. It was hard to believe that someone would go to that length just to get him off a case that wasn't looking solvable any time soon. But he couldn't see any other explanation. Frustration gnawed at him. "There's something here that we're not seeing. We've got a suspect in the serial killings sending me a film of those two boys being gunned down. And now this set-up." Ash dropped to the table from the burning end of the forgotten cigarette. "And however bad it looks, I *know* it's a set-up. Something's linking all this, but we're just not getting it."

Ramsey looked at him. "Okay, so let's say this is a set-up. How would they have got your sperm?" There was no accusation in his tone, simply curiosity.

Cass shrugged. "Fuck knows. They must have gone through our rubbish. Got a condom."

"You and your wife use protection?"

"She doesn't like the pill and I didn't want a vasectomy." He paused. "Can't beat safety first in this day and age. I've seen people with Strain II. It's not pretty."

"You think your wife was sleeping around?"

"No." His smile was bitter. "But I know what I'm like. She probably does too, and you hear too many revenge-fuck stories these days." He finally remembered the cigarette and pulled on it. The smoke was hot and tasted of old dirt. He stubbed it out and immediately regretted it. "Don't even try to understand my marriage. We don't understand it, and we're in it. It's a fuck-up. I damaged it when I was undercover and it's never recovered. If we didn't use condoms, then that would mean that we trusted each other." He paused. "No, that's not right. It would mean *she* trusted *me*." He smiled slightly. "And *I* don't even trust me. Not like that."

There was a long silence.

"So what now? Are you going to arrest me or hold me?"

"No, neither. But the DCI says you need to take a week's paid leave. They'll call it compassionate."

Cass laughed. "And he's all about compassion."

Ramsey shrugged. "You know how it is. They can't have you working either of the cases with this hanging over you. You need to prove you weren't there. No one really believes you had anything to do with this awful thing, not even Bowman, under all his aggression. But if the media got hold of it and you were found to be still working the Jackson and Miller case, they'd be baying for blood."

Cass nodded. He'd seen it coming the minute they'd started the formal interview. He'd been in the same situation ten years ago, knew what was likely to happen, but it didn't stop feeling like a punch in the gut.

"So basically, they're suspending me."

Ramsey's silence said it all.

Claire had been waiting for him in the corridor, and she kept pace as he stormed outside.

"Fucking suspended." Even though the sun was shining, the air was still damp. It smelled of mud and tasted of the earth as Cass sucked it in. His anger had left him almost breathless.

"I heard it was compassionate."

They were halfway down the stairs in front of the station before she managed to stop him.

"That's just semantics, and you know it."

Claire pushed a strand of hair out her face. "It's a fuck-up, that's what it is."

Cass almost laughed in surprise at the curse, and it calmed him down. "Careful. You're starting to sound like me."

"Well, the whole thing's just insane." She frowned. "Bowman's loving it. Maybe you were right about him."

"Oh yeah, I'm right about that bastard."

A shadow fell across the steps. "Inspector? DI Jones? Can I have a word?"

"Not now," Cass answered before he'd even seen who it was. His mind didn't change when he recognised the young man as the ME's new assistant.

"It's just that I—"

Cass turned back to Claire. "My mobile will be on, so keep me informed on both cases. I want to know everything Bowman knows, and if possible I want to know it *before* he does." The lab assistant shuffled from foot to foot behind them. He could wait. He probably just wanted to apologise for that stupid photograph, and Cass was in no mood for simpering sorrys.

"And look at that film again. Keep looking at it." He shoved his hand in his pocket, relieved to feel the data pen still there. "I'll do the same."

Claire nodded. Her eyes searched into his, full of a care he knew he didn't deserve. "And you stay in touch. If you need anything then just call me. Any time."

"I'm sure the new boyfriend would love that."

"He'd get over it." She looked away. "He's been a miserable bugger these past few days anyway."

"Working for me can do that to a bloke."

She smiled sadly and he squeezed her arm. "Don't worry about me, Claire. I'll be fine."

"Um, excuse me—" .

"What?" Cass finally turned back to the skinny young man on the step below him. What was his name, anyway? Jim? Josh? Josh Eagleton, that was it. The ME's assistant licked his lips.

"Get on with it, man."

"Well, I—" He hesitated, his eyes sliding from Cass's face to somewhere behind him.

"I . . . uh . . . I was just wondering if you'd seen Dr. Farmer." He waved a manila envelope. Cass could see sweaty fingerprints where he'd been gripping it. "And there he is."

The assistant had at least lost his irritating cockiness. Cass turned to see the ME coming down the stairs, Bowman pushing open the door a few steps behind.

"Great," Cass muttered. He looked at Claire. "And give Bradley my card. Just in case he gets another visit, or remembers anything else. It's unlikely, but just in case."

She nodded.

Farmer passed them without any acknowledgement and Cass smiled bitterly. What did he think? The shit would somehow stick to him too, just for a nod and a wave?

"What are you doing here, Josh?" The ME frowned at the boy.

"You wanted these results ASAP. From that domestic? I brought them. They're as expected."

"Well, they could have waited. You know there's such a thing as being too efficient." Farmer pulled him down the stairs and away to their cars, but not before the kid sent a look back in Cass's direction. He was too far away for Cass to read his expression, and then Bowman was upon them and the moment was forgotten.

"Sergeant May. You'd better get back inside and help Blackmore update my case file. I want to take everything home, including the Jackson and Miller case evidence." He sent Cass a disdainful glance. "What there is of it. The film too."

Cass bit his tongue. He wasn't going to add to his problems by getting in a fight with the other man. He might have lost weight in his few days in hospital, and he was pale as a ghost, but Gary Bowman still looked smart. His suit had to be tailored, it fit so well, and his shirts were the expensive sort, done up with cufflinks rather than buttons. His face was smoothly handsome, the complete opposite to Cass's own rugged looks; hard to believe the two men were about the same age. He was a smug, pretentious bastard, that much was for sure. Cass didn't need to be a head doctor to know that.

Bowman watched Claire head back into the building and Cass wondered if he had let his eyes map the outline of her shape with the sole purpose of winding him up.

"We all know you've fucked *her*," Bowman said idly, "but I never took you for the sort to fuck your own brother's wife." He grinned, his cheekbones sharp as razors. "What am I saying? Of course I did. You're scum, aren't you, Jones? You always were."

Cass smiled back. "I'm capable of a lot of things, Gary. We both know that." He leaned in closer, as if about to whisper a secret, and was pleased to see a twitch of something close to fear in Bowman's own expression. "And another thing we both know is that I'll always be the better fucking copper. So keep my case warm for me and I'll see you when this is sorted."

Cass turned and walked away before Bowman could speak. He hoped he couldn't see his clenched fists in the pockets of his own off-the-rack suit jacket.

Kate was pacing the sitting room, talking quietly into her mobile when he got home. She glanced in his direction and then turned her back on him to finish her conversation. He stood in the doorway watching her as she lowered her voice, but still heard her say, "Cass's back. I'll call you later."

Her face was still blotchy and Cass thought fresh tears had been shed that day. He felt the hollow pit inside himself and wondered where she found all that grief. Who was she crying for? Christian? Jessica and Lucas? How well had she known them really? Christian wasn't *her* brother. Maybe she was crying mainly for herself. He didn't like that thought. His own pain was locked inside and it was making him mean.

"Who was that?"

"None of your fucking business."

Her voice was cold and his heart sank. Of course, someone would have been round. Maybe they'd even searched the house, looking for more evidence. He took a few steps towards her.

"Look, Kate. I wasn't there—"

She slapped him, hard, and for a few seconds the room was filled with the echo of the attack.

"How *could* you, Cass? With *Jessica*?"

So it was out.

"Good news travels fast." His face tingled and he felt the decayed skeleton of his marriage finally crumble. Who the hell would have told her that? He ground his teeth together and his eyes burned. He knew they'd tell her evidence had been found, but who at the station would think to tell her about the affair? When this was all over, he'd find the bastard and make him pay, that much was for sure.

Kate shook her head and turned away but not before he caught the smell of brandy on her warm breath. He looked down at the coffee table and the tumbler with the thin brown layer at the bottom.

"I'm sorry," he said finally. "It was a long time ago. If I could take it back I would."

"We all have things we'd take back, Cass." Her back was still to him but he could hear the thick tears in her voice. "But we can't." She paused. "I think that there's just something wrong with you." She looked at him over her shoulder. "You know? Deep inside?" She shook her head a little. "I don't think you can help yourself hurting people."

Her words sliced into him. "Maybe you're right."

"Knowing it doesn't make it okay, Cass." She let out a long sigh, her flash of anger replaced with exhaustion. Cass wondered just how much of the afternoon she'd spent drinking.

She sniffed and straightened her shoulders before turning to face him. "I'm going to be out for most of the day tomorrow. You can come and get your stuff then."

More tears welled up in her eyes, and she wiped them away before staring defiantly at him. "But I want you gone tonight. I don't want you here. You disgust me."

He stared at her. There were a thousand things he wanted to say, all on the tip of his tongue: that he loved her, and that he'd always loved her, even though she'd never see it. He wanted to tell her that he disgusted himself. That every morning he stared into the bathroom mirror and saw a desperate pair of eyes looking back that were trapped in the events of one night ten years ago. He was haunted by the ghosts of himself and Charlie Sutton, two people in one man. He lived in Hell, and his own need to punish himself, to never allow himself joy, had dragged down everyone around him. He wanted to tell her that she was too good for him, and that he hated that she always saw blood on his hands, no matter how many years passed. He wanted to say a thousand things, but he chose not to. His guilt wasn't hers to share, and his feelings had been trapped inside him for so long he wasn't sure he'd know how to get the words out any more.

"I need to ask you about the bathroom bin."

"What?"

"The bathroom bin. How often do you empty it?"

Kate sat down heavily on the sofa. "What do you want to know that for? Now?"

"Condoms." He ran his hand through his hair and leaned into the doorframe. She hated him already; nothing he could ask now was going to make much difference. "It's the only place whoever did this to me could have got what they did."

"Jesus Christ, Cass." She shook her head. "Like I'm supposed to believe I'm the only person you've been fucking?" Her laugh and sob mixed into a phlegmy cough.

"Please, Kate. Help me out with this."

She drained the glass and stared at him. "If you must know, they don't stay in the bathroom. I put them in the main bin outside in the mornings when I get up. I don't want Mrs. Cooper to have to deal with them when she comes in." She sniffed and wiped her nose with the back of her hand. "That would be tacky."

He nodded. Mrs. Cooper, the cleaning lady. Like they needed one. That was Kate's problem, she wanted a life he couldn't give her. No job, tennis club, and a cleaning lady to come in and "do" for them. When was she going to get that for most people, that world was gone? When had she stopped wanting something real for herself? As he stared at her, he realised that he'd never known what Kate had wanted to do with her life. Had she ever wanted more than just a nice home, good clothes, and beautiful things around her? It had always been about *his* career, and then *his* downfall. Who the hell was his wife really, and why had he never taken the time to get to know her better?

"Thanks. It'll help me—"

"I don't want to help you, Cass," she said softly. "I used to, but not now. Now I just want you to go."

Whatever it was they'd clung to together, some piece of driftwood memory from their youth, it was broken now. The anchors of his life were being ripped up one by one. Christian was dead, his job was dangling by a thread and now Kate was finally kicking him out. Maybe that's what he'd been pushing her to do for the past decade, with his affairs and his coldness. He couldn't walk away himself; he loved her too much to do that, even if he knew she deserved better. Instead he'd just pushed and pushed, until finally here they were at the final straw. He could hear it snapping in the silence between them.

He left her where she was, slim, fragile, sitting hugging her knees, and headed up the stairs. He felt sick, a cold kind of queasiness that pricked at his insides. His world was unravelling. He recognised the feeling from that time so long ago. Then it had come in one sudden moment, and he had done it to himself. This time, some other bastard was doing it to him. And he intended to find out who that was.

He slung some clothes, underpants, a pair of jeans and a T-shirt, into a holdall he yanked out from under the bed, and grabbed some essential toiletries from the bathroom. He'd come back tomorrow for the rest, just as she'd said. Anger and hurt danced in his guts. The décor and most of the shit in the house she'd chosen anyway, and he wondered if this cold, sleek look reflected the inner soul of his elusive wife. His clothes were all he'd need to take. She was welcome to everything else.

Halfway back to the stairs, he paused. Something caught the corner of his eye and he turned to look. He froze. The door to the spare bedroom, the room where he'd slept the previous night, not knowing that it was to be his very last chance to lie beside his wife and listen to her breathing, was open. The last inch or two of the double bed stretched into view, the rest hidden beyond the wall.

Cass stared. His mouth was dry, and he felt it drop open. Someone sat on the bed, very still. In the narrow strip of the double room that was visible, all that could be seen were legs, dressed neatly in dark suit trousers, bent over the side of the divan. They sat primly, held together at knee and ankle, the line between perfectly straight. Cass could make out a glimpse of black socks above the highly polished laced-up brogues. The air suddenly felt heavy around him, a glutinous gel holding him firmly in place. His pupils flickered and widened as he noticed how splashes of something, not quite black, more deep crimson, spoiled the sheen of the leather surfaces. He could just make out a pale white hand, resting on the left thigh, the wrist emerging from a blue shirt. A glint of gold flashed on the third long, elegant finger.

The moment held. Nothing moved. The world emptied as Cass stared, silent. Someone was sitting on the bed—no, he corrected himself, not just someone: *Christian* was sitting on the edge of the bed. His dead brother was sitting on the spare room bed. His own beating heart thumped loudly against his ribs. It couldn't be Christian. Christian was dead. There were no ghosts. He stared at the pale hand and tried to ignore the trembling in his own. After a few minutes, Cass swallowed hard and, very slowly, turned away. He left the unmoving figure where it was and headed down the stairs. He refused to run. There was nothing there, just his brain playing tricks and he didn't have time for any surreal head-fucked shit today.

Kate was on the phone again as he left. He didn't look into the sitting room, and he didn't say goodbye. He noticed she didn't pause in her conversation, apart from to sniff loudly and wipe her nose on the back of her hand. On anyone else, that would look dirty, but Kate could make even that slutty movement elegant, he thought to himself. Outside, the air was still damp. All he wanted to do was go and get drunk, but it was Friday and he needed to make sure the bonuses got delivered first. He was tired of having that envelope of money stashed under the seat of his car and people would be waiting for their cash.

He almost dialled Claire's number, but instead found his finger scrolling up from May to Blackmore. Claire would do it, but even though she took her share he knew she didn't like it. Blackmore would be the better choice. He could give it out himself, but he was fucked if he was going to put himself through all the questions and the looks. He'd had enough of that for one day.

Blackmore answered on the third ring. The conversation was short; they'd meet in Soho, and Blackmore would collect the envelope and take it to The Swan that evening to divvy up the dosh. Every week, all

over the country, no doubt, money trickled into the palms of policemen, each firm securing their manor for another few days, and as he
switched on the car's engine, he wondered if Claire maybe had a point.
Criminal was criminal, and where did you draw the line? Still, he figured, he hadn't started the system; he just used other people's lines.

He headed back into the city, the money tucked under his holdall
on the passenger seat. As the world flashed by, people and buildings
nothing more than a passing blur, he mulled over the interview, and
the crazy evidence that had been allegedly been found at his brother's
house. The way things were shaping up, the cash bonuses, moral or not,
might not be his concern for much longer.

CHAPTER NINE

Moneypenny's was primarily a girly club, but from time to time Artie Mullins used it as a venue for a floating poker game. Time stopped, there in the basement, away from the busy streets. The booze flowed and the cards turned and there was no sense of the hours outside passing.

Artie never cared who won. He always got his percentage of the pot, and his fee for security and venue, and though it was strictly pin money, the games were a nice little earner every now and then. Artie Mullins was one of a rare breed: an old-school player who'd learned to move with the times. He still ran a fair share of London from his various business outlets, but as he'd said to Cass, a good businessman knows not to turn his back on easy money, however small the amount. You may need it one day.

There was a late afternoon game going on when Cass came down the stairs. The money had been safely deposited in Blackmore's hands and now he had business to attend to. The nation's no-smoking law was one of many that didn't appear to apply to Artie Mullins and his guests and the bar was heavy with smoke, even though the air-conditioning unit on the wall was rattling away. Cass ignored the game around the corner of the L-shaped room. He had other fish to fry; the gamblers could keep their anonymity tonight.

Artie sat on his stool at the end of the bar, from where he could see the whole of the club. As soon as Cass appeared he stood up.

"If you'll excuse me, gents, I'm going to retire to my office," he called to the players, speaking around the cigar clamped firmly between his teeth. "Can I remind you there's just over one hour of play left before I need my pussy parlour back." He grinned as murmurs of assent rumbled back at him.

He picked up a bottle and grabbed a couple of tumblers, then gestured at one of the thickset gentlemen sitting against the long wall. "You're up, Brownie. I'll be in back."

The big man rose and silently took Artie's place at the end of the bar. His suit jacket was stretched tight across his shoulders, and Cass wondered just how many hours in the gym and pills popped it took to get that big. Everyone knew about the new-generation steroids out there, but he didn't think even they could create that kind of muscle mass. He looked closer; the man's eyes were sharp, too, and it looked like he was carefully studying every move at the out-of-sight table. If he'd been on the 'roids, he wouldn't be functioning so well. Cass had seen far too many domestic murder scenes brought on by 'roid rage. Artie had chosen well; Cass wouldn't want to go up against someone like him, that was for sure. Just looking at the man's muscles made him feel like a scrawny kid all over again.

"Big fella, isn't he?" Artie smiled. "In all departments, I'm assured." He tilted his head towards the office. "The birds love him."

"If I was a woman I think he'd scare the crap out of me." Cass lifted the wooden flap that cut off the small reception and coat-check area and followed Artie into his office.

"That's the thing with birds, though. They're not like us. Don't even try to understand them."

Cass thought of Kate crying at home. "Yeah, I'm with you on that."

Artie sat on his leather desk chair and with the bottle and glasses down on the desk finally took the chewed cigar out of his mouth. It had gone out and he dumped it in the ashtray.

"From what you said on the phone, I think you're a man in need of a drink."

Cass nodded, and Artie poured them two large measures of a very nice single malt.

"Didn't sound good," Artie said, leaning back as the chair swayed slightly.

"Trust me, it isn't." Cass clinked glasses and lowered himself onto the leather sofa. He leaned forward. "They've suspended me—although they're calling it some compassionate shit. Some fucker's setting me up and I just don't know why."

"That business with your brother and his family was on the radio. Sorry to hear it."

Cass wrapped his defences hard around his heart. Now wasn't the time. "Thanks—although I just can't see Christian doing that, whatever they say. And now they've found this crazy evidence that I was there when I fucking wasn't. This whole thing is badly screwed."

"So what are you going to do about it?"

That was what Cass loved about Artie. There was none of this bullshit feelings crap, just out with it and on with the action. If you believed something, then you went with it, even if the rest of the world was against you.

"Well, tonight I intend to get completely shit-faced, and then tomorrow I'm going to clean up and start figuring out what the fuck is going on, and who's out to get me."

"Sounds like a plan." Artie grinned and stretched out his palms. "*Mi casa es su casa*, or whatever that Spanish shit is."

Cass drained his glass and let Artie refill it before lighting a cigarette and then rummaging in his pocket for the small wrap he'd vowed he'd throw away. He tossed it on the table. Artie pulled out his wallet and used a platinum credit card to chop out two chunky lines. He rolled a twenty and handed it to Cass. With one nostril held closed, Cass breathed in hard through the other. The powder raced through his nose and down the back of his throat, the initial burn immediately replaced with pleasant numbness. He ran one finger over the grainy remnants and rubbed them into his teeth. His heart thumped and his head tingled. Tiredness ebbed away. He washed the drugs into his system with a large mouthful of burning liquor. Artie did the same.

He felt comfortable with Artie, who reminded him of Brian Free-man in so many ways. There was some relief to be had in a place away from the constraints of the law, in a world where men made their own rules, most of them unwritten. It made him wonder at the part of him that had worked so hard to stay in the force, and wanted so much to be good, to make up for everything—to find some redemption. That word again. It echoed in his head, spoken in Christian's dead voice down the phone. Even from behind the wall of his rising buzz, his heart ached. What kind of redemption could Christian have been look-ing for?

He squeezed his dead brother's memory to one side and felt it in-stantly replaced by the cold fingers of the murdered dead that quietly pulled at him. It felt like they'd torn a way through his skin as easily as digging up through the soft earth of a grave. Coke was a fucker like that. When it woke you up, it woke *all* of you up.

He looked over at Artie. "Have you ever heard of someone called Mr. Bright?"

"Why do you ask?"

"The name came up with a witness today. Whoever he is, he's play-ing games with me, I think. He sent me something."

Artie's eyes slid away and Cass saw his mouth twitch hesitantly.

"You *have* heard of him." Cass put his drink down, his plan to get rat-arsed momentarily forgotten. His heart thumped, a relentless rave beat, and it was only partly the drugs.

"You know London." Artie shrugged. "There's a lot of faces in this city."

"You're saying he's with a firm?"

Artie smiled and shook his head. He didn't speak for a moment while he relit his cigar. Finally, he asked, "What do you know about The Bank?"

"What, apart from it's supposed to save us all from financial Armageddon?"

"Yeah." The older man's face wrinkled up as he smiled. "Apart from that shit."

"I don't know too much. Christian would have known more. He

worked at their London headquarters." He sniffed, feeling pleasantly numb. "When was it formed? 2010?" Cass continued to scour his fading memory for details. Sometimes it felt like The Bank had always been there.

Okay, he'd found those errant details. "America and the UK billionaire poster boys Gates and Branson own it in partnership with the élite from Japan, the new Chinese super-rich and Russia. And that means they now own most of the Western world's property and bank accounts, in one form or another. How am I doing?"

"Not bad, though you're missing out one thing: The Bank runs the whole fucking world, mate. It's virtually the government now." Artie shook his head. "The so-called *elected* government asks The Bank's permission to wipe its own arse. All that shit in Russia and Chechnya? The Bank's behind that. And the African oil business. Those hundreds who died? Who the fuck do you think shut them up?"

Cass stayed silent, listening and learning, just like he'd done with Freeman all those years ago, when he'd been Charlie Sutton most of the time. "Hard to equate some of those personalities with that kind of shit, though," Cass said eventually. "Or maybe I'm being naïve."

"The thing with powerful men"—Artie leaned forward, his voice was slow as he ruminated—"and I mean in all walks of life, the thing with *really* powerful men is that you never really know who they are. They're never the names of the figureheads. Me? I know my place in things. I may seem like the top dog in town, but if I really was"—he wiggled a finger at Cass and winked—"my name wouldn't be on any of your files. I'd be invisible."

Cass frowned. "Are you saying this Mr. Bright works for The Bank?"

"Everybody works for The Bank, son, in one way or another. But maybe not your Mr. Bright."

"I don't get it."

"Maybe The Bank works for him."

"I'm still not following. You're saying he's one of the founders of The Bank?" Cass was aware he sounded incredulous.

Artie shrugged. "I'm just saying that I've heard stories. Most of them third-hand, like Chinese whispers, the kind of stories told in shadowy places about shadowy people. Like those urban legends they make into crappy films, where birds run around half-naked until some fucker finally shuts them up with an axe, or whatever his weapon of choice is." He laughed, but his eyes were cold, and deadly serious. "The thing is—I've heard that name, and I've heard it in a lot of places both legit and otherwise. Fuck, I'm not even sure it's his real name, but I know I've never heard it spoken without a hint of fear and a heavy measure of respect." He puffed on the cigar, sending out a cloud of pungent smoke to hover in the air between them.

"Everything has layers, you know that, Cass. There are layers in your world and in mine, and sometimes they even overlap." He nodded. "You've been there. You're one of those who live on the overlap. They're everywhere: the government, The Bank, the world . . . and the layers normally just stick to their own, you know what I mean?" Artie didn't wait for an answer. "Your Mr. Bright, though, he seems to have been heard of in all of them." He leaned back. "If he's fucking with you, then there is some serious shit going on. That's all I'm saying. Who he is, what he does? I don't know. And more to the point, I don't want to know."

The smoke between them had cleared, but Cass's thinking was still fogged up. He wasn't sure he understood Artie at all. So who the hell was this Mr. Bright? It felt like Artie had said a whole lot, without telling him much at all. His brain ran over the information, but it was shooting in too many different directions for the rest of him to follow. Maybe he should have left off the coke until after they'd had this conversation. He realised he was grinding his teeth again and he dry-swallowed as the remainder of the drug trickled down the back of his throat and into his system. He needed to stick to the detail. The bigger picture could wait for tomorrow.

"Do you think he could be a killer?"

"Fuck me, Cass, we're all killers."

"I mean, a serial killer. The psycho fuck-up kind." It perhaps wasn't the clinical description Hask would have given, but Cass figured it would do.

"Ah, the dead birds. So you think the same bloke's doing them?"

Cass nodded, and forced the image of Carla Rae's pathetic corpse back into a corner of his mind. Her cold fingers were harder to shake. "Can't give you details, but I figure they'll be in the papers soon enough."

"Well, I'm no expert, and I've never actually met the man—and have no wish to do so—but I wouldn't put money on it being him." His eyes darkened. "I don't think he cares enough about people to kill them like that."

"Well, I just don't get it then." Cass ran over all the information that was scattered like jigsaw pieces in his mind. None of the edges matched up. "I just don't fucking get it. He's either taunting me or trying to tell me something, but either way it's not working."

Artie nodded. "We all get fucked with, Cass. It's part of the game." He sipped his whisky. "Just remember, son, sometimes it's not the obvious things you need to look at, and sometimes you can't see the obvious when it's staring you right in your ugly mug."

Cass watched the other man carefully. "Are you trying to tell me something, Artie? Because if you are, I could really use it told to me straight right now. I'm pretty fucked off with subtlety." His patience was fried, and although the coke was waking him up, his nerves felt like electric cables dancing on water. Mr. Bright wanted to tell him something by sending the film. The killer, Bright or otherwise, was trying to tell him something with the fly eggs and the scrawled message. *Nothing is Sacred*. Someone had sent a pretty strong message in the planted evidence. And he even had the distinct feeling his dead brother was trying to tell him something. The last thing he needed was for Artie Mullins to start talking in riddles.

"I'm just sharing an old bastard's wisdom, Cass. You don't get to survive as long as I have without picking up a few worthwhile gems along the way." He winked. "I should sell them to some Chinese fortune cookie company." His quiet laugh was a throaty rattle, and Cass figured he'd earned that like everything else he had: the hard way.

"I'll take it on board."

"You do that," Artie said. Inside the club the card game was wrapping up and men's voices filtered through from the reception area where no doubt the vast bulk of Brownie was handing back expensive overcoats and ensuring everyone left as politely as they'd arrived.

The old gangster grinned and his hooded eyes danced. "Now, let's forget all this shit and have a fucking drink. What do you say?"

Cass raised his glass. "I say I'll fucking drink to that."

Cass sat at the corner table, his arms spread wide across the back of the padded leather seats. His brown eyes shone black, the colour of his irises eaten up by his expanded pupils. His blood raced through his veins, the ever-present throb of the cocaine high blurred by whisky, leaving his limbs feeling strangely heavy. It didn't matter. He wasn't in the mood for movement, or talk. He didn't want any company, despite Artie's thick fingers pointing out this girl or that one.

His body seemed perfectly still, but unlike Carla Rae's, the quiet was only on the surface. Inside, the machine was working overtime. His skin was hot. His throat was dry and the burn at the back of his nose had grown steadily worse with each thick line of white powder he'd snorted. His gram was long gone. He was on Artie's hospitality now. His lungs felt cold from too many cigarettes; he'd lost track of how many as the hours had ticked by. It didn't matter. He'd probably smoke some more before the night was over.

He fought the urge to look at his watch. Time had flowed quick and slow, until he could only get a vague suggestion of how long he'd been there from the emptying of a fresh cigarette packet and by how many lines he'd had, and he'd lost track of both of those. He didn't care. The hangover was going to be a killer in the morning, whatever time it was. All that mattered for now was that it was late, he was fucked, and for a little while at least the fingers of the dead had let him go. He let the music pump into his veins, buzzing through him as it went. He didn't know the tune, but it didn't matter. It sounded good, not too fast and not too slow. It was seductive, calling to the darker side of him. He almost smiled. Tonight the music wasn't required to unchain the shadows in his soul. He'd already set them free to party.

The room swirled in a mass of heat and colour around him as his eyes darted from table to table, taking in the scene and sucking it back through the haze that separated him from the outside world. His frantically active mind tore at each image, unpicking it then sending the findings further inwards, to where the essence of Cass absorbed it.

At the table across from his, a beautiful blonde laughed at something the middle-aged man beside her said. They'd finished one bottle of champagne and were halfway through their second. To look at it, they were both well on their way to being drunk. The girl leaned in towards her companion and stroked his face with one hand. Cass watched as his eyes dropped to her cleavage, accentuated by the tight, low-cut dress and her body position, and for a flicker of a moment Cass thought he saw a yellow wash stream from her partner's eyes. The woman laughed and tilted her head back, and while the man was absorbed in the view, her hand slipped the champagne glass beneath the table. Still smiling at the man beside her, she tipped more than half the contents onto the dark carpet before leaning in and kissing the mark on his nose, distracting him as she brought the glass back up, and then made a show of draining the dregs.

His eyes shifted. A plump girl at a table of four refilled their glasses and while the men's attention was elsewhere, swiftly upturned the still half-full bottle into the bucket of ice. Her fingers clicked for the waitress as her smile suggested that another bottle should be ordered. It was.

Artie sat at the end of the bar, smiling. Everywhere around him, the girls were chasing the money. They hustled men to their seats, ordering over-priced food that wouldn't be eaten, bottles of champagne that would never be finished, and all on a promising smile that never reached the eyes.

The drugs sent an involuntary shudder through Cass's body. Nothing was as it seemed. Everything was an illusion. In the dim lighting, and dressed provocatively, each girl was a beauty, a land of promise that drunk men would pay hundreds to explore. How would they be in the morning? As ordinary as Carla Rae. As cold as Kate. As homely as Jessica. His heart ached.

After another line, his only measure of time, the whole world was dancing. The girls' smiles stretched too wide. The men laughed too loudly, as they sweated and tried to keep the rhythm of their writhing, gyrating partners. Cass wondered if even the women were finally succumbing to the alcohol. Up on the stage a black girl in a thong wound herself sinuously around a pole. Her eyes were bored.

The room stank of warm champagne. From in his seat, Cass could feel his own hot sweat sticking his back to his shirt. He lit another cigarette, barely tasting the smoke in his numb mouth. He didn't feel sorry for the men whose credit cards and company expense accounts were feeding hundreds of pounds into Artie's coffers. They weren't stupid. They bought into the show, happy to play their parts in it, just as long as the fantasy was delivered: deception within deception. It was a false world.

Cass found himself almost laughing, and then he stopped, suddenly. His eyes were puzzled and his mind struggled to unpick the sight that caught his attention: a pair of shiny black lace-up brogues were at the centre of the dance floor, pointed accusingly in Cass's direction. Around them bodies came together as the track shifted into something slow. The feet remained still. Cass stared.

Not now. He blinked hard. The shoes were still there. Cass wondered if the lights came on, whether he would be able to see fresh blood on them. His pounding heart slowed. His eyes moved up from the shoes, following the neat line of the trousers. At the waistband, the pale blue shirt was half tucked in and half hanging out, the expensive material creased. A couple moved in front of the still figure in a clumsy parody of a waltz, leaving only glimpses of pale shirt and dark trousers as they passed. Cass's eyes moved up, a sense of dread gripping the chill inside him. A flash of blond hair. A blue and golden eye, still behind the mass of dancing forms.

"Another line, mate?" Artie's thick body suddenly blocked his view. "You look like you're falling asleep there and we can't have that."

For a second Cass couldn't speak. He slowly raised his gaze back to Artie, very much part of the here and now. "I think I'm fucked," he spat out eventually.

"You and me both, mate."

There are no ghosts, Cass thought and focused instead on his host. Artie looked a long way from fucked. The older man's leathery skin must house a solid constitution. He wondered if he'd have a tolerance like that if he lived that long, or whether you had to take the whole way of life to earn it.

"Always room for another," Artie continued. "Anyway, it's only two-thirty. We've got another hour to kill before closing, so let's finish this gram off."

Time suddenly had its place in the night, and the sense of the surreal slipped away. The world was what it was, and so was he. Cass pulled himself to his feet and followed Mullins back to the office. The figure on the dance floor was gone. Of course it was. It'd never fucking been there; just an insubstantial ghost of the imagination, brought on by stress and grief and too much shit in his head. As he passed the bar Cass caught a glimpse of his reflection in the long mirror at the back and for a brief moment his eyes shone blue and gold, like Christian's had. It was definitely time for another line.

He opened his eyes to a sea of nicotine-stained cream and for a moment his head was beautifully and perfectly clear. It lasted the full fifteen seconds before he looked away from Artie's office ceiling and over at the man himself. A swift bout of nausea battled with the rush of the ache that set up camp at the base of his skull and sent advance parties out across his head. By the time Artie had poured two mugs of coffee Cass was feeling every bit as bad as he'd predicted. He hauled himself up into a sitting position, rubbed his face and then looked over at Artie.

"You look disgustingly healthy. What time is it?"

Artie nodded up at the clock. "Just gone nine. I've been up two hours. Never manage more than a few hours' sleep these days." He laughed. "Got too much to do. You know how it is."

"Tell me about it." Cass thought of the day ahead. At this point he couldn't see much beyond getting his stuff from the house and checking into a hotel somewhere.

"So," Artie slid the coffee across the desk, "you got all that out of your system?"

Cass nodded. "Oh yeah. My brain feels like it's trying to escape through my ears."

"That'll be the fags. You smoke too much."

"That must be it." The coffee was hot, and the back of his throat was still raw from the drugs. It tasted good, though. "I need some painkillers."

"I've got something better than that to pick you up."

He slid a piece of paper over the desk and Cass took it. There was a name on it he didn't recognise. Ali Khan.

"Ali Khan? Who's he when he's at home?"

"He, my son, runs a burger stall down the Elephant and Castle. Just round the corner from the Ministry. He makes a fortune from all the clubbers on their way home."

"And what's he got to do with me?"

"He's your alibi."

Cass frowned. His brain wasn't awake enough to move this quickly. "My alibi for what?"

"Well, you couldn't have been at your brother's house because you bought a burger from him at quarter past midnight that night. He re- members you because you complained that it wasn't cooked properly and demanded a fresh one. He remembers your flash car too." Artie grinned. "'A moody dark-haired bastard in an Audi A8.' Can only be one of those in the city." He lit a cigar and the pungent smoke made Cass's delicate stomach flip. The effort it took to swallow his bile back down made his headache punch a fresh hole through the soft tissue of his brain. Great.

"What you need to do is give that pretty sergeant of yours a bell and tell her you've got a vague memory of stopping for food at the Elephant. She'll track old Ali down soon enough. And Artie's your uncle." He laughed into his coffee. "I'm good to you, boy."

"Cheers." Cass passed the paper back. "I'll do it, but they'll never believe it. Not Bowman, anyway. That bastard's really got it in for me."

"Whether they believe it or not doesn't matter. It's all smoke and mirrors. We know that you weren't there, and now we've created a fact to prove it." Artie shrugged. "A small lie to shake a bigger one down."

Cass laughed, despite the flashes of pain that shot across his face. "I love your thinking, Artie."

"You're welcome."

They drank slowly, sipping as the hot liquid cooled. Finally, Artie said, "You going to be okay, Cass?" His face softened. "You want any coke or anything? On me?"

"Thanks, but no thanks." Cass grinned. "It's time I cleaned up for a while. I need my head straight while I try and get to the bottom of all this mess."

Artie nodded. "You take care of yourself, son. And you know where I am if you need me."

The old man's mobile rang and he went out to take the call. Cass stayed where he was on the sofa, letting the coffee slowly bring him round. He wondered what business Artie was doing: arranging some deal or another, maybe organising some violence to teach someone a lesson—nothing would surprise Cass; the only thing that did surprise him was that the only person aside from Claire who appeared to believe a word he said was a man who lived on the other side of the law. The world was a funny place, that was for sure.

CHAPTER TEN

It was nine-thirty on Saturday morning when Claire May and Mat Blackmore got to the scene, which wasn't bad going, given what they'd been in the middle of when the call came in. Not that the good mood had lasted. It was her weekend off and Mat had told her she should stay behind, but there was no way she was doing that. She didn't see the point, for one thing. She'd only be thinking about the case at home if he was working, and they'd only end up talking about it when he got back. She hadn't seen what his problem was until he'd called her "Jones' little spy in the camp." She'd just gritted her teeth and got in the car. She didn't want that argument, partly because she was sure he'd said it out of some stupid male jealousy, and partly because it was true. She would keep Cass in the loop, every step of the way. The two cases had collided, and Cass deserved to know what was going on. There was no way in hell he'd been involved in the shooting of his own family.

She pulled the plastic shoes on over her own, happy to be in the midst of the hubbub. The car journey to Charing Cross Hospital had been a silent one. She could almost hear Mat's jaw clenching tight as he drove. She knew he was jealous, of what she and Cass had done, but it had been brief and now it was over and there was nothing she could say to make it not have happened. And maybe he had a reason to be jealous: she liked Mat, sure, she liked him a lot. But was there magic? No. Cass Jones might not have felt it, but for her, he'd been thunder and lightning, and probably always would be. Maybe one day the slow burn she felt for Mat would grow, but deep down inside she had a horrible feeling that he was her rebound guy, and she just hadn't realised it before.

The Strain II wing where the fifth woman had been found took up most of one floor of the hospital, and in spite of a low buzz of conversation from the plastic-shrouded police officers littering the corridor, there was a deathly hush. Claire shivered. She couldn't help herself. Strain II was the new plague, and the nurses who worked here had her utmost respect.

She followed Mat past the two officers on the door to a small ward. A naked woman lay on the bed in the centre, the green curtain pulled completely back, exposing her dead body to whoever cared to see. Had the screen been left like that by the killer, or had Dr. Farmer opened it up? *NOTHING IS SACRED* was daubed in red across the top of the woman's full breasts. Claire fought the urge to cover her up. DI Bowman leaned against the side wall, looking ill. At least he was in the right place if he took a turn for the worse. Beside him, Dr. Hask gestured, acknowledging their arrival, and then returned to staring at the scene of the crime.

"Sorry, excuse me—"

Someone fully clothed in plastic pushed between Mat and Claire: Josh Eagleton, the young lab assistant. He almost dropped the camera he was carrying in his hurry to get to the bedside.

"You're late." The ME stared coolly at him.

"I had no change for parking. I didn't think. I'm so sorry . . ." The boy's eyes slipped away from his boss's. He was sweating and flustered and Claire felt rather sorry for him. Cass could be a bastard to work for at times, but Dr. Farmer was much worse.

"You can work through your lunch. Now start the photos."

Bowman pushed away from the wall and looked at his own assistants. "Two for the price of one?"

"I thought the more the merrier, sir," Claire answered, cutting in before Mat could speak. "I'd only have to catch up on Monday, anyway." She glanced back at the bed, drawn by the first camera flash.

"Who is she? A patient?" She couldn't help the slight jangling in her nerves. Strain II was far more contagious than the original HIV/AIDS.

"No," Dr. Farmer said, "she's got far too much meat on her for Strain II."

"Charming as ever," Bowman interjected. "She's a specialist nurse here. Her name's Hannah West, thirty-eight years old. She was on the night shift. Matron found her when she came on duty at eight this morning."

"Jesus." Mat's nose wrinkled. "How long had she been here?"

"According to the charts, she completed her last round with meds at two a.m. Her shift was set to finish at six. Her husband rang at seven forty-five to see where she was. He had to get to work and she was supposed to be home in time to watch the kids. They live in Kentish Town."

"He works on a Saturday?" Claire asked.

"Yeah, in a supermarket, apparently. He used to be in sales, lost his job a year or so back. Anyway, the day shift came looking and they found her in here. Matron took it upon herself to call the husband and tell him after she'd called us. Luckily, we got here first."

"Where is he?"

"A couple of uniforms have him stashed somewhere. They're taking a statement now that the poor bugger's finally calming down. He didn't get in here, at least."

"This is a big room for just one person," Claire said. "I thought there was a bed shortage going on?"

"There were three patients in here, but the occupant of this bed died yesterday and they were going to move in someone new today."

"But our man got here first," Mat muttered. He shook his head. "How could he have done this with other people in the room?"

"I wouldn't consider the other two as people," Dr. Farmer said, dryly, "not in the sense of witnesses, at any rate. They're not exactly in full control of their faculties. They're completely out of it, on a cocktail of drugs that includes a hefty dose of morphine. They're both advanced cases with not long left." He looked over at Bowman. "And even the less ill patients are heavily sedated at night. The hospitals are short-staffed and operate a skeleton crew at night. If everyone's asleep, it makes the job much easier to do." He peered upwards. "The curtains were drawn around her when she was found. If either of the other two had noticed anything—which is doubtful—they'd probably have just thought a new patient was being brought in."

"The hospital must be short-staffed if no one noticed her missing until her husband rang up," Claire said.

"A lot of nurses refuse to work with the Strain II cases. They don't get paid enough to take that kind of risk." The ME looked up and smiled. "I'd say she died not long after she finished that two a.m. round, or so her liver temperature would have me believe."

"I'm presuming by the words that he hasn't changed his *modus operandi* in the past few days?" Bowman stepped slightly closer. Claire thought he looked almost as pale as the body they were studying.

"He's injected her in her right arm, same as the rest. Her eyes are open. But look—" He signalled Bowman closer and pointed at the red words on the woman's chest. Claire stepped forward and peered over the DI's shoulder.

"Look at the edges." There was something close to awe in the ME's voice. "He's painted the words in blood, as usual, then he's outlined his words with the eggs, one behind the other in an absolutely perfect line."

Claire looked. Although the words themselves were uneven, the ME was right: exactly as he described, the tiny white grains were laid out with the tip of each just touching the one before and the one behind. *"Incredible,"* she breathed.

"How has he done that?" Bowman asked, incredulous.

"God only knows. It's like the eyes. He gets them in there perfectly too. Josh and I tried for hours, but we damaged some every time." He looked up at his assistant, who nodded from behind the camera.

"He's getting more ambitious." It was the first thing Dr. Hask had said. Unlike the rest of them, he hadn't moved but remained with his back against the far wall.

"I've listened to the analysis you did with Jones," Bowman said, turning to him, "and it sounded good, but maybe you're off the mark a bit? This stuff about displacing them, putting them where they don't belong?" He spread his hands. "This is a hospital, and she's a nurse. This one's hardly out of place, is she?"

"But she is," Claire cut in before Dr. Hask could answer. She could see it clearly. "She's a nurse, not a patient. She shouldn't be on a dead patient's bed. She's here to help them. She's not infected. She's a world away from the people that are patients in this wing."

The profiler nodded. "That's exactly right. This might be more subtle than the others, but she's definitely somewhere she doesn't belong. There's almost an irony with this one. Maybe he's starting to respect the opposition a little more. Whatever the reason, he's definitely upping the ante."

"Oh, great. That's just what we need." Bowman stepped back.

"Show-offs invariably take a tumble, Detective Inspector. Let's just hope this one does it sooner rather than later."

The SOC team loitered in the doorway, eager to get on with their job, and Claire followed the three men out into the corridor. She could understand Bowman's concerns. They were the same as Cass's had been, primarily the press, and the ability they had to destroy careers. With this murder the killer had taken the cards out of police hands.

The corridor they were standing in was sealed off now, but it didn't take a genius to figure out that the details would be all over the papers by tomorrow. Nurses' salaries were low and the red tops would pay well for a story like this. This new victim was a nurse and a mother, and was murdered in the hospital itself. Add that to the other details and you had a juicy by-line for any up-and-coming hack, and a guaranteed splash and spread. Claire could practically see the headlines.

"The DCI tells me I'm holding a press conference this afternoon." Bowman headed slowly towards the stairs at the end. As the others followed it sounded as if they were walking through snow, their plastic soles crunching against the lino.

"He's no happier about it than I am, but we've got no choice. We've been lucky enough so far with keeping a lid on it, but someone in this building will call it in, and we'll have no way of knowing who that will be. And you can bet that as soon as the papers have one story, then everyone who's kept quiet over the others will realise this is a serial and want their share of the media pie." He turned to the profiler. "You can help me figure out what we're going to say—what to leave in, what to leave out. If there's anything we can mention that might make our man mad or draw him out."

"Not a problem."

Claire felt a hand tug at her sleeve and she turned. It was Josh Eagleton.

"How's DI Jones?" His voice was low, and Claire didn't blame him. Cass's name was mud around here.

"He's okay. This mess will all get straightened out eventually. It's just bad timing—he hasn't done anything wrong." She was aware of how defensive she sounded, but she couldn't help it. Everyone else was too damn keen to believe that Cass was lying. She knew Cass's faults, probably better than any of them, but she also knew that if he'd been there when things had kicked off with Christian, he would have stayed and dealt with it. She knew his record. She knew what he'd done. But that was a long time ago, and a very different situation.

"Come on, Claire." Bowman had reached the door. "If you're working, you're coming back to the station with us. Otherwise, go home."

"Sorry." She smiled at the young man. "Got to go."

"I think he's innocent too," Josh said, almost whispering.

She'd already turned away, aware that the others were waiting for her. "Thanks. That's good to know." Maybe the ME's new assistant wasn't as bad as Cass had thought. She gave him another brief smile goodbye before picking up her pace and catching the others in the doorway where they were pulling off their shoe covers and dumping them in the bin.

"Claire, find wherever the constable is with the husband and get his account of her day yesterday. Also, talk to some of her colleagues. See what they say about her," Bowman said. "Then grab a lift back to the station with a uniform."

"Yes, sir." She glanced back, and as the double doors swung closed she saw the geeky young man still watching her from the corridor, looking skinny and awkward in his plastic overalls. The plastic hood tight over his head wasn't helping.

"Has he got a crush on you or something?" Blackmore frowned.

"Maybe." She grinned at him. "He wouldn't be the first, and he won't be the last."

She left her lover staring after her as she took the stairs down to find poor Hannah West's husband. The reply had been unusually cocky for her, but Mat deserved it for being such an asshole for the past few days. And anyway, someone had to keep the Cass Jones spirit alive at Paddington Green until he got back. It might as well be her.

He knew Kate wasn't there the moment he shut the front door behind him. The house felt empty, as if it had somehow been switched off and was waiting for some human content before becoming a home again. Cass called his wife's name anyway, but there was no reply; even the house remained silent, with not even a click or whir from any of the kitchen appliances, or water gurgling through the radiators. He waited in the hallway for a moment. She'd said she'd be out, so it shouldn't have come as any surprise, but he still couldn't fight the small wave of disappointment. But at least there wouldn't be another argument, no more accusations. He was in no state to face them right now.

He'd planned on taking a shower before getting his stuff together, but now that he was back in the house he figured he'd take a raincheck until he got to whatever hotel he'd end up checking into, despite how grungy he was. The house was already beginning to feel as if he didn't belong there, and getting naked in the bathroom would be weird now—especially if Kate came back before he was done. He'd just have to bear the grime and cigarette smoke from his night's excesses for a couple of hours longer.

He went into the spare bedroom and hauled down a suitcase from the top of the wardrobe before heading into the master suite. He stopped in the doorway. The bed hadn't been slept in. Kate had obviously changed the bedding, but the creases ironed into the pillowcases by Mrs. Cooper were still clear. The same with the duvet cover. His stomach tightened. There was the possibility that she'd changed them this morning before going out, but that wasn't Kate's way; she wasn't a morning person. She'd have got up, showered and dressed and gone out before he'd got here. That would have been it. He went into the en-suite and felt the bristles of her toothbrush. They were dry.

He went back in the bedroom and stared at the bed for a few moments before throwing the suitcase on it. As he opened the cupboard and looked at the racks of clothes, not knowing what the fuck to take and what to leave behind, he felt a twinge of something close to jealousy. If Kate hadn't slept here at the house, then where had she slept? And with whom? It annoyed him that he immediately wondered if she'd found a male shoulder to cry on . . . but maybe she had. He couldn't exactly blame her if she had gone and slept with someone else; it wasn't like he hadn't done his share. But emotions didn't work like that. He took a deep breath. He was overreacting. She'd probably just gone to one of the friends she was constantly on the phone to. He thought about his own brief relationship with Claire during their split. Maybe Kate had found someone too, and perhaps she'd now rekindled it. He couldn't help the twist in his guts that came with that thought.

He looked at the neat pillowcases again. If she'd had no intention of sleeping in their bed that night, then why the hell had she insisted on kicking him out? He knew that his anger was probably unreasonable, but that didn't stop him giving it free rein. Anger was better than pain, and unreasonable was what Kate and the rest of the world had come to expect from him anyway.

After shoving most of what he needed in the suitcase he added his phone charger and electric razor and zipped it up. Anything he'd missed he could come back for, or buy. He headed back downstairs.

The lounge was filled with too many expensive knick-knacks that he hadn't chosen and wasn't even sure that he liked. There was nothing there that he wanted to take, and even if there had been, a small part of him was still hoping that maybe once all this was sorted, Kate would relent. Maybe he'd even agree to whatever counselling it was she kept pushing for. If he started taking things from the home, well, that was like admitting the marriage was dead. He hadn't accepted that in all these years, and he wasn't quite sure he was ready to cave in yet.

He carefully pulled Christian's slim laptop bag out from behind the large TV attached to the wall. His brother and he were so different in so many ways; you only had to look at their houses to see that, but on some level he wondered if Christian's home was as much of a façade as his own. It was the laptop Cass had taken to try and find a way inside his brother's mind, not anything from his easy, comfortable home, nor the hard drive from his PC that sat on his desk that Jess and Luke had access to. If something was bothering Christian, he would have hidden it in his private files somewhere. He was too organised to put it anywhere else.

The phone rang, cutting through the quiet. The shrill sound demanded attention, but Cass let it ring out. The only person who'd ever tried calling him at home was Christian. Everyone else knew that his mobile was the best bet. He wasn't even sure Claire or anyone at work even knew the landline number, and he preferred it that way. With the laptop bag over one shoulder, he went back into the hall and grabbed his suitcase. He was just at the front door when the answer phone kicked in.

"Hello? Cass? Are you there?"

His hand dropped from the latch and he turned. Could that really be who he thought it was? There was a pause and he could hear the caller's hesitant breath.

"Oh, that's such a shame. I was hoping I'd catch you in. I don't have another number for you, so I hope this is still the right one. It's Father Michael."

Something tugged at Cass's insides. The last thing he needed was platitudes from some blast from the past, but at the same time the priest sounded so concerned. He remembered that about Father Michael. He *cared*, genuinely. He'd tried to speak to Cass twice since his parents had died, but Cass had avoided him, in the same way he'd avoided Christian recently. Maybe that thought was what stopped him from just leaving the answer phone running.

He picked up the phone. "Hi, you just caught me. I was on the way out the door." He paused. "How are you? It's been a long time."

"Oh, I'm so glad you're there. I know how busy you must be."

Cass frowned. "You do?" He'd expected the priest to launch straight into apologies for his loss, and perhaps mull over the old times from when Christian and Cass had been regulars at Sunday School.

"You always did like to be doing things rather than thinking about things. Especially at times like this. Do you remember when little Briony Holmes got run over by that train? How old were you? Ten maybe? You and Christian were both fond of her, but I think you liked her a little—"

"Like you said, Father, I am pretty busy." The conversation may have started out unexpectedly, but the old man was already drifting into the past, and Cass wasn't sure he had either the time or the inclination to go there. He stared at the suitcase. He needed to find himself somewhere to live.

"Of course, of course. I'm sorry." Cass could hear a crackle of age in the priest's voice that hadn't been there all those years ago. What would the priest make of Cass if he could see him? Lined and unshaven, he was a far cry from the boy of his youth.

"I just wanted to say that I heard about Christian, and how shocked I was. Such a tragedy. He was only down here a couple of weeks ago, and he seemed fine." He paused. "Perhaps there was something there that I should have seen. I'm sorry, Cass, but I didn't. He was so . . . animated. I thought he was okay. A little odd at times, but okay."

Cass felt the world shift a little. "Sorry, did you say you'd seen Christian? Recently?"

"Well, yes." The priest seemed surprised. "Didn't you know? He'd been coming down to your parents' house."

"He'd been *what*?"

"He'd been coming down to your parents' house, on and off for the past three or four months. But his visits had definitely become more frequent. He'd been staying over some weekends, and I've even seen his car outside some weeknights."

"With the family?" Cass couldn't get his head round this: what the hell was Christian doing going home? It felt weird even thinking of his parents' house as home, it had been so long since he'd spent any real time there, but the word came naturally all the same.

"No, on his own," Father Michael answered. "Didn't you know? I thought maybe he was trying to answer some personal questions. He seemed very curious about your parents, the past. We've had some long talks." He paused. "It's been nice to catch up. I was very fond of you both when you were children and since the funerals even Christian had stopped coming home."

Even Christian. The old man wouldn't have meant it to sound like an accusation, but Cass felt the sting. Even Christian, the good son. Not the prodigal killer, who hid away and fought his father over his beliefs every time they met up, for no other reason than because he couldn't think of any other way to deal with all his pent-up rage and anger at the fuck-up he'd made of his life. His father, with all his faith and calm acceptance, had been a good punch-bag. Neither had been very good at understanding each other, but at least Cass hadn't pretended. The age-old irritation fizzed back into life in the pit of his stomach, but he was no longer sure if it was aimed at his father or simply at himself. He swallowed it and concentrated on the curve ball that Father Michael had just thrown into the mess that surrounded him.

"He didn't talk to you about this?"

"No. No, we hadn't talked much recently."

"I'm sorry. I really am." He hesitated again. "Maybe you should come down to the house. Take some time to yourself. It might be good for you."

It hadn't been exactly good for Christian, had it? Cass bit back the snotty remark. Father Michael didn't deserve his bitter defensiveness. He looked down at his suitcase and his head filled with the image of a sleepless night in a shabby hotel room. What the hell had Christian been doing at home? His life was here, in London, with Jess and Luke and his job at The Bank. He thought of Artie's elliptical comments on Mr. Bright and The Bank. He thought of some bastard planting evidence to discredit him in his brother's house. His brain bubbled with activity. Was Christian somehow linked to Mr. Bright? What was so important that it had led him home for answers? The floor almost rippled under him and he gripped the handset.

"You know, I think I might just do that. I'll come down today. They've offered me compassionate leave if I want it." A man with more shame might have felt more than a twinge of guilt at lying to a priest, but Cass saw it as a mild twisting of the truth. And his soul was too far gone to be bothered by the odd white lie. Truth was only ever a matter of perception.

"Good. Good, that's great!" He sounded genuinely pleased, and Cass was surprised to feel an echo of that sentiment lift his mood. "It's been a long time, Cass. I'm looking forward to catching up. I'll put some basics in the house for you."

"No, really, you don't have to worry—I can manage."

"You can pay me back when you see me. I'll keep the receipt." The short laugh was soft and full of affection. "You always were so independent, Cass, but all of us need to go home sometimes, to remember who we really are."

As he ended the conversation, Cass realised with a strange ache that Father Michael was probably the only link to his family left.

The buildings became less grand as Cass navigated his way through the centre of town and out through the poorer boroughs to the arterial roads. First they became rows of rotten, broken teeth; the edges uneven and surfaces grimy-grey, coated with years of pollution, but slowly, the nature of the landscape changed. The flats all crammed together turned into houses, their outlines against the backdrop of the sky becoming more uniform as the suburbs sprawled alongside the slow-moving dual carriageways. These houses epitomised normality, each the same as the next, the only individuality expressed through a poorly thought-out pebble-dash or a cream instead of white coating of paint. These were the homes of the fiftysomething middle-class: close to the road and within reach of a good school, somewhere you could keep up with the Joneses—because everything they had was the same as yours.

Cass almost smiled at the irony as he opened the window slightly and lit a cigarette. Not the Jones family that he came from, of course: there was nothing uniform or normal about them. The woman in the car next to him watched as he smoked, and frowned, a look that implied that if she had more time she'd call the police and report him. He could tell she was the kind of woman whose life had never been tainted with crime. Cass stared at her. She'd have to be if she thought the police would give any kind of shit about someone smoking in public. He

grinned at her and she looked away, a sudden flush rising in her sag-
ging cheeks, her mind no doubt filled with stories of road rage and
maniacs. He inhaled hard and blew the smoke out of the window in
her direction.

His mobile rang and he recognised Claire's number. He patched it
through the hands-free unit and tapped the answer button. "Hey."

"We've got another one," she said.

"Another dead woman? Already?"

"Yes, they found her this morning. She was a nurse called Hannah
West." She talked him through the details of the murder, and how the
profiler was convinced the killer was upping his game by where he'd
left her. And she told him about the almost impossible outlining of the
bloody words.

"I'd agree with Hask," Cass said. "He's speeding up. Maybe the
initial thrill isn't lasting so long."

"Great."

"Yeah, not good for us." *For you, I should say,* he thought. *I'm per-
sona non grata.* "No link to the others?" He wasn't hopeful.

"Well, I've just finished typing up what the husband had to say and I
can't see where she might have met the other four women. They're all so
different." She paused. "He did say that she sometimes went into town
early before her shifts started. She liked to go to Covent Garden."

"Was she a shopper?"

"No, not according to the husband. He said she just liked it there.
She said it helped before work. She found it peaceful. He said he'd never
really questioned her about it. They both work long hours and they
have kids. I guess they were probably more like ships passing in the
night than a couple that got to spend any quality time together. She'd
been doing extra shifts since he lost his job—nursing pays more than
sitting on a till at Asda, so the husband's been doing more of the stuff
with the kids. They're a pretty ordinary family." She paused. "Sorry.
There's not much to go on."

"I wasn't expecting much, to be honest. Maybe there's something
in this Covent Garden thing. See if you can talk to any of the relatives
and friends of the other women again. Find out if they went to any cof-

fee shops or anything there regularly." He couldn't picture Carla Rae in the kind of Italian cafés, with their expensive lattes and espressos, that filled Covent Garden, but you never could tell.

"Bowman's got a press conference later," Claire said. "I think it's scheduled for half-twelve. They can't keep a lid on the story for much longer."

Cass glanced at his watch. It was only just eleven. "I'm heading down to Kent for the weekend to sort out some stuff at my parents' place. I should be there in time to catch the first airing. Speaking of the odious twat, where's Bowman now? Don't let him catch you on the phone to me. He'll give you hell."

"We're safe. They've brought Macintyre back in and Mat and Bowman are interviewing him. I went to take them this report but they looked like they were going at him pretty hard, so I figured it could wait and I'd call you instead."

"Good girl. At least they're still working my case as well as their own."

"Bowman doesn't look well. His appendix was fine, but apparently some infection has inflamed his stomach—a bad case of food poisoning or something. The doctors aren't even sure."

Cass laughed. "Poor bastard. Can't say I've got that much sympathy." He paused, reminded of his conversation with Artie. The white lie to Claire was going to feel worse than the one to the priest, but he continued anyway. "Speaking of food, I've been thinking about the night Christian died. I've got a vague folk memory of stopping for a burger. Somewhere down by the Elephant and Castle—maybe near the Ministry of Sound, because I can remember seeing the clubbers going in and out."

"Good, anything else?" Her voice had brightened; here was something she could do.

"Yeah, I think I complained about the burger being not cooked properly. I might have demanded a fresh one." He tried to sound a little shamefaced. Claire May was thorough; she'd find this Ali Khan.

Claire laughed. "I'm surprised he didn't kick your head in. You went for a rat-burger and complained about it?"

He tried to laugh along. He would rather she knew the full story, but then Claire wouldn't have gone for it. She believed that the truth would always out of its own accord. One day she'd learn.

"One more thing you can do for me."

"Fire away."

"Don't share this with the others yet, because I don't want to have to say who I've been talking to. See if you can find out if this Mr. Bright works for, or is in any way connected to, The Bank."

"The Bank? It's a big organisation, and that's quite a common name."

"Yeah, but use the age and physical description that we got from Bradley."

"Sure." She paused. "Why do you think he might work for The Bank?"

"I'm not sure he does, but he might be associated with them. I don't know how, and it might be all a wild goose chase. I'll explain if we get a lead on him there. Sorry."

"Not a problem. I'll get on it."

When Claire said it wasn't a problem, he knew she meant it. She was uncomplicated. If something pissed her off she came out and said it. There were no games with Claire May. There was good and bad and right and wrong. He wished he could have loved her for it. He wished he could have explained that he could never love her, exactly because of that. But the time for those conversations was over and they'd both moved on. Right now Claire May and Artie Mullins were the only two people who believed in him; he wondered what Dr. Hask would make of these opposing personalities trusting in Cass Jones.

The phone beeped: a call holding. It was Ramsey.

"I've got to go, Claire. Stay in touch."

"You too. And take care."

He switched to the second call.

"Hi. What can a suspended DI do for a fully employed one?" If they'd found any more planted evidence against him they wouldn't be letting him know with a phone call; it would be blues and twos with sirens wailing behind cutting a path through the train of irritated traffic behind him.

"Well, it's a funny thing." Ramsey's tone was light. "Your brother's employers have been in touch."

"The Bank?"

"Yes. They first expressed their sympathies. Then they were very clear that they wanted his work laptop back, ASAP." Despite his American drawl he spoke the acronym like a Brit, sounding out each letter. Cass liked him all the more for that.

"Laptop?" He matched the American's easy tone and glanced down at the slim bag on the passenger seat next to him. "Surely that must be in the house somewhere."

"You'd think so, wouldn't you? But it's the damndest thing. It seems to have gone missing."

Cass could hear in his tone that Ramsey knew exactly where the laptop was, but unlike Bowman, he wouldn't come in screaming accusations. Cass almost smiled; he was enjoying the game for once. "Maybe he left it in the office somewhere?"

"That would seem a reasonable assumption, but in the crime scene pictures it's on his desk in the dining room. Somehow, it's not there now."

"How strange."

"You could say that. It occurred to me that you might have accidentally picked it up when you went to see the place the other night?"

"Admittedly, I was quite emotional." Cass flicked the finished cigarette butt out the window. "But I'm sure I would have noticed. Unless it got stuck to my shoe and I didn't realise in the dark."

"Well, it seems to have gone walkabout, one way or another, and its owners want it back. They were very insistent."

"If I come across it somewhere then I'll let you know."

"Yes, you will." Ramsey became serious. "I've told them you're on compassionate leave and out of reach until Monday. If you could find the laptop by then, that would be helpful."

"I'm sure it'll turn up. Just out of interest, who was it that rang from The Bank?"

"You know I can't tell you that, Jones."

"Oh, come on. You know you'll only be saving me a couple of calls."

Ramsey sighed into his ear. "Okay, but don't cause me any trouble.

Remember, I'm on your side on this. The first person who rang was your brother's assistant, Maya Healey. The second, an hour or so later, was his boss, a man called Asher Red. He sounded foreign, maybe Middle Eastern. He didn't sound overly sorry for your loss. He was more concerned about his."

"Two calls? They must really want this laptop back."

"Like I said, Jones. Monday."

"You'll have it."

Finally free from the city's grasp, the road emptied a little into normal weekend traffic and Cass was able to put his foot down as he pulled onto the M20. The road was pretty empty, with lorries the only traffic trundling down to the ferries now. With no passenger ferries or cross-Channel trains running, the cheap airlines had cornered the market in European travel.

The motorway still had the signs up pointing traffic towards Ashford for the Eurostar Passenger Service, but it was merely a grave marker. Everyone knew the tunnel would never reopen after the terrorist attack the year before. Cass shuddered at the thought of those trains stuck in the Chunnel when the bombs went off. The public had completely lost faith in travelling beneath the sea, for now anyway, which was probably a good thing for the government, because they sure as fuck didn't have the money to repair it all.

He headed towards Folkestone, driving almost on autopilot while his conscious mind mulled over his brother and The Bank and the elusive Mr. Bright. He thought about the film he'd been sent as heavy clouds moved across the sun, sending dark shadows across the road. Brilliant flashes broke through the jet clouds—the weather, Cass thought, also had no idea what to do next.

He looked down at his phone and scrolled through the numbers until it reached JACKSON HOME. It was worth a try; hopefully the Jacksons and Millers wouldn't yet know that he was technically off the case. He pushed the green call button.

"Hello?" The wary answer came after just four rings.

"Mr. Jackson? It's DI Jones. I'm sorry to disturb you. I just wanted to ask you something."

"Of course." The dead boy's father sounded slightly vague and Cass wondered if Isaac Jackson had resorted to pills, or was relying on a stiff drink or two before lunchtime to help see him through the rest of the day. He thought it was probably the latter. Women took antidepressants. Men found other ways to cope.

"How can I help?" Jackson didn't mention Cass's sudden exit, even though he must have heard what had happened to Christian and his family. Cass didn't mind. Platitudes made him uncomfortable, and he knew how selfish a bubble of grief could be. Isaac Jackson had enough to cope with in his own nightmare. He wouldn't be thinking about anyone else's.

"I just wondered if you'd ever come across a man called Mr. Bright. He might work for The Bank."

"We don't work for The Bank." A hitch in the man's breath filled the slight pause. "Why would we know someone who works for The Bank?"

Cass frowned. That was a bit strange. "Well, everyone knows *someone* who works for The Bank these days. And you and Mr. Miller both work in investments, don't you? I just wondered if the name meant anything to you. That's all."

"I'm sorry." Jackson just sounded tired again. "I haven't been sleeping. You think this man may have something to do with what happened to our boys? Does he know that gangster?"

"I really wish I could tell you. I'm just following up a lead. It might be nothing."

"Well, the name doesn't mean anything to me. I'm sorry."

"If you could check with your wife and the Millers and let me know if they've heard the name anywhere, I'd be grateful."

"Of course. Who is he?"

"It's just a name that came up. It's like I said: I'm just following up whatever leads I can."

They said their goodbyes and hung up. So Jackson didn't know the elusive Mr. Bright. He wasn't surprised. That would have made it too easy. He sighed in the gloom. Questions tugged at him, each one tangled in the grip of the dead, and he didn't have any answers to make them let go. He pushed his foot down and took the turning for Folkestone. Home, then. Maybe he'd find something there.

CHAPTER ELEVEN

The village of Capel-Le-Ferne sat about three miles outside of Folke-stone. With the window rolled down Cass could smell the fresh tang of the sea in the air. As he drove through the narrow streets it didn't look like much had changed over the past few years. The front of the butcher's had a new coat of green paint, but that was about all. Time slowed in the country. Or maybe it was that the people who lived there liked things to stay just so. The calm might appeal to some, but Cass wasn't one of them. Already he missed the grime of the city, even when surrounded by these picture-postcard houses and neatly mown green lawns. He couldn't help it; it was in his blood now.

The house was a couple of roads back from the tiny high street, and he followed the twists and turns of the road until he pulled into the pebbled drive and finally stopped the car. He looked down at his keys. Amidst the bundle was the gold Chubb to his parents' house. He couldn't remember the last time he'd used it, certainly not in the five years since the funeral, but when he'd bought the new car he'd auto-matically transferred the key with the rest onto the silver Audi keyring Kate had bought him. He wasn't quite sure what to make of that.

The clouds overhead were slowly dispersing and clean spring sun-shine bathed the house, making the glass in the windows glint. Thick hedges rose high between the house and the road. Cass had wanted to sell the house, but Christian had said the market wasn't good. Cass knew his reasons were more sentimental than that. Only in a tiny village in the country could a house stand empty for five years and remain undamaged—though it was likely that Father Michael had been keeping an eye on it for Cass and Christian, probably popping in once a week or so and checking nothing was broken or pipes hadn't leaked. For all Cass knew, the priest and his brother had come to some arrangement, or maybe Christian had even organised a cleaning lady. The empty space that was his brother's life ached in the hollow of his stomach. Maybe he'd find some answers here.

The light shifted and he grabbed his suitcase, the holdall and the laptop from the car. As he walked to the door he glanced upwards. Ivy clung to the red brick, covering one side of the front of the house and creeping across to the right. Cass frowned. He'd always hated the ivy. His mother had planted it, and as a child he'd been quietly convinced it was suffocating the house. He found that as an adult, his opinion hadn't changed. Not that it mattered. It wasn't as if he intended spending long here. When all this business was sorted out, maybe he'd even sell it. He'd probably have to if Kate decided she wanted a divorce. He pushed that thought aside. This trip was about Christian, not Kate; she was a whole host of other problems. His eyes followed the ivy upwards. The chimneys at either end of the hundred-and-fifty-year-old house still stood straight, pointing skywards.

Always look up, Charlie. The thought came out of nowhere and Cass immediately brought his head down. Brian Freeman and his words didn't belong here. Cass turned the key in the lock and went inside.

The pale walls and wooden floor kept the house light and airy, just as it had always been. Cass had expected to feel more, but leaving his stuff in the hallway and peering into the front room, there was only a sense of curious familiarity. After the funerals Christian and Jessica had come down and cleared away all the personal items and knick-knacks and bagged up his parents' clothes for charity. Cass hadn't joined them, and not only because of what he and Jessica had been doing while Christian had been trying desperately to reach them the day their parents died. He couldn't face it: that was the truth. In many ways, quiet Christian had been stronger than Cass. Or perhaps it was just that the younger brother had a lighter load on his soul.

The basics were still in place—TV, sofas and bookshelves—but all the personal things had gone. There were no ornaments on the mantelpiece, and the pictures and prints from the walls had disappeared. The house was like a place in limbo, his home and not his home, as if it had been sold and packed up, but the removal men hadn't arrived yet. In the kitchen the microwave and coffee machine were still in their normal places, and a quick inspection found cutlery in the drawers and crockery in the cupboards. Maybe Christian had been considering renting the place out, and never got round to it.

A note rested up against the kettle. *Come to the church tomorrow? About one? Michael.*

Cass smiled. It seemed strange to see the name without its title. He would forever be Father Michael to Cass. He peered inside the fridge. There was milk, bacon, eggs, mushrooms, a bag of salad and a pre-made lasagne that was big enough to last two days. He closed the door. On the side behind him was a small box of teabags and a jar of coffee, as well as fresh bread and a very nice bottle of Rioja. It looked like the priest was happy to have him back.

He took his suitcase upstairs. It was just coming up to twelve-thirty, but there was no satellite or cable TV in the house so he'd have to wait until the one o'clock news to see Bowman's press conference. A shower would fill the time. He hovered on the landing momentarily, unsure which room to take. His first instinct, to go to his own room at the far end of the corridor, didn't appeal; after spending the previous night on a very uncomfortable sofa he didn't much fancy his old single bed. And his parents' bedroom had an en-suite bathroom, so it made sense to use it. Still, he couldn't shake the sense that he was trespassing as he pushed the door open and dumped his suitcase on the bed.

He opened the curtains and let the sunshine stream through, catching the dancing dust in its beam. That was better. It was just a room. He looked in the cupboards and, as expected, they were empty. There was no clutter on the dressing table, nor in the bathroom. Christian and Jessica had been thorough. Still, it was a long time ago, and he wasn't quite sure what he had expected—that everything would have been left just as it was the last time he was here? His parents were dead and gone . . . and now Christian, Jessica and Luke were gone too. Even though he had identified the dead bodies himself, Cass found he couldn't quite grasp that he was the last one left. He and this house were the wreckage of the Jones family. The rooms around him felt suddenly emptier. He shook away the chill that came with a great surge of loneliness and turned the shower on, welcoming the hard noise of the water on ceramic tiles. Anything was better than the silence, and the feeling that the dead were watching him from the shadows.

The press conference was the lead story, and with the volume up and a hot coffee in one hand and a cigarette in the other, Cass felt the quiet emptiness of the house creeping away as the building adjusted to being occupied again. The shower, a shave and clean clothes had done him good; he was feeling almost his old self.

He watched Gary Bowman walk towards the central seat, Blackmore on one side and the DCI on the other. The long white table separated them from the journalists. There was no sign of Hask, but that wasn't a surprise. Ironically enough, on the rare occasions the headshed were prepared to fork out for profilers, they always kept them low profile. Technically, they were civilians, and as such they needed to be protected. Bowman sat down carefully and Cass noted how pale he looked. What the fuck was he doing back at work? Brown-nosing for a promotion, probably. He waited for the noise in the room to subside before resting his arms on the table and leaning forward. His cufflinks glinted in the flash of a camera as he raised a hand to get silence.

"This isn't going to take long, and I'm not going to answer any questions at the present time, so listen carefully. This morning we found the dead body of a female nurse in Charing Cross Hospital. We believe that she was murdered."

He paused as the expected buzz of noise made its way round the room before continuing, "We believe her death may be linked to those of four other women found dead in the central London area over the past few weeks." This time Bowman just raised his voice and talked over the hacks until they finally shut up. "We believe that the individual committing these crimes is a white male over the age of thirty. He may move jobs quite frequently, and he is probably something of a loner."

Cass recognised the profiler's analysis in Bowman's words. He sipped his coffee and watched.

"He may recently have gone through an upheaval, or perhaps a crisis of faith."

"Is it true he's written on them in blood? 'Nothing is sacred'?"

The voice cut through from the back of the crowded room, and despite his dislike of Bowman, Cass didn't envy him having to deal with this pack of hounds.

Bowman stared, but the camera didn't cut to whoever it was had called out. After a moment he said, "You know I can't disclose any information on the killer's methods."

"But has he—?"

Next to Bowman, DCI Morgan leaned forward and spoke into the microphone. "You'll either listen, or we'll terminate this press conference right now," he growled. "And thank you for no doubt adding to the number of false confessions my officers will have to waste time sorting through. Maybe I should send your newspaper the bill?"

He had the kind of voice you didn't want to argue with, even though Cass had managed it several times. Was it only yesterday that voice had been directed at him in the interview room? Felt like longer . . .

"He may be socially awkward," Bowman continued, "and we think he's probably below average intelligence."

Cass sat up. This was not what Hask had said; he'd distinctly said the man they were looking for was probably highly intelligent, not below average. He'd also said that he was probably quite charismatic, despite being a loner. Cass stubbed his cigarette out in the saucer he was using as an ashtray. He understood what they were doing: they'd be trying to get a reaction from the killer, to force him into making an angry mistake. They didn't have enough clear information to make

any true description worthwhile, so they were using the press conference both to appease the papers and to see if they could draw him out.

Cass thought it was a long shot. He doubted their killer would be
so easily wound up. He turned the TV down as the three men got up
to signal the end of the press conference and the screen cut back to the
studio. He wondered if the smart and stylish Mr. Bright had seen the
news. Was he the killer they were looking for? After what Artie had
said about the man's reputation Cass wasn't sure himself, but he was
most certainly involved in this mess in some way. He was eager to hear
what Claire had managed to find out about any links he might have
with The Bank.

But right now, he had another task. He slid Christian's small laptop
from its bag and opened the lid. It was a make he didn't recognise, but
its elegant shape, size and light weight indicated expense. Many of the
founders of The Bank came from IT backgrounds, and it wouldn't
have surprised him if they had a range of equipment solely for use by
its employees.

He pressed the On button and the crystal display came immediately
to life. He'd been right. This machine was good. Against the black and
silver backdrop a command box opened, demanding a password. Cass
stared. He typed in Jessica. It failed. He tried Luke. It failed again. He
frowned. Christian was predictable. Whereas Cass's passwords, as and
when he ever needed them, were always completely random, he was
pretty sure that Christian would fall into most people's habit of using
a loved one's name. He typed in JessicaLuke, all one word, and almost
pressed enter, but his fingers paused above the keys. Christian's password would never be made of words. Christian loved his wife and
child, or at least he had until that final night, but he thought in numbers. Cass deleted his typing and instead inserted the two numbers 7
and 4. There were seven letters in Jessica and four in Luke. He pressed
enter and the red screen disappeared, instantly replaced with a clear
homepage. He grinned. Maybe he still knew his brother a little after all.

He wasn't sure what he should be looking for, so he clicked on Start
and began to rummage through the files. He started with the email

application, but as he scrolled down they all looked entirely bland, all work-related. Efficient as Christian always was, the history only went back about six weeks, so anything further back was probably deleted or backed up into the system in The Bank's London HQ. Most of what remained were from Maya Healey, the assistant Ramsey had mentioned, checking on the progress of various audits and account transfers. Occasionally there was one from his boss, Asher Red, but those were always short and polite, and, to Cass, relatively pointless. Whatever Christian was doing at The Bank, it was impressing the bosses. Mr. Red's communications were all asking Christian if he needed anything, or congratulating him on doing such a fine job. Cass wondered if maybe Asher Red could give DCI Morgan a tip or two on how to talk to your staff.

The last email conversation was from Christian to Maya on the day that he died. Cass looked at the times. It was probably only an hour or so before he'd called Cass. He was querying some transfers and personal details on accounts. Cass frowned. *"Please double-check these. This can't be right."* Something had been bugging Christian. The sentences were too short and to the point. He scrolled down to Maya's response, which was to confirm the transfers and details were correct and to ask what he was doing auditing small businesses rather than company ones. Christian answered that a batch had arrived on his desk and he was just working his way through them. Someone must have been off sick. He then asked for a printout of all movement from one of the accounts to take home and look at. Surely, if Christian had taken the statements home, they would have been in the laptop bag, but that was empty.

He typed the two numbers into his phone. Maybe it was something, maybe nothing, but they would be worth checking out.

He searched both the Inbox and Outbox for anyone with the surname Bright, but there was no result. He tried a search on the contents of all mail files, but there was still nothing. He gritted his teeth. It was never going to be that easy. His finger moved over the narrow touch-sensitive mouse pad, clicking on various files, most of which contained accounts or reports on various companies. Some of the names he rec-

ognised as being part of The Bank group; others came as a surprise.
There was also a file with companies that were about to become viable
for future purchase. Cass scanned the pages. All joking aside, maybe
within ten years everyone would work for The Bank in some form or
another. No wonder the moguls that headed it were always smiling.

He left the individual files alone and explored the drives. There was
very little in the way of anything personal, and not a lot that Cass really
understood, but nothing struck him as out of the ordinary. He peered
at an icon down at the bottom of the list. He almost hadn't seen it;
without a file name attached and in the middle of so many others, it was
almost invisible. He clicked on it and as another dialogue box opened
the screen behind vanished back to silver and black.

FILE: REDEMPTION.

He stared at the word. Redemption. What was it Christian had said
to him on the phone that night? *It's about redemption. That's the key.*
His heartbeat quickened. Whatever his brother had wanted to talk to
him about, it was in this file. He typed 7 and 4 into the password box.
The dialogue box changed. PASSWORD ONE: ACCEPTED. Beneath
it a blank space flashed next to the command PASSWORD TWO.

Fuck. He lit a cigarette. He added Christian's name in numbers, 9, to
the tally. Nothing. He tried rearranging them. There was nothing again.
For ten minutes he tried various combinations of words he thought
might be significant to Christian, right down to the name of his first
pet, a short-lived hamster called Woolly. Nothing worked. He'd even
tried CASS but, as expected, that had failed. He sucked on the butt of
the cigarette until it was damp, and then ground it out. What the hell
would Christian have used?

He shut the computer down and leaned back in the chair for a moment. There was no point in just typing in random words; he'd end up
trying for all eternity. Christian had been coming down to the house
for a while, that's what Father Michael had said. Maybe the clue to the
password was here somewhere. He looked around at the bland lounge.
Whatever it was, it wasn't in here. The sun had dispersed the last of
the clouds and Cass opened the window slightly to air out the smoke
before heading back upstairs.

What had been his own bedroom as a child was pretty much as it was the last time he'd been here, made up as a small spare room and completely impersonal. It hadn't housed any of his junk since he'd left home. Once his parents had moved his stuff into the attic—or chucked it out—they'd given it a lick of paint and bought some new furniture. There was nothing of Cass left in it. He paused in the doorway, remembering dark blue walls and the stars his dad had painted on the ceiling. Even when he'd hit his mid-teens he'd kept those walls. He'd pretended that he couldn't be bothered to change things, but really he loved them. It was the smallest room in the house, but he'd liked its position at the other end of the house from the rest of the family. As the older brother he should have claimed the biggest bedroom, but it had never crossed his mind. With a small smile, he pulled the door closed and headed down the long landing to his brother's room.

As they had done with Cass's, his parents had also redesigned their youngest son's room into a nice spare, with a small double bed at its centre. This was obviously where Christian had slept on his visits. One of their dad's old suitcases was open on the bed. Cass looked at it. This wasn't a case that had been used for holidays in the years before they died; the scuffed tan surface looked more like a relic from the sixties or seventies, with flight labels dirty with age stuck to its rough skin. Inside it was lined with frayed pink silk.

Cass sat on the bed. It was full of old photographs: a case full of memories. For a moment he didn't touch them. His mouth dried. In the far corner a sepia-tinted image stood out, showing a stiffly dressed couple smiling awkwardly, their hands resting on a small boy's shoulders. Cass didn't recognise them, but they had to be grandparents, maybe even great-grandparents. He'd known none of them, on either side; his family were cursed when it came to living to a ripe old age. He felt the ache inside again. They were all gone apart from him, even little Luke.

He swallowed and reached into the case, ignoring the older black and white photos, instead picking up a handful of the coloured ones. The gloss on some had stuck them together and he carefully peeled them apart. His mum and dad twinkled at him from under their Christmas cracker paper hats. They were laughing. The next one had been taken on the same day, probably by his mum. It was his dad, him and Christian. He stared at the teenager he'd been. His skin was smooth and his smile was open. Although he was looking into the camera, his father and Christian were both staring at him. His dad looked proud and Christian had something close to awe on his face. There was a lot of love in both their eyes, you'd have to be blind not to see that.

He picked up a different picture, his father again, now as an older man. He was in the garden doing something to a rose bush, thick gardening gloves covering his calloused hands. His skin was rough like Cass's, but it was cracked in a kind smile. Silver glittered in his dark hair. Cass swallowed. This must have been taken not long before they died, maybe a year or two at most. He looked like his dad, he suddenly realised. Christian was blond, like their mother, but he and his dad had the same shaped face, same build, even similar mannerisms. How had he never noticed this resemblance before? He looked more closely. Their eyes were different though: both dark, yes, but his dad's were gentle. Care shone in them. He wasn't hard like Cass.

"Come home, Cass. We can talk about it. Please come home. It wasn't your fault."

His father had called a lot after the shit had well and truly hit the fan during his undercover time. After all the debriefings and the six months spent holed up in the middle of nowhere while the rest of the world cleaned up after him, his dad had kept on calling, saying the same things over and over. Come home. We can talk about it. Cass didn't want to go home, though, and what was there to talk about? It was done. He remembered the soft kindness in his dad's voice. Maybe if Alan Jones had got angry Cass would have gone home, but the kindness would have killed him. And really, what could his dad have said—it was all okay? He should forgive himself? It was far from okay, and he didn't think he could ever forgive himself. He couldn't see how.

Aside from what he'd actually done that night, there was some poor stiff who had been dragged out of the Thames and buried in a grave in London under the name of Charlie Sutton. Cass wondered about that poor sod's family. They'd never know what became of their boy; he was nothing more than a convenient dead body to get a copper off the hook and lay a fucked-up case to rest. Guilt scraped the inside of his skull. They always said not knowing was the worst thing. And that family would never know.

He looked back at the picture of his dad. Regardless of how similar they might have appeared on the surface, by the time that shit had happened he and his dad were far apart. The old man would have wanted to bring God into the equation, and Cass would have laughed at that. Those that were kind would never understand those that were cruel, and the cruel ones could never really respect kindness. He didn't know if it was a Freemanism or not, stored away by the part of his mind that was happiest being Charlie, but it summed up Cass and his dad.

The next picture was of his mum loading up the boot of the car for a weekend away. Cass thought his insides were slowly solidifying into lead. Everything felt heavy, as if the thin sheet of shiny paper were made of some dense matter that was dragging him down. He cursed his dead brother for excavating this suitcase from its resting place in the attic, where surely it had been left to be discovered by the next generation of Joneses . . . although there wouldn't be one now. He was it. In the picture, his mother's fine blonde hair was pulled back in a ponytail and she wore a pair of denim shorts. Her legs were long and slim. She was in good shape for a woman who must have been nearly sixty when the photo was taken. She rested one arm on the picnic basket in the open boot and smiled.

The bed felt strange beneath him as time in his mind stretched between this moment of the present and one five years in the past, with the even older picture drawing it all together. The car Evelyn Jones was standing next to was the same Volkswagen that would later collide with a lorry and flip itself over and over until it came to a crumpled stop in a ditch almost a hundred feet from the road. Eventually, with his parents stuck inside, bleeding and broken, it would catch fire. His mother had been unconscious and his father had used all his energy to call 999 from his mobile. Then he left a message on Cass's phone, telling him there'd been an accident and that they both loved Cass very much. He called his youngest son after that, and it was Christian who stayed on the phone with their father for the few minutes that must have seemed like forever until he started screaming, and the phone died in the heat.

While his brother had been listening to his father screaming, Cass had been busy getting hot and sweaty and fucking Jessica in a seedy hotel in Argyle Square. By the time either of them had picked up their messages from Christian, the blaze was out and his father was dying in agony in the hospital. The doctors said that bits of the steering wheel had melted into Alan Jones' chest. They didn't understand how he was even still alive. The woman who smiled out from the photo had briefly regained consciousness, only to scream in pain for a moment or two before she died in the ambulance, a burned husk of something that had once been a smiling beauty with long, slim legs and golden hair.

Cass had told Christian that he'd been with an informant, and had no signal. Jessica arrived a few minutes later and said she'd been at the gym. Christian didn't doubt them for a second—why should he? He leaned into Cass's shoulder and sobbed, and Cass could even now remember flinching with guilt, and the fear that Christian would smell his wife's sex on his skin. He remembered his disgust at himself, his pity for his brother, and the huge sense of relief that he hadn't had to be the one on the end of the phone. Amidst the memory of all those teeming emotions he couldn't recall his grief for the loss of his parents. What had he felt then—nothing? Just guilt?

As he looked at the photo again he thought he could taste petrol. He felt *something*, he knew that. He just kept it too far down inside to acknowledge from day to day, just like he would with Christian's death. It was only in his dreams that the feelings surfaced. Perhaps Hell was here on Earth, a plane in his subconscious where nothing was ever truly over and done with. Cass's nightmares had punished him for his parents' drawn-out blazing deaths and the thing that happened in Birmingham . . . sometimes he'd woken up convinced his hands were on fire from where he'd been yanking at that Volkswagen door, desperate to pull his burning parents free.

He carefully put the photo down and noticed his hand was shaking. What was the point of this? The past was done. He sniffed hard, ignored the tears that threatened his vision, and pushed the suitcase away. There was nothing in there that was doing him any good. A sliver of white peered out from under the edge of the case, where it had been shoved aside.

Cass bent down and pulled it free: a large white envelope made of high-quality paper that felt like linen under his fingers. Even empty, this envelope was heavy. Three words were written in ink in Christian's neat handwriting, each letter perfectly aligned to the next, as if measured with a ruler. *GIVE TO CASSIUS.*

His watery eyes cleared; his breath stopped for a moment. Outside, the sun shifted lower in the sky, beams cutting like lasers through the knotted branches of an old tree, sending a kaleidoscope of patterns in through the bedroom window. A stream of white sliced through Cass's hand and as he squinted against the sudden burst of brightness, a shadow fell across the suitcase on the bed. A new shadow, from within the house. Cass took a sudden deep breath as he stared at the soft outline, at odds with the sharp edges of the photos and mad lines of sunlight. It was out of place. It was wrong.

The moment stilled, like a whisper half-spoken. Cass slowly turned his head, knowing what he was going to see. In the silence of their family home, Christian stood in the doorway, neither in the bedroom, nor in the hall, but somewhere in between. His polished shoes still carried the heavy drops of crimson, and his blue shirt was still half in, half out of his trousers. There were bloodstains on his right shoulder, but his head was mercifully intact. The hallway yawned darkly behind him.

Dust motes danced in the space between the brothers. Cass could feel the sun on his skin through the glass. Somewhere deep inside, his heart was thumping madly as he stared at the figure. There were no real ghosts, only those in his head, gripping at him and refusing to let go. But this one seemed so real. Was this madness? Whatever it was, real or illusion, it wanted Cass to know something.

Christian smiled and raised his left hand to his ear with his thumb and little finger extended, as if holding a phone, and then let his arm drop. Cass noticed how blue his little brother's eyes were, and he could see the large freckle just below his wrist. He'd forgotten Christian even had that.

Cass swallowed hard, though his mouth was so dry it hurt. *There were no ghosts.* He turned his head back to the suitcase and squeezed his eyes shut. He breathed deeply, counting to three. When he opened his eyes and cautiously looked towards the doorway again, his brother's ghost was still there. Christian smiled and raised his hand to his ear once again, then stared at Cass for a minute or two. Then he turned and walked silently along the corridor, his feet making no sound on the old floor. His arms were stiff at his sides. Cass watched him until he disappeared around the corner and down the stairs.

Finally, he let out a breath. His whole body was trembling and his head felt like it had been douched with ice-water. He clumsily pulled his mobile phone out of his pocket and scrolled down to Christian's number. He pressed the call button and held it to his ear. It didn't even ring before clicking through to the answer phone declaring that the mobile was switched off. Cass cancelled the call and almost laughed at himself. What had he expected? His dead brother to answer? The O2 service was good, but he didn't think it could make calls to the other side quite yet.

The adrenalin that was pumping through him slowly subsided. *There were no ghosts.* Christian was dead. Whatever his eyes thought they were seeing, Cass told himself, it was all made up inside his own head. He slumped forward a little and rubbed his hands together. He didn't believe in ghosts. He didn't believe in life after death. When you were gone, you were gone. That was it. Whatever he was seeing or not seeing was coming from his own mind playing tricks on him, so he could either go quietly crazy, or just ignore it and get on with the crap involved in living his own life. With Cass, it was always going to be the second option.

He shivered a little and then looked at the envelope. He cleared some more space on the bed and, with another deep breath, and making a determined effort not to look towards the doorway to see if Christian was watching, he emptied it out.

There wasn't much inside: a few photos and a letter. Cass picked up the picture closest to him. It was a Polaroid and it took a moment for him to recognise the two men standing with their shirts off and with one arm round each other's tanned shoulders, grinning against the backdrop of a desert and a military-looking Jeep. He checked the back and the scrawled writing there confirmed his guess.

Alan and Mike. Lebanon 1970.

His dad and Father Michael. He looked at it again. 1970. His father had been sixty-five when he'd died in 2010. Cass did a quick calculation in his head. He would have been in his mid-twenties in the picture, nearly ten years before Cass had even been born. He wasn't even sure that his dad had met his mother by then. How strange that Father Michael had known him all that time. He'd never really given their friendship that much thought. He looked at the two men again. They were like strangers, more than ten years younger than Cass himself was now, and with the boundless enthusiasm of youth screaming out of their white smiles and hippy hair. He carefully put the photo to one side.

The next was one of him and Christian in the garden at the back of the house. He recognised the spot; if he craned his neck he'd be able to see it out of the window. This picture had been taken in the 1980s, on a roll of easy-wind film. Their mother was crouched down, hugging her knees, between her sons but slightly behind them. As she smiled at the camera Cass could see her face was filled with excitement. Cass himself was on the right of the picture, a few inches taller than his blond brother. They both wore shorts, and judging by Christian's chubby face and knees, his little brother couldn't have been more than maybe three or four, which would put Cass at six.

His smile faded as the more he studied it, the more he realised what a strange photograph it was. It was the way that they were standing that was odd, facing each other, their expressions serious. Each had an arm raised, with one finger pointing at eye level at the other. It was an unnatural pose for children of that age, who were more often squealing in the mud or pulling worms in two. A memory shifted in the dust in the far recesses of his mind, but he couldn't quite pull it free.

He turned the picture over.

The boys see the Glow! Yay!

The words were scrawled in his mother's hand, but someone—Cass wondered if it had been Christian—had circled round the two words *the Glow*. The memory growled, sucking him back for a second into the faded landscape of the picture. He had a scab on his knee that itched. He was six years old and his dad was telling him to look harder. And then there it was. He could see gold coming from his brother's eyes, pouring out in the brightest light. It made him feel warm just looking at it. The surprise he felt was mirrored in his brother's face. They had both raised their arms at the same time, and their mother had laughed.

He squashed the memory. It had been a trick of the light, nothing more than a childhood game. Still, it tickled maliciously at him, and he couldn't deny the hint of fear in the pit of his stomach that he couldn't explain. He put the photo carefully on top of the first. Something else to ask Father Michael about tomorrow.

It was the third picture that stopped him dead. On the surface, it was just a snap of his mum and dad, who had obviously met by then, although they still looked like a pair of young hippies. His mother's hair hung in two long plaits and his dad stood behind her, his hands wrapped round her bare waist in the gap between her flared jeans and tie-dyed shirt. With his thick wavy hair that reached his shoulders and the short beard and moustache, Cass thought his dad looked like he'd spent the seventies doing a very good impersonation of Jesus. Beside them stood a middle-aged man, probably in his fifties, with silver hair and a sharp smile. His linen trousers had impeccable sharp creases. They were standing in front of some kind of office, and Cass had to bring the picture close to read the dusty sign. SOLOMON AND BRIGHT MINING CORPS.

Mr. Bright. He looked again at the man beside his young parents before quickly turning the image over.

"Me, Evie and Castor Bright. South Africa 1973."

Underneath, in the same blue Biro that had circled *the Glow*, Christian had scribbled "Bright? But how?" Cass noted that his brother's writing had lost some of its neatness. He turned it over again and stared, trying to imagine the middle-aged man in a suit and overcoat. He'd look just like Adam Bradley's description of the man he met in the Newham flat. Mr. Bright. He looked again at Christian's question. "But how?" The answer was simple. It couldn't be the same man. It wasn't possible. Even if he was still alive, the man in the picture would have to be in his nineties by now. One thing was established, though: there was a definite link between a Mr. Bright and Christian, and this picture had obviously freaked his brother out. He looked at it again. What the hell had been going on in Christian's world?

The letter was interesting. It was addressed to Christian at his own office, although the paper itself had no header. It was creamy and expensive, just like the envelope Christian had used. The typed message was short: The Bank would be interested in employing Christian, and he should go to the head offices at Vauxhall Cross. There was a date and a time, and a signature scrawled in black at the bottom, written with what looked like a calligraphy pen. The name was printed under it. *Mr. C. Bright.* Castor Bright? The same as the man in the picture? He paused, trying to get his brain to stop spinning. Whoever had got Christian his job at The Bank was related to a man who had known their parents—and now Christian was dead, and someone called Bright was sending videos of botched gangland assassinations to Cass . . . What the fuck was going on?

Cass stared out of the window. The brief spell of sunshine was fading and in the true spirit of British March weather dark clouds were pulling in towards each other, slowly covering the sky. He needed to think. He gathered up the photos and the letter and as he headed back downstairs thunder rumbled overheard.

In the kitchen, Christian was sitting perfectly still at the island in the middle of the room. His pale face gazed towards nothing. He didn't move as Cass paused and turned to watch him. Rain started to fall outside, but within the house the steady drip of thick blood on leather was louder, even though no fresh stains appeared on Christian's shoes. Cass sighed and turned away. He took a seat at the small glass dining table with his back to his brother's ghost. His mind could play whatever tricks it liked. Cass would just look the other way. He looked over his shoulder. It didn't seem to be bothering Christian very much.

He emptied the envelope out on the table again, shuffling through the images. Some were older, random faces of men he didn't recognise.

Some were posed, others looked as if they'd been taken secretly. On the back of each his father had written, *Network?* but the word meant as little as the faces. He added it to the list of possible passwords to try on his brother's laptop.

He picked up his mobile and typed out a quick text to Claire. "Bright initial probably C. Try first name Castor. Thanks." He didn't want to call her: it was Saturday, and she'd either be still at work or at home, and either way Blackmore would be with her. A call from Cass would likely cause an argument between them, and he had few enough friends left without making trouble for Claire.

He stared at the evidence that meant something and nothing spread around him and wished he had a computer of his own. His BlackBerry had internet access, but its small screen wasn't up to showing much on full searches. He didn't want to use Christian's computer in case he left evidence of his searches—he might be a bit of a Luddite but even he knew that whatever you did on a computer you always left a trace, even if you wiped the hard drive, and he did not want The Bank knowing what he'd been looking for.

He stared at the pictures that meant something and nothing. What he did know was that Christian had concerns about Bright. He looked at the other pictures. *Network?* What the hell was that about? His head ached and rain pounded against the window. It was time for a break. He also realised he was hungry. This time when he turned round, Christian was gone. Cass couldn't help the slight wave of relief. Bacon and eggs for one then.

Once the fry-up was done and the house filled with the mouth-watering scent of bacon fat, Cass opened the bottle of red that Father Michael had so thoughtfully provided and added it and a glass to his tray and went back into the sitting room. The room was empty of ghosts and he demolished the food in minutes, wiping up the dregs of runny egg with a thick slice of bread and butter.

It felt good to have a full stomach. He lit a cigarette and poured his second glass of wine before turning the TV back on; it was nearly time for the evening news and he wanted to watch Bowman's piece again. The wine hit his system almost immediately and Cass enjoyed the warm buzz. He probably still had booze and drugs inside him from the previous night, but the wine was calmer than the whisky and cocaine. It was like a good woman's arms wrapping round him, soft and warm and full of promise. His eyes felt heavy.

He opened up Christian's laptop and found his way back to the RE-DEMPTION file. He put in the first password, and when the second password prompt came up, he tried Network, the Glow, Network-Glow, BrightGlow and various other combinations of words and numbers before giving up again. It could wait until morning. His brain was fucked.

With the computer put away, he leaned back and put his feet up on the coffee table, pushing the tray with his plate on it slightly to one side to make room. He should take it out and wash it up. The suggestion was a blend of female voices: his mother's, Kate's, Jessica's, even Claire's, all rolled into one. *If you don't wash it straight away it'll stick and take ages to scrub off.* That voice was purely his mother's. As a boy, he might have done as he was told, but now he just relaxed into the sofa and took another long gulp of wine. Let it stick. How many plates did a dead house need? Maybe he'd just chuck it straight in the bin.

His eyes grew grittier as the evening ticked round into the gloom of night. The news came and went and Cass half-watched as Ant and Dec took over the country's Saturday night, still as irritatingly chirpy and cheerful as they had been when they hosted that jungle shit. The audience let out a tinny round of applause after one or other of them made some lame joke. Cass had never figured out which was which. He sipped more wine. They were feel-good people. They must be hell to live with.

Night fell as the black drops of rain tapped at the window, blown in each gust of wind, and Cass's brain drifted between the cases, focusing on nothing in particular but letting the thoughts and images come and go. It stopped the childhood memories that were threatening to overwhelm him: Saturday nights in front of the TV, his mum and dad laughing together over a bottle of wine, and Christian rolling his eyes over-dramatically when they kissed. He sighed, trying once again to focus on the TV. The house was full of ghosts. His tired eyes were threatening to close, and he wondered if maybe his dead family were watching him pityingly. The one they left behind. It was a maudlin thought, and a mildly drunken one. A glance at the bottle showed that it was nearly empty, though he couldn't remember refilling his glass more than twice. The time glowed bright on his watch, not even nine o'clock yet, but if he sat there much longer he'd be out for the count on the sofa, and his joints would seize up and he'd spend tomorrow cursing himself for repeating the experience. The soft arms of the genie in the wine bottle were dragging him down sleepwards, but he didn't mind. At least they were warmer than the cold fingers of the dead.

He took his phone and cigarettes and pulled himself to his feet. With the TV off, the house finally succumbed to darkness. It was soothing on his eyes and he left the lights off as he climbed the creaking stairs. He plugged his phone in, but didn't bother brushing his teeth before peeling off his clothes and collapsing into the comfort of his parents' bed. Kate was right. He was a slob. But for now he didn't have to worry about anyone noticing or caring. It was good to let his eyes shut and his muscles relax. It had been a motherfucker of a week. He idly wondered if one last cigarette was in order, just to add to the morning flavours his mouth would hate him for, but the dark behind his eyes claimed him before he could reach for it.

CHAPTER TWELVE

He has been sitting on the edge of the low, narrow bed for hours, just staring at the cracks in the paint on the walls. It doesn't disturb anyone. He has his own room in the hostel now. It wasn't what he wanted when he started out. He moved from the luxury penthouse, first to a bedsit, now this. Next, he'll maybe try spending his nights under the bridges. He'd wanted to rest in the large, overcrowded, stinking dormitory, with all the dregs of humanity, but after a few nights the softly spoken, well-intentioned volunteers had moved him.

They said it was because of the good work he was doing with the vicar at the church, and that he needed a quiet space to sleep, but he knows better. He can see it in their honest faces. It's because he upsets the rest of them. He makes the junkies and drunks and damaged people cry out and cause trouble. Perhaps the more feral a man becomes, the more he can see the truth, or what's left of it. They can see he doesn't belong among them . . . or maybe it's simpler than that: they just can't stand the buzzing in their dreams while they toss and turn and dream of the next bottle.

He can't control the flies so well when he's sleeping any more. The more human he becomes the more they break free. They don't live long. He's dying, ergo they're dying. Some spin in mad circles for a few scant moments before falling to the floor. He looks down and as if in testimonial three are lying near-dead at his feet. He watches them wriggling on their backs before they die, legs waving frantically in the air. There was a time when he could have felt each one, but no longer. He stretches his fingers out and concentrates. A tiny smooth egg slides out from under his fingernail. He smiles. He still has what he needs for his messages, even if it drains him.

The walls are closing in a little and he stands. It's nearly morning. He hasn't settled all night. There are wheels within wheels, games playing out. The pawns move; the king must be protected. He frowns as he lets himself out of the small room. He was surprised by the press conference. The wrong man was at the desk, after he'd worked hard to make sure it was the right one. Still, that can be fixed. And it's pleasant to be surprised, especially when humans get involved in the game. His feet hurt. It feels as if they thump heavily on the ground even though each step is silent. He is tired and his old bones ache. He wonders when it will be over, and how—though he thinks he knows. Wheels within wheels. There really is only one way for him.

He heads for the entrance. He wants to enjoy the beauty of the creation as the sun rises. The door is locked every night, but he hears the slight metal click as it undoes itself for him. It makes him smile. Maybe it's only his coming death that is truly human. He wonders if he should be more afraid. It's been so long, and they are dying so far from home. In the street, grey cracks of light are finding their way through the night and the air is fresh and clean in his lungs. He has always loved London mornings, even when they were rank with smog so thick you could barely breathe, let alone see.

His feet finally make some sound as the heels of his shoes click on the pavement. So much time has passed. At least his fear isn't making him want to find a way back, unlike some of the others. They made their choices a long time ago, and he will live, and die, with the consequences.

His legs feel lighter now he's striding through the centre of town. He wonders what Bright makes of it all? Their private battle has over-

whelmed the bigger picture for now. Bright always seemed so un-touchable: the architect in his ivory tower. He would be at least a little piqued now, and that was something to live a little longer for.

He makes his way to the church gardens and finds the gates are al-ready open. No need for his magic here. It's only six-thirty, but the first service during the Sundays of Lent is at seven. He wonders how many actually turn up so early to hear the kind vicar's words when there are hangovers to sleep off and lazy mornings to enjoy. The physical so of-ten gets its own way. He pulls the pay-as-you-go phone out from his pocket. He had taken a handful of them before he'd walked out of the offices and his old life for good. Its number will be logged in some sales invoice somewhere. That makes him smile. Another small screw loosened. Slowly, slowly, catchee monkey. Bright wanted to leave this man be for a while, but he is intent on giving all the players in the game a chance to see for themselves before he dies.

From within his jacket he takes a small moleskin notebook. In it is all the information he stole from the system, everything he thought he might need when he left to devote the rest of his own personal journey to playing with Bright's plans. Two birds with one stone. His elegant fingers flick through the cream pages until they find the number. He's always trusted paper and handwriting over computers.

Why he's calling from here he doesn't know, just like he doesn't know why he finds comfort in the peace of the church when its founda-tions are built on such a bad retelling of the old story: man's great tem-ple to wishful thinking. Still, he thinks, it's a pretty place, and maybe he doesn't need any more reason than that. He types in the number and presses the dial button. Time to call the King.

The rain eased to quiet drizzle in the dark of the night. Cass slept fit-fully, tossing and turning, sweating in the blackness. Ghosts crowded his mind and he called out as memories played, the incoherent sounds cutting through the silent house until he finally fell still and only his lips moved against the pillow as he whispered, "Well, what are you waiting for, Charlie?"

* * *

"Well, what are you waiting for, Charlie?"

Cass stares at Brian Freeman as his heart races too hard in his chest. He thinks he might throw up or pass out or both.

Brian "the Brain" Freeman looks about a hundred years old. He's sitting in a chair in the office in the back of the snooker hall. Even in the dirty light Cass can see that the old man's Marbella tan has drained away with the blood that is soaking through the makeshift bandage. A light sweat coats his forehead and his breathing is rapid. His eyes are angry, and very much alive.

"Don't worry, son, I'll live," he says. "Now sort that one out for me. Like the son I never had." His hand doesn't even shake as he takes a long swallow from a bottle of brandy. Cass wants a drink more now than he's ever done in his life. His mouth is screaming for it, but Brian doesn't part with the bottle. His hand doesn't feel like his own as he slowly pulls out the gun from where it's tucked into his jeans. He wonders how he can buy more time.

It's a fuck-up from the moment his mobile rings at five a.m. and he hears George say, "Get up. We've got a problem. Picking you up in five. Bring your wallet."

No, he thinks, as his brain races and Brian and George and the boys stare at him and wait. That wasn't the fuck-up moment. At that point, shit-scared as he was, he'd known what to do. His hands were shaking and sweating, but he'd quickly switched the sims and dialled his connect while struggling to pull on his trousers.

The connect didn't answer. That was the fuck-up point. He should have been there. Cass had cursed into the answer phone. "Bring your wallet" was not good; that was code. Bring your gun. He spat out a message after the beep, though he wasn't sure how much sense he made. He'd known this moment was coming. He'd felt it building. Everyone got tested to see what they were made of, and there was no way Charlie Sutton would be treated any different, no matter who his uncle was. Charlie was always going to be tested, if only because Brian liked him so much. He'd already fucking told the connect as much. Much good that'd done him.

He'd rung another number even as he waved down at the waiting car. His London SO10 co-ordinator's phone was turned off. Cass had been almost crying in frustration as he took the heavy gun from the back of the wardrobe and dug out the clip from the drawer by his bedside. He checked the bullets. All present and correct. He should have put the original sim back in the phone, just in case, but he was going to have to take the risk and leave the other in. If the connect managed to get his shit together in time he'd need to be able to track the phone to locate Cass. He turned it to silent and hoped for the best. He dry-heaved a couple of times, then pulled out a cigarette to calm his nerves before leaving the flat. Didn't want the boys to see him shaking. He was smoking hard as he got in the car.

He didn't know that the connect had been drinking on duty after a fight with his girlfriend. He'd passed out. Things had been quiet on the Freeman case and he'd got slack. It had never happened before, he swore that. And his SO10 boss had been curled up in bed with a pretty young thing named Nicholas. He'd turned off his phone so his wife wouldn't be able to interrupt his pleasure. Like the connect, he claimed it had only been for an hour, two at most. Things had been quiet. It was just plain bad luck that it all kicked off while those two rare moments of dereliction of duty collided—luck, or fate, or choices made by people who were too far away from the action. Whatever it was, these things would save Cass's career, if not those of the men who should have been by their phones . . . his career, if not his soul.

No one had spoken in the car as it raced through the quiet early morning streets. No one ever talked on the move. You never knew who was listening. But Cass only had to look at George's face to know this was deep shit. Mac was at the door of the snooker hall to let them in. He was a skinny guy, Brummy born and bred, and Brian had invested in his hall and bought him new tables, given the place a shiny new make-over. All he asked for in return—as well as the obvious cut of the profits—was the occasional use of the space at the back.

Mac had looked like he'd rather be anywhere than here, and Cass silently sympathised as he followed George through the empty maze of tables towards the room behind the bar. Andy and Jez had been standing guard in the corridor. They'd pointed George in the direction of the storeroom. All tooled up, Cass thought, and when he caught the flash of metal as they followed them into the room and took their places by the door, he shuddered inwardly. He'd been right.

Bile rises up in his chest. It burns like hell. He is standing here looking at Brian and the poor beaten boy tied to a chair in front of him, and he knows without doubt that this is a fuck-up of the first order. It is the mother of all fuck-ups. And it's all happening too quickly. There's an unfamiliar man slumped in the corner. Dreadlocks cover his face and blood covers his chest. The only way he's ever going to move again is if someone hauls his corpse out of here.

"Fucking Yardies," George mutters. The man in the corner doesn't react. The boy in the chair is shaking.

Cass licks his lips. He must buy more time. "What the fuck happened?" he asks.

Brian winces. "Fuckers come up from London and think they can do us over on a deal. Like they think we're fucking born yesterday." He glares at the boy in the chair. "Fucking learned now, haven't you? Your dad should have just stayed on the fucking boat, you black bastard."

Cass can see the fear in the boy's eyes. He's sobbing, and sweat shines on his dark forehead as he twists in the chair. He's fifteen, at the oldest . . . Cass hopes he's fifteen, but something tells him the kid is just a boy really, no more than fourteen, thirteen even. He's got dreads, like his dad, but they're almost fuzzy, still growing in. He's not old enough to be a player yet—well, not tough enough, at any rate. The bile burns and he swallows it down.

"How long have you been here?" Cass asks.

"All fucking night," Brian sniffs. "Tell you something, these bastards will take some pain before they talk." He laughs, and George and the others join in. It's not a happy sound.

"Why didn't you call me?" He can't bring himself to laugh with them. His mouth is too dry, and he knows that if he tries, he'll look nervous and guilty; he'll be Cass, not Charlie. And this fuck-up is bad enough without adding to it.

"Lad like you needs your beauty sleep. We had it all under control." He sips from the brandy again, and the humour goes out of his dark eyes. "Now, though . . . thought you might like to do the honours for me, Charlie. Time to take the step up to the next level."

"You want me to shoot him?" Cass sounds dumb and he knows it. He can't seem to stop himself saying, "He's just a kid." Time ticks slowly, though his heart is pounding nineteen to the dozen. He wonders if the fucking connect has picked up his message yet. He wonders if police cars are even now racing here. He wonders how much longer he can drag this shit out.

It's George who laughs this time. "Fuck me, boy, are you a fucking retard or what?"

He opens his mouth to answer, but it's Brian who defends him.

"Leave him alone, George. He's a good kid. He's just not that bright in the mornings. Late night, was it, Charlie?"

Cass nods. "Something like that."

"It's been a long night for all of us," Brian says, sounding sympathetic. "Look, son, it's not pretty, but it's the only messages these Yardie bastards understand. His dad was the stupid fucker that brought him here." The boy in the chair moans, but Brian doesn't even notice, just carries on, "Let's get this thing done, so we can clean this place up and all go home. I need a fucking doctor to get this bastard bullet out of my shoulder."

Cass feels all eyes on him. The turning world stops. He thinks of Kate, fast asleep at home in London. She has no idea how much he loves her. He thinks of the rule book, and how all that training has come to fuck-all because there are some situations you just can't prepare for.

Finally, he pulls the gun out from where it's tucked into his belt. He's sweating all over now, and the metal is warm where it's been lying against his skin. The room is silent except for the boy's low sobs and his own breathing, fast and raw, like he's running even though he's standing still. He looks at the kid, all snot and tears and grey-black skin. He's shaking so hard with every sob that even if he was trying to say something, it's incomprehensible.

For a moment Cass wonders if the boy had ever thought, even for a moment, that it might end like this when his dad asked him to come along. Had he felt like a hard man? Was he planning to go back and brag to his mates on whatever stinking estate they came from? Or was he just a kid, thinking his dad was just a regular guy, like all the other kids' dads? Cass wonders a lot of things, not least: what the boy would think if he knew a copper was holding his life in his hands.

Cass raises his arm. It feels like he and this kid are alone, separate from the rest of the room. This moment is theirs, and theirs alone. He moves the slide back and hears it click into place. That surprises him a little, because his fingers are sweating so much he can barely grip the weapon.

"Please, please . . ." There's nothing of Trenchtown in the kid's accent; he's London through and through. "Please don't—Please . . ." Cass finds the words hard to decipher through the hitching, panicked voice, though he gets the sentiment. That's coming through loud and clear.

"Came in here, all Jack-the-fucking-lad. Not so brave now, is he?" George snorts. Cass hears him and wonders if he's talking about the poor Yardie kid or him. The Yardie, of course. He wonders if Charlie is slipping away on the outside as much as he is on the inside. He's running out of time. He swallows hard. This is a different rule book now.

"Charlie?" Brian's voice isn't so soft now. "How can I trust you if you don't do this, Charlie?" Cass can hear danger, loud and clear. Brian Freeman has vouched for him. He's taken him under his wing. If Cass doesn't do this thing, then at the very best he's out, but Brian will feel like a mug, so who knows how far he'll go? He'll start to look into Charlie Sutton's imaginary life, and Cass knows, without a shadow of a doubt, that Brian will figure the set-up out, and then he'll come after Cass with all he's got. And Cass won't die quickly, not like this boy. Cass knows this, because he knows Brian.

All this has run through Cass's fevered head in a heartbeat. The police aren't coming, he knows that now, and there is no way he can shoot George and Jez and Andy before one of them has filled him full *of holes. He can see goosebumps rising on the back of his hand. This is survival, pure and simple. Him or the Yardie kid, fuck the police, fuck everything outside. There is only this decision: whose life is more important?*

He looks into the eyes of the boy in the chair. They haven't changed; the kid is still terrified; his eyes are pleading with Cass to save him. He might be speaking, but Cass can't hear him. The boy has no Glow, that's what he's thinking now. He doesn't know where that contemptuous thought comes from, or what the hell it means, but he thinks it anyway. He has no Glow. Somehow that seems important, but it's the thought that follows that is the decision-maker: I value my life more than his. I am more important. *It's cold and clinical, and it calms his heart.*

He pulls the trigger. He doesn't even shut his eyes.

The noise fills the room and in the echo Cass is lost. The boy is no longer recognisable.

"Jesus Christ, Charlie," Brian breathes, "you shot him in the fucking face! That's fucking disgusting!"

The eyes that had been staring so desperately at him are gone, replaced by a hollow, shiny red cavern. Small fragments of bone are protruding here and there from the mess framed by soft, fuzzy dreadlocks. After a moment the body slumps forward. Time ticks out in the drip of blood. Cass slowly lowers the gun.

He's still staring at the body when the door bursts open.

Mac stares at the wreck in the chair for a moment, then looks around. He has a more urgent fear. "Fucking coppers!" he shouts. "Outside!"

Cass thinks he should laugh, but he can't bring himself to move. One squeeze of his finger and his life has changed irrevocably. He can almost feel his insides rotting. He drops the gun.

It's several seconds before he realises George has his arm. "Take Brian and get out the back! Charlie! Mate, we need you! Go!"

Gunshots ring out and now he looks up. He expects George to have no face either, but George is alive and sweating and hauling his brother onto his feet and leaning him on Cass. And then he's gone, leading the way. Brian is heavy, and he's wounded. Cass has to half-drag him to the back, where he leans him against the wall so he can open the fire-escape door. Despite his confidence, it's obvious Brian's lost a lot of blood. He is very weak.

"Why the fuck didn't you go to the fucking doctor's, Brian?" Cass finds he cares. He's a little surprised at that.

"Business before pleasure, son." Brian coughs out a weak laugh.

Dawn is turning into morning as they half-jog, half-stumble into the parking lot. Cass expects to see armed police everywhere, but for the moment they are alone. They are halfway to the wall when the first car screeches in and policemen start screaming at them to get down on the ground, hands on heads, chuck away your weapons. Brian grips him hard, pulling him in by the neck and holding him so close that their noses are almost touching. Cass can smell brandy and sickness on him.

"Run, Charlie," Brian whispers. He pushes Cass away, and immediately crumples to the floor. "Run, Charlie!" he says again.

And Cass does. The obligatory shots are fired amidst the calls for him to stop, but he knows they won't hit him. As he scrambles over the wall, he takes a minute to glance back. Brian is grinning under the three plain-clothes who are pinning his damaged body down. On the other side, Cass hits the ground and starts running. Tears stream down his face, and he can't bring himself to stop.

Cass thought it was sirens that woke him. He sat upright in the dark and turned this way and that, his heart pounding fiercely, looking for the blue flashing lights to burst through the curtains. There was nothing but the grey early morning light creeping around the edges of the heavy material . . . and the steady hum of his vibrating phone. Who the hell would be calling him so early? Claire. Had they found another body, or got a break in the case?

He pulled the handset free from its charger and frowned. There was no name on the screen, and the number didn't look familiar. When he answered there was nothing at first except for a faint buzzing.

"Hello?" he repeated. Maybe it was a bad line.

The buzzing smoothed into soft breathing.

"Were you asleep?" The voice was smooth, easy on the ear. "If so, I'm sorry. I don't sleep so well these days and the mornings are always so beautiful I hate to miss them."

"Who is this?"

"I didn't see you on the news. It was supposed to be you. I thought I had that all sorted out."

Cass's skin tingled. The man was talking about the press conference.

"I asked who you were."

"You know who I am." A weary sigh filled Cass's head, and the other end seemed to buzz for a moment before it faded. He felt wide awake.

"Are you Mr. Bright?"

"Oh, he'd love that." The caller's laugh was dry, melodic, and somehow ancient. "Even he might smile at that thought."

"You know him?"

Again the sigh. "He looks for me, I watch him. I couldn't resist playing with him."

Cass hadn't even turned on the bedside lamp. He was locked into the phone call. Sleep and the dreams of the night had fallen away and his brain felt like it was on fire. He wished he had a pen and paper handy, but made notes in his mind instead. *Not Bright—but knows him—at least knows of him.*

"Do you believe that life is sacred, Cassius Jones?"

Every hair on Cass's body stood upright. "Don't you?"

"Maybe once, a long time ago. Some lives, anyway." There was that slightest edge of humour that made Cass wonder if he was being mocked slightly. "But you know what I think now; I've spelled it out clearly enough."

"Nothing is sacred?"

"It would appear that way."

"Anyone who heard the press conference could have that information." Cass kept his own voice light and conversational. "Tell me something no one outside the investigation would know."

The man tutted. "So untrusting. Maybe I will, and maybe I won't." He sighed again, and this time there was something in that sound that made Cass shudder. "I'm sorry about your brother," he continued, and this time there was almost sadness in the voice. "That was nothing to do with me. Or us. No one would hurt family."

Us? Family? "Tell me who you are."

"I am the Man of Flies."

Cass's breath hitched. No one knew about the fly eggs. His gut screamed at him that this was their man; this was the killer they were hunting. He had thought so right from the opening of the conversation, but this gave him proof, here was something he could take back to the brass. If they'd let him in the bloody building, of course.

"Don't trust them, Cassius Jones. They have their own agenda."

"Who?" Cass glued the voice to his memory. It was almost completely free of any hint of accent, and it tickled his ears like sandpaper against wood. It was strange and compelling.

"Don't spoil the game. One thing at a time." Somewhere in the background Cass thought he heard birds. Whoever he was, he was outside. "Think of it as a series of tests. Testing people is so interesting, don't you think? They're so often found wanting. They prize nothing other than themselves." The buzzing overwhelmed his voice for a moment and Cass flinched. What was that? A bad line? It sounded more like insects flying around the handset . . . Flies, he thought. It sounds like flies.

"Is that why nothing is sacred?" he asked when the noise had faded.

"I'll be in touch."

And then the caller was gone.

Cass grabbed his cigarettes and ran downstairs, rummaging through the kitchen drawers until he found a pen and a notepad. He brought up the number and saved it, and wrote it on the pad, followed by everything the caller had said. Who was it that he shouldn't trust? And what had he meant about Christian's death, that it was nothing to do with him? Not just him, *them*. Was he saying that someone had driven Christian to do what he did? Or was there a more sinister hint that maybe Christian and his family had been murdered? Someone had

SARAH PINBOROUGH

certainly planted that evidence against him. The question now was: did they kill his brother and his family as well?

The caller had used Cass's private mobile number, and that irked him. Some front desk idiot must have given it out, no doubt. He wished that all police thought like policemen, but like every profession the force had its fair share of dunces and slackers, the type who preferred to sit on the desk and file paperwork rather than actually engage their brains. It wouldn't take much of a story to get a mobile number from some of them.

He looked at his watch. 6:40 a.m. His first instinct was to call Claire, but professionalism took over and he tried Bowman first. The man riled him, but it was his case. His phone rang out, but there was no answer.

So he'd done the right thing. Now he could ring Claire.

She answered within three rings.

"Yeah?" Her voice was thick with sleep. A man muttered something in the background. Blackmore was there, or she was at his, one or the other. He wasn't surprised. He had an altruistic moment when he wondered if Blackmore would be good enough for her. He wasn't convinced.

"I've tried Bowman but can't get an answer." He paused. "I think I've just had a phone call from our serial."

"What?" She was alert now. He thought he could hear sheets rustling as she sat up. He definitely heard a muttered conversation taking place, and Blackmore's voice getting excited too.

"What happened?" Claire was back on.

He talked her through the call, not needing to glance at his jotted notes once. The whole surreal conversation felt like it had been recorded in his head. When he'd finished, he gave her the caller's number.

"It's a mobile, so I'll guess it's a pay-as-you-go, but see if someone can track where it came from, and what shop sold it. It's a long shot, but you never know; it might give us something."

"We're on it."

"Sorry I've messed up your weekend off."

"Not a problem. Mat's working anyway, and I'm finding I just can't switch off these cases, even when I'm not supposed to be working."

"I know the feeling." Claire May might still believe that good would triumph over evil, but she was a career copper through and through. Cass wondered if that was part of why he'd been drawn to her.

"One more thing," he said. "At the end of the call, he said he'd be in touch."

"You think he's going to call you again?"

"Or just leave us another body."

"Always the optimist." She paused. "Any idea where he was calling from?" In the background Blackmore was asking questions and Cass couldn't help feeling pleased when Claire *ssshhed* him.

"Outside somewhere. I heard birds, I think. There was some buzzing on the line at times, so he might have been in a bad reception area. He wasn't on long enough to have got a location even if we had been able to trace it. My guess is that he was in the city somewhere. I didn't hear much traffic but it was pretty early and a Sunday morning so I don't suppose there'd have been much about."

"And you think he knows Bright?"

"Yeah, I know he does. We need to talk this through with Hask, see what he makes of it. He's getting paid enough." And Cass trusted the psychologist's judgement, not least because he had backed Cass himself.

At the other end there was a pause, then Claire lowered her voice slightly. "Mat's in the bathroom. Didn't want to say this with him here, because he wouldn't understand and I don't need a row right now. I sent a couple of guys out to find your burger man last night. It was on their own time. Nice to know you still have some fans in the office—other than me, obviously." She laughed a little. "Anyway, I should hear back from them later. Let's hope for the best."

Cass smiled. He didn't deserve a friend like Claire, not after everything. He wanted to tell her about the things that had drawn him home: the photos, the possible links between Bright and his own family, and the fact that something had really been bothering Christian and he'd wanted to talk to Cass about it. Shit, part of him wanted to tell her that he kept seeing his brother's ghost, but all of that was a conversation for another time. And until he'd spoken to Father Michael, he didn't have much of a clear picture to offer anyway. He needed Claire to be concentrating on things she could actually do something about.

"Are you okay?" she asked.

"Better than I expected to be."

"Have you heard from Kate?"

"No." His defensiveness kicked in and he changed the subject. "Look, I've got some bits and pieces to do here, then I'll probably head back to London tonight. Tell Bowman I'll be in the office as a civilian witness first thing tomorrow morning. He'll love that."

"Once he hears this he'll probably want you in ASAP."

"He can wait. There's nothing more I can tell him than I've told you."

"Oh, one more thing." She was rushing her words and Cass assumed that Blackmore had finished his shower. "I put some feelers out on Bright yesterday afternoon. We'll see what comes back."

"Good work, Claire." He paused. "Thanks."

"No problem, guv."

He smiled as they said their goodbyes. It felt good to have Claire at his back. The minute he'd ended the call, his phone started to ring. It was Bowman. Sod him, Cass thought. What's good for the goose . . .

He left the phone ringing on the breakfast bar and went upstairs to shower.

He left the coffee brewing as he dressed, then filled a mug and lit a cigarette before taking the notebook and pen into the sitting room. It was time to get to grips with the three cases jumbled in his head. He pulled the coffee table close and made three headings across the top of one sheet: **MAN OF FLIES CHRISTIAN JACKSON&MILLER** and underneath, he jotted: *Link between all three—Mr. Bright. Sent tape to me, sent Christian the letter and Man of Flies knows him. May have family link to Jones.* He paused, then added: *He needs to be found.*

It felt good to be using his brain. From the corner of his vision he saw a pair of black shiny lace-up shoes and the hem of dark trousers by the armchair over to his left. He ignored them.

He did look at the **CHRISTIAN** heading, though. Underneath it, he jotted: *Someone setting me up. Why?* The answer was obvious. *To get me out of the way.* That raised another immediate *why*, but he left it for a moment to think about the *how*. Had someone killed Christian and his family and planted the evidence at the time of the crime, or did Christian shoot his family and himself and someone then took advantage of the situation, with the evidence being planted afterwards? Whichever way round it was, it was planned. Someone had been through his rubbish and dug out a condom. Maybe that was lucky. He figured with his record a fingerprint on a gun would have been enough to get him a few days off at the very least.

Still, the idea that the evidence had been planted *after* the event was the most unpleasant, and not because it would mean that Christian had done this terrible thing, but because whoever placed the fingerprint and bodily fluids there would have to be either one of the SOC team, a police officer, or an attendant at the morgue. It wasn't a pretty thought, but times were hard and most people were open to offers if the price was right. He knew as well as anybody how easily evidence—and even bodies—could be left unattended at a critical moment. What had been done was tricky, but far from impossible. He looked over at Christian's shoes for an answer and followed the trouser-clad legs up until his own dark eyes found his brother's blue ones.

"Did you do it, Christian?" His words sounded strange, spoken to an empty room. Christian didn't answer. He didn't even raise his hand in that strange telephone gesture that he had become so fond of. Cass almost smiled. Maybe even his own figment of imagination realised Cass didn't need any distraction right now.

He looked back down at the scribbled *Why?* and added several frustrated question marks. It couldn't be the Man of Flies case. The caller had hinted that he *wanted* Cass on that case, and as it was, Bowman had dragged himself into work even if he still looked sick as a pig, so there was no need for outside interference. It was Bowman's case and he'd taken it back. Cass was off it. That just left the Jackson and Miller shootings. The failed Macintyre hit.

He had put his data stick into Christian's laptop bag and now he grabbed it and turned the machine on. He was missing something—he had to be. Even on Christian's pin-sharp screen, the film was still grainy. He watched it twice, his level of frustration rising. What wasn't he *seeing*? He pressed play for the third time. Once again the waitress served someone on the other side of the glass. Once again a man's sleeved arm raised his coffee cup, his cufflink causing a glitter of light on glass. The fat woman still stared longingly at the cake. Macintyre arrived, his hair still hidden by the black hat, and lit a cigarette at the same time as the man on the screen did. Cass couldn't help but compare him with the old-school gangsters like Brian Freeman and Artie Mullins. Macintyre had none of their class. Cass narrowed his eyes as the car pulled up in the street and the two laughing schoolboys drew almost level with Sam Macintyre. They didn't even see the gun emerge from the window. However many times he watched it, Cass wasn't sure he'd ever be able to stop that lurch of his stomach when the first bullets hit Justin Jackson. Macintyre had rolled away, behind or under the nearest car.

Cass grimaced. No, Macintyre was *nothing* like Freeman or Mullins: they would have pulled one boy down to safety with them at the very least.

The film ended and the screen froze and Cass pressed play again. He didn't want to think of Brian Freeman. His dream was still with him, like a sour aftertaste in his mouth. A lot of years had passed since he'd been under Brian Freeman's wing. A lot of years since he'd learned to look up.

"Don't just look at the obvious, mate. Look around it." Freeman's words echoed in his head. He pushed them away and tried to concentrate on the film playing out yet again on the laptop.

Another voice replaced Freeman's in his head: Artie Mullins, a far more recent memory. Just two nights ago, after Cass's world had got turned upside down, he'd called Cass "son," and told him, "Sometimes it's not the obvious things you need to look at, and sometimes you can't see the obvious when it's staring you right in your ugly mug."

Cold trickled across his skin. For a moment he sat completely still. Outside, a burst of sunlight flooded through the bay window, its brightness making the screen invisible. Cass watched as goosebumps rose on his forearm. He remembered Isaac Jackson's voice on the phone yesterday, the edginess, and the stiffness in the men's backs as they stood behind their crying wives. Cold erupted through his pores, and he felt clarity washing over him, through him. His heart thumped. The *obvious*: it was right there in front of him, and he hadn't seen it. He tilted the screen forward, out of the glare, and pressed play again.

Maybe Macintyre just happened to be there as he had always claimed or maybe not, but these were professionals. If they weren't, they'd have sprayed the whole street with bullets trying to hit Sam Macintyre, and it would have been a massacre. He watched as Justin Jackson's body danced in the gunfire before falling to the ground. For a brief second, John Miller stood alone, and then he was down too, thrown back into the door of the café, silently smashing it, under the power of the bullets. Cass looked at his scuffed school shoes, sticking out on the pavement. The two boys were dead, and no one else on the relatively busy street was so much as injured. The car had disappeared.

His mouth hanging half-open, he sat back against the sofa. In the armchair, Christian mirrored his actions. Cass barely noticed. The obvious was horrific, but it had been staring him in the face for two weeks and he just hadn't seen it. What if the hitmen *had* made a clean kill? What if they'd got exactly whom they'd been paid to kill? *What if the Jackson and Miller boys had actually been the targets?*

His hand was shaking as he lit a cigarette. Adrenalin buzzed through him. He hadn't bothered to do any checks on the Jackson and Miller families, because they had all been so focused on the boys as tragic victims in the wrong place at the wrong time. He cursed himself.

He picked up the phone, but paused before dialling. His first instinct was to call Claire and bring her up to speed, but he stopped himself. He'd given her quite enough to do that hadn't been approved by the

DCI or Bowman, and the last thing he wanted was to get her into trouble. And there was the darker consideration that someone, somewhere, had set him up over this case. Right now it was safer to keep any developments out of the office. He didn't feel guilty—they'd bloody suspended him, after all.

He scrolled through, looking for the right number. Perry Jordan owed Cass a favour. He'd been a bright PC with a promising career ahead of him—until one of his mates was brought in for a urine sample. Jordan, young, stupid and thinking himself the man, did the sample himself. He got caught. End of career.

Cass had liked the boy—he had that edge that you only got being London born and bred, and his mistake had been misplaced loyalty, not personal gain. He'd have made a good copper, given time, but there was another use for his talents. Cass knew a PI who was looking for someone, smoothed the way. Six years on, Perry Jordan was pretty much running the business, and doing well. It was the force's loss.

The phone was answered with a grunt.

"Did I wake you?"

"Jones?" A muffled yawn.

"It's gone nine. Wakey wakey, rise and shine."

"Easy for you to say. I've been doorstepping a dodgy house in Bermondsey all fucking night."

"Anything interesting?"

"Ha! I wish. Rich bloke with a cheating bird who likes a bit of rough on the side."

Cass gave him a second to wake up fully. "I need you to do something for me."

"Don't tell me you think your missus is cheating . . ."

A small knife turned in Cass's gut. Who knew what Kate was doing? Definitely not him. "No, it's nothing like that. I need you to do some digging around on two families for me. I want their financial details—mortgage payments, bank loans, personal histories, you know the drill."

"It'll be a pleasure to use my brain for a change. Names and addresses?"

Cass told him.

There was silence for a heartbeat as the penny dropped at the other end. "The boys that got shot. You want a full file."

"That's right." He tried to keep his tone light.

"Can I ask why you've come to me?" Jordan asked after a moment. "Surely you could get this done in-house—not with my flair and brilliance obviously, but you've got more manpower, and it'll be free."

"I want to keep this under the wire until I know what I'm looking at," Cass said. He paused. "And if you could keep it under your hat I'd be grateful."

"Don't need saying, mate." The PI sounded fully awake now and Cass knew he'd got the subtext clearly enough. "But even with my genius I'm going to need a day or two."

"Understood. Thanks." He knew Jordan would prioritise it; he doubted he'd get the work done quicker in-house, or as thoroughly. As he ended the call, Cass was buzzing. Maybe at last he was getting somewhere. He realised Christian had vanished at some point during his conversation with Jordan, and he wondered if he should be concerned about how laissez-faire he'd become about the random presence of his dead brother. He decided that with everything else going on, the ghostly visitations came pretty low on the list of things to be worried about—and he couldn't help but admit to himself that seeing Christian's face every now and then was easing the pain of his loss.

He made some toast and drank more coffee before tidying the house so he didn't need to mess around after seeing Father Michael, he could just pick up his stuff and head back to London. The idea of staying in some grotty hotel wasn't very appealing, but everything he needed to do—finding Mr. Bright, stopping this self-proclaimed Man of Flies, working out who'd framed him—was back in the city. And if things had worked out as planned, Mr. Ali Khan would have been found by now and Cass would be back at work by tomorrow latest.

As he made the bed, he thought that even after just one night it didn't feel so strange being home. Maybe Christian had felt the same, and that's why he'd never got round to selling the place. He closed up the suitcase of photographs in Christian's room, but left it where it was. When all this was done he intended to come back and take a proper look at them. Maybe the photos would help lay some ghosts, maybe not, but Cass was surprised to find his curiosity about his family had been piqued.

Downstairs, he put the envelope of photos on top of the laptop and put his suitcase in the hallway. That laptop was still bugging him; he needed to find the password for the Redemption file before he gave it back, and he had only a few hours. There was no getting out of that either, the tone of Ramsey's voice had made that clear. Cass could respect that. He'd removed evidence from the scene—that alone could get him the sack, especially with his chequered past.

Across the village, church bells pealed out. To Cass, they felt like a summons to his past.

CHAPTER THIRTEEN

It was only midday and already it felt to Claire like it had been a morning of two halves. Her enquiries about the elusive Mr. Bright had resulted in a big fat zilch; as far as she could ascertain, he didn't exist, which struck her as odd, given how common the name was. Ms. Middleton, the police liaison officer at The Bank, was a stern woman in her fifties who had made it clear that it would take some considerable time to search The Bank's employee database for anyone with that name, and if they wanted to include The Bank's subsidiary companies, then they would have an even longer wait. Claire wasn't sure if the woman was being obstructive just for the fun of it, or if she had had her orders from higher up—after all, how long could it really take for a name search on a computer database belonging to the most efficient and highly resourced company in the civilised world?—but her over-the-top reaction immediately made Claire want to push deeper.

Claire took over from the constable who'd made the original enquiry and called Ms. Middleton back. This time she gave the full name: Castor Bright. So much for the "difficult search" and "lengthy wait" her DC had been promised; within five minutes a one-line email response had pinged into her inbox: *There is no one with the name Castor Bright on our employee database.* Claire forwarded it to Cass's email account. The queries she'd put out to her journalist contacts were all coming back blank too. It was intensely frustrating.

On the upside, however, Cass's burger man had been found, and she was now reaping the rewards. Blackmore was looking at her as if she'd screwed someone else, Bowman was so angry that his pale, sickly face was sporting two feverish spots of colour, and Ramsey's expression was that of someone who was beginning to think he'd ended up in a *Twilight Zone* episode.

"I can't believe you thought it was okay to do this behind my back." DI Bowman was almost spitting at her.

"It wasn't behind your back, sir," she tried to explain, "I just didn't see the point of bothering you unless the man could be found."

"If I didn't know about it, May, then it was behind my back," he shouted. "You do not have the right to tell *my* staff what they should be doing unless you have cleared it with me or my senior officers first." He was almost incandescent with fury.

"They were off duty," she said. "It was a favour." She couldn't work out why he was so wound up about this—it was clear that he and Cass Jones had no time for each other, but given how understaffed they were, she'd thought he'd be happy to have Cass back to take up his own caseload.

"Sir," she said, keeping her tone apologetic, "maybe I didn't go about it the right way, but it was with the best of intentions. The man's come in to be interviewed, and his description of DI Jones and his car are pretty spot-on—so Cass Jones couldn't have been at his brother's house if he was in the middle of a drunken argument with a burger van man at the Elephant and Castle, could he?" Facts were facts, after all, she added to herself.

"He never did have any class," Blackmore muttered.

Claire fought the urge to bite back at her boyfriend's dig at her ex-lover, choosing instead to ignore the jibe. "Sir, surely it's enough to get him back to work, don't you think? We need him here—especially after the phone call—"

"She's right," Ramsey broke in, "we should get him back. You guys need him to talk you through this phone call he's had." He rubbed his head. "And on top of that, I just can't see him having anything to do with what's happened to his brother—call it gut instinct or whatever, it's just not fitting in my head. And Dr. Hask agrees."

Bowman snorted, and Ramsey gave a wry smile before continuing, "Trust me, I wish to God he had been there, because now my nice tidy murder-suicide is looking suspiciously like a triple homicide with planted evidence, and I really could have lived without that headache. I've got quite enough work on back at my own nick."

Bowman finally nodded, but he still looked unhappy. "Well, at least yesterday's interview tied up the Macintyre case. Jones can dig in on the serial case." He gave a bitter smile. "After all, he's now the Chosen One in our killer's eyes."

"Solved, sir?" Claire looked quizzically at Blackmore. How come he hadn't told her this?

"Don't look so put out, given how much you've been doing without keeping anyone else in the loop," Bowman said. "We didn't get confirmation of what Macintyre admitted yesterday until an hour ago. He neglected to tell us about a 'disagreement' he'd had with some Chechens. Money, of course—drugs or money, isn't it always? They probably put out the hit. We're pulling in some names now."

As the door opened and DCI Morgan peered in and called, "May? A word?" her heart sank. Maybe this was going to turn into a day of three parts. The way things were going, her career was heading for the same path as Cass Jones'—straight to the stagnant pond of no promotion.

She stepped into the corridor, Sam Macintyre and his "Chechen disagreement" temporarily forgotten. "Sir?"

Morgan leaned in. "I hear you've been trying to locate this Bright character your witness claims gave him the film to deliver?"

"Yes, sir, but I'm not getting very far."

"You won't." His voice was cool, and he was close enough that she could smell tobacco on his breath, which came as a surprise given what a big deal he'd made about giving up when the smoking laws changed. She thought he'd succeeded. You never could tell what was really going on with people.

"Sir?"

"It's a wild goose chase. There is no such man. Your witness must have got the name wrong."

"No, he was pretty clear—"

"I said," DCI Morgan cut in, "that he got the name wrong."

This wasn't making sense. She ploughed on, "With all due respect, sir, how can you be so sure?"

"Because, young Sergeant May," he said, looking at her with old, tired eyes, "I've been told to be sure." His shoulders sagged. "Just leave it alone. If this Bright exists, then he's nothing to do with your case. Bowman says we're closing the Miller/Jackson case, and now Jones has had a call from the killer we're looking at a different man, yes?"

Claire nodded, dumbly. She didn't know what else to do. Who the hell *was* this Castor Bright, to have got the search on him closed down so fast?

"So no more of our limited resources wasted on this, right? Make the most of the leads you've already got."

Claire's mobile started to ring but it did nothing to dissipate the tense atmosphere. She stared at her DCI, still trying to find answers in his face, but he remained inscrutable.

"You'd better answer that." He turned and walked away.

She watched him as she dragged the phone from her pocket. It might have been a Sunday, but the station was buzzing—Cass's call from the serial had them all fired up. If only the boys out reinterviewing the first four victims' friends and families could find some links to Covent Garden, then maybe they'd even have a chance of catching the killer. She wanted Cass back, and not only for that private comfort she got from having him around. If anyone could do it, then he could. She turned her attention to the phone.

"Claire?"

"Yes, who is this?" She couldn't immediately place the voice, and she was distracted by Mat Blackmore peering angrily round the door. It was obvious who he thought the call was from.

"It's Josh Eagleton. Are you at home?"

"No, at work. We've had some developments so I came in."

"Oh." As Josh's voice dropped so she could hear raised voices in the room behind Mat; Ramsey's defence of Cass probably hadn't gone down well with Bowman. Great. Blackmore glared at her again.

"What do you want, Josh?" She tried to keep the snappiness out of her voice, but failed. At least Mat might stop looking daggers at her now she'd made clear she wasn't on the phone to Cass—her *boss*. His attitude was beginning to seriously piss her off.

"I need Cass Jones' mobile number." The young man spoke hurriedly.

"I can't give you that."

"But I—"

She needed to get back and find out what was going on before it all came to blows. Maybe Ramsey had suggested something sensible—like sending Bowman home to rest. She glared back at Mat. She was tired of him being so angry at her. Maybe she shouldn't have been so honest when he'd asked her about her past with Cass, back when they'd first started seeing each other. It wasn't as if either of them had been virgins. Cass always said she was too honest, too trusting. Perhaps he had a point after all.

"I'll text him your number and tell him to call you. That okay?"

"Yes. Yes, thanks."

Claire cut off his stammered thanks. He was a strange kid, that one. It was up to Cass if he wanted to call him back. Josh was probably just running an errand for Dr. Farmer, but Cass was technically on compassionate leave so they couldn't have it both ways. She typed a quick text to Cass, attached the number and pressed send.

"Who was that?" Mat blocked the doorway.

"Just the ME's assistant. Wants to talk to Cass about something." His glare faltered slightly and she knocked his arm hard—only partly accidentally—as she pushed passed him and headed back into the fray.

CHAPTER FOURTEEN

Looking at Father Michael's face was like looking at a crumpled photograph. Cass could see he'd aged in the five years since the funerals, even though he didn't remember much about that day. He'd turned up for the service, and left with both his heart and his conscience heavy. The Father Michael he saw behind his eyes was the one from his childhood, somewhere between the young man in the picture he'd seen this morning and the old one standing beside him now.

Father Michael had taken him out to the bench in the small graveyard to make the most of the sudden spring sunshine. "Will you bring Christian and his family to rest here?" he asked.

The soft words were like a punch in the heart. Cass hadn't even thought about the funerals yet. "The police haven't released the bodies yet." He looked away.

"Bear it in mind. I think he would have chosen to come home." Father Michael patted his arm gently. "To be near your parents."

"I didn't realise how long you'd known my dad until I saw some old photos Christian had dug out." Cass wanted to steer the conversation away from the personal. He was still buzzing from his discoveries, and Claire had texted to say the burger man had been found and he was wanted back at work. It hadn't come as any surprise, but it had made him smile. She'd sent him Josh Eagleton's number, but it just rang out and he didn't bother leaving a message. If the ME had found anything good, he'd have called himself. He needed to head back to the grimy city he loved—but first, he wanted to try and make sense of this stuff, whatever had been winding his brother up so much.

"That doesn't surprise me." Father Michael smiled. "It's the nature of young people: they can't imagine a world that existed before they came into it. Just like they can't imagine that they could cease to exist and the world would still continue." He waved an insect away from his face. "In a way your father and I were adventurers together. We met when I was spreading the word of our good Lord in some war-torn part of the world."

"Lebanon?"

"Yes, it might have been. Your father was relishing in the journalistic opportunities of war with as much enthusiasm as I was trying to stop the conflict. But we both drank and smoked, and we both loved the danger of wandering off the beaten path." He shook his head wryly. "We garnered ourselves something of a reputation, travelling together as we did. I think he got the stories and I got the converts simply out of the people's curiosity."

It felt like the old man next to him was talking about a stranger. His dad had always been so placid. It had been a major cause of friction between them.

"Doesn't exactly sound like the dad I remember."

"He was different then, and people change. Back then he had no faith, and I'd given up trying to persuade him. He was quite wild, you know." His smile faltered a little. "But he was always a little odd. I sometimes thought he might be indulging in LSD, though I never saw any evidence of it."

"What made you think that?" Cass almost laughed aloud. His dad on acid: now there was a sight he wouldn't mind seeing.

"Oh, the things he used to say when we'd been drinking . . . how different he was to other people . . ." Father Michael's face clouded. "I'd forgotten all about it until Christian turned up talking about the same things."

Cass's stomach roiled. On the other side of the graveyard Christian had appeared, his back to them. Cass could see the crumpled blue shirt tails hanging down. He bowed his head in front of their parents' graves.

Cass tried to blink him away. It didn't work.

"I was there when your parents met," Father Michael said. "Alan and I were in South Africa—there was plenty of work for both of us there." He shook his head. "Some things don't change. Anyway, we were at a party, and your mother, Evie, was there with her boss, a man called Castor Bright. She was his personal assistant."

The ghost was forgotten as the words cut through: *his mother* had worked for Castor Bright?

Beside him, the priest hadn't noticed Cass's start at the words. He was lost in the memories of the past. "Mr. Bright was quite a man. Very charismatic. He didn't have much time for me. I always felt as if he was laughing at me and my beliefs in some way. Or perhaps that was just my own inexperience, my youth. He was a powerful man and looking back I doubt he even noticed me much. Evie was fond of him though." His brow furrowed. "He was an elusive man. Even now I don't really know what to make of him. He owned a mining company there, as well as several other businesses—and it turned out he had a share in the newspaper your dad worked for. Coincidences, eh?" The priest chuckled.

Cass smiled with him, but the expression was tight. *Coincidences?* He wasn't so sure.

"David and Evie clicked straight away. In fact, they more than clicked; I'd say it was love at first sight. I think she bought into his funny ideas too." He laughed again. "Perhaps they'd both spent too long in the sun!"

"Funny ideas? About what?"

Father Michael sighed. "Your father believed that he could see—well, a sort of halo on some people. It's what made me think maybe he was on something. When he was drunk he'd bang on about how some people were different, that something came out of their eyes. He called it *the Glow*. Apparently Evie could see it too. He said no one had it as strong as him and Evie—apart from Castor Bright." For the first time the priest looked searchingly at Cass. He said nothing. He was here to get information, not give it, and he doubted Father Michael needed anyone else spouting strange shit at him. *The boys see the Glow! Yay!* Despite his racing heart, he kept his face neutral.

"Anyway, they got married, a lavish do that Mr. Bright paid for—your dad was spending a lot of time with him by then—and I left soon after that. My own mother was dying and I'd decided it was time to settle down. After all the atrocities I'd seen, all that pain and suffering and sorrow, my soul was weary. I felt I'd challenged my faith enough and it was time I tried a nice quiet parish back at home, somewhere with smaller problems, where I might actually be able to help." He spread his fingers. "And here I've stayed."

"And my parents?"

"I didn't hear anything from them for a while, until they turned up here just after you were born. Your dad had changed. He was quieter. And he'd found religion."

"Did he say why?"

"No, but I think it was something to do with this Bright fellow. When I left I had the sense that he was grooming your dad for something. He'd been trying to get him to work for him in a kind of public relations role. I don't know what happened. Your dad wouldn't talk about it, but he said he wanted to live in the shadow of a good church. And I think he trusted my faith." He smiled sadly. "I was flattered, but I'd rather have had my friend back without the haunted look. We stayed up drinking for several long nights when he first arrived here, but we didn't laugh like we had before. Instead, he asked me a lot of questions about fate and destiny. I couldn't answer most of them." He stopped and looked down at his steepled fingers.

"What happened after that?" Cass didn't remember anything particularly disturbed about his dad, so something must have straightened out his thinking.

"After a couple of months, his mood lifted. One day I found him in the church, praying. He looked peaceful. He said he and Evie had talked about it and that even if the world wasn't what we all thought it was, he knew there was a God. His exact words: *he knew it for a fact*. And he intended to use his own free will." Father Michael peered into the distance, right through Christian's ghost. "He didn't talk about it again, but he came to church a lot." He smiled. "And there were the names he chose for you and your brother. Cassius and Christian."

Cass looked confused.

"Cassius was the surname of one of the oldest families in Rome. They were ambitious, vain and ruthless. Gaius Cassius plotted to assassinate Julius Caesar. Your dad loved history, particularly the history of Rome. We explored no end of ruins in the Middle East, and he drank up the stories, so when he turned up with a son called Cassius, I wasn't surprised."

Cass was genuinely surprised—he had always hated his name, that's why he'd shortened it. Most people didn't even know it was short for something. "He always told me I was named after Cassius Clay," he said, shaken.

"That was a white lie, I fear. By the time you were growing up, he probably wished it was true. His love of the cruelty of imperialism had gone by then. Hence Christian's name."

"And what did Christian talk to you about?" In the distance, his brother wandered through the long grass and disappeared through the trees. He didn't look back.

"He was talking about the Glow, the one your father said he and Evie could see." He looked at Cass. "He was agitated and curious, but I didn't think he was depressed. If I'd known—"

"I didn't see it coming either," Cass broke in. "You're not in any way to blame. At least you spoke to him. He'd been trying to reach me, but I was too busy." It was the closest he'd come to admitting his own guilt, and Father Michael nodded.

"No one ever really knows the secrets of another man's soul." He leaned back on the bench. "I wasn't concerned when he started asking questions about your parents. It's natural to want to know all about those we've lost. But when he started to talk about this Glow thing, I was surprised. He said that he could see it too, had seen it ever since he was a child." He looked at Cass. "He said you could see it too, but you closed it off. You *refused to see it*, that was how he put it."

Cass shrugged. "I don't remember."

"He said Jess could see it too. And he knew your parents had been able to, though I don't know how."

Cass did: that photograph. Or maybe it was more than that—maybe Christian had talked about this while their parents were still alive.

Father Michael was still talking. "I told him that perhaps it was genetic. People are capable of strange things, after all, but he laughed at that. He said it might be genetic, but not in any traditional way. He seemed a little paranoid. He said that he was starting to believe that his life was being manipulated, and that perhaps it always had been and he hadn't seen things clearly until recently." He paused, as if searching for the exact words. "Until they'd started to show themselves."

"Jesus Christ." Cass shook his head.

"I know. Hearing myself now, I should have picked up the warning signs. But these things came in tiny snippets, in what were otherwise perfectly ordinary conversations. Most of the time he sounded happy just listening to me talking about the old times with your dad, and then he'd tell me how his family was doing, and we'd just shoot the breeze, as the Americans would say."

"When did you last see him?"

"A couple of weeks ago, after Luke's last set of tests. I was saying how lucky it was that The Bank gave him private healthcare. He said they gave him more than that, but he didn't look happy about it. He wouldn't be drawn, but I got the feeling that he was worried about Luke, and not because of this lethargy he was suffering. It was something else. All he would say was that Luke had never seen the Glow."

Cass pulled out his cigarettes and offered one to the priest who took it. Cass noticed the other man's hand was shaking slightly.

"The old ladies of the parish would kill me if they saw this." He took in a long lungful. "That's better. It's just that . . . thinking about those conversations with Christian: they were like the talks with your father all over again. Uncanny."

Cass knew what he meant. He'd come looking for answers, and all he'd found were more questions. Who *was* this Mr. Bright? And why was this *Glow* so important? Cass dealt in hard evidence, in life and death. You just got on with it. He had no time for the crap that your mind could produce to fuck you up. He gazed over at the far headstones as they sat in silence, smoking.

Finally, he asked quietly, "Do you believe in ghosts, Father?"

"Depends on the kind you mean. Why?"

"I've been seeing Christian."

The priest said nothing.

"I've tried ignoring him, but he won't go away." He paused. "I think he's trying to tell me something."

He turned to look at the old man, all he had left to connect him with his family, and found kind eyes looking wisely back.

"Then maybe you ought to listen, son."

"Trust me, I'm trying."

"Then eventually you'll figure it out."

Cass smiled. "I hope so."

"How's Kate?"

The question threw him and he laughed, more from surprise than humour. "Well, put it this way: I'm heading back to London tonight and I'll be checking into a hotel rather than going home."

"I'm sorry to hear that." The priest sounded genuinely surprised.

"Shit happens."

"Yes it does." Father Michael threw his butt down and ground it out, then bent to pick it up. "You'll have to come back again, Cass. It's been good to see you. It's a shame it's such a short visit, but I imagine you're at your best when you're working."

"Something like that."

He stood up and shook out his cassock, and with it went the gloom that had settled over them. "Come inside for a moment. I think I might be able to help you with your accommodation problem." He winked. "It'll be perfect for you."

Back at the house Cass made himself coffee and once again sat himself in front of the slim laptop. He opened it up and sighed, staring at the screen. Part of him wanted to throw it across the room and smash it up, venting his frustration in violence, but that wouldn't get him anywhere other than hauled up on another disciplinary, and there were only so many of those what was left of his career could survive. He rolled his shoulders and thought hard.

Christian had always been cautious. From what Father Michael had said it sounded like he'd started to veer towards the paranoid, but Cass didn't believe his brother would have hidden and double-passworded these files if they weren't important. He was pretty sure at least some of the answers he was looking for were here, and he was running out of time to find them. The laptop had to be back to The Bank tomorrow, there was no getting out of that.

"Come on, think," he muttered under his breath as the empty password box flickered, almost taunting him. It had to be something he knew. It *had* to be. He tried *Father Michael*. No access. The blank screen mocked him and as he looked away his eyes fell on the envelope of pictures his brother had left, his own name printed clearly on the front. Maybe the clue was inside and he'd missed it.

He paused before opening it, staring again at the writing, so neatly lettered. His full name: not Cass, but *Cassius*. It looked strange. He never used it—and after a few decisive fights at primary school, neither had anyone else. If Christian were going to use his name as a password, he'd be formal and spell it properly. Just like he had on the envelope.

It was with a vague chill that he realised that the man who'd called him this morning had used his full name too, and that wouldn't have been easily available. Someone had been doing their homework. Maybe it was a sign. He typed in CASSIUS and pressed enter.

ACCESS GRANTED.

Cass smiled as a surge of excitement ran through him. *Bingo!* He looked up, half-expecting to see his brother's ghost standing smiling over him, but Christian obviously had haunting business elsewhere.

"I love you too, little brother," he muttered into the empty house. A sub-directory opened up on the small screen and Cass reached for his data pen. Whatever all this stuff was, he intended to copy it. On the table his phone started to buzz: the ME's assistant calling him back. He let it ring out. Whatever the boy wanted could wait; Cass needed to concentrate on what was in front of him. By the time the message tone beeped, he was so engrossed in figuring out what Christian had downloaded from The Bank's mainframe that he didn't even hear it.

Josh's hands were sweating as the call rang out and went to the answer phone. "This is DI Cass Jones. Leave a message." That was something. At least Jones had returned his call earlier. He spoke rapidly into the handset, and then paused before adding a final comment. It wasn't ideal, but hopefully it would do.

"Everything okay?" Dr. Farmer peered through the door from the lab to the small office.

"Yeah," Josh said, "just had to return a missed call." He smiled. "Telephone tag. I missed them this time."

The ME nodded. "That's normally the way it goes." He paused, and Josh felt himself flush under his boss's scrutiny.

"You okay, son?" There was a box of surgical gloves just inside the door and he pulled on a pair. "You haven't been quite yourself these past few days."

A knife of guilt twisted in his gut. Maybe he should have gone to Dr. Farmer first. There was probably a perfectly reasonable explanation for everything. The words sounded hollow, even inside his own head. If there was, then he was having a hard time seeing it. The DI was the only person he could talk to. But still, Dr. Farmer was his boss.

"I'm just not sleeping that well. I think it's this serial guy. The thing with the flies is bugging me." That was partly true, but that wasn't what was stopping him sleeping. He shrugged, sheepishly. "And I stayed up late, thinking I was getting a lie-in today. Wanted to crack the next level."

"Ah, so that's why you're tired." Dr. Farmer's face crinkled into a smile. "Just remember, we charge double for our weekends, and our clients don't mind if we work slowly." He sighed. "Not that we've got that luxury today. So come on." He turned back to the door. "Let's lay these two to rest. I want them done by five so we can play with fly eggs some more. You're not the only one who wants to know how that bastard does it."

Josh slipped his phone back into his pocket. If he'd been at home like he'd expected when he'd called Sergeant May then he'd have not missed the DI's call, and that would have been a weight off his mind—but he'd done his best. He waited for his hands to stop trembling before he headed to the door. God, this was shit. He liked this job. He really wanted to make a career of it, and as much as he could be stupid sometimes, like that dumb stunt he'd pulled at the Carla Rae scene, he was learning to have a great respect for the dead, and the mysteries their bodies held. He'd never have expected to be in a position like this. He wished he'd never . . .

"Come on, Josh, this liver won't weigh itself." Farmer didn't sound as if he was smiling any more. Bloody double suicide, Josh thought as he went through to face the internal organs of the overweight couple who had decided that this Sunday morning was a good day to die. If they hadn't been dead already, he'd be tempted to kill them himself. Still, he thought, as he shivered in the cool air of the morgue, Cass Jones would get his message. Despite the diseased liver in his hand, he was starting to feel a bit better.

Cass's head thumped as he worked his way through the files. There was too much to take in at first glance, and more than once he found himself wishing he had Christian's mathematical mind. The sun slid slowly down the sky, but he barely noticed the time passing.

The Redemption folder, unlike the other work folders Christian had stored on his laptop, was not Windows-based; it looked like it was some sort of a sub-directory, a whole separate system of its own running underneath The Bank's main computer system. How the hell had Christian even found it? What had happened to have made him go looking?

Each file housed what he presumed were bank account numbers. Money was flowing in and out through a tangled web of transfers both internal and external, but at the heart of this financial web there appeared to be twenty primary accounts. None of them had names attached to them; they were identified simply by the letter X and a number, 1 to 20. Each account had records going back two hundred years, logging vast sums of money moving in and out. The opening balances were huge too, so somewhere there had to be paper records that hadn't been input into the system. How far back would they go? The pit of his stomach was icy. Four hundred years? Further? Whose money was this?

The only account with no outgoings was the final one: X20. All the rest had an annual amount paid in that added to the already huge sums listed. What was that account—some kind of joint savings?

He put his questions to one side and concentrated on what he could see. Six of the accounts had been closed within the past three years and the money they contained had been divided up equally and transferred into the remaining accounts. Against X3 was the tag FROZEN. Cass couldn't see why; whoever X3 represented was not short of a few billion in cash. The sums he was looking at were extraordinary: who the hell were these people? Were these the private accounts of the businessmen who had collectively set up The Bank? Or was he looking at something else entirely? Maybe each number represented a group of people—but how could they go back so far? The one thing he knew about people was that they disagreed, especially where money was concerned. If these were joint accounts, then at some time over the past couple of hundred years most of the groups would have fallen out: it was human nature. Even families had a tough time staying together when money was involved. The idea that each of these accounts belonged to a single individual was even more disturbing. Unnamed people in control of such huge wealth meant that whoever they were, they had power. But why were they anonymous?

He looked at the transactions again. Most of the external transfers involved what looked like traditional bank account numbers. Businesses? Foreign bank accounts? And several paid into the same accounts, proving further collaboration between these invisible players other than their contributions to the X20 account.

His foot tapped and he wished his brother's ghost would return and maybe give him a hand. If Christian thought Cass could figure all this out just by looking at the numbers, then he'd vastly overrated his older brother. How was this money flowing in and out of the main system?

Someone on the other end must know where it was coming from. He looked again at the numbers. The receiving bank accounts outside of this hidden system must be the key. If he could track them, if he could see how all this money was being used, then maybe he'd get an idea of who these people were.

He exited the account files and browsed through some of the others. He had the distinct feeling that this was only the tip of the iceberg. Some files refused to open, or displayed only computer-generated nonsense text, perhaps corrupted when Christian had tried to copy the information over. One file that did open was a database of what looked like company names. He scrolled down, but it was endless. Some had been famous names in their time, now no longer trading, but most he'd never heard of. Then his eye snagged on one: the Solomon & Bright Mining Corps. Next to it was a series of numbers, the registered company number, maybe, and start and finish dates and shares held, that sort of thing.

It was going to take someone with a wider understanding of the corporate world to fully comprehend what he had here, but he knew enough to know that it was important. He also knew that no X account holder would have a list of companies unless it was because he or she had a vested interest in them. What was this, some kind of new world order? He thought about the dates on the computerised accounts; maybe not so new.

He looked again at the Solomon and Bright entry. Could Mr. Bright be one of the account holders? Once again, everything came down to this name. He hoped to hell that Claire had dug up some information to share when he got back.

Each of the saved zipped files was labelled only with an incomprehensible series of numbers or letters, with no clue to content in the name. Most were corrupted, but the last one opened and the coded title vanished to be replaced with one word. POTENTIALS.

There were fifteen folders, and as Cass looked at the names on the first few—Adams, Begum, Boyle, two lots of Smith—he realised they were surnames. He opened one. A DOS-style screen opened and flashed the words *File deleted. Potential voided 1988.* He clicked another. The

message was the same, except this time the voided date was 1996. He
went through the rest. The fourteenth declared the "potential" voided
in 2003. At the fifteenth, the name on the file was JONES, the usual
DOS screen appeared, but this time there was a series of options: heritage, employment, medical, surveillance. His stomach churned as he
clicked on the first. He looked through the list of names, not recognising most until he came to his own immediate family. Some names were
in red—his parents, him, Christian, Jessica and Luke—but Kate was
in green. If he hadn't felt so invaded he might have laughed: even in
some bloody computer system they were separated. He went into the
medical folder next, and frowned. He knew Luke had been seriously
ill, but if the figures next to the various dates were medical bills, then
the boy had been through a shitload of tests. But this couldn't be right.
There were dates going back to his birth. Cass scrolled down, trying
to make sense of the dates and the numbers. Under the initial batch
was another heading: SECONDARY, with a single line, *See main employee directory*, as explanation. Cass began to nod to himself: Christian's medical cover was provided by The Bank, one of the many perks,
so whatever medical costs he'd incurred, like Jess's pregnancy care,
would be in The Bank's main files. Cass couldn't see what was so special about the medical costs listed here that someone had to hide them.
Questions upon questions.

The surveillance folder appeared to be a spreadsheet of accounts, a
mixture of large payments interspersed with smaller ones: an annual
billing system? So who were they watching—Christian? Him? *Both of
them?* And, more importantly, *why?*

He looked up from the computer. This was their family home, and
suddenly it no longer felt safe. A chill of paranoia crept into him, a familiar, quiet fear that he hadn't felt in a long time. After Birmingham
he'd lived with that watery sensation in the pit of his stomach for a year
or more. Every time someone moved quickly around him, he thought
he'd been found, and that the lie of the body in the river had been uncovered. If the nightmares didn't wake him, then the slightest breeze
outside the window would. Eventually, time passed and the world moved

on, and he'd slowly learned to relax. But now it had flooded right back, feeling like oil in his guts.

He slipped the data pen into the slot on the side and came back to the start menu. He dragged the file over to the box, and was dismayed when the computer flashed up: COPY FAILED.

He tried again.

COPY FAILED.

He swore quietly under his breath and clicked the help icon. FILE NON-TRANSFERABLE. Well, that was just great. Without the files he had no proof. He rubbed his face, his fingers sinking into creases that felt as if they'd deepened over the course of the day. Proof of what, exactly? That The Bank had accounts dating back hundreds of years? That Mr. Bright had a vested interest in the Jones family? That the whole company was some kind of front—for *what*? If he started spouting stuff like that they'd lock him up. Whatever was going on here might have some bearing on the three cases, but for now he'd keep this all to himself, and see where the normal investigations led. He reopened the files. All of this must have been what Christian wanted to talk to him about. But he had an hour before he had to leave. There was nothing wrong with taking some notes to look over later.

As he scribbled, lost in the Redemption file and the conversation with Father Michael, he completely forgot about the two account numbers he'd stored in his phone the previous day and the missed phone call of earlier. The small message icon pulsed quietly in the corner of the screen, unnoticed.

CHAPTER FIFTEEN

"You should be quite comfortable here." The rector smiled. "As long as you can live without television during your stay."

Cass laughed. "I wish I had time for telly." He left his suitcase in the small bedroom and followed the older man out. He'd half-expected the roof to cave in when the Reverend Terence Abercrombie had shown him the small chapel. Father Michael hadn't lost his sense of humour, sorting him out with a room in a seminary. Still, he was grateful; the large complex was right in the middle of Westminster, and aside from a small donation, the rector had refused any other payment. God only knew what the premises were worth now—the buildings had housed priests for well over a hundred years, surviving all the twentieth century could throw at them.

"Feel free to stay for as long as you like. You're more than welcome." Revd Abercrombie had the kind of thin face that should have looked mean, but somehow didn't. He smiled too much, and there was too much kindness in his eyes. It didn't make Cass feel particularly relaxed.

"Thanks, but I should be sorted in a couple of days. And I'll be out most of the time." He shrugged. "Police work isn't exactly nine to five."

"I understand. Our good Lord keeps strange working hours himself."

The sun was setting, but the sky was clear, and only just turning a deep midnight blue. As the two men stepped outside, at the back of the main building a security light came on, shining brightly over the slightly overgrown garden, where plants fought for space in overcrowded borders framing a lawn. Cass was glad to be outside. He wasn't up on all the commandments, but he knew some of the big ones: thou shall not commit adultery, thou shall not covet and thou shall not kill. If there was ever a man who shouldn't be seeking shelter in the House of the Lord, Cass knew it was him.

A tabby cat yowled as it crept out from the undergrowth, heading straight for the rector and wrapping itself around his legs. Its fur was scruffy, and it was thin.

"Seminary cat?" Cass asked.

"No, she's a stray. There are too many people with allergies, so the trustees don't allow pets." He leaned down and stroked the creature until she started purring. "Every day I say that I'll call one of the animal rescue people to come and get her, but every day I find myself putting out a bowl of food instead."

He smiled up at Cass. "I'm sure the Holy Father won't mind a few pennies going to help this little homeless one. We're all his creatures. And all life is sacred."

The rector's innocent words sent a chill through Cass. There was at least one man in the city busy proving the priest wrong. Cass bent over to pet the small animal, but it hissed, ducking away from his hand and retreating to the bushes. Its eyes glinted amber from among the leaves.

"Sorry about that. She's been out on the streets too long, I think." The rector sighed. "In hard times people can be cruel to strays. Still, she's getting friendlier."

"And she knows better than to bite the hand that feeds." Cass stared at the bush where the cat was hiding. A stray. Something about that bugged him, but his brain was too tired to figure it out. Somewhere inside a bell rang out.

"That's the bell for evening prayers. If you want to unpack, dinner will be in half an hour in the refectory. I'll collect you, shall I?"

With one eye still on the hidden animal, Cass followed the rector back inside. A thought niggled abstractly at the corner of his mind, refusing to come to the fore. He looked back as the doors shut. Nope. He couldn't see it yet.

It finally came to him at 6 o'clock the following morning, as the seminary stirred into life around him. A ringing bell shook his brain alert and he sat up in the narrow single bed that took up most of the space in the small room. The stray cat and his craving for a cigarette filled his head in equal measure and he reached for his trousers and a T-shirt. Outside for a smoke, and then the shower.

He padded past the fresh-faced young men who smiled as they headed towards the chapel. He felt surprisingly alert himself, and realised that he'd had ten hours of solid sleep for the first time in a very long while. The garden shimmered with dew, but the sun was already brightening the sky. It was going to be another glorious day. As the nicotine rushed into his grateful system, Cass peered around. There was no sign of the cat. The niggling thought he hadn't been able to grasp the previous night had suddenly exploded in his head. If it turned out to lead somewhere, then he'd buy that mangy moggy a month's worth of Felix.

By the time he'd hunted down some coffee in the refectory and showered it was half-past seven, and students and teachers alike were hurrying to finish their breakfasts and start the daily lessons. Cass left them to it and went back outside to ring Claire.

"Animal sanctuaries," he said the moment she answered.

"What?" In the background he could hear traffic. They were obviously on their way in to work. He was surprised they weren't already there.

"Ask Mat if they checked all the animal sanctuaries and rescue shelters to see if they'd had any pentabarbitone stolen. I can't remember anything saying they did in the files."

"Animal shelters?"

A flurry of wings sent three small birds skywards as the cat appeared on the far wall. It stared at Cass, watching him curiously.

"Yes, that's what I said." He frowned. She sounded distracted. "You okay?"

"Not really. We just had a phone call from Dr. Farmer. Josh Eagleton was in an accident last night."

Cass froze. "What happened?"

"I don't really know. He got run over. Not far from his house." Her breath hitched. "They left him for dead. The driver didn't even call for an ambulance."

"Is he okay?" The tips of his fingers tingled against the phone. Eagleton was just a kid.

"No, he's in a bad way. He's in St. Thomas's, and he's in a coma. It's touch and go, Dr. Farmer says."

"Jesus." His good mood vanished into the sunshine that continued to shine brightly, oblivious to a young man fighting for his life. Maybe individual lives weren't so sacred after all.

"Did you speak to him yesterday?" Claire asked.

"No." Cass paused. "I didn't get round to it. I'll see you at work in half an hour or so."

The call ended, he stared at the small message icon that had waited patiently for him to notice it since the previous afternoon. He drew a deep breath and dialled the answer phone.

"Detective Inspector Jones?" Cass recognised Josh Eagleton's voice straight away. "I'm sorry to bother you."

He sounded nervous. Quiet. What was Josh afraid of? Being overheard? Cass listened intently, not only to the words, but the nuances between them.

"I just . . . I just really need to speak to you. It's about your brother's wife."

The tiny hairs all over Cass's skin rose as one.

"I mean, there's probably a good reason, but something's not making sense. Not to me anyway." The words were coming out in a rush, but they landed like tiny ice-cold drops in Cass's head.

"Can you meet me at the Farmer's Arms in Chiswick at about nine?" There was a breathy pause. "I was here first, you see, when they brought the bodies in. And I . . . Well, I'll explain later."

The call clicked off.
Shit.

By eleven it felt to Cass like he'd never been away from the office at all. He'd had an awkward conversation with Morgan, who'd made it clear that he still thought Cass should be off the case, at least until this "evidence issue," as he referred to it, was cleared up. But the Commissioner had thought otherwise. The DCI had made it clear he wasn't happy about that, but as it was Cass the killer had called, he had to agree it was better having him and his phone at work. Cass had sat quietly and let his boss go through the usual list of demands: don't rock the boat. Do as you're told. No smoking on the premises. Help Bowman where you can; he's back to being the officer in command unless he goes off sick again.

Cass had nodded, but he was only half-listening. The station had always felt like the closest thing to a real home he'd had, but now that feeling had shifted. It was like a bubble, and he was now somehow on the outside of it. He could feel people watching him as he strode through the corridors, and he knew what most of them were thinking: *no smoke without fire.* But for every suspicious glance that came his way, he was sending one back. Someone had tried to set him up, and it was most likely they were in this building.

As he'd been leaving Morgan's office the DCI had called him back. His voice sounded lighter, as if what he was about to say was almost inconsequential. "Oh, and this Bright business? I've told your sergeant to leave it alone. It's clear from all the evidence that he's not your killer. We need our limited manpower to chase more pertinent leads." Morgan had peered over the paperwork he was hiding behind. "Okay and understood?"

Cass had nodded, his face calm. That old Columbo "one more thing" routine wasn't fooling him. Claire had already reported her conversation with Morgan, and the DCI was, all unwitting, giving him some answers. Mr. Bright was an important person, that much Cass knew, and if he was controlling one of the X accounts, then he would have more power and influence than Morgan could even begin to imagine. Someone on high had told the DCI to stop that thread of the investigation, that was written clearly across Morgan's pinched face. And he was willing to bet they hadn't given him any reasons.

Cass had also seen the email the police liaison woman at The Bank had sent, and he'd smiled at its clever answer. *There is no one of that name in our employment database.* Cass was certain there wasn't: he didn't yet know quite what Mr. Bright was in relation to The Bank, but he certainly wasn't any ordinary employee. As it was, with everything he'd discovered or worked out over the weekend, he was happy for that line of investigation to stop. At least within the office, and for the time being. Mr. Bright and his family were interwoven in some way and so that would be a private investigation.

After leaving Morgan's office, he'd sorted through the piles of paper that had mounted on his desk, and caught up on the autopsy reports on Hannah West. He stared at the close-up picture of the tiny fly eggs, lined up so perfectly along the edges of the words written in blood. He needed to find this man. He'd put everything else aside—the photos, the Redemption file, his brother's death, even the Jackson and Miller case—he needed to find this man. He remembered the way the killer had laughed on the phone when Cass had asked if he was Bright. The two men knew each other, and that sent a chill through his bones. If Mr. Bright could pull strings to get a major police investigation off his back, then could this man do the same? It would take more than Morgan forbidding him to stop Cass from doing his best to catch him.

Apart from taking a long look at the photos inside, he'd ignored the Jackson and Miller file. He was itching to hear back from Perry Jordan, but that call wouldn't come in today; even Jordan wasn't that fast. So Macintyre had allegedly made some confession yesterday, but he wasn't buying it. He could believe that Bowman had paid the gangster to give him some names to bring a nice tight closure to the case, not to mention a big fat bonus and probably a promotion for Bowman himself.

He bit back his annoyance at the other man. He'd wait and see what Perry came back with before making any noise. From behind his desk he could feel the invisible barrier between him and his colleagues growing thicker. He was keeping too much to himself, he knew that, but who could he trust? For now, this was just the way it was going to have to be.

The days of interview tape recorders were long gone; now, when the record button was pressed, the interview was saved directly into the computer mainframe. Back-ups were on disc, of course, and the files were stored and available for anyone with the correct clearance to access as and when required, from the comfort of their own desktop. Cass was about to listen to the Macintyre interview when Claire came to collect him for the briefing. He followed his sergeant past the hive of activity in the Incident Room to the smaller conference room at the other end. Blackmore and Bowman were there already, as was Charles Ramsey.

Cass raised an eyebrow. "Didn't know you were on this case."

"I'm not." The American smiled. "But right now, *you're* all I've got for *my* case. So I'm sticking with you. I figure if I follow you around long enough, we might find some time to talk." He paused. "And did you find that laptop?"

Cass grinned. "Funnily enough, I did. I'll get it back to them today."

"Yeah." Ramsey smiled back. "I'll make sure you do."

Cass liked the man. And what he liked best about him was that he wasn't from Paddington Green nick. He was outside the bubble too.

The moments before Hask arrived were filled with awkward chat. Bowman pulled out a chair, draped his jacket over the back and slumped in it. He was dressed as smoothly as ever, but he looked pale, and patches of sweat were slowly spreading out from the armpits of his expensive shirt. The air in the room was cool and Cass figured he had to be running a temperature.

"I heard about young Josh Eagleton," Ramsey said. "From what I hear he's got the makings of a good ME himself. Bright kid."

Cass had forgotten that Farmer and his team did Chelsea's bodies too. "Let's hope he pulls through."

Blackmore looked up. "By the way, I asked Farmer what Josh had wanted to speak to you about yesterday, but he didn't know anything about it."

"Neither do I." Cass shrugged, keeping his shoulders loose. "He didn't leave a message. Can't have been important."

The door opened and Hask's huge frame squeezed into the empty space. "Sorry. Just had to print something out." He sent a beaming grin in all directions. "Have I missed anything?"

"No, we waited for you," Bowman said. He gave the large man time to wedge himself into the second seat before nodding at Blackmore. "Let's get everyone up to speed on what we've got."

"Okay, the first thing we chased yesterday was Claire's possible Covent Garden link between the victims. Hannah West's husband says she often stopped there on the way to her hospital shifts, but he didn't know whether it was to browse the shops or have a coffee or what."

Cass was pleased that Claire had been able to run with his suggestion. She glanced up at him and he winked. She obviously felt bad about taking credit, but he didn't mind. She could hardly have told Bowman it had come from him. That would have gone down a storm.

"We've had people out reinterviewing and it looks like there might be something in it. Emma Loines had temped at a solicitors' office in Garrick Street. Carla Rae's sister works as a waitress in Ponti's, in the Jubilee Market, Amanda Carlisle had a disabled aunt she visited there, and Jade Palmer occasionally worked at a jewellery stall."

"So that has to be it." Bowman looked up. "It's the only thing that we've found that connects these women. Somewhere in Covent Garden he's selecting his victims."

"But where from?" Cass frowned.

"I doubt they're random," Hask added. "He'll be taking them from somewhere precise."

"We've borrowed some local constables to take photos out and see if people can remember seeing the women and where. They'll be out for the next couple of days on the street." Bowman shrugged. "It's the best we can do, and it's better than nothing."

Cass couldn't argue, but he didn't hold out much hope for someone remembering all five of them, especially as they'd gone missing at different times.

"We're trying to track that pay-as-you-go number, and we're also calling all the animal sanctuaries in the Greater London region to see if any of them have had any drug thefts." Blackmore gave Cass a quick nod of acknowledgement. "We missed those first time round. The team have been on the phones all morning so hopefully we'll get something."

"That leaves this phone call Cass was blessed with," Bowman said.

Was that a slight tinge of jealousy in Bowman's voice? Psycho-envy? Cass thought he'd heard it all now.

"Yes, this is interesting." Hask smiled. "He must see you as his adversary. I've got the notes of your conversation here." He was enjoying himself, and Cass didn't blame him. There was a real buzz in tracking a killer, no one who worked on a murder could deny that. "Something prompted him to ring, and from what he says, it has to have been the press conference."

"Because we called him socially awkward and stupid?" Bowman asked.

"No." Hask shook his head and his jowls wobbled for a moment or two more. "I think it was because he expected to see Cass running it." His thick forefinger stabbed at the paper. "He said as much. But what really got my attention was this phrase: 'I thought I had it all sorted out.'" He looked at Bowman. "When did you start feeling ill, Detective Inspector? I'm guessing it was about the time this case started, maybe just before."

Bowman slowly nodded. "About a week or so before the first body. I just ignored it for a while. Why? What are you implying?"

Cass stared at Hask. "Are you saying that this guy did something to get Bowman off the case before he'd even started?" That hadn't ever occurred to him. And what the killer clearly didn't know was that there was no way the DCI would put Cass in front of the cameras. He'd had an occasional fuzzy photo in the papers, but even after ten years the last thing any of them needed was someone recognising him from the Birmingham fiasco.

"It's definitely possible." The profiler slapped Bowman cheerfully on the back. "Don't panic. I think if he'd given you anything lethal then you'd be getting worse rather than better. What did they say you had in the end?"

"Some gastric virus."

Some of Bowman's natural cockiness had slid away and Cass fought the urge to warm to the killer.

"Maybe you'd better get over to the hospital and get yourself checked out once we're done here," Hask said. "That would be a wise precaution. I doubt the hospital would have checked for a full spectrum of poisons or toxins—although I'm sure whatever it is has done its worst already."

The sweat patches in Bowman's armpits were growing. He didn't seem too reassured.

"But *how* would he have done it?" Blackmore asked.

"I'm not sure, but you policemen are creatures of routine. He just had to watch you for a while. Maybe he slipped something into your pint or wiped some toxin on your car door handle."

"Jesus," Bowman whispered.

"He really did plan this to the letter, didn't he?" Claire said.

"But as with every plan, you can't factor in the unexpected actions of others. Cass took on the case, but after what happened with his brother's family, Bowman had to come back."

Cass liked the way the profiler skimmed over the minor details of accusations, murder, suicide and the planting of evidence without even skipping a beat.

"Why Jones?" Bowman asked. "Why does he want *him* on the case?"

"I don't know. Maybe when we find him, we'll find out." Hask moved the papers and peered closely at them in a way that suggested he should be wearing glasses, before looking back up. "This comment about Bright is interesting. '*He looks for me, I watch him.*'" The profiler seemed unaware of the tension that rose, at least in the part of the room that Cass and Claire occupied.

"It could hint at a potential for multiple personalities, in that he and Bright are one and the same . . . but I'm not convinced." He tapped his fingers on the table. "I think we need to take it at face value. It would certainly explain why your body turned up in the same flat the video was sent from."

"I don't get it," Blackmore said.

"It doesn't matter if you do, or don't," Cass cut in. "The Bright line of enquiry is closed down."

"Really?" Hask watched Cass carefully. "That's interesting in itself."

"Not really. The DCI says it's not relevant." Cass gritted his teeth to force the next sentence out. "Bowman's apparently solved the Mac-intyre case—"

"No *apparently* about it," Bowman snapped. "We've got two of Macintyre's men coming in this afternoon to give their statements. They were paid by one of the Eastern European firms trying to get in on Macintyre's turf to say exactly where he was going to be that afternoon."

Cass raised his hands. This was an argument for another time, after he'd heard back from Perry Jordan. "Maybe that came out wrong. What I meant was: as that's looking closed, the need to find Mr. Bright appears to those above to be a waste of resources."

"Even with the mention of him on the phone?" Ramsey frowned.

"Well, I actually mentioned him, not the caller." Cass shrugged. "But whatever the reason, he's out of the immediate picture."

There was a moment's silence. They were all clever people, even Bowman, for all his sharp suits and smug veneer. This wouldn't sit right with any of them, but if the headshed had spoken, there was nothing they could do about it.

"I have to say I find your bosses' motivation strange, but if that's what they want, let's move on." Hask sighed. "He calls himself 'the man of flies.' This obviously ties in with the leaving of the eggs on the bodies, but it's also an interesting variation on the Lord of the Flies."

"Lord of the Flies?" Bowman asked. "Isn't that a book?"

"Yes, by William Golding. It's an allegorical story about how soci-ety created by man will always fail. It explores our duality: that we have an instinct to follow rules, but at the same time, we desire to force our own will on others. Some literary theorists feel that the novel sums up the history of our civilisation."

"You think he's trying to make a point about civilisation?" Bowman was incredulous. "Jesus Christ."

"The phrase is also a more obvious variant of the Hebrew Ba'al Zebub, translated literally as the Lord of Things that Fly, or as we would put it, Lord of Flies."

"Ba'al Zebub?" Claire repeated. She leaned forward. "Is that Beelzebub?"

Hask laughed, a light sound that didn't match his physical bulk. "Got it in one. Once the god of the Philistines, and now considered interchangeable with Satan himself."

"Our man thinks he's the devil?" Blackmore said. "Oh, that's great."

"No," Cass said, "he called himself the *Man* of Flies, not the Lord. There's an important distinction there."

The profiler folded his hands across his middle. "Perhaps he thinks he's the devil's chosen man on Earth. Someone to send his message out."

"It fits with him having some kind of religious connection," Cass agreed. He frowned. "He just sounded so . . . sane."

"Some people would say that only the truly insane believe their own sanity."

"Enough," Bowman interrupted. "I want to get down to the hospital, so let's leave the mind shit until later and keep to what you've got to tell us."

"Sorry." Hask smiled. "It's just so interesting, I was curious about what he says about testing people and finding them wanting, how we are only ever interested in ourselves. This ties in with the concept of the duality of our natures, but perhaps it also ties in with his selection of victims."

"Maybe he's tested the women somehow?" Claire asked.

"How could Hannah West be found wanting?" Cass asked. "She worked with Strain II cases."

"I don't know," Hask said, "but he's been testing someone. He doesn't say it's the *victims* he was testing, but something's happened to make him feel that nothing is sacred. He's reached a personal conclusion about that. Oh, and I found something else out for you yesterday." He grinned at them all and pulled out a sheet of paper. "The music that was playing at the Carla Rae scene? It was a 1990s heavy metal band. The Dog-Faced Gods. They weren't overly famous, from what I gather. The CD was called *Random Chaos Theory in Action*." He let out a short laugh. "You've got to admit that our man has a very dry sense of humour along with his paranoia and superiority complex. One of the songs is called 'God over All.'"

"You think he's being funny?" Blackmore asked.

"Maybe not funny ha-ha, but I think he's definitely making a point."

A quick rap on the door was followed by the appearance in the doorway of a uniformed constable, a tall, thin man in his twenties.

"Sir—" he started. His eyes darted around the room. He obviously wasn't sure where he should aim his words. He settled on Bowman. Cass didn't blame him. "We've got something. The pay-as-you-go phone was one of a batch that was ordered in bulk through the Carphone Orange Warehouse. They're going through their records now to find where the order ended up."

"How long till we know?" Cass asked. Carphone Orange Warehouse, with its irritating orange cow logo, was now the biggest mobile phone and web company in the country, having absorbed most of their weaker competitors over the previous year. He dreaded to think what their systems were like as they absorbed all the extra customer information.

"They say this afternoon, but we'll see. You know what phone companies are like." The constable came a little further into the room. "But that's not all. We just had a call back from someone at the Limehouse Rescue Shelter. The big one? He said they reported a theft of pentabarbitone to their local station about three months ago. They never heard back."

Cass looked over at Bowman, who frowned. "If it was in the system, then why didn't it flag up months ago?"

"It's not in the system, sir." The young officer shook his head.

"Whoever took the call mustn't have logged it. The manager over at Limehouse said they reported it when her partner vet found it was missing. It was called in around four in the morning."

"Fucking great." Cass sucked air in through his teeth. The constable didn't need to say any more. Some bloody night sergeant took the call and decided they had no chance of catching the thief, so what was the point of adding to their unsolved figures? He'd have given out a dummy incident number and left it at that.

"The manager said she thought the police hadn't paid much attention because there was no sign of a break-in, so it was the shelter's problem to solve. And they didn't notice it was missing until a week after it had been stolen."

"Taken by someone in-house?" Cass's stomach fizzed as the thrill of the chase kicked in. He looked at Bowman. "Do you want me to deal with this while you get yourself checked over?" He kept his tone light, but he didn't have to worry. Bowman had started to crap himself the minute Hask had mentioned that maybe the killer had something to do with the DI's illness.

"I solved your case. I guess you can have a go at solving mine," Bowman said.

God, he was a condescending bastard. Cass gestured to Claire. "Come on."

"Wait up." Ramsey followed them out into the corridor. "We take the laptop to The Bank on the way. My phone's been buzzing in my pocket and I know who's on the other end."

"What laptop?" Claire asked.

Both Cass and Ramsey ignored her. "Tell you what, we'll take it with us," Cass said. "But going to The Bank is going to have to wait."

Cass grabbed his jacket and the laptop bag that was tucked under his desk. He held it up to Ramsey. "Funny the things you forget you have."

"Ha bloody ha."

"I can't persuade you to stay behind?"

"No chance."

Cass laughed. "Well, let's go then." With Claire's slim frame between them, they strode out in the sunshine towards the Audi. Traffic willing, they'd be at Limehouse by midday.

The director of the rescue centre was a middle-aged woman called Sheena Joyce. She walked with a slight hunch, and Cass wondered whether it was arthritis or another degenerative condition, or an accident. As she shut out the barking that had accompanied their walk past the rows of kennels that led to her offices, she leaned on the door for a moment and sighed.

"Sorry about that," she said. "I think the place was designed so that anyone visiting would have to see the animals, and hopefully take pity on one. Unfortunately I have no room for more at home, but I still have to pass them every time I need to use my office." She dropped into the chair behind her desk. "But to be honest, that isn't often."

Cass didn't envy her. However much you loved animals, that constant noise must drive you mad. It was a tatty old place. He'd noticed a lot of the dogs were two to a kennel, and he figured it would be the same with the cats. The director looked like she could use a make-over as much as the building. Now that they were in the well-lit office, he could see that she couldn't be more than fifty, and she had the look of an ageing Brigitte Bardot, her thick grey hair piled into a loose chignon, though without the heavy make-up, not even a lick of mascara. He wondered if she'd look better after a decent night's sleep; she was obviously running on fumes. Despite all that, she had what was probably a completely unintentional quirky bohemian look.

"So, this is about the Pentobarbital theft, is it?"

"That's right," Cass said. "We're sorry that it got lost in the system."

"Why are you all interested now?" Her eyes were tired, but they glittered with intelligence.

"Why didn't you chase up the report?" Cass ignored her question. "Pento's a controlled drug—and a lethal substance at that—and it's not like whoever stole it wanted it for a good purpose, is it? I'd have thought you'd expected at least one visit from the police."

She watched him steadily for a moment and then leaned back in her chair. "I suppose I didn't want to draw attention to malpractice within the shelter." She shrugged slightly. "A scandal could lose us funding and things are tough enough as it is. If I'd been here, the theft probably wouldn't have been reported in the first place."

"Malpractice? What happened?"

"The business of running a shelter has never been easy, even at the best of times. It's almost impossible now. The first thing people dump when money's tight is the family pet. First the cats, and then the dogs; our intake has more than tripled. The bigger problem is the sheer number of strays out there: they're not getting neutered, so they go on reproducing. The feral animal population has increased massively, especially in these poorer areas. People used to say wherever you were in the city, you were never more than a few feet away from a rat. Now it's cats. Keep your eyes open. You'll see what I mean."

"At least the cats must be keeping the rats down," Cass said with a wry grin. "And how does this affect the theft?"

The director ignored his poor attempt at humour. "I'm getting there. This could be the end of my career, so let me tell it in my own time." She paused as the door opened and a young girl in scrubs brought in a tray with four mugs of coffee and a jug of milk. Cass took one and sipped it gratefully.

"You have better coffee than we do." He smiled. He liked this tired woman with her crisply efficient voice.

"Better behaved inmates too, I should imagine." She added a little milk to her own cup. "Anyway, as our numbers have been increasing, so our funding has been decreasing. Battersea's the high-profile London shelter, always has been, so we're left with the scraps, even though we have twice as many abandoned animals to deal with, not to mention a much poorer local constituency. As well as having to run this place on very limited finances, I'm also chief veterinary officer. We can't afford many full-time staff, so most of our helpers are volunteers, like young Stacey who brought the coffee in. She's a student, comes down when she's not at lectures, but we also have a lot of unemployed people who want to feel useful. To be honest, without them, we couldn't keep going."

"And one of the volunteers took the drug?"

"It's not as simple as that." She looked around the dilapidated office. "Pentobarbital is a controlled substance, for veterinary use only, and we keep it locked up." She paused. "Normally." She took a sip of her coffee and went on, "We have two vets onsite, but as I've been saying, times have changed, and we can no longer keep every animal that's brought in to us. We certainly can't care for all the newborns that get brought in—or are left dumped on our doorstep." For the first time her eyes slid away from Cass's.

"We vets, we train to save animals. But we've had no choice but to go back to the dark old days, when any unwanted animal is automatically put to sleep. And trust me, it's not a job I'd wish on anyone. It's soul-destroying." She looked back up. "It'll be easier for you to understand if I show you. You'll want to see where the drug went from anyway. Follow me."

She took them out through the kennels and into a separate block where the cats were kept. Cass was relieved to note the felines were far less interested in them than they were in sleeping.

"Here you go." She typed in a code to a room at the back and opened the door. "There's my afternoon's work once you've gone."

A cacophony of tiny mewls and squeaks filled the room, escaping from the cardboard boxes that littered the floor. Cass crouched and opened one to reveal eight tiny black and white kittens stumbling over each other. He looked around him.

"There must be ten boxes in here—twelve maybe," Claire said. "You have to put all these to sleep?"

Ramsey stood in the doorway, saying nothing, but Cass could see her revulsion mirrored on his face. He closed the box. It was the innocence that did it. He could feel bile curdling at the back of his throat.

"We had a new volunteer. He was only here a month. He wasn't like the others." Sheena Joyce sat on the bench and looked mournfully at the boxes that awaited her. "I was working in here"—she let out a small, sad laugh at the irony of her words—"and I must have not shut the door properly. Anyway, suddenly he was just standing there. I had the syringe in one hand, a kitten in the other, and I was crying." She stopped, and swallowed. "He had a presence about him. A stillness. He sat beside me and told me it was all right, and before I knew what had happened, he had the animal in his hands and he'd injected it. He told me I'd done enough, that he could take care of this." She took a deep breath to control the tears welling in her eyes. Her voice shook. "And God help me, I let him."

"That's what this man did for you?"

She nodded. "I shouldn't have let him. None of us should. Even these days you still need a euthanasia licence to put animals to sleep. But I just couldn't do it any more. I needed a break. Neither I nor Martin—the other vet—could reconcile ourselves to spending half the day trying to save animal lives and then the other half quietly taking them before they'd even begun." She chewed her bottom lip. "And he was so kind and calm. If I'd thought he was getting any kind of thrill out of it, obviously it would have stopped immediately." She lifted a hand and rubbed her lip. "It was just such a relief." She sighed. "But then one day he just didn't show up. We tried to avoid all this"—she waved her hand at the cardboard boxes—"and managed about a week, but there was no way we could feed them all, let alone look after them as they needed. Martin was working a night shift when he came back to start taking care of it. He noticed the 500ml of Pentobarb was missing."

"Not before?"

"No, we keep separate supplies. There's 400ml down in the hospital area, and more up here, obviously. He'd taken the largest bottle and a box of syringes."

"How many animals could he kill with that?" Claire's question was careful, and once again Cass was grateful he had such a clever sergeant. This poor woman had enough to deal with already; she didn't need to know that her weakness might have helped get five women murdered. Not yet, at any rate.

"Recommended dose is 4ml per 10 kilos."

Cass did the sums. *Jesus Christ—how many women was this bastard intending to kill?*

"What was his name, Ms. Joyce? And have you got an address for him?" He'd probably have used a false name, but the address might give them something, even if he'd moved on already.

"Yes, of course, I should have said. His name was Solomon. Mr. Solomon. I've got the address in my office." She frowned a little as something dawned on her. "I never got his first name."

Cass's mouth drained dry. Mr. Solomon. *The Solomon and Bright Mining Corps.* He turned and stared back through the doorway, picturing the photograph of his parents standing in front of that sign. It had been taken thirty years ago. Could Bright and his partner *both* have sons who were somehow now linked? *Don't trust them*, that's what the caller, *Solomon*, had said. *They have their own agenda.* Don't trust who? The police? The Bank? This shadowy X-account organisation both Bright and Solomon had connections with?

"Something you want to share?"

Ramsey's question broke the moment and Cass looked up. For an instant he thought he saw pale yellow light shining at the corner of the other detective's eyes. *The Glow.* He blinked it away. What the fuck was going on? He could feel Christian, Bright, and now this Solomon winding themselves around him, tangling him in a web of murder and lies.

"No. It's nothing." He forced a thin smile. Kittens mewled at his feet. "I was just trying to figure out if I knew the name from somewhere. But no. Sorry." He shut the door firmly, hearing the lock click back into place, and pushed past Ramsey to catch up with the director.

"How old was he, Ms. Joyce, this Mr. Solomon?"

"Hard to say exactly. My gut instinct is to say about thirty, but really, he could be anywhere up to forty-five." She smiled a little. "He was a good-looking man. He had thick golden hair . . . but he had old eyes." They made their way back through the barrage of barking towards her office. "They say some people are old souls, you know that expression?" she added.

Cass shook his head.

"I've got a friend who believes in reincarnation; she said there are people whose souls have lived many times. If there are such people, then I'd say Solomon was one of them. He was a relatively young man, but he had the air of someone tired, and wise beyond his years."

"He had quite an impact on you," Claire said.

"Oh yes. He was quiet, but he spoke well—I got the impression that before the economy collapsed he must have had a very good job." She tilted her head reflectively. "He drew you to him, somehow. I wouldn't have given him the responsibility that I did if he hadn't had that certain something."

"Charisma?"

Sheena Joyce smiled a little wistfully. "Yes, I suppose that was probably it."

Cass registered Claire's quiet excitement as the director turned away to rummage through a filing cabinet. She was thinking of Hask's profile: over thirty, charismatic, intelligent. *Solomon and Bright.* Wheels within wheels. Solomon must have watched Bright organise the film to be sent to Cass, then left a body there, just to get at the other man. These two men were obviously playing some kind of game of their own, and he and his family were involved somehow. He didn't like it, not one bit.

"Ah, here we go." She handed the form over. "It's a Whitechapel address. Arbour Street. Shouldn't take you long from here."

Cass handed it back, but she shook her head. "I presume you're going to need it for your records. I know what I did was terribly wrong, and I imagine I'll lose my job over it." Her eyes clouded over and Cass knew her thoughts were back in the locked room in the cattery. "In many ways that will be a relief . . . but if you could try and keep the shelter out of things as much as possible . . ." She turned her head away, trying to hide her brimming eyes. "It's not the fault of the animals," she said softly. She tugged out a tissue and blew her nose, regaining her balance. "Right. I'd better see you out."

"I'll try my best, Ms. Joyce," Cass said, and he meant it. "I'll keep it as quiet as I can, but I can't promise anything." Unfortunately, he meant that too. If they closed this case, the papers would be tearing the world apart for the details.

The smile she gave him quite transformed her face, and Cass was relieved to see no unnatural light in the corners of her eyes. Ramsey's were normal again too. It was just psychosomatic, he told himself. You're tired and overwhelmed. There was no Glow. There never was. His dad had been deluded and that delusion had infected Christian. A long-buried memory rose in a dark corner of his mind but he crushed it before it could blossom into a thought and he headed out into the noise.

Dogs leapt at the wire mesh cage fronts, every one of them wagging their tail furiously and barking for attention. It was a huge relief when they stepped out into the sunshine, shutting the racket away. Ms. Joyce followed them down to the car park and waited as they found the Audi and pulled away. As her figure diminished in the rear-view mirror, she looked fragile, Cass thought. He hoped she wouldn't become another of Solomon's victims, destroyed in his wake rather than by his touch.

When they pulled up outside 54 Arbour Street, Cass looked up. Old habits. Tiles were missing on the roof and the whole façade could have used fresh paint and some pointing around the windows, just like the rest of the terrace. He could see why Solomon had come here. This was not the kind of area where you took the time to get to know your neighbours.

"God, what a dump," Claire muttered as she followed the two men past the overflowing black bin shoved against the wall in the tiny front garden. There'd been no phone number with the address, but five minutes' gruntwork from someone back at the station had got them the landlord's home number, and he'd agreed to meet them at the property. He said he needed to make a visit anyway. A couple of the tenants had complained that something was stinking in the drains. He sounded disgruntled. Cass didn't know what he was complaining about. He only lived five houses away. Perhaps it was just the prospect of having the police in his building that bothered him. Judging by the state of the place, the odd bit of ganga-smoking would be the very least of the sins taking place within those four walls.

Claire's phone rang as they watched a scruffy man dangling a large bundle of keys make his way towards them. It didn't take a genius to figure out he was the landlord.

"Sir?" Claire shut the phone and spoke quietly as they nodded their hellos and followed the irritated man inside. "That pay-as-you-go number?"

"Yeah?"

"It was part of a batch." She paused for effect. "Bought by The Bank."

He stared for a second, a ripple of excitement running through him. Everywhere he turned, something led him back to The Bank.

"Apparently, twenty sims have been stolen from their stock—they didn't even know until we called. They keep them in reserve for convenience."

Of course they do. "Make sure you find out who had access to them." He didn't hold out much hope; no one bothered much about stationery cupboards—who really gave a shit if a bunch of envelopes and Post-it Notes went missing? And while you might count in and out laptops and data storage devices, who would bother with sim cards? Still, it was another small step forward, and one more link to The Bank, and he was not going to bitch about that. He followed the landlord through the door.

Inside, the walls had been painted nicotine-brown, maybe to save worrying about stains. And it was apparent no one ever had: by the payphone someone had thrown something like coffee, leaving rings of darker colour that had never been wiped away and were now there forever.

"His room is on the second floor." Mark Manning's reedy voice irritated Cass almost as much as his poor décor choices did. "Dodgy, is he? He couldn't give me a reference but he gave me six months' rent in advance. Seemed a bit posh for here too. I thought he'd just fallen on hard times or been kicked out by the missus." He paused on the landing. "Don't you need a warrant or something?"

"I think it's likely your tenant is no longer here." Cass was sure of it. After stealing the drugs, Solomon wouldn't have stayed at the same address. It would have been too risky. Thus far everything their killer had done had been planned meticulously. "And I'm sure you want us out of your way as soon as possible. Some of your other tenants might not like the idea of having Old Bill lingering for any longer than we have to."

Manning's face tightened. "I've never had any trouble. My tenants keep themselves to themselves."

Cass figured the landlord and tenants had a happy blind-eye relationship. If Manning hadn't checked on Solomon in all this time, then he probably never came into the property unless it was to collect money. The state of the whole building told him the kind of person who'd be living here. Solomon could have been killing the women in the room and no one would have complained at the noise. The thought wasn't pleasant. This would be no place to die.

"I can't believe he's moved out and not asked for a refund." Manning sniffed. "Or at least bloody told me. I could have had a new tenant in here."

Cass smiled grimly to himself. Sounded as if the room might be just as Solomon had left it, rather than having any trace of him wiped away by someone else's life, as he'd feared. Not that he expected it to provide much, but you could never tell. They'd found Bradley through trace evidence and a police record. Maybe they'd come up with something here too.

The stairs, barely covered by a threadbare carpet, creaked as they climbed. The paint on the banisters might once have been white, but had faded to a dirty cream, flaking away to expose the wood; Cass tried not to touch it.

The first-floor landing had three doors leading off. From behind one came the steady thud of some hip-hop reggae street blend. Behind another, someone was shouting at a crying child. On top of all that was a vague smell that turned his stomach.

Cass tried to keep the disgust off his face, but Claire was having less success. Ramsey followed behind, staying in the background. It wasn't his case, and he knew better than to become involved. Once you were in, it was hard to get out, and Ramsey's bosses over at Chelsea wouldn't be happy with him putting think-time into Paddington's cases.

On the second floor, Manning rummaged through his ring of keys until he found the right one and slid it in the lock. He threw open the door. "It's all yours."

It was the stench that hit him first. Sweet and nauseous, and all too familiar.

"I think we've found the cause of the complaints." His head twisted away, seeking the stale air of the corridor that was fresh and cool in comparison to the damp warmth inside. Jesus. The small room contained a single bed along one wall, a tall cupboard made of some dark wood and a scratched pine chest of drawers. Almost next to the bed was a small breakfast bar of chipped Formica, with an old oven underneath. Behind that was a sink, with a precariously hung immersion heater above it. There was barely room to walk from the sink to the bed, and Cass wondered if it was even legal to rent it out like this—but he doubted Manning was aiming for clientele with prospects.

But none of that was what had made him catch his breath. His eyes dropped to the flies that covered every surface. They were scattered across the floor like mouse droppings and heaped on the furniture. There must have been hundreds of them. Thousands. *The Man of Flies.*

"God," Claire said behind him.

No, not God, Cass thought. Not God at all, just a fucked-up man.

"What the hell is that smell?" Manning said.

Cass didn't answer as he stepped carefully into the room. He was aware that he was crushing evidence beneath his feet, but it was impossible not to. There were too many husks of dead flies for him to avoid them. How had Solomon kept them in here? Had they started as maggots or eggs, and he'd just left them behind? What on God's good earth could they have fed on? The dead insects covered the windowsill and the kitchen area, too. He stared at the oven. It was set to fifty degrees. Low, but enough to fill the room with warmth if left for a few days. The oven was where the noise was coming from. A low buzzing. There were some flies in the room that were definitely still living. He stared at the greasy door. Something was rotting in there. He turned the oven off, but he left the door shut. *Save the best till last.* One thing was for certain—if the flies in the oven were alive and feeding on something, then it meant that Solomon had returned at some point recently to leave it there. For whom? Cass wondered briefly, before accepting the obvious answer: for them, of course.

He crouched down by the bed and, doing his best to ignore the dead flies, peered under it. "I've got something," he muttered, trying to hold his breath against the dusty stench that permeated the filthy fabric. He pulled out a pen and tried to jockey the notebook towards him until he was able to pull it out.

"What's that?" Manning frowned.

"Nothing of your concern." Cass smiled up at the irritating landlord as he took Ramsey's proffered cotton handkerchief. He carefully flicked through a couple of pages. There wasn't much in the book, just a series of numbers, account numbers, maybe, written neatly in blue ink, and then some pages of scribbles.

"So, what else did you know about this Solomon?" he asked, getting back to his feet. "Did he tell you anything that might give us an idea where he'd go?"

Manning twitched slightly. "I didn't talk to him much, only when he moved in. I didn't have to collect rent from him like I do with the others. All I know is that he said he used to work at The Bank."

Bingo. Cass looked over at Ramsey and smiled. "Maybe it's time to take that laptop back."

"But first maybe you should see what's cooking?"

As Cass did so the flies swarmed free, a great cloud that rushed past, myriad wings brushing his face, spreading the sweet rotten scent as they beat their way out into the corridor and away to freedom.

When Cass opened his eyes again the room was clear. At first he wasn't sure what the dead thing in the oven had once been. He held his breath and leaned forward, peering into the darkness until he could make out some tufts of fur on the maggoty skin, and the remains of one ear flopped forward.

Mr. Solomon had left them a puppy.

He despatched Manning to find Claire a cup of tea, which earned him a glare; there was no way she was going to be touching anything that grubby landlord had had his hands on. While the man was out of the way he quickly copied down the page of neatly printed numbers into his own notebook. There were twelve in all, and next to each was printed PASS or FAIL. He frowned as he wrote. Were these part of the tests Solomon had mentioned on the phone? There were only two passes in the twelve. Is that how their killer had judged people to "be found wanting"? He didn't recognise the notes that filled some of the other pages. It looked like poetry. He wrapped the book up in Ramsey's handkerchief and handed it to the sergeant.

"Once the forensic team are here, get this to the lab boys. Find out what all this shit is he's written in here. Looks like poetry. Get it to Hask too, this is probably his field. I want the report on my desk by the end of the day." He paused. "If Bowman's back then let him see it, but make sure we keep it—he can have a photocopy for the file. I'll be on the mobile."

He felt a bit of a shit for leaving Claire behind, but he had no choice. She could handle Manning, odious little prick that he was. Apart from his recent trip back to leave the poor puppy, Solomon had been gone for months, but the SOC boys should be able to pick up some trace evidence from the room—maybe it would tell them something, maybe it wouldn't, but they couldn't look sloppy on this case. DCI Morgan might scream at the mounting costs, but once the hacks were on it even he had to accept that all the angles had to be thoroughly—*publicly*—investigated.

The atmosphere wasn't exactly awkward without Claire in the car, but Cass could feel Ramsey studying him as he drove. He lit a cigarette and opened a window, glad to hear no disapproving noises.

"So," Ramsey finally said, "I know you probably don't want to talk about this, but I've still got a case of my own to close, and a DCI on my back about it. What do you think happened with your brother? And don't tell me you haven't got a theory, because I'm not that stupid."

"I've got a couple." Cass stared at the road and thought carefully about how much to share. "I think maybe he uncovered something he shouldn't have at work and someone shut him up for it."

"Like what?" Ramsey shifted in his seat. "Some kind of embezzlement? Did you find something I should know about in that laptop?"

"I don't know. I haven't figured that part out yet." It was an honest answer. Although Christian had obviously been digging around in The Bank's records, and he had discussed personal concerns with Father Michael, Cass couldn't believe that Bright and some mysterious sub-Bank organisation would have murdered Christian and his family in such an obvious way. It was too crass. And then there was what Solomon had said to him on the phone: that he was sorry about Christian's death; that it wasn't anything to do with him . . . Or *them*?

But neither could he believe that Christian had killed his own family. It just refused to ring true. He was missing something, and as much as Mr. Bright and Solomon were entwined with his own family's lives, this was about something different. He was sure of it.

"Just about everyone is into The Bank in some way or another—personal or business account, loan, mortgage, insurance—you name it, they've got it."

"I tried the laptop," Ramsey said, "and couldn't get into it. I take it you figured out his password?"

"Yeah—but it all looked straightforward to me." Cass didn't look at the other man. He wasn't about to start trying to explain hidden files on his family, or photos with people in them that couldn't be there. That was private business. That was an investigation for another time.

"What about the evidence against you?" There was nothing accusatory in his tone.

"That's more of a sticking point." Cass found that he didn't mind opening up at least a little to Ramsey. He liked him, and he had to talk to someone. "The only reason someone would want to do that would be to get me off a case, and the only one I'm working that I could think of was Jackson and Miller."

"But isn't that now solved?"

"So they say."

"You think there's more to it?"

Cass flicked the butt of his cigarette out into the street. "Let's just say that I'm making further enquiries. But whichever way I look at it, some person or persons unknown wanted me off that case, and they used the deaths of my brother and his family to make that happen."

Ramsey sighed deeply. "And there's only one way fingerprint and bodily fluids could have come to be where they did."

"Exactly. Someone's been paid to make me look dirty. And let's face it, it could be any number of people."

"Yep, it's the same all over. You can always find someone to do something for money, and these days it's even worse. In every nick I'd say half the coppers are bent double, rather than the little bit we all are." He paused. "Fuck. This whole thing is a mess."

"That's policing," Cass said. He didn't need Ramsey to elaborate; they'd be taking *bonuses* in Chelsea too. "How come you believe me?" he asked suddenly.

"Well, aside from your very convenient alibi," Ramsey said with a slight grin, "I just don't think you'd be so stupid as to have fucked your brother's wife without a condom, then gone back and shot them all and left a fingerprint on the gun while you were doing it."

Cass almost laughed out loud. "I'm glad my intelligence gets your vote, even if my morals don't."

"Think nothing of it." Ramsey smiled. "But seriously, it's the fingerprint that's saved you. Whoever did that was stupid. If they wanted you out of the way, for whatever reason, then the sex would have been enough. You could have denied it all you liked, but with your reputation, you'd have been suspended straight off. It wouldn't have looked good in the press if it got out. But the minute they put your fingerprint on the gun, it was a set-up. Even Bowman, who *really* doesn't like you, would have a hard time finding a reason for you to have done all that. Bang. You're in the clear."

He was right, it was a stupid mistake, and that normally meant that whoever had done it hadn't had much time to think or plan, but had worked fast. He gritted his teeth. Whoever it was, he'd get the bastard. Jackson and Miller seniors? Was it them—and if so, *why*? He had a good reputation, but he wasn't Sherlock Holmes, and he hadn't been anywhere close to finding answers in the shootings when Christian had died and he'd been set up.

He gritted his teeth and hoped Perry Jordan was working for him today. He wanted some fucking answers.

CHAPTER SIXTEEN

The Bank's London headquarters were in central London, overlooking the Thames. The SIS Building had, until four years previously, been the home of MI6, until, with terrorism on a sharp increase, both at home and all across Europe, the government decided it would be better if the secret service went back to being a little more secret, which coincided with The Bank's desire for a suitable site for its British and European headquarters. The Prime Minister and each of the ever-changing Chancellors had made a lot of noise about how good it would be for the world's new economic champion to be calling London home, and suddenly The Bank was setting up home in the SIS Building.

With hindsight, Cass wondered if maybe MI6 were pushed, rather than leaving of their own free will. Money corrupted, and the men who had put together The Bank would know that better than most. The building had state-of-the-art security, and while the Service would have taken some of it with them, all the wiring and structural work was already in situ, ready for cameras and card-swiping systems and rooms that needed top security clearances to enter. He thought again of the files Christian had copied. Maybe it was the men behind the men who founded The Bank who had secured the eviction of MI6. That kind of available funding could definitely talk.

Four women sat behind a long, sleek desk. The front panels were brushed glass decorated with black and silver, the colours synonymous with The Bank wherever in the world you travelled. Behind them was what looked like a room made of black glass, keeping the security men and the camera monitors neatly and very stylishly out of the way of prying eyes. To their left, the way to the lifts was blocked by a series of card-swipe machines and high clear plastic barriers. Not only did they look far more modern than the usual silver turnstiles, the gates were too high for anyone to leap over. On the right, several black leather sofas and armchairs were positioned around brushed steel tables. No one was sitting on them. They must have come at a quiet time—or maybe The Bank was so efficient that no visitor had to wait for long.

Only three or four minutes had passed since one of the women behind the desk had spoken softly into the phone when a lift slid open and a smartly suited Asian man stepped out. His hair was combed straight back, accentuating the fine features of his angular face. Behind him was a rather dumpy young woman whose blue skirt pulled too tightly across her hips. Her low heels clattered on the marble as she tried to keep up with the smooth stride of the man in front. The man exuded cool sophistication, but she was a bundle of nerves. Maya Healey didn't look like The Bank's type of employee—how the hell had she got a job here?

When they were standing in front of Cass, he could see that under her make-up, the young woman's eyes were red and puffy. He understood that look; he'd seen it on Clara Jackson and Eleanor Miller: these were eyes that had cried themselves out. Her foundation was flaking over the delicate sore skin, where she must have applied too much to cover it up. She kept her head down. The man smiled. His teeth were perfect.

"I see you found our laptop." His accent was straight from Eton or Harrow, but Cass caught the edginess of the gutter in the hardness of his smiling eyes.

"You must be Asher Red?" Ramsey said as he handed the case over. Cass stood slightly behind him. Ramsey had stayed out of his way at Limehouse; it was his turn now, to start with at least. "And Maya

Healey? As I said on the phone, we'd like to take a look at Mr. Jones' office."

"Of course." The grit in Mr. Red's eyes turned to stone.

"And we'd also like to look in his computer."

"You can, of course, see inside the late Mr. Jones' office. But his computer may be more of a problem."

Asher Red turned and with a flick of his wrist produced two clip-on Visitor badges from somewhere within his stylishly cut suit. He gave one to Ramsey and then one to Cass. They were bright red, as if even a visitor in the building could be perceived as some kind of danger. "Please place these where they will be visible. Your suit lapels would be best."

"Why might the computer be more of a problem?" Ramsey asked.

Asher Red nodded to Maya, who swiped her card to open the barrier. It slid open soundlessly into the one next to it: barely noticeable precision engineering that came at a cost.

Cass smiled at Maya as he walked through and she gave him a brief flicker of a grateful smile back. Her nails were chewed down. Asher Red probably didn't like that either.

"It's company policy to wipe an employee's computer account when they are no longer with The Bank. The accounts Mr. Jones was working on will still be in the system, of course, but I'm afraid all his personal files, including his email files, will have been deleted."

"You didn't think to check with us first?"

"Well, I didn't think it was necessary." Asher Red maintained his smile as the lift doors closed around them. "You did, after all, have his laptop. I presumed that you would have found all the information you required on that."

Cass cringed inside. Ramsey obviously hadn't told them who had the laptop—that would have made the whole investigation suspect, and open to accusations, should anything further come to light about Christian, Jess and Luke's deaths. He'd done Cass a huge favour by not coming after him for it, and Cass was only just realising how big a favour that was.

But before Ramsey could respond, Mr. Red said smoothly, "But of course, you wouldn't have had the necessary passwords." His smile was tight. "It will take our people some time to find them. Our laptops, especially those used by employees as highly valued as Mr. Jones, have very sophisticated security systems. The passwords are user-specific, unlike the desktops, whose passwords are logged."

Cass didn't look at the man. He didn't want the smug bastard to get even a hint that he had found a way into Christian's laptop.

Asher Red's fingernails were perfectly manicured, the white tips of each nail of identical length. He pressed a button for the eleventh floor. The buttons were in two banks of ten on the silver plate, with a gold oblong dividing them: an over-the-top design feature for a company that appeared to be all about understated elegance, Cass thought.

From the corner of his eye, Cass could see Ramsey's foot tapping. It was the only external sign of the irritation he was feeling inside, and for a moment Cass felt a cramp of guilt, but it passed. The Bank would have deleted Christian's account whether Cass had taken the laptop or not. That was just an excuse. And most of the information on the laptop was personal: Cass's business, no one else's.

"Miss Healey, you were Christian Jones' assistant, weren't you?" Ramsey asked. His voice was surprisingly gentle.

"That's right." She picked at the skin around her thumb with her forefinger.

"Well then, perhaps we could look at your computer files instead," Ramsey said. "Most of Mr. Jones' emails would have been cc'd to you, I presume? And you were responsible for typing his letters? So most of what we are interested in seeing will be on your account too. It's important that we get a feel for any work situations that might have been affecting him."

Maya's mouth moved silently and she looked at her boss. The lift doors opened onto the floor.

"I'm afraid I would have to ask permission from my superiors for that to take place," Mr. Red said as he waved them out and onto the thick black and silver carpet. "And I am afraid they are unavailable today."

"They are *all* unavailable?" For the first time Cass could hear a hint of irritation creeping into Ramsey's laid-back drawl.

Asher Red shrugged and led them past another reception desk and down the silent corridor. "It's often the way. The higher one reaches in an organisation, the fewer superiors one has. Ergo it becomes harder to have someone readily available to approve an important company decision." He smiled again. His eyes stayed cold. "I am sure it must be the same in the police force."

Cass figured that even if Asher Red had given a shit about what it was like in the police force, he certainly wouldn't consider Ramsey high enough in its ranks for his point to apply. He was a smug, smarmy bastard and his flash suit made Cass think of Bowman, even though this bloke's tailoring made Bowman's Armani look like Matalan seconds.

"I'll have to get on the phone and organise a warrant then." Ramsey smiled. "That will take the responsibility of decision-making away from you and your elusive superiors."

"Yes." Asher Red didn't miss a beat. "That would probably be for the best."

Cass could have punched him. Red obviously knew it would take them twenty-four hours to get a warrant—at the earliest. This wasn't a crime scene, there were no obvious murder suspects, and if a judge were to look at all the evidence, he would most likely still say it looked like a simple murder-suicide, and if warrants should be issued to look at anyone's files it should be Cass's. It was hard to reconcile this arrogant fucker with the emails sycophantically praising Christian's work. He doubted handing out praise to anyone other than himself came easily to Mr. Red or his type.

Email. The word lingered in his head as Asher Red opened a heavy, old-fashioned oak door. Cass clung on to the image and dug for its relevance in the mess of information tangled in his mind. There had been something in the emails he'd read on his brother's laptop that had got his attention before he'd become distracted by the photographs and the Redemption files. Christian had wanted some details on two accounts. His heart thumped slightly. He'd written the numbers down in his phone. What was their relevance? He gritted his teeth. He'd find out some way, but this was probably not the time or place to raise it, not without risking far too many questions about how he'd come to find the information.

"Come in. The office is exactly as Mr. Jones left it."

Cass bet it was: exactly as Christian had left it—but with all useful information removed. He was quite sure Asher Red had had his security goons deleting any scrap of useful information the moment news of Christian's death had come through, and Ramsey obviously knew it too. He didn't ask Red to leave, but he did smile and accept the offer of coffee from Maya.

At the nick coffee came from the vending machine either with sugar or without, but Maya gave them a list to choose from. Cass was tempted to ask if they had any instant, but that might be seen as childish. Not that Asher Red's behaviour was anything other than sophisticated childishness. He was stopping them doing their job simply because he could, and they all knew it. The reputation of the police was tarnished in some circles, but when it came to serious crime, they still worked their arses off to bring the bad guys to justice. And if they were making this request of any other company in the country, they'd be getting exactly what they'd asked for. Asher Red was making a point about power.

Cass idly wondered how powerful the slim man would feel with his perfect nose spread across his face.

He looked round the vast room that had been his little brother's office and couldn't reconcile it in his head. The last time he'd been anywhere Christian worked it had been a tiny, understaffed office overloaded with piles of paper. People bought their suits from Burton's, and dry-cleaned them twice a year, if they were lucky. This was a few years and a world away from that—shit, this was a world away from *everywhere*. His own cubbyhole of an office would fit into this and leave most of the room over. The size was emphasised by the lack of any excess furniture.

A large desk filled the far end. A sleek flatscreen monitor looked as if it were embedded into the wood, like it could be closed in much the same way as a laptop. A small pile of documents sat on the blotting pad in the centre. Ramsey pushed the large leather chair to one side and rifled through the papers. Cass scoured the floor for any sign of other furniture that might have been moved out, but the thick carpet showed no indents from a heavy filing cabinet or anything else. The Bank wasn't a big supporter of the paper trail, it appeared.

Maya brought in the coffees. Cass took his and wandered over to study the huge canvas that covered one wall. Paint splatters flew in all directions, and for an instant he saw only the blood that had sprayed all over his baby brother's dining room when his brains had been blown out. He flinched and turned away, half-expecting to see a pair of shiny black lace-ups daubed with crimson, but they were not there. He squeezed down a wave of grief, crushing it back into a small place deep inside.

Mr. Red had taken a seat in one of the two wing-backed chairs. They reeked of expensive leather. He crossed his legs carefully before sipping his espresso. Maya lingered awkwardly in the doorway.

"I'm very sorry about your brother, Detective Inspector," Asher Red said, "but I am surprised to see you here with Detective Inspector Ramsey. Surely you are not part of this investigation? Your presence here could be seen as something of an irregularity."

Cass smiled, and walked behind the desk. So Mr. Red knew who he was—but Cass had the upper hand. A pile of white business cards sat in a small box next to the computer screen. He picked one up. The card was richly textured, like the envelope Christian had left for him.

"Oh, but I'm here on another matter entirely, Mr. Red," he said as he slid the card into his top pocket. "I should have said." He grinned at the slight look of discomfort that flitted for a second across the man's face. "I just thought I'd let Detective Inspector Ramsey get his work done first."

Behind him, Ramsey yanked open a desk drawer with far more force than was required, as if to support Cass's point.

"And what would that business be?" Asher Red studied him. "Perhaps I can help you?"

"I want some information about an ex-employee of yours. A Mr. Solomon."

There was just the briefest tightening of fingers around the delicate china espresso cup. "Solomon? Do you have a first name?"

"He stopped working for you approximately three months ago. And no. I don't have a first name. But I'm sure your highly efficient computer system is capable of finding him."

Asher Red tilted his head slightly in a reluctant nod. "And might I ask what this is regarding?"

"No," Cass said. "You may not."

Mr. Red stared at him for a moment, his polite smile frozen on his face. "Just let me make a phone call and see what I can find out for you," he said eventually.

"Thank you."

Ramsey sighed. "If this office is exactly as Christian Jones left it, then I can't see how he did any work." He stared at Mr. Red, who had risen from the chair. "Your boys really did clear him out, didn't you? There's not even a photo of his family, just a bunch of stationery and an empty diary. Very efficient." He raised an eyebrow and turned to Christian's assistant. "But please do expect that search warrant, Ms. Healey."

Asher Red didn't even bother with a hint of an explanation or apology. "Let me take you downstairs then, if you're quite finished, and I'll search out that employment record."

He nodded at Maya. "Miss Healey, if you could clear these cups away, then you may continue your work."

She disappeared without even a murmured word of farewell. The three men rode the lift down to the ground floor without speaking.

They waited in the cool lobby, no doubt under the scrutiny of those hidden within the black glass box, while Ramsey rang through to Chelsea to start the paperwork for the search warrant. When he'd finished he looked at Cass, the closest to a glare he'd yet come. "If you found anything on that laptop of your brother's then you'd better use it wisely and carefully, and keep me in the loop."

Cass nodded, thinking of the numbers he'd stored in his phone. They were the only bits of information that he could imagine sharing with Ramsey, and he couldn't do that yet. Ramsey would go through the proper procedures, and until Cass knew who'd set him up, everything outside of the serial case was going to be kept private.

Asher Red appeared silently in the corridor. He scanned a printed-out sheet. "Yes, we did have a Mr. Solomon working here: David Solomon. A single man, according to our files. He worked with us on the merging of Abacus Entertainment into the Virginity Division of our corporations. He left about three and a half months ago." He looked up. "It appears he just rang in one day and said he was leaving. Some people find the pressure that comes with working at The Bank too much to cope with." He paused. "Perhaps that was part of what prompted poor Christian's actions."

"Can I see that?" Cass asked. He had no wish to discuss his brother with this odious bastard. All he wanted to do was break his nose, and then maybe throw him into the murky Thames outside.

"Certainly." He handed it over.

Cass scanned the sheet. The information on it was minimal, and there was no mention of any Solomon and Bright Mining Corporation. There couldn't be two families with this unusual surname linked to The Bank, which meant that what was printed here was probably unreliable.

"This Canary Wharf address—this is where he lived?"

"Yes, but the property belongs to the company." Mr. Red shrugged gracefully. "I understand another employee was assigned the living space as soon as Mr. Solomon moved out."

"That part of town isn't cheap. I don't recall Christian being offered a flash pad to move into."

"We expect a lot from our workforce, Detective Inspector, and we are very generous in return. Your brother was indeed offered company housing—and at a far more prestigious address than that one. He chose to stay in his own home. In return, we substantially reduced his mortgage payments each month."

"There's a lot missing from here. Bank details, prior addresses. Not even his National Insurance number."

"I have released the information I can give you without first—"

"—without first getting your superiors' permission," Cass finished for him, and grimaced.

Mr. Red smiled again. "We understand each other."

"One more thing. A pay-as-you-go sim card that was one of a batch stolen from this company has been used to make calls we believe may relate to a crime. Where do you keep these items?"

"Ah yes. I believe someone mentioned this earlier today. Each department has its own supply centre. The sim cards were taken from Mergers."

"The department that Mr. Solomon worked for?"

"Yes." Mr. Red relinquished the word almost unwillingly. It was the first piece of solid information he'd actually provided.

Cass stared at him. "Well, thank you so much for all your help." He looked over at Ramsey. "Although I'm sure we'll be seeing you again, aren't you, Detective Inspector?"

"Oh, without a doubt. Just as soon as that warrant comes in."

They didn't bother with formal goodbyes, instead ignoring Asher Red's proffered hand and heading back to the car. Clouds had covered the sun and the breeze coming in from the river made Cass shiver. There was more to David Solomon than just some office exec who had burned out. Cass had seen the Redemption file. He'd seen the photos of Bright with his family. And Solomon had laughed at the mention of that name. This employment record was a fake; whoever Solomon was, he was far more intrinsically linked with The Bank than Asher Red was letting on. Cass thought about that smug bastard for a moment. Was it possible that he didn't even know the record was a dummy? His brain itched for answers.

He drove from under The Bank's shadow, he and Ramsey both lost in their own frustrated thoughts. He needed to get back inside the building unsupervised to find more information on Solomon, and he needed to know more about these two accounts that Christian had pulled out. And he could think of only one way to do that. But first, they had to get back to the office.

Bowman was still at the hospital. Either they were running some major tests on him, or even policemen with suspected poisoning and access to NHS couldn't move to the front of the queue. Out in the Incident Room there was still a lot of activity, one person marking up all the new information on the board as others talked quietly or manned phones. The end of the room that had been dedicated to the Jackson and Miller case was silent; someone had already started dismantling the board. He ground his teeth together. How could anyone actually believe that Bowman had managed to get some kind of shitty gang war story out of Macintyre after one interview when Cass hadn't after days of grilling the Irishman and his known associates?

"Sir?" Claire stood in the doorway. "So far no luck with people recognising our victims over in Covent Garden, but we've got a list of places that are open to the public that they might have all gone to."

Cass scanned down the sheet. There were several cafés and restaurants, a church, the rock venue, the Opera House itself, and a number of pubs. It wasn't a short list and most of the locations were not the sort where you would notice a new face or an occasional visitor. Covent Garden was filled with strangers most days. They probably had more chance of catching Solomon before they figured out how he selected his victims.

"Well, if we've got the manpower, then keep them on it. I'm not too hopeful, though." He paused. "Any news on Josh Eagleton?"

"No change," Claire said. "I rang them about an hour ago. They say they'll know better after this initial twenty-four-hour period if there's likely to be any permanent brain damage."

The kid's message played over in Cass's head and he kicked himself for not taking the call. Something Eagleton had noticed had freaked him out, and he could only hope the kid recovered so he could share it. He made a mental note to find time, and a reason that didn't look suspect, to talk to Farmer and get the breakdown of that day's events. It wouldn't be tonight, though. This evening would be all about getting back inside The Bank.

"What about the notebook?"

"They've got prints from it and are searching the database. So far, nothing. The words are from *Paradise Lost*. Hask has the notebook now and he is going through the individual quotes, as well as seeing what he can get from the handwriting. That guy really is the expert's expert." She paused. "It's strange that Solomon left it behind, though, when he was so careful to clear everything else out."

The same thought had occurred to Cass. "Maybe that's what the puppy was for. To make sure if we didn't get there of our own accord, someone in that building would smell it and report it. Hask says he's clever. He'd paid up front and it wouldn't have taken a genius to see that the landlord was a lazy bastard who was hardly going to be checking his tenants were happy every five minutes. Maybe we've found everything exactly when he wanted us to." He shrugged. "And on top of all that, who knows what makes this one do what he does? Sure as fuck, not me. Maybe he was testing us. He seems to like tests, this guy."

"I've got something else strange for you. I just had SOC on the phone. I asked them to look out for blond hairs—Sheena Joyce said he was blond, so I figured it would save some time."

"Good thinking. Well done."

"Well, the problem is"—and Claire shook her head, bemused—"they haven't found any."

"Nothing?" Cass stared. Hair was normally the most abundant trace evidence found. The average person shed a hundred hairs a day, and in a dirty bedsit they should have been everywhere.

"None that would fit the description. They've found dark hair, and some long blonde hairs with dark roots. None the right length to be our man's."

"But that's simply not possible!"

"That's what I said to SOC. If he'd cleaned the room of his own hair, then surely they wouldn't have found any other hairs under the flies or in the bedding." She paused. "They said that was our problem."

"Charming."

"Maybe he was wearing a wig," Claire suggested.

It was a possibility, but Cass didn't buy it. Sheena Joyce would have noticed. They didn't make wigs that good, even for the movies.

"And just to add to the confusion, apparently there are no pupal cases in the room. There are in the oven, but none outside of it."

"Pupil cases?"

"Not pup*il* Pup*al*. It's what the flies hatch out of. If he'd had them there growing on something from eggs, the flies would have left these small dark shells behind."

Cass had a vague recollection of Farmer talking him through the life cycle of a fly when he'd first come onto the case, but it had been pushed aside by more important information. "And there weren't any of these cases in the bedsit?"

"No. It's like the flies just appeared, and died. Or maybe he brought them in already dead and scattered them there."

"Perhaps they're part of the message. He's left eggs on the victims; maybe this and the notebook are a message to us. The dead flies are the opposite end of the cycle. Maybe he's saying something different to us. Maybe the dead ones represent him finishing something. Get the SOC photos over to Hask. That's his department."

He shut the door behind her and after a moment pulled out Christian's business card from his top pocket. His brother's name was typed in a small, elegant font and had no title underneath it. Having seen his office, that didn't surprise Cass much. Christian was probably too high up in the company to have just one title. Underneath it was Maya's name, and the title Personal Assistant, and under that was a number. He dialled it.

"Maya Healey." It was a soft, sweet voice. The kind that oozed "Victim."

"It's Cass Jones."

There was a pause that suggested that if she hadn't been such a polite person she would have hung up. As it was, she just let out a breathy, sharp sigh. It took Cass less than five minutes to persuade her to meet him after work for a drink to talk about Christian. She didn't want to, but he pulled at her heartstrings until she said yes, he could pick her up round the corner from work when she finished. She said she finished at six-thirty. Cass decided he'd be there at six, just in case she let her obvious anxiety get the better of her and decided to flee a little earlier.

With the phone still in hand, he chewed his bottom lip. "Fuck it," he muttered, and dialled his home number. There was no one there.

After a moment he tried Kate's mobile. The phone rang out and just as he'd given up, she finally answered.

"What do you want, Cass?"

He could hear her sniffing loudly at the other end. Surely she couldn't still be crying about Christian and Jessica?

"I just wanted to—"

A siren wailed loudly in his ear, cutting his sentence off. What did he want to do? Talk to her? Make everything right? Come home? Were either of them capable of that? Another siren joined the first and it was a long minute before it was quiet enough for them to speak.

"I wanted to check you were okay." It sounded feeble. Shit, it *was* feeble.

"This isn't the right time, Cass. I can't talk now." She sniffed again. "I don't want to talk." Her breath hitched. "It's all your fault. I can't sleep and it's all your fault. If you hadn't . . ." Her sentence tailed off.

"If I hadn't what?" She sounded so angry, and it tugged at some place inside him.

"It doesn't matter," she sighed, the fight gone from her as quickly as it had flared. "I've got to go."

She didn't even wait for him to say goodbye before hanging up. Cass stared at the receiver and thought for a second about calling her back before replacing it in the cradle. Even if he did, she wouldn't answer. He needed to concentrate on the things he could actually do something about. Kate wasn't one of them right now.

He flicked on the computer and typed *Paradise Lost* into the search engine, then scrolled through the results to find an example of the text. His eyes moved over the words, but he took nothing from them. Fucking poetry. He'd hated it at school, and it still left him cold. He navigated away and browsed through the many sites that claimed to explain it as the story of Satan and his followers and how they fought God and were cast down from Heaven. He scrolled through, skim-reading for ten minutes or so. His dad wouldn't have liked this. For at least part of the text Satan was portrayed as some kind of hero taking on a despotic God, before creating Pandemonium out of Chaos. The last word rang a bell and he thought of the music that had been playing when

poor Carla Rae had been found. Hadn't Hask said it was called something to do with chaos? Well, he didn't need the profiler to tell him that
David Solomon clearly had some issues with organised religion that he
was addressing in his own dark, perverse way.

The later sections of the poem focused on Adam and Eve and their
eviction from Paradise, but it was all heavily worded and nothing leapt
out at him. After scanning through the notes on the screen he shut the
computer down. He'd seen enough. Analysing it in any detail was
Hask's job; he was an eminently better person to do it than Cass.

He went into the station database and searched for the most recent
Macintyre interview. He turned the volume down low before clicking
play.

"Interview commenced at 11:45 a.m. Those present: Samuel Macintyre, Detective Inspector Gary Bowman and Detective Sergeant Mat
Blackmore." Blackmore's voice was tinny through the small speakers
on either side of the screen. Cass listened as Bowman took over, firing
questions at the gangster, demanding answers. Papers shuffled and
Blackmore announced that DI Bowman was showing the suspect a series of photos of the dead boys. It was all routine stuff, and it had all
been done by Cass himself over the course of the previous two weeks.
Then came the application of pressure, the threats that the police would
be like a second skin on Macintyre's arse until he had no businesses left
if he didn't tell them what the fuck had happened that afternoon.

Bowman moved on to the subject of Artie Mullins, but not in the
way Cass had expected. Instead of pushing the blame onto the rival
crime lord, Bowman hinted that if Macintyre didn't give them something to go on, then they'd make sure that Artie heard that Sam was
implicating him in the attempted hit. It was a good tactic, Cass gave
him that, but it wasn't enough to make Macintyre suddenly give up the
info that he might have been set up over a dispute with some Chechens—
which was exactly what he did next. And then to suddenly drop the
names of two villains who had admitted they'd been conned into revealing his plans for the day? None of it rang true. It was all too slick.

For a start, if Macintyre thought some of his own men had been
dumb enough to almost get him killed, they wouldn't be walking around,

let alone be able to come in and give statements. They'd be fucking lucky if they got away with just having their kneecaps smashed. It was far more likely that their bodies would be washing up on some Thames mudbank, bloated and rotting. People like Macintyre dealt with their own shit. They didn't hand it on a plate to the police.

He tapped his fingers against the desk in frustration. He could see why the DCI and his superiors were going along with it. Everyone was screaming for an end to this case, and Bowman had delivered it. Macintyre walked away, no doubt some poor Chechen fucker would turn up dead from some kind of "accident," Bowman could close the case, and the whole thing would go away, with no one ending up in prison and everyone in pocket. It was shit. He played the interview again. Something else was bugging him, but even after listening through it twice more, he couldn't place it.

It was only when he got in his car to head back to The Bank to meet Maya Healey that he realised what was wrong. It was the timing. Blackmore gave the start time of the interview as 11:45 in the morning. It didn't fit. When Claire had rung him, he'd been driving down to the house and it had only just gone eleven, and she'd said that Macintyre was already in the interview room. He pulled too fast out of the car park, almost colliding with a Panda coming the other way. Without even waving an apology, he steered into the road. The fuckers. They used that first forty-five minutes to set up with Macintyre how the recorded interview would proceed, and then started the official interview afterwards. Dusk was creeping over London, light and dark fighting for supremacy of the sky. He thought of the interview, and Bowman, and his own life. Maybe that grey area was all any of them could hope for, but if Perry Jordan came back with something on either Jackson or Miller, then Detective Inspector Bowman was going to regret trying to clean up too soon.

He parked up in one of the side streets, fed the meter with a ridiculous amount of money and leaned against the corner wall, his tall frame swallowed up by the shadows of the encroaching night. Although the

SIS Building was most dramatic when seen from across the river, Cass thought the rear view, with its sharp, angular lines, was equally impressive.

His eyes moved upwards, taking in the sleek slash of steel against the black backdrop of the fallen night, juxtaposed with the shining glass windows, lit from within. He counted up the floors to the eleventh, where Christian's office sat empty, waiting patiently for a new executive to fill it. His eyes drifted upwards again and then he frowned. He counted again from the floor to the top. The numbers were wrong. The lift had buttons for twenty floors. He was tallying more than that. He checked twice more. The count came back the same each time. Even if he took out a couple for the computer system base and archives, there would still be more than the twenty floors numbered in the lift. Why would they have floors that weren't accessible? Was there a separate lift, or a staircase that he hadn't seen? It didn't make sense. He breathed quietly, his brain whirring.

Buildings were something that he understood. In the black months after Birmingham, he'd spent a lot of time studying architecture. He had needed the solidity of buildings, the reality of them, and he couldn't shake that last instruction, to "look up." His brow furrowed. Maybe when the place had been MI6 HQ they'd needed some separate floors for security purposes. The question was: what was The Bank using them for now?

He was still staring upwards when he realised the plump figure of Maya Healey was about to scurry past. She jumped slightly as he reached out of the gloom and touched her arm, and even when she realised who it was, her face stayed tight with tension. She didn't start to relax until they were sitting in a pub around the corner from her home, several safe miles from her place of employment. He couldn't blame her. He was quite certain Mr. Asher Bastard Red would not be impressed to learn she was meeting the troublesome policeman away from his watchful gaze.

"Thanks for meeting me." Cass slid the large glass of white wine across the table to her. She'd asked for a Diet Coke, but he'd persuaded her that they should have a drink for Christian. She hadn't argued. Cass wondered if Maya had ever argued with anyone in her life. He doubted it.

A smile flickered briefly as she clinked her glass quietly against Cass's pint mug. "You don't look like Christian," she said and a flush mottled her neck, as if perhaps she should have started the conversation with a more expected nicety.

"We weren't really very similar, in either looks or personality. I think he was the better man—in both departments," Cass said, a little surprised at himself for revealing that.

"He was a good man." Her smile stretched sadly. "He was a very good man. I shall miss him terribly." Her eyes flickered across his. "It must be awful for you. I can't even imagine."

Cass nodded awkwardly. "That's why I wanted to talk to you. To understand his life better. Did you work with him ever since he joined The Bank?"

"Oh no, I worked with him before then." She took another sip, the alcohol or the mention of Christian relaxing her slightly. She was like a nervous cat creeping ever so slightly closer to an offered treat. "I was his assistant in his last job, when he was at McGowan's." She leaned across the table slightly. "When he was asked to join The Bank, he insisted that I come too. I would never have got a job there otherwise." Her face twisted bitterly. "I'm not their type."

Cass didn't comment. There wasn't anything he could say. Timid, she might be, but he doubted she was stupid. She was right: she probably wasn't their type, but maybe one day she'd realise that that wasn't necessarily a bad thing. There were far worse things to be than ordinary. He smiled.

"Well, Christian obviously valued you highly, and that's worth more to me than The Bank's opinion."

The flush rose higher on her neck and her eyes darted downwards. Cass swallowed a mouthful of beer. "Did you notice anything strange about Christian recently? Did he talk to you about anything that might have been bothering him?"

A hand fluttered to her neck and the tightness formed again, wrinkling the thin skin around her eyes as they narrowed.

Cass refused to drop his own eyes and let her off the hook. "Please, Maya. I'm his brother. I'm just trying to understand all this. He tried to speak to me and I wasn't there for him, and now it's haunting me." It was the truth, although Cass thought she'd run a mile if he mentioned the crimson drops on black lace-up shoes, but something must have resonated with her.

She took another swallow of wine.

"He did change. After Luke got sick."

"What happened?"

"He wanted to see the results of the medical tests and talk to the experts. The Bank insisted on treating him in their own centre, which they never did for me when I had to have my gall bladder removed." Again the bitterness threatened to twist her plump sweetness into something mean. "I know Luke's better now . . ." Her breath hitched as she realised the awful irony of her words, but Cass just nodded at her to continue. "At the time your brother was really worried."

Cass had a vague memory of Kate talking to Jessica on the phone, and him waving away the silent suggestion that maybe he should talk to Christian. He wasn't good with illness. He couldn't cope with it. It was better that Kate handled it.

"It turned out to be anaemia, didn't it?" he said. "It was treatable."

"Yes, but at first they were worried that it was leukaemia. It was awful. Christian said that Jessica's parents had both died young, from blood-based cancers, and of course it played on their minds that Luke had somehow inherited the potential for it."

Cass nodded, encouraging her to continue while he tried to ignore the pangs of guilt that were tearing at his heart. How had he missed all this? How had this little fat woman supported Christian more than he ever had?

"Anyway," she said, "I think he did some research into the doctors' names that were on the reports, but he couldn't find anything out about them. He wanted to get a second opinion from a specialist at

Charing Cross, but it caused quite a fuss and it never happened. *They* wouldn't allow it."

Cass wondered if she realised that her voice had dropped to almost a whisper, even though there was no one close to them in the quiet pub.

"He didn't tell me what went on, but you know how it is in an office." She shrugged. "It's easy to overhear the odd thing. Even in a place like The Bank, you just can't help it sometimes. From what I could make out, I think he was told that there would be no second opinions, and that there was nothing to worry about. I sensed he was being pressured to feel grateful and not rock the boat. It didn't stop him though. He tried to make an appointment for Luke through the private practice, but they wouldn't do it. They said they had no appointments for at least six months."

She stopped to take a larger sip of her wine. She sounded more confident now. "Christian didn't believe them. He thought they'd been told not to give him an appointment, and he couldn't understand why."

"Did he tell you this?"

"Yes, one night after work. When we were at McGowan's, we'd quite often go out for a quick drink when we were done. We didn't do it so often after the move, but about three months ago we did. Maybe a bit longer than that, I'm not sure. Luke was doing okay and the medicine seemed to be working, but Christian was obsessing about the way the whole thing had been handled. I'd noticed he was more agitated. He'd started to question instructions, and he was staying a bit later, digging around in the computer for God only knew what. I think to start with he was looking for the records of Luke's medical costs, but I think it went beyond that after a while. I think he was trying to understand The Bank better."

She peered at Cass over her glass, making sure he was following. He was. "He'd never been sure why they'd headhunted him in the first place. I told him it was because he was brilliant with figures, which he was, but I think he convinced himself that there was something else going on." She paused. "I think he was getting a little paranoid." The blotches on her neck flared red at her own disloyalty.

"Anyway, out of the blue about two months ago, he was told he was going on some kind of management weekend course. I didn't know any of the details, which I found odd, as I was his personal assistant, but sometimes they're just like that at The Bank. What I found stranger was that no one else seemed to be going—even Mr. Red wasn't invited. Christian thought maybe his opposite numbers from the other headquarters across the world would be there, but I never found out."

"Didn't he tell you when he got back?"

"No." She shook her head, visibly upset. "He changed after that. He didn't really talk to me about much any more. He just withdrew. He was quieter. He still stayed late, and I'm sure he was still doing his own research into the company, but he didn't open up to me. He looked tired, and then he began taking long weekends. I wondered if maybe Luke was ill again, but when I asked, he always said he was fine. After a while, I just stopped asking if he was okay, because it was pretty clear that whatever was bothering him, he didn't want to talk to me about it." Her eyes brimmed with tears, but she carefully wiped them back. "Maybe I should have pushed harder. Shown him how much I cared."

Cass realised that Maya had been a little bit in love with Christian. He wondered if his brother had even noticed. Probably not.

"You couldn't have known. And if anyone should have been there for him, it should have been me." He paused, giving her time to collect herself. "There is one thing you could help me with though."

She looked up.

"Just before he died, Christian asked you to find some information out for him about two accounts. He seemed to think that there was something slightly wrong about the transfers, I think?"

Maya looked at him blankly and he pulled his phone out and found the numbers. He jotted them down on a piece of scrap paper, along with his own phone numbers, and slid it across to her. "It was in his emails to you. I saw them on his laptop."

"I'm sorry, but I don't remember. We deal with so many different accounts."

"Could you have a look for me? Something about these two had obviously bothered Christian. And I just want to make sure that there's nothing suspicious about them."

"Okay," she said, "if Christian had asked me for the details then I'll have them to hand somewhere." The wine was obviously making her braver. "But tomorrow I'm in a meeting with Mr. Red. It might be the afternoon before I can get back to you."

"That's fine." Cass smiled. "I guess I'd better make sure you get home safe. If you need the loo before we go, I'll keep an eye on your bag."

"I guess I can trust you." She smiled back at him. "You are a policeman, after all."

He waited until she'd disappeared around the corner before unzipping the large leather purse and rummaging inside it until he found the pass that she'd tucked into the inner pocket. Bingo. He quickly tucked it into his jacket and replaced the bag exactly as it had been. When he was done he'd drop the pass in the doorway on his way out, try to minimise the trouble she might get into. With any luck she would persuade herself that it must have fallen out of her bag somehow. He was abusing her trust, but he didn't feel that bad. It was in a good cause—and after all, he'd done much worse in his time.

Even though it was nearly eleven, there were still plenty of lights blazing out from the building. The Bank, with all its global interests to manage, was a company that obviously didn't believe in sleep. Cass kept his head down slightly as he walked with brisk efficiency into the foyer. He gave the girl behind the desk a quick, confident smile which she returned with impersonal professionalism before returning to whatever was occupying her on the small computer screen.

Maya's pass let him through the clear barriers and he headed towards the lifts, half-expecting armed security guards to leap out of the stylish black central office and drag him out of the building. The heels of his shoes sounded louder against the marble than they had earlier, as if the building was aware of his illegitimate presence, even if the security team hadn't yet noticed him. He waved the card again to call the lift and the doors slid open immediately. Inside, he pressed the button for the eleventh floor and wondered where in the panelling the security cameras might be. He stayed facing straight ahead. There was no point in worrying. If they decided to double-check if Maya Healey had been in the building, he was sure there would be no shortage of cameras showing his face. What he'd do then—well, he didn't yet know. All that mattered right now was to get into the computer system and see what information on Bright and especially Solomon he could find. If he did find anything, then maybe the commissioner wouldn't give a shit that he'd entered the building unauthorised. Or at least he could hope as much. Right now, his career wasn't an issue. He just wanted answers.

The quiet corridor was softly lit by silver spotlights embedded in the ceiling, and Cass hoped that the lack of any noise meant that all those who worked in this section had headed home for the night. He didn't imagine that there were too many people with offices up here. There were few doors breaking the antique white walls, maybe six on either side. He made his way carefully to what had been his brother's office. The door was open and he went in, closing it behind him. For a moment in the gloom he thought he saw a figure seated behind the desk, one dark arm rising to mimic making a phone call, but as he flicked the switch on the wall there was only the chair pushed in close behind the vast desk. No Christian. Just an echo of a memory.

Aware that his intrusion could be noticed at any time, Cass flipped open the lid of the embedded computer and hit the power button. The screen lit up immediately and demanded a password. He typed in the number seventy-four and hit enter. Nothing happened. He tried again, this time with his own name. Again, nothing happened. Shit. The dawning realisation of how stupid he'd been slowly hit home. They hadn't just wiped Christian's personal files from the system; it looked like they'd wiped the whole computer clean. Of course they had. Why wouldn't they?

He thought of Maya Healey and the way he'd stolen her pass so thoughtlessly, and all for nothing, and then he looked at the pass again. Maybe it still had some use. He closed the screen down and went back into the corridor, carefully trying each door as he passed it, hoping that the plastic rectangle would open Maya Healey's office when he found it. He'd seen that glimpse of love in her eyes earlier. If he was right, and if he could get to her computer, he'd be willing to bet she'd used his brother's name as her password. Finally, the small panel next to one heavy wooden door flashed green. He smiled. The expression didn't last. He turned the handle, but the door refused to budge. It was only when he peered closer, swearing quietly under his breath, that he realised there was a second lock: a good old-fashioned one that required a key. Bollocks. Whatever they did on the eleventh floor, they obviously didn't want anyone unauthorised getting in.

With nowhere else to go and his mood darkening, he recalled the lift. He'd fucked up big time; he'd just not thought the whole thing through properly. How the hell had he thought he was just going to waltz into The Bank and get into their system, simple as that? It had been fucking stupid. He pressed the ground-floor button and the machine slid into silent action.

He was still silently cursing his own stupidity when the lift eased to a halt a few seconds later. He frowned. The lit button in the row above the double doors read five. His guts sank an inch. Great. Not only had he entered the head office of the world's biggest financial institution under false pretences, and attempted—very badly—to hack into their computer system, but now he was stuck in the fucking lift. It was almost laughable. Whatever was left of his career was creeping away.

The light on number five went out and a breath later the machine's engine whirred. The lift was going up again. In the panel against the wall the ornate middle section that had jarred with him earlier in the day glowed green at its edges, as if a light underneath it had switched on. Was that some kind of concealed control button? But he hadn't pressed it. Cass jabbed his finger on the ground-floor button, trying to override whatever command the machine was following, but the round disc remained grey. His heart thumped. Wherever this lift was going, he was along for the whole ride.

Finally, it stopped. The green light behind the panel changed to a pale pink and the doors slid open. Cass's hand automatically reached for the ground-floor button again, hoping to get the doors closed and moving again before anyone on the other side could either get in or recognise him, but he paused. There was no one waiting to get in, and as he looked out, he felt his feet moving forward. This wasn't a floor like the others. This was very different indeed. He stepped out of the lift. Maybe his trip to The Bank wouldn't be in vain after all.

The wood beneath his feet shone cherry-red with age, and it absorbed his footsteps almost as well as the carpet on Christian's floor. To his right, beyond the low chesterfield sofas and armchairs that made a lounge from the middle section, rose a wall of books, their spines red and green and blue; books from an age ago that had only their titles embossed in gold on the front, to encourage readers to open them. Alongside the bookcase, a wide spiral staircase of burnished bronze led up to a second floor that was swallowed in darkness. His mouth dried.

Pools of light shone out from various lamps creating a subdued, shadowy atmosphere so different from the sharp business floors below. Were they below? Or maybe they were above. Cass realised he had no idea exactly where in the building this place was. The heart of it, that's where he was. Even through his shoes he could feel the quality of the vast rug that stretched over to the far wall, the pattern in reds and creams looking to his untutored eye like a vague blend of Oriental and Middle Eastern characters. Heavy velvet drapes the colour of claret hung from the ceiling to the floor, covering what Cass could only imagine would be a bank of glass windows from which most of London could be seen. He turned to his left. Two thick wooden doors framed an inset modern fire where blue and yellow flames flickered from the stones sitting within the square steel frame. It was the only thing Cass could see that looked like it belonged in the present century.

He took a step closer and peered at the small bronze plaques attached to each door. His heart stopped and for a few seconds silence reigned completely, both within the network of his veins and in the stillness of the room. *Mr. Bright* was embossed in black on one, and *Mr. Solomon* in matching writing on the other. His heart burst back into life. *Solomon and Bright*, with offices here in the heart of The Bank . . . His mouth was dry, but his palms leaked hot sweat as he stepped to his left and pushed open the doorway into Mr. Solomon's room. He stared.

It was a far cry from the filthy bedsit where they'd found the flies and the notebook. A thick red carpet, so dark it was almost as black as clotted blood, covered the wooden floor. A vast desk was the main centrepiece of the room, behind which sat three large plasma screens, side by side on the wall, their screens black, dead. The desk was cleared and the waste paper bin empty. On a low table in the corner sat a huge globe of faded yellow, the map lines of the world drawn in ink a hundred years or more before. A vast painting hung on the left-hand wall, and Cass stared. It was beautiful, and ignorant as he was about art, he knew without a doubt that it was the original.

In the gloom, the paint appeared almost luminescent, the pale skin of the recumbent man like marble. The naked figure lay on one thick wing, and an angry eye peered over the raised arm that hid its face. Ghostly winged figures filled the sky above where this creature lay on the burned earth. Cass stared at it, for a moment all thoughts of Solomon and Bright forgotten.

"I think I shall have that moved into my office."

Cass's skin almost lifted from his body as he jumped at the sudden intrusion of sound. *What the fuck?* He turned to see a silver-haired man standing at the top of the spiral staircase.

"It's too good to just hang there with no one to see it." The man's feet tapped out a quiet rhythm on the metal rungs as he came downstairs. "Although, who knows? Perhaps we'll find someone to take over Mr. Solomon's position soon enough."

He reached the bottom and smiled at Cass, his perfect teeth gleaming white in his tanned face. Cass understood what Adam Bradley had meant when he said there was "just something" about Mr. Bright. He was shorter than Cass, and thicker around the middle, but there was an air of contained danger and energy in his confidence.

Cass stayed where he was.

"Mr. Bright, I presume?"

Again the flash of that smile. "I'm impressed with you, Cass." On the other side of the room, Mr. Bright folded his arms. "You've found us quickly."

"As far as I was aware, the lift brought me here. I didn't push the button."

"I was speaking in a more general sense. Of course, I brought you *here*. But I thought you'd earned it."

Cass didn't like the tone of amusement. It made him feel like a child, and he hadn't been one of them in a long time. There was a familiar twinge in his jaw as his teeth ground together. He wouldn't bite back. If this man underestimated him, then all the better. Still, he couldn't shift the unease from the pit of his stomach; this man looked identical to the person in the photo with his parents, far beyond what you'd expect from even the most similar father and child; this Mr. Bright was an exact replica of the one his father had known.

Questions filled his head and he spat out the only one he could form coherently. "What the fuck is going on?"

Mr. Bright's laugh was like hot water on ice. "You wouldn't believe me if I told you."

"Try me."

"No." The laugh hissed into a soft sigh, and for the first time there was just the hint of age around the man. "I think I'll just keep guiding you until you get there for yourself. I'm not in a hurry. Not yet." He pulled a remote control from the pocket of his expensive suit and pressed a button. The curtains slid away and he walked over to the vast window that looked down over the city. "Some people like the river view best," he said. "I prefer to see life." He paused for a long moment. "You've always fought it."

"Fought *what*?" *With you,* Bright had said. Who else had he tried to lead?

"Fate. Destiny." He didn't face Cass, but his reflection shone in the glass.

"There is no fate. There are only choices."

Even reflected in the glass Bright's teeth sparkled. "No, Cass, in that you're wrong. There are rarely accidents or coincidences." He turned. "Not for someone like you. You've always refused to see it. In many ways I've admired that in you."

Cass tried to keep up, his brain analysing each word and phrase. *Always?* How much did this man know about him? He remembered the figures in the Jones folder on the Redemption file. There had been money allocated in there for surveillance. Had this bastard been watching him? For how fucking long? And why? Were there films somewhere of his marriage as it slowly crumbled? A grainy shot filled his head: two boys dying in a busy street. The cold fingers were back and the rest could wait. This man had information he needed.

"Why did you send me the film?"

The slightest shrug. "I wanted you to see it."

"Why?"

"That's for you to figure out." Mr. Bright leaned over a box on the coffee table and pulled out a cigarette. He lit it, the sound a snapped twig in the brief silence. Cass fought the urge to smoke one of his own. He didn't want this bastard seeing he was unnerved.

"I'm enjoying watching you work," Mr. Bright continued. "Don't spoil it by demanding answers. Perhaps you should see this as a kind of test." He smiled. "And it's not one I'm expecting you to fail. I have high hopes of you, Cassius. We all do."

"Isn't that what Solomon is doing when he kills these women? Some kind of test? Who's he testing? Me?"

"Mr. Solomon, unfortunately, I cannot account for. He's become . . ." He hesitated, then said, "He's become something of a liability. He thinks he's dying." He raised an eyebrow. "Perhaps he is. He's certainly having a crisis of faith."

"We're all dying. He's just making it happen too fast for some people."

"I think he's hoping you'll stop him." Mr. Bright's gaze was enigmatic through the haze of white smoke. "I think he likes you. I think he thinks you'll understand him." He paused. "Just don't trust him."

An echo of memory stirred. "Funny. He mentioned something about not trusting people too. You two have issues." Cass refused to let his own eyes drop. "And frankly I don't give a fuck about trust. I just want to catch him. Do you know where he is?"

"No." Bright shook his head. "I'm rather hoping you'll find him for me. He's become something of an embarrassment for all of us, and he's drawing far too much attention to himself."

"What was it that made him crack?" Cass looked back at the vast office. "Corporate mental breakdown? Office not big enough?"

Mr. Bright laughed again, his head shaking slightly. He didn't answer the question.

"Who is he, this Solomon?" Who are *you*? was what he really wanted to ask, but he already knew he'd get some infuriatingly ambiguous answer.

"Solomon?" Bright paused, and the cigarette smoke he exhaled settled in every tiny fine line that covered his tanned face, suddenly ageing him a thousand years. "I suppose he is my brother. Of sorts."

"Of sorts?"

"One day you'll understand."

Cass didn't think he would. Black shoes. Crimson stains. His heart ached. "Did you or Solomon have anything to do with Christian's death?"

"No, not at all." Mr. Bright's eyes widened slightly in surprise and he almost recoiled as if at the thought.

Cass thought the sudden display of emotion looked genuine, but how could he tell with this enigma of a man? He'd seen the way Artie Mullins reacted at the mention of his name. Mr. Bright was not to be underestimated himself.

"He was perhaps too much like your father and I didn't see it. I let the others panic me, and told him too much too soon, and then once he started digging he found things that didn't concern him." He ground the cigarette out. "I think he wanted to help you."

"Help me?" Cass glared at the man who clearly knew so much but wouldn't share it. He wanted to stick him in a cell and kick the shit out of him until he couldn't scream the information out fast enough. What help, and what with? Police business or his personal life? Cass had thought that Christian had wanted help, rather than trying to give it. Had he underestimated his little brother that much?

"I should have told him about the film. And he should have trusted me."

"How would the film have helped him?"

Mr. Bright shook his head. "Don't spoil the game. I trust you'll get there eventually."

"Solomon will kill more people if you don't help me."

"People die all the time, Cass. It's in their nature."

"Perhaps I should get a warrant and come back here tomorrow."

Mr. Bright laughed; a sudden tinkle of light. "We both know that's not going to happen. The only reason you even know about me is because I wanted it that way. How else to get a policeman's attention but to provide an over-the-top wall of silence? Everyone's traceable, Cass. An untraceable man would just leave a false trail. To give you nothing was sure to grab your attention."

The idea that he'd been suckered into looking for Mr. Bright didn't sit well. His fingers clenched at his sides. "Why can't you just tell me what the fuck is going on?"

"One day I will." Mr. Bright stared at him for a second and then smiled. "But I think for now it's probably time we said goodbye. I'm sure we'll meet again soon enough."

"What?" Cass was ready to punch him when he turned the remote to the lift. The doors slid open.

"Unless of course you want me to call security and explain your presence?" Teeth glinted in the soft light. "And don't doubt that I would, Cassius Jones. In some ways it might add a little something to the game, putting you under the extra pressure of losing your job so spectacularly."

"You're some piece of work." Cass's impatience boiled over. "Why are you so fucking interested in me and my family? Who the fuck are you?"

"All in good time." Mr. Bright raised an arm to usher Cass to the open lift. "But you have nothing to fear from me."

"Really?" Cass almost spat the words out. "Is that why my father ran from a man called Mr. Bright? Is that why my brother's now dead?" He strode towards the lift. "In fact, *don't* fucking tell me. You're right. I'll fucking figure it out for myself."

"And that's exactly what I want you to do." Mr. Bright's smile was almost humourous, as if Cass's rage simply wasn't there. "Now if I could just have Miss Healey's pass back?" He held out a smooth pink palm.

Cass had forgotten about Maya. His stomach turned slightly. "This wasn't her fault. She doesn't know I've got it."

"I know. But I'll take it and make sure it's returned to her in the morning." His eyes twinkled. "We wouldn't want it falling into the wrong hands, now, would we?"

"Will she get in trouble for this? I made her meet me. She didn't even want to. She's done nothing wrong."

Mr. Bright laughed. "I would never blame her for simply being human. What she did was perfectly natural." The card slid into his suit so quickly he could have been a master magician. "In fact, she did exactly what I expected of her." He shrugged. "So how could I blame her for that?"

Cass watched the strange man and couldn't fight the slight awe that leavened his anger and frustration. "Does everyone do as you expect them to?"

"When you've lived as long as I have, there are rarely any surprises left." He paused. "You, though, Cass, you may prove the exception to that rule."

Cass stepped into the lift. "I fucking hope so."

"You don't have to like me, Cass." Mr. Bright's smile didn't waver. "But think of me as your guardian angel."

The doors slid shut and Cass stared at them. The world was unsteady under his feet and it had fuck all to do with the lift's descent.

CHAPTER SEVENTEEN

It was gone one a.m. when he finally got back to the seminary. The corridors were dark and quiet. Beneath his feet the wood was scuffed and dull from overuse, but he found something earthy and clean about it compared to the highly polished floor he'd left Mr. Bright standing on. For the first time he felt some sense of peace rather than discomfort in the building. He didn't believe in any kind of God, and even without that faith he felt he was the last person to feel at home in a place dedicated to goodness, but the calm of the seminary and its sense of purpose helped to ease his mind's furious struggle to pull all the pieces together. Maybe there were no gods, but there was something of the best of mankind in these corridors. A hope for something better, perhaps. Whatever it was, he needed a dose of it.

For the first time he actually looked at the small paintings hung at wide intervals on the walls. There was a massive difference, in size and cost and sheer opulence, to the vast canvas hanging in Solomon's office, but the theme was the same. His eyes snagged on an image of a naked Christ nailed to the cross. His face showed a perfect image of agony and self-sacrifice. Blood oozed from where thorns punctured his forehead and ran thickly through the painted crevices of his contorted face. In the sky above the dying man angels waited, garbed in white and clutching harps and bows, ready to take the Lord back to his place in Heaven when his suffering on Earth was done.

The angels looked like children's cartoons to Cass, floating regally above the Earth. The pain and suffering though: that looked so very real. He tilted his head and his heart felt heavy. Had all that suffering been worth it? The man in the picture, the thousands of others who'd burned and died and killed in his name—was there really a point to it all? What was it about this agonisingly painful death that drew the young men who now slept in the cells around him? Where was the goodness to be found in this? He wished he could understand it, he truly did, if only to have had a better relationship with his father—but it would never be. The Earth was the Earth was the Earth. There was nothing else.

Footsteps clicked against the floor behind him and Cass turned to see the shadow of a figure in the gloom. The black suit trousers turned the corner out of sight, a flash of crumpled blue hanging at the waistband. The painting was forgotten. Cass's mouth went dry. He followed as Christian's heels rang out in a steady, even tread. Cass's own were merely a whispered thump, echoing the steady beat of his living heart. His brother was just out of sight until Cass reached the tiny chapel at the back of the building. The door was open and the rows of pews were half in shadow. In a small alcove a few candles guttered. To his left, a young man with an eruption of acne on the back of his neck knelt, praying hard. His lips moved, but Cass couldn't hear what he said. He didn't look up.

Cass stayed where he was in the doorway and stared at the figure that stood in front of the altar. Christian's back was towards him and his head was tilted upwards, gazing at the small stained-glass window that in the morning would catch the light from the courtyard and bathe the small chapel in dazzling colour. The Virgin Mary cradled her child, surrounded by smiling angels. It was still beautiful, Cass thought, even without the illumination of the sun creating a halo around their image.

As if suddenly realising Cass was there, Christian turned and smiled. Cass recoiled slightly, his breath hitching. The praying boy didn't move, his eyes squeezed shut as he repented for whatever sin it was that had kept him awake in the middle of the night. He was in his own world. The two Jones brothers were in another entirely. Cass stared at Christian. Above his smiling mouth, his eyes were red hollows. Blood ran down his pale face in slow streams, dripping crimson splashes on his black shoes. It was dead blood, thick and dark, and it had no right flowing at all.

Cass didn't move. They stood at each end of the small aisle: one blond, one dark. One dead, one alive. One innocent, one guilty. Still smiling, as if his bleeding eyes were the most normal thing in the world, Christian raised his arm and once again mimed a phone call. His fingers were paler now, as if death were finally taking hold of the apparition. After a moment his hand fell back to his side and he turned back to the altar and raised his head, once more surveying the beauty in the glass. Cass trembled and clenched his hands into a fist. His fingers were icy-cold. It had been a long day—too long. There was no ghost, and wouldn't be, no matter how many times he saw it. It was just his mind, wanting him to work something out. He turned and headed back to his room. No footsteps followed him, only the hushed tread of his own filled the corridor.

He'd just got dressed and was heading outside to clear the minty taste of toothpaste from his mouth with the first cigarette of the day when Perry Jordan rang.

"Morning, Cass. Up and at 'em."

"Already am." He clicked the lighter and inhaled before opening the car door and getting in. The kid sounded cocky. That was a good sign. "What have you got for me?"

"Mate"—the laugh in his ear was throaty—"you're gonna love me."

"Go on." His gut tingled.

"Both families were fucked financially. And I mean majorly fucked. They were a mess. Miller was four months behind on the mortgage and Jackson was three. And that was after remortgaging." A lighter clicked at the other end and he could hear as Jordan sucked in hard before continuing, "Looks like they'd both had a major run of luck, then a series of dud investments, some of them even more major. Their salaries have been cut too—I figure it was that or redundancy. From what I can see they've both had holes in their boats for quite a while, but this year was when they started sinking."

"Great metaphor, mate."

"I aim to please."

"So if they've been screwed for cash for that long then how have they been able to keep up their lifestyles?" Cass wondered.

"They sold some assets: private sales of paintings and jewellery. Bits and pieces here and there. Some of it was pretty pricey, according to payments I traced back to the auction houses."

Cass remembered the picture hanging at a slight angle in the Jackson house. Recently rehung? A fake, maybe?

"Do you think the wives know?" he asked. His skin tingled, and it had nothing to do with the nicotine.

"You're ahead of me." He laughed again, clearly enjoying himself. "My guess is no. Both families have two lots of bank accounts, with money being transferred from the main one held in only the husband's name to a joint one, which is where the women do their spending from. And boy, do those women spend. Their luxury items come to more than my salary and that's considerably better than it was before you lot did me a favour and kicked me out. They've got health spas, central London gym memberships, top hairdressers—and don't even get me started on the clothes.

"They haven't reined, not one bit, since their husbands fucked up, so every month they've been adding a couple of grand to the problem. Both families were right on the edge of losing everything. I'd love to have heard *that* conversation." He laughed drily.

"So they're broke."

"No. They *were* broke."

"What do you mean?"

"This is where it gets interesting. Six months ago Miller and Jackson each received three payments of fifty thousand pounds over the space of one month."

"How much?" His back stiffened against the seat. "A hundred and fifty each? Where from?"

"That's the fun bit. I can't trace the money. Not fully. But that alone tells us plenty."

"How could that amount of money suddenly appearing in someone's bank account not flag up any enquiries?"

"These days the banks are so glad to have any money coming in that they don't look far. And banking's a nanny state now anyway. The Big Brother of all banks does the regulating, so if the money's coming from The Bank itself, who's going to dare to run secondary checks?"

"The money came from The Bank?"

"Well, it was transferred *out* of there, at any rate. Each transfer came from a separate account there. The info cost me, which in turn means it'll cost you, but I got the details. Neither of the two accounts had ever been used for any other banking—basically, they were a tunnel to get this money into the Jackson and Miller private accounts without raising any eyebrows."

"Explain."

"The Bank has layers of accounts. It would have to, being as big as it is. It operates as many subsections, as well as a whole. But it has to run one numbers system so it can audit itself. It uses different sequences of account numbers that can be recognised quickly, both in-house and in the wider financial sector, and they're allocated on importance, or priority, or however you want to put that. Some of those account sequences make people jump higher than others. These two tunnel accounts started with the digits 251, and that's considered pretty high-up in the system."

"How the hell do you know this shit?" Cass took a deep breath. His jigsaw was finally coming together.

"I told you: it cost me. I'm like you, Cass, I've got friends in lots of places, and they're not all the kind to get themselves nicked on a DUI charge either. Anyway, my contact did some probing for me, and he got the number of the accounts that transferred the money into the 251 accounts. And this is where you're now on your own."

"How do you mean?"

"The accounts started 7777. No one I know, not in the banking or the financial sectors, has ever heard of a 7777 account. Not inside The

Bank, not in whatever's left of the economy outside of it. And trying to trace it from within The Bank caused my mate's computer to crash. More than once."

"What were the account numbers?" Cass's heart was thumping as he dragged his small notebook out of his pocket. "Have you got them on you?"

"Sure. Hang on."

The rustling of paper at the other end matched his own as he flicked through the pages to find the numbers he'd scribbled down from the moleskin book they'd found under the bed at Solomon's bedsit. His blood chilled and then raced as Jordan read the numbers aloud. Both were listed on the page, and both had *failed* written next to them. He grinned. Bingo.

"Perry Jordan, you're a genius."

"They mean something to you?" He sounded surprised.

"Yes, they do. Send your bill and a copy of everything you got over to me at the station, will you?"

"Already on it, mate. The courier's on his way."

"I'll see him there. And Perry, mate, I owe you."

Cass could almost hear the grin.

"Yep, you do!"

The DCI sat behind his desk and stared at Cass. "But what about Macintyre? I thought this was done and dusted yesterday?"

Cass didn't glance at Bowman, who was leaning against the back wall trying to look nonchalant. Cass knew what he wanted to say. He wanted to say that Bowman didn't have the balls or brains he was born with, that he was so fucking ambitious that he'd just wanted a quick result and the glory of closing the high-profile case. He wanted to say he'd opted for the easy way, as he always did. He wanted to say that he thought that Bowman and his flash suits and flash lifestyle was a Grade-A cunt. He didn't say any of that, though. For once he toed the party line.

"Maybe Macintyre *has* got some shit going down—it would be hard for him not to imagine that this had something to do with him.

Maybe his boys gave up the Chechens because they wanted them out of the way."

DCI Morgan nodded. Cass knew what he was thinking; he'd be mentally wading through the damage and looking for ways to limit it. As things stood, their position was okay: the press hadn't been informed yet, and the parents were out of the loop. If it did come out that Bowman had got it completely wrong, well, it wouldn't look too terrible for the DCI with the Commissioner, not as long as he'd been the one who encouraged the discovery of the truth.

Cass slid the open moleskin notebook across the desk so that it sat next to the bank account information Perry Jordan had traced. The DCI looked from one to the other.

"But this notebook came from Bowman's case? The serial killer?"

"Yes, but we've known for a while the two cases have links. Solomon used to work at The Bank, we've got proof of that, and this money definitely passed through The Bank, even if we don't know exactly where it came from. Plus there's the man who sent in the film of the shootings from the same flat Carla Rae died in. This Mr. Bright, who apparently doesn't exist and couldn't possibly have anything to do with this, but who Solomon had definitely heard of when I asked him on the phone."

He paused and was pleased to see that the DCI at least had the good grace to look awkward. After a moment he went on, "The way I see it is this: if we don't pull Jackson and Miller in and this all comes out later, which it probably will because if Perry Jordan could find this stuff out then the press can pay someone like him too, then it's going to be another fiasco of police incompetence. And these are dead children we're talking about here. The newspapers love that shit. They'll follow the family and they'll dig. You know how it is. Build 'em up and then burn 'em down."

"What do you think, Bowman?" Morgan looked at his other DI.

Bowman shrugged, his shoulders stiff. "We should probably talk to them," he mumbled.

Cass hadn't expected anything like good grace. He'd had to agree, of course. On the way up to Morgan's office, Cass had casually asked about the interview times with Macintyre, and after a moment said he must have got the time wrong when Claire rang, though he thought he'd checked his watch. Bowman had said nothing. He hadn't needed to. Cass could see he'd got the message from the blanched look on his already pale face. Cass wondered if it was forgivable to wish the hospital had found some trace of actual poisoning in Bowman's blood, instead of the vague suggestions of unidentifiable abnormalities. At least that way he'd be confined to a hospital bed and out of Cass's way.

"Okay, I agree." Morgan brought his attention back to Cass. "Bring them in. But tread carefully. These people have lost *children*."

Cass was already out of the door by the time his boss shouted those last few words. The boys' *mothers* had lost children. What these fathers had done with them, he wasn't so sure.

It was quiet down on the basement levels of Paddington Green Station, away from the noise and bustle of the offices and main holding cells above them. These interview rooms were rarely used except by the Anti-Terror Division for overflow or by the Murder Squad in extremely high-profile cases.

If they were lucky enough to catch Solomon, they'd interview him down here. Cass figured that while Isaac Jackson and Paul Miller might not be serial killers, they could use the quiet space. He was pretty sure these men hadn't had any since their children had died, and there was nothing like feeling cut off from the world to make you reassess your inner demons. Cass understood that.

He peered through the small hatch. Isaac Jackson sat perfectly still in his seat, staring ahead. Like Paul Miller, two doors down, he seemed much smaller than he had the last time Cass had seen him, standing stoically behind the plush white sofa. Without the grand house and the beautiful wife and the luxurious furnishings surrounding him he looked like just a broken man weighed down with guilt. That had been clear when Jackson had opened the door to the grim-faced officers and the waiting police car. Cass had seen that look before: a mixture of relief and expectation. It was the expression of the ordinary man who'd done a terrible thing and was ready to pay for it. On Jackson it had been as clear as day. Jackson would break first.

The wives, distraught and uncomprehending, had immediately called their solicitors. Paul Miller had his man in with him, but Jackson had refused to see his. Cass reckoned he was having five minutes with his conscience, and weighing up how much he could still keep secret. He was pretty certain once Jackson started talking, he wouldn't be able to stop. He wouldn't know then that talking about it just created a second version of the horror. It couldn't get rid of the story etched on your soul. Cass knew that. Your stories always stayed on the inside.

Cass took a moment to enjoy the quiet himself while Claire fetched coffee. Upstairs, the front desk would be manic while the Incident Room staff fielded continuous phone calls. The press were gathering outside the station, starting to bay for information, for blood. There was nothing his team had been able to do about that. There was no way they could take the men from their homes without bringing the pack back with them—they'd been camped outside since the boys had died. Even though the men—the *fathers*—hadn't technically been arrested, that tired old cliché of "helping the police with their enquiries" was fooling no one. Across the city, newspaper editors were putting together instant spreads, covering both sides, one tearing the families apart, the other vilifying the police for their brutality in the face of tragedy. They'd wait to see the outcome before deciding which way to run: good guys hard done by, or evildoers destined to rot in Hell, that's how they'd be portrayed, regardless of the fact that most people were somewhere in between.

Claire appeared with a tray. "Sorry. Had to go upstairs." She looked over at the door. "You ready to go in?"

Cass nodded. He was more than ready.

Isaac Jackson looked up when Claire placed the hot coffee in front of him and then turned on the audio recorder and gave the time and date. She spoke clearly. This was one interview that was not going to be fucked up on a technicality.

"Have you spoken to Paul yet?" Jackson's voice was hollow.

"I thought I'd start with you," Cass said. "Mr. Miller is talking to his solicitor."

He nodded, moving like an old man trying to pretend he's still young. Life had taken its toll on Isaac Jackson.

"I want to make it clear for the record that you are speaking to us without your solicitor and of your own free will. That is correct, isn't it?"

He nodded again and Cass looked at him. He cleared his throat and said, "Yes." His voice was dull, defeated.

"And you understand the implications such a decision may have on any subsequent trial?"

"Yes." He would be aware of what the outcome might be. The death penalty had been reinstated for first-degree murder cases two years previously, but with the chronic overcrowding in prisons and the massive rise in lesser crimes, there were movements within government to shift the boundaries further still, adding second-degree, manslaughter and accessory after the fact to the roster. If Jackson and Miller *had* had anything to do with their boys' deaths, they'd be a gist to that group.

"Mr. Jackson, during the course of this investigation we have discovered that both you and Mr. Miller have had some financial difficulties over the past two years. Is that correct?"

"You could call it that." Jackson let out a short laugh, devoid of emotion. "I'd call it financial meltdown. Neither of us have ever saved, but we had a knack for picking the right investments to keep ourselves afloat. But we started to make mistakes. We were too cocky. The world had changed and we had not accounted for that. Everything was high risk and we started to make some losses. Big ones. We tried to rectify our mistakes and we made it worse." He looked at Cass. "You probably know all this already."

"I have the paperwork, but I'm no financial genius. Explain it to me."

"You don't have to be a genius to see when sums like that don't add up." He leaned back in his chair and wiped his eyes as he sighed.

"Does your wife know?"

"What do you think?" After a second he answered his own question. "No, we decided not to tell Clara and Eleanor."

"Why? You thought they would leave you? Both of you?"

Again the slow shake. "Oh no, much worse. They'd be disappointed. *Let down*." He sipped the coffee for a moment, then looked at Cass again. "Paul and I are reinventions of ourselves. We created the image of ourselves we wanted to be: successful, confident, men who could take on the world and win. Those were the men our wives fell in love with. Only Paul and I knew that we weren't exactly all that on the inside."

"Everybody's different on the inside," Claire said. "Even your wives."

Jackson smiled at her pityingly, as if there were no way she could ever understand.

"You thought they wouldn't love you any more?" Cass frowned. "That's crazy."

"They wouldn't love us *the same*. We wouldn't be the men who *took care* of things. It would have broken everything." He looked down at the desk. "Maybe it sounds crazy, but at that point we still thought we could save everything and they would never need to know." The clipped accent had slipped since he'd started talking.

Cass wondered how much of his life had been pretence—sometimes he himself still heard that harder edge of Cockney that was Charlie Sutton in his head. He wasn't unsympathetic. "So what happened?"

"Paul met someone in a casino."

"Where?"

"I don't know exactly. Some high-class place around Baker Street."

"He was gambling? He had money for that?"

"Of course he didn't. But it's the last station of hope for a desperate man, isn't it? To play the odds on the cards or wheel? And it was easier to pretend to be working late than going home. The strain of keeping up appearances was unbearable." His eyes narrowed slightly. "I think we were starting to hate each other. You know how it is, it's easier to blame someone else. Anyway, he got drunk and started blurting out all our problems. He says he doesn't remember much about what he actually said, but the man gave him a card. Plain white, expensive. All it had on it was a mobile phone number."

"Who was this man?"

"I don't know his name. Paul never told me—he said he didn't remember. But he told Paul that if we called that number there might be a way out of our problems. He said that he'd been in a similar situation and the man on the other end had saved his life, turned it around."

"So what did you do?"

"We called the number, of course."

"And who answered?"

Jackson smiled softly, though his eyes were cold. "He said his name was Mr. Solomon."

Claire's eyes darted to Cass, but he didn't look back, despite his own rising excitement. A business card, plain white, expensive . . . he knew the feel of a card like that. Threads were weaving together in his head. *Nothing is sacred.* People had been tested and found wanting. That's what he'd said. What test had Solomon set these men that they had failed so spectacularly?

"Where did you meet him?"

"Two days after the first call he rang Paul and told us to come to his penthouse at the Wharf."

"And who was he?"

"He said he was an investor."

"Did he work for The Bank?"

Jackson was about to answer and then hesitated. "I'm not sure he *worked* for them. He said he invested heavily in The Bank. He didn't strike me as someone who worked for anyone."

Cass thought of the empty office and the huge canvas that filled the wall. Jackson had nailed Solomon pretty well. It was also close to the description that Adam Bradley had given of Mr. Bright. He found that didn't surprise him either. Bright and Solomon were bound together in his head, two parts of a whole, twisting around him and his family and his past.

"And then what happened?"

Jackson shifted in his seat and leaned forward. "Have you ever seen *The Godfather*?"

"With Marlon Brando? A long time ago. Why?"

"We went there expecting to be offered a loan at some extortionate rate." A bitter smile flashed across his face as if at a bad private joke. "But it was like the opening to that film. We explained our situation and he just nodded and listened. Then when we were done he said he wanted to speak to us each separately. I only know what he said to me."

"Which was?"

Jackson sighed. He almost stank of shame. "He said he would lend me one hundred and fifty thousand pounds to get myself straight, with no interest on the loan. But I had to cut my cloth accordingly. He said I should talk to my wife, about my work and money problems . . . and if I didn't do those things, there would be a charge to pay on the money within a year. He was insistent we should learn from our mistakes." He looked at Cass. "He told me not to discuss any of this with Paul. He suggested it would be better if we eased up on our friendship."

He stopped for a bit, his head hanging, then added, "It was like talking to some kind of counsellor rather than a loan shark. I've met some powerful people in my time, but this man was different. He couldn't have been much older than us, but there was something about him that was completely different—I just can't put my finger on why. Sitting with him, I had every intention of doing what he asked me. I couldn't imagine *not* doing what he asked me."

"And then?"

A small shrug. "We went home. We didn't talk about it, but I could see Paul was happy too. We cleared our debts and slowly started spending less time together. I broke away gradually so that Clara wouldn't notice. I think he must have had the same instruction because he didn't say anything about it."

"I've seen your bank accounts," Cass said. "It doesn't look like you told your wife."

For the first time tears appeared in Isaac Jackson's eyes. "I didn't—I *couldn't*. Paul obviously hadn't told Eleanor, so how could I tell Clara? They're best friends. It would have killed her"—he stumbled a little over the phrase—"if Eleanor were able to maintain her lifestyle while Clara couldn't. She'd have been humiliated."

Tests. It was all about tests, and these men had failed. Cass could see it unfolding so clearly. Paul, and Jackson too, probably, supposed to talk to their wives about their overspending, both watching and waiting for the other to do it first. An absolute classic case of having to keep up with the Joneses, and both wives blithely unaware of the cost—but at *what* cost?

Jackson's defeated voice intruded on Cass's thoughts as he continued, "A month or so ago my phone rang. It was Solomon. He wanted us to meet."

"Back at the penthouse?" Surely Solomon wouldn't have met the men at the bedsit?

"No, not this time, in a restaurant. An ordinary place, one of those steak chains. It was in Soho. Solomon looked different. He wasn't so smartly dressed. He seemed less . . . *contained*. Maybe it had all been there the first time, but I hadn't seen it. I'd been too worried about myself then to see the madness in him."

"You think he was crazy?"

Jackson laughed for a full thirty seconds. The sound was at odds with the bleakness of their confines and his tale. Eventually, he continued, "Oh, he was crazy. And I think he made me crazy too. I'd gone in there knowing he was going to ask for something. He'd said at the first meeting there'd be a charge if I didn't tell Clara we needed to cut back, but I'd allowed for that. Investing on my own I'd made some extra money—nothing major, I'm not as brave as Paul, so the choices I'd made were less risky. But I'd kept the money, put it aside for when this call came." That sour smile flashed again. "I thought I had it covered. How wrong can you be?"

"Tell me." Cass had an awful feeling in his gut. *Nothing is sacred. We'd been tested and found wanting.* What did Isaac Jackson and Paul Miller do?

"He said that my wife's life was an illusion. I'd failed to be honest with her and allow her to share in reality as he'd told me to do." He paused and swallowed hard. "He said that he'd made that clear when he'd given me the money. He said that her life was the charge." His eyes met Cass's, the horror of reliving those moments so clear that Cass felt he could almost see the film running in a loop deep in those chocolate-brown eyes.

"I didn't understand what he was saying at first. I kept babbling about the money I'd put aside for him. He waited until I'd finished. Then he just said, 'I'm going to kill your wife.' As simple as that." Jackson ran his hands over his head and then rested his face in his palms, his long fingers pressing against his mouth and nose as if that could somehow stop him from finishing this story.

"But your wife is still alive."

Jackson's nod was almost imperceptible. "And sometimes, God help me, I wish she wasn't," he whispered. "I begged and pleaded, and in the end, he gave me a choice." A whine crept into his deep voice, and Cass recognised it: it was the sound of someone who badly needed forgiveness of some kind. He'd heard it a thousand times before, in a thousand squalid police cells, and just like then, suddenly he was the Father Confessor. It was always the way, but he could offer no forgiveness; all he could do was to mete out justice. His face stayed impassive, but his stomach churned. He thought he could see where Isaac Jackson's story was heading.

"A choice?" Claire asked softly.

"He said a life was forfeit." His breath was ragged, the calm of earlier fading. "He said that if it wasn't Clara, it had to be someone else. At first I thought he meant Justin and that almost sent me over the edge . . ." Now tears flowed unchecked down his face and he stopped for a while until Cass prompted him again. "He started talking about Paul, and how the mess I was in was as much his fault as mine. As if he knew what I'd been thinking, why I didn't tell Clara. Then he gave me my choice. Clara or Paul's John." He buried his head into his hands again, and Cass could barely hear him when he said, "God help me, I chose little John." Snot ran from his nose and the words dribbled out with it: "I chose John."

Cass stared. He was feeling so much he almost felt nothing at all.

He was numb in the face of what had happened. Solomon had set them a test, and they'd failed. Pride, vanity, stupidity, and the craziness of one rich man: all these things had collided to create a tragedy, and two boys died. And even right at the end Jackson hadn't offered up his own life to pay for his own weaknesses, no, he chose the life of *someone else's child* over that of his wife. Did he even once say, "Don't take either of them, take me"? Would things have been different if he had? Maybe that would have been Solomon's Get Out of Jail Free card: offer the ultimate sacrifice and all will be well. Perhaps that was one high-risk bet that Jackson wasn't ready to take.

"And then when it happened, I knew." Jackson's mournful gaze could have cracked ice. "Of course Paul and I both knew. We'd made the same choice. Our beautiful boys were gone, and now the devil is dancing with our souls. I can't look at him any more. Nor he me."

Cass couldn't help the disgust that rose up inside him. He wanted to show him the tape. Perhaps he would. Maybe both men should live with the sight of their boys, friends to the last, gunned down side by side. Maybe then they'd see the reality of what they'd done. He glared at the sobbing man.

"If I could take it all back I would," he was repeating, "oh God, I would." He was a broken man.

Black shoes. Crimson spots. There was one more thing Cass needed to know. "If you feel so bad, then why did you try and set me up?"

"What?" Jackson's head slowly rose and revealed a face riven with guilt . . . and now confusion. "What do you mean?"

"My brother and his family. The evidence that was planted."

Jackson stared at him and then glanced at Claire before looking back at Cass. "I don't know what you're talking about," he said.

"This was the only case I was working. It had to be you or Miller." He leaned in and growled, "Things cannot get any worse for you. You and your good friend—your *best* friend—just killed each other's children."

He enjoyed the visible recoil as the statement hit home. "Just tell me why. I need to know."

There was a long pause. Jackson looked helpless. "But I really don't know what you're talking about. I haven't tried to set you up—Christ, I was *relieved* when you came for me. That's the truth."

Seconds ticked past silently. The problem was that Cass believed him. Compared to killing his best friend's kid, this was *nothing*—he had nothing left worth lying for.

Miller didn't take long to break after that. Cass saw the horror on his face when he realised Jackson had told him everything. It took less than thirty minutes of increasingly abject "no comment," most of which Cass thought was the last vestiges of self-denial, before Paul Miller was in tears as well, blabbing out his version of events much less coherently than his former friend had. Cass wondered if there wasn't something more honest in this loss of all self-control than there had been with the stoicism Isaac Jackson had displayed when he started his interview, his completely unjustified sense of "doing the right thing."

As he left his second sobbing man of the day behind he figured it didn't much matter. There was no good way of accepting what they'd done. Cass felt sick, any brief moment of sympathy he'd had for these men and the mess they'd created long gone. They weren't bad men, just weak, and somehow that made what they'd done more terrible, unforgivable. Their children had died for their weakness. Acid burned up his throat.

He felt the cold fingers of the two boys tightening around his heart as Claire came outside and stood next to him. The truth might be out, but how could that ever be enough to satisfy the ghosts of those boys' lost years? That haunted him.

"You okay?" Claire touched his arm. Her hand was hot, or his own skin had gone cold. He couldn't tell which.

"Yeah," he lied. "You?"

She smiled wanly. "You got them. You were right."

He tried to smile back, but the victory was hollow. Children killed by their own fathers; unwittingly sacrificed. There was no pleasure to be gained from that. He wished Bowman had been right, that it had been a botched hit on a gangster. A terrible accident was something they could all live with. As it was, this would be one of those cases that stained everyone who came near it, even innocent Claire, with her touching faith in right and wrong and black and white. Once the thrill of closing the case had passed she'd find her sleep restless, and she wouldn't be able to put her finger on why: a silent haunting down through the years until she finally came to realise—as she would, in this bloody job—that black and white are easy to live with; it's the shades of grey that give you nightmares.

"Get Blackmore to show them the film," he said.

"What?"

"I've got to go out." Despite his calm voice, his hands were trembling at his sides. "Bowman can explain to Morgan exactly how he fucked up, and I want Blackmore to sit in each of those fucking cells and show those bastards what they did." God, he needed a cigarette. "They've fucking earned that right." The small, cold fingers slowly released their grip and slid away into the darkness inside him. The dead were vengeful; Cass thought perhaps he'd given them what they wanted. He'd given them everything he could, anyway.

He couldn't look at Claire; he didn't want to see her looking at him as if she saw something bad below the surface of his skin: a man she didn't understand at all.

"What are you going to do?"

"I have to go and see their wives and tell them what their haircuts have cost them."

She flinched. "That's not fair, Cass. They didn't do this." So much pity in her voice. Was it for the families, or for him? "They've lost their children *and* their husbands in one fell swoop."

"I know. I'm sorry. You're right, of course. Clara Jackson and Eleanor Miller are victims too." So why did he feel so angry at them? Was this his own resentment at Kate coming out to play? There were parallels between them, that was for sure. Kate had always pushed him to climb the ladder. She was desperate to fit in with the best people, to have the best things. She wanted him to be *successful*. Well, it hadn't worked for him, and it hadn't worked for Isaac Jackson or Paul Miller. He remembered Kate's face when those dreams had been destroyed.

He remembered the feel of the trigger as he squeezed it. They were all steeped in blood.

"Just make sure they see that film."

Claire nodded. Even she wouldn't argue with him in this mood. He walked away without looking back.

He had one more thing to do before heading out to wreck what was left of the women's lives. He went to the busy first floor, where people were too busy running around chasing reports of domestic violence and stolen cars to pay any attention to a phone call. He flipped open his mobile and called Artie Mullins. If Jackson and Miller hadn't set him up, whoever had was still out there. Only one person appeared to have any idea about who that might be, and he was lying in a hospital bed.

Artie was as straightforward as ever, and with no real questions asked. Cass knew that one day he was likely to call in a huge favour, and that he was going to have to oblige, but worrying about that could wait.

"What's this kid's name?"

"Josh Eagleton. He's in a coma in the ICU."

"Not a problem," Artie said. "I'll get some people over there."

"Nothing obvious, though. I don't want anyone asking questions."

"Trust me, your lot won't even know we've got anyone there—but your boy will be safe as houses." His strong London accent didn't mask his genuine concern. "You getting all this shit sorted out, Jonesy?"

"Let's hope so, Artie. Let's fucking hope so."

Ramsey was loitering outside the building. Cass saw him flick a cigarette aside before he turned to go back inside. He didn't smile; his face was a mask of tight lines.

"I didn't know you smoked," Cass said.

"I don't. Just once in a blue moon, when I think my choices are that or punch someone more senior than me. The cigarette becomes the lesser of two evils."

"What's up?" Cass wasn't sure he wanted to ask. He was weighed down with enough this afternoon.

"It turns out no one's in that much of a hurry to get me that search warrant for your brother's computer. Not that there'll be anything left on it by now." He grimaced with frustration. "I've just sorted out another CSU to go through the house again and see if there's anything they missed that might give us a clue who tried to make you look dirty, and how. There must be *something* they didn't pick up on." He sighed. "It looked so open and shut—sorry, Cass—that maybe the team didn't hunt so hard first time round. You know how it is. Everyone wants it to be easy."

Cass lit a cigarette of his own and now Ramsey really looked at him.

"You're not in too great a mood yourself. What's up?"

"I'm just going to see Clara Jackson and Eleanor Miller, to tell them that their husbands are responsible for the deaths of their children." His fingers were still cold and trembling.

"*Jesus Christ!* What the fuck happened?"

Cass looked at the other DI. In the late afternoon sunlight it looked as if the slightest yellow wash was drifting into the air from the corners of Ramsey's eyes. He didn't want to look at it. It wasn't there. He shook his head. It was all he could manage.

"You know what," Ramsey said, "I've got an hour to kill before anyone even thinks about giving me any paperwork that's any use. I'll drive you."

"It's okay. They've both got WPCs with them. I'll be fine."

"This isn't about you." Ramsey started down the stairs towards the car park. "I want to hear the story, and I'm fucking bored of just hanging around here doing fuck all—what a waste of a great police brain." He laughed drily as a car bleeped and flashed its lights in friendly greeting. "Get in."

CHAPTER EIGHTEEN

The late afternoon is warmer than he expected, as if the sun has come to pay its final respects. He looks around and sees the faded beauty of the earth, and he smiles. The flowers are dancing in the slight wind. The grass grows in the lawn that runs between the beds and the concrete. He wonders if perhaps this day is truly more wondrous than all the countless thousands that have gone before, and whether perhaps this is something that is felt by all who know their final hours have arrived. He finds he is glad to leave the world while there is still some beauty left amidst the rot.

He breathes in, and fills his lungs with damp air so full of the scents of humanity that he can barely taste how it used to be. He feels strange. Not afraid, just disconnected. Over his sweater and cords he wears a long brown mackintosh, to keep out the damp. He checks its pockets: the bottle of blood and a paintbrush in one; in the other two syringes, one large and one small. He says a silent goodbye to the gardens and the earth and the air and the citadels beyond and turns to go back inside the church. His bones ache with the movement and he wonders if they're turning to dust inside him already.

The heavy doors shut with a thud that vibrates through his long fingers. He looks at the old wood for a long second, surprised by the sudden wave of sadness. The world on the other side is gone for him now. He will look upon it no more. Although his sadness surprises him, he knows it doesn't matter. Nothing is sacred. *It is a rotting world. Nothing is good, nothing is bad. None of it should ever have been. Even its Gods are dying.*

The vicar is at the altar, arranging some flowers brought by someone who enjoyed the music. He is placing them carefully in a large vase of water, but there is no point. The stems are cut. They have only the scent of death. He wonders if that is what it means to be human. As soon as the cord is cut they start dying. He sighs. They really didn't think it all through properly at the start. As he walks down the aisle his skin under his shirt itches. The flies can feel the end is coming and they're fighting it, even though they're dying within minutes now when he sets them free. But he is in charge, and he will not rage against the dying of the light.

The vicar turns. He has a name, Brendan Carpenter, but he will always be "the good Reverend." He sums up all the best of those who have dedicated their lives in service to a God who was only ever an illusion, a long-ago memory. He is goodness and kindness and weakness rolled in one. But still he does not Glow. He is simply human. And they were only ever pawns in the game. They tagged along when there was nowhere left to go. The rejects. The ones who failed the first test.

The vicar recognises him and his face bursts into a smile. He is not an old man, and there are times he can look quite boyish, even in the sombre uniform of the church. Solomon smiles back and the good Reverend's expression falters. The women had been the same, their adoring faces dropping in that moment of realisation that this man was something they could never *understand. But still they had done as they were told, mute in his presence.*

The eggs are hard under his fingertips and flies squirm beneath his skin. The vicar doesn't move as he approaches, but his mouth drops open and the flowers fall, forgotten. The power surges. He feels stronger and taller. He is a God among men. It pulses for the last time inside him. His smile widens.

When he is done he watches as the vicar's body stops jerking. The panic goes out of his eyes as soon as the needle has thrust its merciful death into his right arm. He stares for a moment at the ceiling of his precious church, and in that eternal last second Solomon wonders if the good Reverend is wondering how this came to be—is he having a moment of black terror, as his faith trembles in the face of the ultimate test? He hopes not. He likes the Reverend. He does this for love, nothing less. He explored the bodies of the first ones, but that was out of curiosity. In recent months he has done this out of kindness. The naked man's face loses focus as his pupils dilate. All thoughts are gone. His limbs relax. His breathing grows ever more shallow until there is only a slight hitch. Then nothing.

Solomon sighs. The church feels empty without the dead man's faith. At least the good Reverend knows the truth now: there is no Paradise. There is no God. All the Gods are earthbound, and lost, and dying. He places the bottle of blood beside the empty body and pulls out his phone. He looks at the dead man who was so kind to him and smiles. They'd be in the void together soon enough. He dials the number. It's time to bring his part in this game to its conclusion—but first he must make his final move and hand over his pieces. Let the king take charge.

The car crawled through the traffic just beyond the Marylebone Flyover. Horns blared loudly, as if they could somehow clear the blockage with their mechanical rage alone. Cass didn't mind. It was better than the silence that filled the car. He'd finished the awful, pathetic story of what really happened to John Miller and Justin Jackson, but he felt as if by sharing it he'd spread the germs of a disease that would infect and rot all those it touched for years to come. His mouth tasted like he'd been spitting out grave dirt with every word. The fingers of the dead were restless, tearing at him from the inside out. Maybe he was finally cracking up.

There was a red heat burning in him that he hadn't felt since those dark days when he didn't know who was more real, Charlie Sutton or Cass Jones, just that they both had blood on their hands. That sense that the world somehow existed apart from him was returning; though he'd somehow forgotten the bleakness of that isolation, it was clawing him back. His family were all dead, his wife was a stranger, and he dreamed most nights of a dead man's eyes meeting his. He, Jackson, Miller, Solomon . . . how different were they? How different was anyone? The world was grey, and all he could see through the glass was weakness . . . so many people with so many weaknesses. It made him feel sick. His hands were still cold.

His phone buzzed in his pocket twice before he even realised it was ringing. He looked at the screen and warmth trickled into his fingers. He stared at the unknown number.

I'll be in touch.

"Jones."

"Do you think the final day is always the most beautiful? Or does it just seem that way?" The words came slowly, followed by a soft laugh. Cass was aware of his other arm reaching over and frantically signalling Ramsey to pull over while the rest of him was sucked into the phone call.

"Perception is a strange thing. It makes truth of lies and lies of truths. Can you spot a liar, Detective Inspector?"

"We're all liars, Solomon. Keep the fortune cookie shit for someone who cares."

Ramsey's eyes flashed as he turned to watch Cass.

"Do you think it's a beautiful day, Cassius, or are you starting to see the world through my eyes? A world covered in so much dirt it chokes us all."

The repetition of that image that had been so fixed in his own head shook Cass badly. He clenched his teeth. He was *not* like this killer. "You set up Jackson and Miller," Cass said, trying to control his anger. "You killed those women, and fuck knows how many more that we don't yet know about. You *are* the dirt, Solomon."

"Jackson and Miller had choices." A sigh. "They weren't even difficult ones. They never have been. But pride overwhelmed goodness. Selfishness won over love." He paused. "Even here, in this place that is so peaceful. Scratch the surface and you will find it is all built on blood and hate disguised as love."

"Where are you?"

The soft laugh was autumn leaves blowing through a dead city. "It's all tests, Cassius. Where am I? Think hard enough and you'll know. I'm waiting to see you before you or I die."

Cass mentally raced through the list of places in Covent Garden that Claire had shown him. Somewhere quiet on a weekday afternoon? That ruled out the restaurants and bars. He couldn't make out any background noises, so Solomon was indoors somewhere. *Peaceful.* He'd used the word peaceful, not quiet.

"Trust your instincts." A hint of humour crept into the voice. "You'll find me. And he'll follow. Wheels within wheels."

Solomon hung up as something finally clicked into place in Cass's head. The low sun was so bright through the windscreen that it almost glowed. He remembered what he'd seen on that list. *Nothing is Sacred.*

"Covent Garden," he said. "St. Peter's Church." He looked over at Ramsey. "Drive!"

Claire's stomach churned. She was tired of being in the bowels of the building, cut off from the busy life above. Maybe it was just her tiredness, but both interrogation rooms were smelling of sharp sweat. She'd smelled fear before, but this was something else: pure guilt, perhaps. Whatever it was, it made her feel sick. If she was honest, just looking at both men made her feel sick, and she cursed Cass for leaving her down here to deal with this shit.

She had studied Isaac Jackson as he watched the film of his son's death, and now she intended to block out Paul Miller's face completely. Jackson had sat completely still, but she'd watched him quietly self-destructing in the twitches in his face and the anguish in his chocolate eyes. The euphoria she'd felt when she and Cass had first heard the confessions was long gone. Now she just wanted a shower. She knew her limitations, and Cass had stretched them by leaving her to deal with this shit. Sometimes he truly was a bastard.

Behind her, Mat quietly told Miller what he was going to be seeing, and he began to sob. Claire pressed play with an angry finger and stared at the screen. Miller muttered something, and Mat snarled at him to watch.

Claire frowned. Something on the screen fluttered like butterfly wings in her mind. There was something on that silent grainy image that she was seeing, but *not* seeing. Something so very unimportant and yet . . .

The moment passed. She fought the urge to rewind the film as that almost-recognition slipped away from her. When she was finally done here, she'd watch it again upstairs. What the hell was it her brain was trying to make her see?

"Please, don't . . . Please stop it—" Miller's voice was thick with snot and self-pity, and for the first time in her career she felt a corner of her heart freeze and turn black: a sliver of dead ice in her chest. He knew what was coming. He knew how the events would unfold, had already unfolded. He'd be seeing this forever, and she didn't like the hard joy that thought gave her.

Eventually it was over and they left the two men alone, with a constable to guard them. Claire was happy to get back up to where the living outnumbered the dead, away from the stinking guilt that had seeped into the walls of the corridors below. She wondered what Morgan would say if he found out what they'd just done. Would he even care, now that he had a result that would keep the papers in exclusives for weeks? She made a quick call to the desk sergeant, putting both Jackson and Miller on suicide watch, and then went to grab a coffee. Outside, the late afternoon sun streaked across the sky, chased by the first dark hints of night. She'd wait until it was a bit quieter and then rewatch the film herself, until whatever it was that was bugging her finally became clear.

Even with a siren attached to the top of the car there were only so many cut-throughs they could take as they tried to weave their way through the rush-hour traffic. The roads were approaching gridlock as buses, taxis and cars all fought for space, and only the bikes that cut up the inside were approaching anything like the speed limit. By the time they'd fought their way down Shaftesbury Avenue and cut down West Street into Upper St. Martin's Lane, Cass was thumping the dashboard and swearing in frustration.

"Pull over," he said at last, "I'm getting out."

Ramsey stopped the car, ignoring the flurry of noisy protest from the stream of vehicles behind. As Cass yanked at the door handle, Ramsey pulled him back. "Hang on," he said, tugging under his jacket, and producing a handgun, a Glock. "It's mine. I'm licenced." He thrust it at Cass. "Take it. If they throw any shit for it, then that's on me. You can't go in there with nothing."

Cass stared at it blankly for a moment, then said quietly, "Thanks." Most of the Murder Squad senior detectives were licenced. Fucking Bowman probably carried, but Cass had never been armed, not since that undercover job went down so badly. Despite the years that had passed, as he took the gun from Ramsey the weight felt comfortable in his hand, the handle familiar in his grip. He looked at Ramsey. He had already crossed one line for him. There was one more thing that he needed.

"I want five minutes' head start before you call for back-up."

"Why? Why would you—?"

"Just five minutes." His skin was burning from the inside out again. This was about more than just catching Carla Rae's killer. This was something personal. Solomon and Bright had been watching his family, and he needed to know why, and that wasn't going to be police business. He wanted no more of his fucking life being added to their files. He didn't wait for an answer but climbed out onto the busy street. The church was only a few minutes away, nestled on the edge of the famous piazza. He ran down Garrick Street, pushing his way through the pedestrians who thronged the area, his badge in one hand and Ramsey's gun in the other.

His breath roared in his ears as he came to a stop. The gate to the gardens was locked and at the other end of the path he could see that the door was closed. This fucker was a planner, that's what Hask had said. He'd have left one way in to find him, and this wasn't it. Cursing, he ran around to the main entrance in the piazza. A sign sat on the top step, declaring that the church was closed. Cass stepped past it and peered at the heavy wooden doors. There was an inch-wide gap between them. How fucking cocky was this bastard, that he would leave the main door open? What if tourists had tried to come in? Would he have just killed them and kept on waiting?

His heart pounded in his chest as he carefully pushed one door open and stepped inside. His feet were silent as he took a few steps forward. He paused. As he stared into the ornate church, echoes of his vision of Christian from the previous night shivered down his spine. A tall man stood at the altar, his back to Cass. A shock of blond hair reflected the golds and yellows of the gilt decoration that ran up the far wall. There was none of the simplicity of the seminary chapel, and this man wasn't his dead brother.

Cass took another step forward and the doors behind him slammed shut with such force that he felt a cold draught beat at his back. He gripped the Glock, ready for Solomon to come for him, but the man didn't even turn around.

Candles burned bright in the alcoves along the side walls. With the doors closed it was suddenly both night and day, and timeless, like being in Artie Mullins' basement club. Whatever was happening in this church was separate from the world outside.

"Solomon?"

The man hunched over the altar still didn't turn around. His brown mackintosh was stretched tight across his broad back.

"Is this where you took them from? The women? Is this how you chose them?"

This time Cass's feet had no hesitation in moving, unlike the previous night, when the sight of Christian had kept him motionless. Now he slowly crossed the tiles until his shoes fell silent on the long red rug that ran the length of the aisle between the dark, polished pews. "From where they prayed?"

"They came for the music." Solomon's voice was soft, and yet it filled the space. "As did I. Beautiful music, performed for anyone who cared to listen, with no mind of caste or creed. Amazing. Something like that can truly touch your soul."

"You killed them because they loved music?" Cass thought of those five very different women, each sitting somewhere in these pews, lost in something so beautiful, and unaware that it would cost them their lives. It was all about the choices. The little things. Go for a coffee or watch the free concert. Life or death.

"No, the music attracted them, but sometimes they stayed behind, just as I did. And then they would come alone, in the quiet times, and just sit."

Finally he turned. Even from halfway down the long aisle, Cass could see he was a handsome man, his high cheekbones offsetting his rugged face as he smiled. His teeth were as white as Bright's, and just as perfectly even.

"Just as I did. That's how I knew they knew." He lifted the bottle of what could only be blood and screwed on the lid before carefully placing it in a small plastic bag lying on the edge of the altar. The paint-brush was probably inside it, Cass thought. He took another step forward, the gun firm in his hand. The naked body placed across the altar didn't demand any rush; the stillness gathering round it only came with death. Others might not be so sure, but Cass had never been wrong about someone past saving. He had the instinct.

"You knew they knew what?"

Solomon pulled something from his pocket, his smile growing as Cass raised the gun higher. It was a hypodermic syringe.

"Don't worry. I don't mean you any harm. I want to help you."

"You'd be amazed how many people are keen to say that to me these days, but I'm not seeing a lot of evidence to prove it." Cass kept the gun raised. The syringe was full; half of it would be enough to kill an elephant. Who did Solomon intend it for, Cass—or himself? The DI was pretty sure he knew the answer, but he wasn't taking any chances.

"What did you know they knew?" There was something in the man's eyes that drew Cass in. There was kindness and strength, and something completely *other* that he couldn't place. It didn't look like madness; if anything, it looked like this man had a terrible clarity. Cass edged forward. Perhaps that was all madness ever was.

"They knew they were lost." He spoke softly. "It was as if even they, so ordinary and human, could see that we are all dying, that everything is corrupting. That there's no going back."

Cass looked at the pale body. "Who is he?" A male victim: the first one, as far as they knew. What would Hask say? That sex had been unimportant, or that Solomon had saved the most important until last? Either way, now it was just semantics. It was over for this man.

"This is the good Reverend. This is his church." Solomon tilted his head and began tugging up the sleeve of his raincoat. Cass watched him. If it came to it, he'd shoot off the man's arm before letting him inject himself. He wanted answers. He wanted a fucking arrest. He wanted someone to say something he could understand.

Solomon sighed. "He was a kind man—a good one—but he had no God, just a poor delusion. He didn't even Glow. Just like the rest of them, he was nothing: the remnant blood of rejected stock."

Cass felt chilled as Solomon's words scraped across his skin. The Glow. Memories flashed through his head: the photograph his mother had written on; Father Michael, talking about his father's funny thinking, and Christian's worries. *Always the Glow.* He didn't want to think about it. He'd never wanted to think about it, and yet here it was, back again, burning into his skin. He had a sudden memory of screaming at his mother: he was small, waist-high, and full of fear and anger. *"I won't see it! I won't see it!"* And then the last: the view of a teenager's desperate eyes down the barrel of a gun, and one clear, decisive thought in the midst of melting panic: *He has no Glow.*

Solomon was watching him. "I think on some level you understand what I mean. You don't want to, but I think you do. You can't help yourself." His eyes ran thoughtfully over Cass's face. "I've never seen it so bright on an ordinary man before."

"I hate to disappoint you, but I haven't got a fucking clue what you're talking about." Cass gripped the gun tighter. The Glock didn't feel like such a powerful weapon against this man.

"I just wanted to help him." The blond man leaned over the dead body and gently traced his forefinger down the uneven line where he'd daubed the familiar message.

A slick wet sound echoed quietly and Cass stepped forward. This poor man had suffered enough humiliation, laid bare on the altar.

What was Solomon doing to him? A steady stream of what looked like white rice oozed out from under the man's fingernail. *Fly eggs.* His eyes widened.

"How the fuck do you do that?" He didn't want to hear the awe in his own voice, but nonetheless it echoed with wonder.

Solomon frowned as the neat line wobbled, the line of eggs breaking and fat black maggots dropping from his fingertips instead. They wriggled madly on the man's torso for a moment and then fell still. He sighed again. He didn't answer the question. He turned to look at Cass.

They were only a few feet apart. Solomon's gaze tore right through him. Something in his eyes reminded Cass of the painting in Solomon's office in The Bank, and there was a darkness in them that reminded him of his own eyes. He felt like time was standing still as they looked at each other. How far away were the back-up team? Had Ramsey given him his five minutes? He still needed answers, personal ones, not the delusions that had pushed Solomon to take these lives.

"What is the Redemption file? Why is there an account in it with my family's name?"

"They think you're so special." Solomon turned away from the altar and slumped into a pew. He pulled a baseball cap from his pocket and tugged it onto his head. He still held the full hypodermic. "They think that you or the other can somehow save all this—this chaos. This pandemonium." He smiled sadly. "Those who don't think they can get back, anyway. Perhaps they've all gone slowly mad over so much time."

Whoever they were, they *must* be mad. Cass couldn't even save his own marriage. His neck prickled.

Solomon's eyes lit up the gloom. "You can't save them. No one can. But they will lie to you to make you try." For the first time, Cass heard an urgency in his voice. "And you must not trust them. Do you understand, Cassius? You must never trust them." He tilted his head. "But you must forgive yourself."

Cass was tired of riddles and puzzles. He was tired of death. And he didn't want this sick fuck telling him how he should feel about himself. Maybe he could live with the mysteries of Bright and his father and the Glow. Maybe for now he wasn't going to get a choice. He did the only thing he could and raised the gun. "David Solomon. You are under arrest for the murders of—"

Heels clicked loudly against the tiled floor at the back of the church and he faltered. For a moment he wondered if it was Ramsey and the back-up arriving, but at the same time he knew the church door hadn't opened since it had slammed behind him. Two things happened at once. The first was that he recognised the smartly dressed man who walked down the aisle, his hands tucked into the pockets of his expensive wool overcoat. It was Mr. Bright. *You'll come and he'll follow. Wheels within wheels.*

The second was that Solomon plunged the hypodermic deep into his bare arm. He sucked his teeth in and then smiled before getting to his feet and moving back to the altar. Cass stared. He'd seen the amount of liquid in that thing. Solomon should have been dead pretty much instantly. What the fuck was this man made of?

His hand wavered, unsure quite where to point the gun. There was something fragile about the handsome man standing next to the dead vicar, and on top of that he had far too much barbiturate rushing through his bloodstream to survive. Mr. Bright, however, was as calm and cool as the last time Cass had seen him, and somehow that terri-fied Cass more.

"How the fuck did you get here? Have you been watching me?"

"Always, Cassius. You should know that by now." Mr. Bright never took his eyes from Solomon as he answered Cass's question. He shook his head slightly at the blond man.

"I never thought it would end like this, Solomon. Not for you and me."

Cass looked from one to the other. It was as if he wasn't even there.

Solomon smiled, and love shone from it. "We've been Bright and Solomon so long I think I've almost forgotten our original names, brother."

He leaned on the altar, the first sign of strength seeping from him. Cass stared. He should be dead. He should be dead, and he shouldn't be able to produce maggots from under his fingernails, and there is no Glow. Thoughts burned under Cass's skin as he watched the two men on either side of him. *The Man of Flies. The Lord of the Flies.* Who *was* this man?

"All this has to end, Mr. Bright." Solomon's smile was almost charming, and Cass could see so clearly why those women would have gone with him, why the good Reverend trusted him. "We should never have started it in the first place. I can't think like you any more. I can smell it corrupting. He's dying and everything is rotting."

"And that's what all this attention-grabbing is about?" Mr. Bright raised an eyebrow, as if the deaths of five women and this vicar were merely the actions of a small child throwing its toys out of the pram in a tantrum.

"I just wanted to watch them die. To see how terrible it is." Solomon's head rocked a little on his shoulders. "I think that perhaps death is not that terrible. We need to stop fighting it." For the first time he glanced at Cass.

"He can't save you. Neither of them can, and he needed to know how you have plotted and planned. Just like his brother found out." His breathing came in short bursts and he punched out sentences with the air. "And that's why I led him to you. At the flat. With the dead girl." Despite the effort, he made the words sound victorious. Mr. Bright, however, just laughed merrily.

"I'm the Architect, Solomon." The silver-haired man's smile sparkled with health. "I was already drawing him in. Your game was just an embellishment, and easy to take care of. You've been too busy with your own tests and toys to keep an eye on the bigger picture." The laughter trickled away. "And now you'll die and it will all be for nothing."

"We're all dying anyway. I can feel it. It hums in the air."

"You think so?" Mr. Bright said. "Look at me? Am I dying? It's all in your head, Solomon. You and the others, you've made your fate. You convinced yourselves. Maybe it's just time and age and ennui." His smile fell. "And now your self-prophecy will come true."

"What the fuck has all this got to do with me?" Cass barked. His back-up would be here soon, and he was tired of being ignored—if he was that fucking important to whatever twisted plans they had, they should at least talk to him. "Why the fuck have you been watching me?"

Solomon gripped the altar and hunched over it, gasping slightly for air.

"Not *watching* you, Cassius," Mr. Bright said, "protecting you. Why do you think you didn't end up dead after that fiasco?" He stepped a little closer. "You think Brian Freeman's people never recognised you in the newspapers, just because Charlie Sutton's body turned up dead in the river?"

It felt like a punch in the face. His brain reeled.

"How do you think you got away with murder, Cassius? And kept your job?" Mr. Bright reached out to touch his arm, but Cass shrugged him away. Mr. Bright's smile didn't falter. "I've been looking out for you. We all have. It's a matter of blood, you see."

"Who's *we all*?" Cass felt sick. He'd been so fucking stupid—so na-ïve. How much of his life had been negotiated behind his back—and more importantly, *why*? Should he have been that poor bastard dragged out of the river so long ago? Were there men who still wanted to do that to him, but who were held at bay by whatever power this strange man wielded? How much was truth and how much was lies? Christian had said the same thing to Father Michael, hadn't he—that he felt his life was being manipulated. The world whirled around him and he just wanted it to stop.

Behind him Solomon hunched further over the dead body. The drugs were winning that battle. "He's talking about the Network." He could barely get the words out, but still he forced himself to his feet. "They've lied to you, Cassius—"

"Shut up, Solomon. You don't know what you're—"

"They've lied, and taken what doesn't belong to them." His eyes were desperate. Something was starting to shine at the edges. There was nothing weak or watery about it, like the vague something he thought he had glimpsed in Ramsey's eyes. "You must find him!" he hissed. His breath hitched again and he pulled the baseball cap from his head. The tips of his blond hair glinted and glistened in the yellow candlelight. Liquid gold dripped in Solomon's eyes and started to shine. A soft buzzing started quietly, growing as he twitched.

"What the fuck is happening to him?" Cass whispered.

"He's dying," Mr. Bright said. "All that he is and ever was is showing itself."

Solomon gasped and flung his head back. Gold radiated from his eyes and mouth, the brightness of it enough to make Cass squint. "What the fuck is that?" He knew the answer before he'd asked the question. The Glow.

"It's what you've hidden from, Cassius, all your life." Mr. Bright's words were almost lost in the building buzz. "It's your destiny."

Cass watched Solomon, dread growing in the pit of his stomach. The tall man's arms stretched out at his sides, a mockery of the crucifixion, his whole body radiating light. For a second Cass thought he heard him moan before the buzzing became a rush of sound and movement that raised a foul wind sweeping down from the vaulted ceiling. Flies swarmed out from under the sleeves of Solomon's cheap mackintosh, a flood of black so thick that it almost deadened the pure light that glowed from every visible inch of the man. Maggots dripped from his fingertips to the ground where they writhed, half-dead, bloated and blackened.

Cass flinched as the dark cloud lost its focus, the thousands of tiny insects moving in all directions, humming madly as they crashed into each other and the walls, darting around both Bright and Cass before finding their way back to the dying whirlwind that surrounded Solomon. Still squinting, Cass looked at Mr. Bright, who stood perfectly still, his hands tucked into his overcoat pockets. Gold shone at the corners of his eyes, but silver ran in his tears.

A terrible silence filled the church, holding them all in it for the briefest of seconds before Cass's breath was sucked out of his lungs, the sound like an underwater explosion in his head. He looked back at Solomon. The Glow, the flies, Cass's breath; they hit the blond man, sending him flying back against the solid stone wall.

Sucking at empty air, Cass fell to his knees. From the corner of his eye he could see Mr. Bright's polished brogues. There were no crimson spots on them. He hadn't fallen. Cass's eyes met Solomon's. They stared long and hard at each other, and as Cass's lungs threatened to explode he wondered if they'd both die here, together on the floor of a church whose beliefs meant nothing to either of them. His face burned in the silence of nothingness, and just when he was sure his head might explode, Solomon's mouth twitched in something that was almost a smile and the last traces of light faded in his skin and eyes.

The air filled with oxygen and Cass gasped in huge lungfuls. It tasted sweet as mountain water. He let his face cool against the tiles, lying there until his breathing grew less ragged. Slowly, he pulled himself up onto his feet. The muscles across his chest screamed as he straightened and walked over to the dead man. Solomon didn't look so handsome now. His skin had sagged and his hair was more brown than blond. He looked old. He looked dead. The flies had disappeared. He was suddenly nothing special at all. Whatever had been there before was gone.

He turned to find that so was Mr. Bright. He looked around him. Mr. Bright was gone, and so was the bottle of blood that Solomon had left on the altar. It didn't surprise him much. Mr. Bright was something else; something *other*. He'd seen a glimpse of something tonight that now echoed through his soul. He stood between the dead men and sighed. What the fuck had he seen? What had gone on here? It felt like the vanished flies were crawling in and under his skin. He trembled.

As the far door burst open and Ramsey ran in, bringing all the noise and energy of the outside with him, Cass thought he might be sick. The world around him had shaken. He was back to being a little boy who could see things he didn't want to. How real was anything? How real was his life? His job? His marriage? There were layers upon layers of reality in his memory. How many of them had been manipulated by Mr. Bright, and why?

"What happened?" Ramsey panted.

"He's dead. Injection," Cass muttered as he slid the gun into the back of his trousers. His hair felt sticky with sweat and his lungs moved slowly, trying to convince him that there still wasn't enough air in the church to breathe.

The next hour or so passed in a slow dream. He called it in and within minutes bodies filled the church, all gloved and careful not to disturb anything. Cass talked on autopilot, delivering an amended version of the truth that could fit with this gritty reality and didn't include flies, and Glow and Mr. Bright. He was in the middle of a bubble of lies. He lied to his sergeant when Claire called briefly, and he lied to DCI Morgan when he turned up. There were congratulations, but Cass didn't feel like celebrating. He waited until Dr. Farmer had arrived and the processing of the scene had started before doing what he'd wanted to do from the moment Solomon had died. Morgan and Ramsey were standing at the back of the church by the door, and Cass paused on his way out.

"I have to get out of here. I need to go home. A shower."

Morgan nodded. "Good idea. I can manage things from here. You've done your share." The DCI looked over at Ramsey. "And you'd better get back to your own nick."

"Sir," Ramsey answered. Cass could have hugged the other man when he saw there was no watery glow in his eyes. What the fuck did that glow mean? *Why did it matter?*

"I'll come back in and file my report later—" He was already walking away as he was speaking; his feet were fighting the urge to run back out onto the gritty streets of the city he loved.

When he finally flagged down a black cab, he wound the window down and breathed in the night air. He forced his heart to slow. The night was real. The streets were real. The glorious buildings that cut through the sky were as real as the men that had bled and died to build them. He drank in its scents and sounds. Maybe the Glow, whatever the fuck it was, was real too. Maybe he was going to have to accept that. But this earth, this city, and the grimy daily struggle of it; that was his religion. People, life and death, and staying mainly on the right side of the line. That was all that mattered.

He tried not to think about the flies that had lived and died inside Solomon. He tried not to think about the line of eggs that appeared from the man's fingertips, apparently squeezed out from the finger itself. There was nothing he could do about those things. He wanted to talk to Kate, to *really* talk to her . . . to see if she'd ever heard of a man called Mr. Bright, and if she still loved him enough to let him make it better. He wanted to hold her and feel the heat of her body, and make love to her rather than just fuck her. And then when that was done, he just wanted to sleep for a week.

Cass let himself into the house and stood in the gloomy hallway. There was a thin wash of light from the one strip that had been left on in the kitchen, but the rest of the rooms were dark. Kate wasn't home. Her absence was palpable. He tried her mobile number, but it went straight to answer phone and he didn't leave a message. The things he wanted to say had to be said face to face so she could see that he meant them.

At his feet was a jumble of envelopes on the doormat and he stooped to pick them up, ignoring the aches that quivered through his body. If the post was still here then Kate hadn't been home all day. Where would she have gone? The memory of their unmade bed when he came back last time tried to rear its ugly head, but he crushed it. It didn't stop his heart sinking a little. Maybe the morning would be a better time to see her anyway, after he'd slept away at least some of the day's horrors. Halfway to his feet he paused. Black lace-up shoes. Crimson stains. He groaned as he rose to face his dead brother. He had no energy left for this.

"Oh just fuck off, Christian."

Christian smiled. At least his eyes weren't bleeding this time. In fact, in the half-light they looked a perfect blue.

Cass stared at him. He was tired of this shit. "Just what the fuck is it you want?" He threw the post onto the side table. "What, Christian? What the fuck do you want from me?"

His brother's benign smile stayed fixed, but he turned his head slightly in the direction of the envelopes. He lifted his hand and mimicked a phone call, just as he'd done every time Cass had seen him since he died.

"I don't know what you—" Cass stopped suddenly as a blue logo poking out from the post caught his eye. The phone bill had arrived. He looked back at Christian before slowly reaching for it. Still smiling,

Christian turned and walked away, his feet leading him steadily towards the kitchen. Cass knew that if he followed, his brother would be gone. Cass had finally got the message. He looked down at the envelope. He didn't deal with the bills; that was Kate's job. As long as they got paid, he didn't care. What was in this one that Christian wanted him to see?

He tore it open and dropped the summary page, letting it drift unwanted to his feet. His tiredness fled as one mobile number came up over and over again. The calls had been made with far more frequency in the past week or so. His chest tightened. He knew the number, and it wasn't one he'd be calling from home. What business would Kate have calling it? He had a terrible sick cramp in the pit of his stomach as he checked the dates and times of the calls made on the night Christian and his family died. The mobile number was the last one dialled, and it must have been just before Cass had got home. The memory flashed bright behind his eyes: coming through the door, tossing the envelope from Mullins and his keys down. Kate, beautiful and cool, hanging up the phone. Hate and rage burned through the cracks in his broken heart. *What the fuck had they done?* And *why?*

On the side table his phone buzzed and for an instant Cass thought a swarm of flies were coming for him. He answered it.

"Detective Inspector? It's Maya Healey." Soft, nervous, awkward. "I've got that information on those two accounts you asked for—the ones Christian was concerned about? Sorry it's taken so long, but he must have taken the original printouts I gave him home, and so I supposed the police must still have them."

"Who do the accounts belong to?" He had no time for pleasantries. His brain was burning and the voice he heard coming from his own mouth was alien. Inside, he wasn't even sure he could form words.

"There were two fronting accounts, but I've got the names of who owns them. It didn't take long, they weren't particularly well set up."

As she said the names, the final pieces of the jigsaw slid neatly into place and he realised exactly what he'd been missing on that film. A glint of light that told a separate story. He needed to get back to the office.

* * *

Claire swivelled Cass's chair from side to side as she sat behind his desk and watched the film. Something about the opening was bugging her; as soon as the two boys came into view, she clicked the mouse to stop the film and start it again from the beginning. She'd been staring at the screen so long that her eyes were burning. Customers sitting at their tables. The waitress moves between them. A man's hand rises as he sips his coffee. His cufflink flashes in the light. Macintyre gets out of the taxi. He stops by the café and lights a cigarette.

Claire stopped it and rewound again, this time just a few frames. She felt a slight tingle as she zoomed in. The picture quality was pretty dreadful, but for this it was enough. Macintyre didn't just stop to light his cigarette. He was also acknowledging someone . . . someone sitting *inside* the coffee shop. Focusing intently, she identified the briefest twist of a smile, and the flick of his wrist at someone on the other side of the glass. She ran it forward, frame by frame. *There*. Just in the corner of the shot, a white sleeve with a cufflink rose slightly in response.

She leaned back in the chair, her mouth open slightly. *The cufflink*. Cold sweat made her palms sticky as she zoomed in as close as she could, until the little piece of jewellery filled the screen. She stared, shaking. The lab boys would be able to clean it up, but she already knew what she was looking at. *Jesus*.

The building was quiet; most of the team had gone to the pub to celebrate closing not one but two major cases in one day. As far as they were all concerned, Paddington Green nick was the stuff of legend, as of today. She stared again at the screen. How were they going to take this? Would they expect her to sweep it under the carpet, shut her mouth and get on with her career? Probably. Cass needed to see this. He needed to know it. *This* was why he'd been set up: to stop him *seeing* this. She was about to reach for the phone when Mat peered into the office.

"You okay? Coming for a drink?" he asked. Other than a couple of constables clearing the boards in the Incident Room they were the last left.

He was at the desk before she could get her act together quickly enough to switch screens. He frowned. "What are you doing?"

"I don't know." She couldn't quite keep the shake out of her voice. "Something's been bugging me—then I realised we'd missed something on the film. We missed who Macintyre had gone there to meet."

Blackmore's eyes widened. "What are you talking about? I thought this was all wrapped up?"

"The shooting is, yes." She looked at Mat, pleased when he took her hand. She needed someone's help, and even if she knew, deep down, that he would never be her true love, if she couldn't trust the man she was sleeping with, then who else was there?

"But I think I know who set Cass up."

"Who?" Blackmore's voice dropped. "You know who did it?"

She nodded at the screen. "You must recognise those cufflinks."

His Adam's apple bobbed as he studied the screen. Eventually he asked quietly, "Is that really who I think it is?"

Claire gripped his hand. "I know this must be awful for you, he's your DI—but it can't be anyone else. And if he was there innocently, then why didn't he say? Can you remember where Bowman said he was when the shootings happened?"

"I can't remember. I can't." He ran his free hand over his spiked hair and swallowed. "Jesus, Claire. *GB*. He's got those cufflinks." He looked back at the frozen screen, then at Claire. "Look, maybe it's someone else. Maybe—"

"Someone else? How likely is that?"

Red blotches were covering his neck and face. "When did you figure all this out, Claire?"

"Just now. Seconds ago," she said. "I need to tell Cass."

"Yes," Mat said, nodding, "we do." He picked up the phone and punched in a number. It rang out and he shook his head. "Straight to answer phone." His keys were in his hand. "Come on, I'll drive you. Where is he?"

"Ramsey called it in; he said Cass'd gone home once he'd secured the crime scene. He was a bit shaken." Adrenalin was pumping through her and her own legs trembled as she stood. Thank God Mat was with her on this, she thought. They jogged down the corridor to the far stairs. "Where's Bowman?" she panted. "Still at the church?"

"No, he's left that to the lab rats. I think he's in the pub." The door closed behind them and he stopped suddenly.

Claire looked at him and frowned. "What's the matter? Let's go." Her words echoed in the empty space.

His hands squeezed the tops of her arms and he pulled her close. For a moment Claire thought he was going to kiss her.

"I'm sorry," he whispered.

The handrail was pressing uncomfortably against the small of her back as she tilted, off balance, and confusion cut through her panic. What was Mat doing? This didn't make sense—

Until he shoved, hard, toppling her over the side of the steps, and she realised how utterly *stupid* she'd been. Her hands clutched at empty air as she tumbled, and she tried to catch her breath to scream. She wanted to click on rewind, she wanted to remind herself that there'd been *two* people in the interview room with Macintyre on Saturday. She wanted to kick herself for being so moronically thick for thinking even for one moment that Bowman could be involved without Blackmore, without his poisonous little sidekick . . . She wanted a lot of things.

But as the ground rushed up far too fast to meet her, she squeezed her eyes shut. Most of all, she wanted not to die.

CHAPTER NINETEEN

Cass knew there was something wrong the minute he arrived at the station. The cab dropped him beside his own car and he walked inside. He needed to watch the film again, and then he'd grab the DCI or the Commissioner and make them see what he knew he'd see on it. He'd tried calling Claire, but got no reply. She was probably in the pub with Blackmore, celebrating. There was no reason for her to be listening out for any calls. The cases were closed . . .

An ambulance was parked in front of the steps and Cass frowned as he made his way round it. Had someone been hurt in custody? That would just be fucking typical on top of what he had to tell the headshed—and on a day when they should be celebrating good, solid police investigation . . .

The reception area was quiet. Everyone waiting with a grievance or a crime to report must have been hustled out. He vaguely recognised the desk sergeant, who looked up from the papers he was shuffling when Cass asked, "So what's going on?"

The sergeant gestured at the main doors. "In there." Whatever had happened must be bad; he obviously hadn't wanted to be the one to tell Cass about it. Cass felt that familiar cold roiling mass in the pit of his stomach. *It wasn't over yet.*

He pushed open the doors to see a small crowd of people gathered on his far left, where the doors to the side stairs were. One of the uniformed WPCs turned at the sound of the doors opening and saw him. She gasped quietly and went white.

That sharp intake of breath. The flash of dark eyes; did they look reddened? Bile rose in his throat as the whole group turned his way. He felt like he was wading through mud, moving inexorably forwards. A hush blanketed them and they silently parted to let him through to the fire doors, which had been propped open, and into the middle of the clicking cameras and huddled detectives. Dr. Farmer was present, his wild grey rock-star hair immediately visible among the more expensively coiffured detectives. He was talking quietly, but when he saw Cass, he stopped. They all did.

It was the shoe that Cass saw first. It was lying on its side under the stairs, forgotten. Not a black lace-up. No crimson stains. This one was blue, with a sensible one-inch heel. It was small and feminine and fragile. His face burned as he turned, peering through the gaps between the living to catch a glimpse of that familiar body sprawled on the ground. This time there was no supernatural wind sucking the oxygen from his lungs. Instead it was his own body simply refusing to breathe as he stared at her.

A large pool of blood formed an uneven halo at the back of Claire's head. She didn't turn to look at him, or smile, that twinkle of fond recognition in her eyes. She remained facing the other way, her head twisted on her bent neck. Her eyes were dull, glazed over, but her mouth was formed into a surprised "O," despite the obvious force of the impact as she'd hit the ground.

Cass almost collapsed onto the second step. Her hair was shiny, the red hints clashing with the thick blood that had burst from some awful wound that was out of sight. His hands shook and now, finally, he forced himself to breathe. *Life to unlife.* All in one shattering instant. He felt sick to his soul.

"What happened?"

It was only when he spoke that he realised how silent it was. Two paramedics slipped through the double doors. They would wait. They had no place here; there was nothing they could do now but carry her to her slab, a freezing bed in a morgue fridge where she would grow colder yet. They wanted no part in explanations or grief. Cass wondered how cold Claire's fingers had to get before they'd start tugging at him. She was facing away from him, with one arm stretched out behind her. He looked at the pale skin and neatly trimmed nails. Maybe she was reaching for him already.

"I said, what happened?" He looked up, now taking in the faces around him. Mat Blackmore was there, leaning against the far wall. He looked small next to DCI Neil Morgan. Another DC—he should have known his name, but right now his mind had gone blank—looked away. He had his hands shoved deep in his pockets. It was the ME who finally broke the silence.

"It was just an accident." Farmer coughed slightly. Cass had never heard him sound awkward before. "She and Mat were leaving to go to the pub. He went to the loo while she was turning off the computer. Someone had spilled some coffee." He stopped briefly, thrown by the look on Cass's face, then went on, "She must have come through the doors and slipped on it and—" He stumbled again, then finished, "She fell over the handrail."

"She slipped on *coffee*?" Cass, incredulous, almost laughed. "But people don't—" He stopped himself. He'd been about to say: people don't slip forwards. They *trip* forwards, they *slip* backwards. It was the basis for every fucking banana skin routine or slapstick comedy that had ever existed. He'd been about to say that, and then he'd stopped. The detective with his hands in his pockets had cast a quick sideways glance at Blackmore, who in turn had looked furtively at Mark Farmer. It all took the briefest of seconds. Farmer kept his eyes firmly on Cass.

"People don't die from slipping in coffee," he finished, allowing some melancholy to flood out in his words. "It's stupid."

He felt it. The slightest ease in tension in the men around him. It made the awful truth clear. Claire hadn't slipped. She'd been pushed. He knew it, and he was pretty damned sure that at least three people there in that stairwell knew it too. He rested his face in his hands and let his shoulders slump.

"If it's any consolation," Farmer's voice was soft, "she died the instant she hit the ground."

Cass gritted his teeth. Anger and grief and death boiled inside him. Yeah, the instant after she'd been pushed—the instant after knowing what was coming. That was some fucking consolation for the death of a woman who was better than all of them put together.

He lifted his head. "Thanks." He looked over at Blackmore. "Are you okay?"

The young sergeant shrugged. "Not good. I just keep thinking, if I hadn't gone ahead. If I'd waited for her . . ." He looked sick. He also couldn't look Cass in the eye.

"Life's not like that," Cass said. "This was an accident. You can't fight accidents."

"Why don't you get home, Cass?" It was the first time his DCI had spoken. Cass watched him, looking for signs of something sinister, but there wasn't anything he could pinpoint. Should he risk trying to talk to him? He stood up, shakily, and looked down at Claire's broken body. He remembered the feel of her, her soft heat, as she'd moved under him and on top of him. He remembered the way she'd looked at him, as if he were the man he would have liked to have been. His fractured heart cracked some more, but he fused it with rage. He'd grieve later.

He couldn't risk talking to Morgan now. He didn't know if he could trust him—anyway, this was something he had to finish by himself. He owed her that.

"Yeah, maybe I will," he said. "I'm fucking tired."

"Take your time." The DCI sounded almost sympathetic. "You've had a bloody awful week." He paused. "And you've done some good policing too. Go home and grieve." The awkwardness in the compliment was genuine. It didn't stop Cass feeling like he was treading through a nest of vipers as he moved between them.

He said a silent goodbye to Claire's broken body and turned his back on her for the last time. He felt her cold hand slide into his, and the sharp edges of those neatly trimmed fingernails dug into his palm.

He should have picked her up and carried her out of there. He shouldn't have allowed their dirty hands to touch her. But still he walked away. Claire was gone. The small crowd on the other side of the doors parted for him again, but he didn't even look at them. Hush now, he silently whispered, lost in the memory of the clean scent of her hair. I will get you your vengeance. And it shall be terrible.

He didn't go back to the seminary. He drove instead to Muswell Hill. Kate wouldn't be there. He was pretty sure about that. The single kitchen light was still on, but now that night had fallen the rest of the house was shrouded in darkness. He smoked a cigarette in the kitchen before pulling out Ramsey's gun. He spent some time checking it over thoroughly, getting a feel for the action. It was fully loaded. He was a little sad at how familiar it felt to have a gun in his hand once more. Then he took the phone from the holder in the hallway and went and sat in the dark lounge. He put his mobile on one arm of the chair, the land line handset on the other.

He lit another cigarette and smoked in the darkness. His eyes were as gritty as his heart. Bowman would either come here, or call. He didn't have any other choice: he needed to know what—if anything—Cass knew. The smoke tasted acrid as he breathed it out and for a moment he wondered, if he looked hard enough, would he see the curious dead in it as it hung in the air? Claire. Christian. Jessica. Luke. Solomon. Even Carla Rae and the two dead boys. Were they all here watching him, wondering what he was going to do? He wondered how much they knew but couldn't share.

Shards of ice formed in his heart as he stared into the darkness. Surely he should feel more than just this cold rage that was filling him? What about anguish, guilt even? Or was he so immersed in that already that there was no room for more? He'd left Claire to make sure the murderous fathers watched the deaths of their sons. If he hadn't done that, then her clever mind would never have spotted what the phone bill and the accounts had shown him.

His mind went in circles. It was his fault she was dead, and hers too, for being so trusting. She must have told Mat Blackmore—her *lover*—

what she'd discovered, and in his panic he did the only thing he could: he killed her. Desperate measures for desperate men. Maya had said there was a lot of money at stake here—easily enough to set him up. And enough to kill Claire for. Was she the only one they'd killed? *Bloodstains in doorways*. Jessica had got out of bed, come running to check on her baby. She'd been thrown backwards . . . Could Bowman have done that? It seemed too extreme, just to set him up, even for that corrupt bastard.

Cass's eyes had adjusted to the darkness and now he was seeing the world in blacks and greys. He didn't look at his watch; he had a while to wait yet. How far did the rot go, he wondered. The news of Claire's death would have cut short the celebrations in the pub. How many whispered conversations were now being had behind closed doors, or in pub car parks and toilets? What the fuck had they all been up to— *and why had they never invited him in?*

He thought of Bright and Solomon, and the Glow. How different was he to other people? Could they sense it? Had that been the problem with him and Kate? Was that what had drawn him to Jessica? A knife twisted in his gut. Kate and Bowman. He remembered himself with Jessica, and Claire, and so many others. Could he really blame her for going elsewhere? Logic said no, but the rage that was freezing him from the inside out said otherwise. And she'd picked *Gary Bowman*, of all men. That made him feel sick. Had they done it in their bed? Had it started during their brief separation and been going on since then?

Rain tapped at the window outside and he thought the dead sighed in the small draught that crept from the sash windows. Cass could feel them so close to him, the new and the old, here in the shadows where nothing really existed. He wondered if they were trying to draw him to them. Perhaps they'd even succeed; maybe that's how this night would end, in his own messy death. He had a gun, but did Bowman? He didn't think he'd much care either way as long as he got to the truth before it was all done. He was finally alone. All those he had ever cared for were either dead or gone. It frightened him, how liberating that thought was. That freedom created too many terrible possibilities. There was no one left to care for, or worry about, or feel a sense of duty for.

He could do whatever he wanted. The gun rested on his lap, its solidity a cold comfort.

He waited.

It was gone half-past eleven when the phone finally pealed out. It was the land line. He let it ring three times. When he answered, the dead skittered into nothing at the sound of his voice.

"Hello?"

"It's me." Her voice was a thousand memories shattering. "Are you still up?"

"Yes." His hand gripped the plastic too tightly. He wondered how she felt to Bowman when he fucked her: warm, wet, eager—forever out of reach? He knew he hadn't really touched her since he'd become Charlie Sutton. They'd both been damaged beyond repair by the aftermath of that single gunshot. All they'd ever got right was the fucking. And that was how she chose to betray him.

"We closed the cases. Both of them." He tried to sound normal. That was easy. Normal with them was always distant and awkward. "But something happened. There was an accident." His voice choked and tears sprang to life in the corners of his eyes. The emotion surprised him and he swallowed the tears down. He would not break now, not until this was done. "It's Claire. She's dead. She fell."

A small gasp. "I'm sorry."

A long pause. They never had been able to talk about the important stuff. Cass wondered where this was leading. "What do you want, Kate?"

"I want to talk."

"What about?"

"Us. Jessica. I want to understand."

Cass sighed. His heart ached, and bled afresh. Did she mean it? Or was she with Bowman now? Maybe he'd played her too, just used her to get to Cass. Maybe she didn't know her lover had been intent on setting up her husband. He couldn't summon much enthusiasm for that argument. Whoever had set him up had got his sperm from somewhere. He hadn't been fucking anyone else, and Bowman was fucking the woman who could get it on tap for him. The thoughts were crude. He wanted it that way: this was all base—base, and human, and gritty, and that he could deal with.

"You want to come here?" he said.

"No." She sniffed, loudly. Surely she couldn't still be crying. "Not there."

"Then where?" His veins fizzed, his blood pumped faster.

"Christian's house."

"What?" His blood cooled. "Are you crazy?"

"You fucked Jessica there." A hard edge. "It's an honest place, Cass. We can't tell lies there."

"It's a crime scene, Kate."

"I don't think so." Softness again. She was mercurial tonight, this wife of his. "I drove past this evening. The tape was gone from around the front. I couldn't see anyone there. I think they're done."

She'd done her homework, but she was probably right. The SOC team would have gone back at Ramsey's request, but the cleaners would have finished and the house would be ready to go to probate, or whoever dealt with the possessions the dead no longer needed. As far as anyone else was concerned, it was a straightforward murder-suicide. There was no reason to keep someone on the door.

"My brother and his family died in that house." He had no intention of making this easy for her, or Bowman, or both of them. "You want me to go back there?" His voice rose slightly. The aggression and pain came easily. "Claire died today, Kate. I've been through things, seen things you just wouldn't believe. And now you want me to go to Christian's house in the middle of the night to fucking talk?"

Another pause. He could almost see the sulky cast to her lips. "It's tonight or never, Cass. If we can't talk honestly tonight, after all this, then we never will." She sighed and sniffed, all rolled into one.

"Okay," he said, and he felt the chess pieces moving into place. "I'll meet you there in twenty minutes."

"Thanks, Cass." The snot turned to tears in her voice and she hung up without saying any more. As if she might perhaps say something she would regret.

He sat still for a few moments more, relishing the quiet darkness and the cool thump of his deadened heart. He would have his vengeance. He made a short call on his mobile, talking quietly and quickly. When it was done, he smiled. It was time to end this particular game. *Wheels within wheels*.

CHAPTER TWENTY

She looked fragile standing in the shadow of the doorway, away from the beam of the street light. She had her arms wrapped round herself to help keep out the night chill. Strands of hair danced in the light breeze as she shuffled slightly from foot to foot. The night wasn't that cold; what was it: nerves or impatience, or perhaps a bit of both? Shadows cut lines across her cheekbones, highlighting her angular beauty. Her eyes glinted and she stood still as he opened the low gate and walked up the path.

She might look fragile, but Cass knew better. Kate was feline, and cats had nine lives. She might be damaged, but she was far from broken. He could see her eyes darting between him and the house. He smiled at her as his heart splintered all over again. They weren't alone. Someone was waiting inside for him, and this beautiful stranger who had been a major part of his fucked-up life for so long had brought him here to face them.

"Hi," he said.

"Thanks for coming." She sniffed and wiped her nose before standing on tiptoes to kiss him on the cheek. Her lips were cool and cracked. A stranger's lips. "Let's get inside. It's cold."

The gun pressed against his back as he reached up with the key. Was Bowman going to blow him away as soon as he opened the door?

His heart raced. Probably not. Bowman wouldn't risk hitting Kate, and if he shot both of them that would be fucking hard to explain. Whether Bowman loved her or not was probably debatable, but either way he couldn't take the chance of making this messier than it already was.

The door swung open and the dark hallway yawned wide, ready to swallow them up. Cass grabbed Kate's arm and pulled her in front of him, ignoring her yelp of surprise.

"What are you doing, Cass?"

He didn't answer but pushed her forward towards the lounge and dining room, following her, and she stepped into the large living space. The house felt empty, as if even the ghosts had left, but the sound of Kate's heels clicking as she stumbled echoed like gunshots. Even in the grey light he could see that the wall had been scrubbed clean of Christian's brains and blood and life. The floor would be clean too. His heart thumped.

"Where are you, Bowman?" he called.

A dark shadow emerged from the kitchen at the far end, forming from the pitch-black. A cufflink glinted against a raised hand.

Cass left his gun hidden as he pushed Kate forward again. "I think this belongs to you now."

In the no man's land between the two men, Kate flashed him a glare. "You bastard."

Cass didn't comment. It was the closest to real emotion he'd seen from her in a long time.

Bowman flicked on a small table lamp, though the warm yellow light didn't stretch far across the room. It wouldn't draw any unwanted attention from the sleeping outside world.

"Well, I guess that answers one of my questions," Bowman said. "You know about us."

Kate stayed where she was, sobbing and sniffing into her sleeve. Cass looked at her again, and in the light, he could see the changes. Her beauty had all but vanished: she had dark bags under her bloodshot eyes and her pupils were so huge he could scarcely make out the bright blue of her irises. Her nose was red and sore. Jesus: her whole body screamed her guilt. He knew that look, he'd worn it himself for long enough. She sniffed again and this time he laughed. Whatever was plaguing her conscience, if she thought that drugs would make it all go away, she had a hard lesson to learn ahead of her.

"So, she's not just a whore." His voice was cold. "Now she's a coke whore." He looked over at the other man. "Nice work. Is that the only way you can get her to fuck you?"

Kate pressed herself against the wall and Cass turned away from her, his attention on his fellow detective. Bowman's hand was up, his weapon pointing firmly in Cass's direction. At least he knew where he stood. And Bowman didn't yet know he had a gun of his own tucked against the small of his back.

"It didn't take much, Jones. In fact, it took pathetically little," Bowman sneered. "Kate just wants a nice life with someone who can give her the things she wants, and a little respectability." He laughed. "Let's face it: that was never going to be you."

"Oh, and I can see just how it could be you." Cass spoke softly, his hatred cold as ice. There was more going on here than Kate. He needed to remember that, keep the rage that tore at him cool, under control. "But she's really not important. You're welcome to her." She flinched. He kept his eyes away from her.

"How long have you been in business with Macintyre?"

"Did Claire tell you that? She told Mat she hadn't told anyone. Funny, she never struck me as a liar."

"No." Cass blinked away the image of the broken body on the ground. "She wasn't a liar. She didn't tell me. Your bank accounts did."

Bowman shrugged slightly. "That would be your brother's fault. He just wouldn't leave it alone. So you've been digging around in his files."

Black lace-up brogues. Crimson stains. A knife-twist in the gut. What the fuck did Bowman know about Christian? His fingers itched for his gun.

"Not that it matters," Bowman continued. "No one's going to care once you're gone."

The implication was clear. Cass felt his stomach tighten. At least Bowman had laid his cards on the table. No surprise, though: they'd killed Claire. They were hardly going to leave him alive.

"Someone will."

"No, they won't," Bowman laughed. "You think this is just me and Mat? You think we'd do all this if it was just us?"

All this. How steeped in blood were they?

"Are you saying you two have some other friends? How sweet. If surprising."

"Sarcasm? It always was the best you could manage, Cass." Bowman's mouth twisted.

From upstairs, Cass heard the tiniest whisper of a creak of the floor-boards. His heart stilled. That was no ghost. Someone else was in the house with them. He didn't react to the sound, and it was unlikely Bowman would have heard it from where he was standing, with Kate's quiet snivelling between them. What Cass didn't understand was why they hadn't attacked him already. He knew *he* wanted information, but what did *they* want now? Whatever it was, he could use it to buy himself some time. He didn't need much.

"Is Morgan involved?"

"No, it's not really a brass thing. You could think of it as a kind of Paddington Green collective. Most of the DIs are in. Their sergeants. The DCs."

"All of them?" Cass's mouth dried. Fuck, he wanted a cigarette.

"Most."

"How?"

"It's the bonuses." Bowman grinned, proudly. "We're all taking money from the firms anyway. We might as well make from it."

"I don't get you." The bonuses were a necessary evil. You just took them and got on with your job the best you could. What the fuck had Bowman turned them into?

"What's the point of a couple of hundred quid here and there? That's spent as soon as we have it. There isn't one. So I spread the word to see if people would be interested in investing the money as a group— you know, buying some product, then shifting it." He was almost preening. "If I say so myself, it's a genius operation. We take the bonuses from the firms on our manor, like Mullins, put the money together, buy the coke from Macintyre and then shift it out to the suburbs where there's no one major to worry about pissing off. It's amazing how quickly you can make some proper money like that. Everyone's doing well out of it: everyone gets their percentage of profits back, then we reinvest and start again. It's a rolling operation, been going for a year now." He grinned. "And you never even bloody noticed."

Cass stared at him. "You're fucking *drug dealers*. This is a fucking *police* firm?" As soon as Maya had given him the names on the accounts he'd known that drugs were involved, but in his wildest dreams he hadn't expected the whole fucking nick to be in on it. Mullins was right: the world was made up of different layers, most of which you never saw. Wheels within wheels.

Another soft creak shivered down the wall of the house. Whoever was upstairs was slowly coming closer.

"Why the fuck didn't I know about it?" Cass asked.

"You?" Bowman snorted. "You're such a fucking martyr, Cass. Would you have come in on it?"

"No." He didn't even have to think about it. "It's too far over the fucking line, Bowman, and you know it."

"Yeah, I've heard your views on fucking shades of grey, Cass. You think just because you blew some Rasta kid's head off that you're the fucking expert on right and fucking wrong?" Bowman's voice rose as he spat out the words. "You think there's a fucking difference between taking the bonuses and what we're doing? Well, there isn't." He took a deep breath. "Light grey or dark grey, it's all the same fucking colour. And why should we work like dogs for a fucking pittance?" He smiled. "But you would never see that, Mr. Cass-fucking-holier-than-thou-Jones. You're far too busy trying to redeem your fucking self—and you know what? *No one fucking cares!*"

Cass almost laughed aloud at the irony, and the bitterness in Bowman's voice. "This has got nothing to do with me and everything to do with you," he said. "You were born dirty, Bowman. You can almost see it on your skin, oozing out of the pores under all those moisturisers and that nice tan. You're scum. You haven't got the bottle to pick your side and stand there, so you sit on the fence and play at both. You're everything I have no respect for." Again there was a shuffle of noise out of sight. Was the final player in this scene making his way down the stairs?

"Well, that just breaks my heart, Cass. If you must know, I've never been that fond of you either."

It was time to end this charade. "What happened to my brother?"

"That was unfortunate."

"*Unfortunate?*" Cass's blood thinned. His eyes burned. Against the wall, Kate grew still.

"He knew about our bank accounts. How, I don't know, but he did. He rang your house that night. You weren't there, but he told Kate all about it. He told her you needed to know."

Cass stared at Kate, but she refused to look at him. *What had she done?* Guilt joined the anger churning up his gut. He should have spoken to Christian. He should have made it home in time for that call. He should have done too many things.

"Kate said he'd been trying to get hold of you for a few days. He'd been talking about weird shit. She said he sounded like he was cracking up." Bowman sounded almost conversational now. "But this was different. She knew if he told you about this, you'd feel honour bound to do something about it. He was kind enough to tell her he would be taking the proof home with him."

A cool shiver prickled along his hairline and down the back of his neck. Cass could see that night unfolding like a movie behind his eyes as Bowman talked.

"Kate told him you'd come round, and he believed her." He shrugged. "She got off the phone and called me straight away. I called Macintyre. He said he'd go round himself, at the same time you were supposed to show. He said he'd try to make Christian see sense. Kate was to make sure you stayed at home."

The bottle of wine. The sex. There was nothing so dumb as a man with a hard-on. Cass looked over at his wife again. Whore. Stranger. Lover.

"When Macintyre got here your sister-in-law and nephew were in bed." Bowman leaned back against the wall. He was still weak; Cass could see a feverish sheen on his forehead. The doctors might not have found anything, but Cass was pretty sure Solomon had done something to the DI.

"Things got nasty and Christian refused to back down. He wasn't prepared to pretend he knew nothing. Macintyre tied him to a chair; he was going to just rough him up a bit, make him see sense, when the wife woke up and called down the stairs."

So it wasn't Luke who died first. He'd slept through it all. It was Jessica who had been disturbed.

"Macintyre went upstairs and shot her. After that, he didn't really have any choice." Bowman left the rest unsaid.

Cass's saliva tasted metallic. *Warm blood.* He could see Christian tied to the chair, something shoved in his mouth, unable to shout any sort of warning. Two gunshots ringing out, and then Macintyre reappearing, splattered in his family's blood. Christian wouldn't have fought after that. Cass would have bet his little brother had just tilted his head back, ready for the bullet, waiting for his brain to be as dead as his heart. He knew how Christian had felt.

Tears stung his eyes. He wondered if they were silver. "You fucking cunt."

"It just got out of hand, Jones," Bowman said. His voice sounded a bit whiny.

Cass stared at Kate. "And you're a fucking piece of work." All that crying, and the brandy: it made sense now. "It's going to take more than a few grams of Charlie to make that go away in your head," he laughed. "That's with you for life, Kate. Good luck with it."

"I didn't do it!" she hissed, spitting out the words as she moved towards him slightly. "I didn't kill them! *I didn't!* I wouldn't—"

Cass took two careful steps back so that he was slightly behind the doorway. The large mirror over the fireplace reflected the dark hallway and the bottom of the stairs.

"But what *did* you do, Kate? You did *something*." He looked at Bowman. "Can I smoke?"

"Sure. Probably better if you do. Make sure you use the ashtray."

It didn't take a genius to work out what Bowman's plan was, and Cass almost smiled as he lit a cigarette and inhaled hard. Suicide in the house where his brother killed himself and his family. Poor Cass Jones, he finally cracked after the tragic accidental death of his sergeant. He'd never been right since that business undercover, no doubt that's what Kate would say, trying to hide her nose lined with a fresh cocaine habit and her nights drained of sleep. That's if they managed to pull it off. As plans went, it was better than throwing someone over the banisters.

He gritted his teeth and enjoyed the feel of metal against his back. Bowman hadn't won yet.

"Don't blame her." Bowman pulled his own cigarettes out with his free hand and lit one. Cass smiled. Mr. Bright was right: people were predictable. If you light a cigarette, then suddenly everyone wants one.

"Mat Blackmore told me about the film coming in. He'd seen me in the shot." He held up the hand with the cigarette in and flashed a cuff-link. "You should take it as a compliment that we were sure you'd spot it, given enough time. I needed you off the case."

In the mirror a white hand shone as it slid down the banister, the wrist emerging from a dark sleeve. Leather, maybe.

Adrenalin pumped through Cass. "So you set me up." He looked at Kate. "*You* set me up."

She brushed aside the lank hair hanging over her eyes and glared at him: hate, rage, love and frustration—it was all there. How had he never seen all that hate?

"Jessica *told* me." Kate wiped the back of her hand across her face. "When Luke was ill and I was going with her to the hospital." Her smile turned into a sad sneer. "She told me about you. She told Christian too. He fucking forgave you." Tears ran from her bloodshot eyes. "She made excuses for you, said you loved me. After everything, Cass, you fucked Jessica. I fucking *hate* you."

Cass stared. She'd been beautiful once, but now she looked hag-ridden. "You *must* have hated me to have started sleeping with him." He paused. "But I did love you, Kate. I never thought I was good enough. I never believed I deserved you." The figure in the reflection had made it down to the hall. For a brief moment the tall frame and gingery-blond hair made him think of Solomon, but there was nothing supernatural about this man. This was just Sam Macintyre, the gangster who had murdered his brother.

His eyes hardened. "Now I know better."

"You bastard!" she cried, and flew at him, her nails clawing at him.

Neither of the other men were prepared for Kate's attack, but it was just the distraction he needed. He pushed the lit cigarette into his wife's pale cheek as he ducked to the left to avoid her ragged nails. Her cry of rage turned to a shriek of agony as she pulled away and stumbled into Macintyre, who wasn't expecting it. Even as he pulled out Ramsey's gun and dropped to his knees in case Bowman fired, Cass could see what was going to happen.

So could Bowman, who started to shout, "Don't—!"

But it was too late, and Cass watched the man's eyes widen for a second in surprise as he reflexively pulled the trigger.

The blast propelled Kate's slim frame back into the room and her hands reached out, her fingers stretching for the life that had already fled her body. Her legs caught on a dining room chair, maybe the very one that Christian had been tied to when Macintyre blew out his brains, and she crumpled to a tangled heap on the floor.

Cass's eyes burned like mercury as rage flooded his veins. Bowman scuttled, panting and wide-eyed, across the floor to the dead body. This hadn't been part of his plan. In the doorway Macintyre was reaching to reload the shotgun. Cass could see everything so clearly as time slowed for him. His teeth gritted, his eyes on fire, Cass raised his own gun and pumped two bullets into Macintyre, one in each elbow. The shots were perfect. He'd known they would be. The burn in his eyes and soul had made it so.

Macintyre stumbled backwards, screaming in agony, and his heavy weapon clattered to the floor. The high-pitched wail signalled the fight was over for him. Cass, on his feet, kicked out at Bowman's head where he was huddled over Kate's dead body. The toe of his shoe connected hard with the side of his skull, then he stamped down hard on Bowman's wrist, crushing his expensive watch.

Now breathing heavily, Cass crouched beside him and tugged Bow-man's gun out of his shaking fingers. The DI might have been licenced to carry, but he was the sort who always got others to do his dirty work. Unlike Macintyre, his reactions were slow, and unlike Cass, he'd never stared into a man's eyes and then pulled the trigger. He would never win in this situation.

Outside, the first sirens wailed. Bowman moaned, trying to focus on Cass. In the hallway, Macintyre was screaming for God, or his mother—or any motherfucker—to help him. Both Cass and Bowman ignored him. With the gun firmly pointed in Bowman's face, Cass lit another cigarette.

"Did you call for back-up?" Blood came out with Bowman's words. Cass must have broken a tooth or two. Still Bowman managed a small smile. "You stupid fucker. Paddington Green is mine. I own it, remember?"

Cass ignored him. He could feel Kate's dead eyes on him, but he couldn't look at her, not yet. Not until this was all finished.

"Why didn't you shoot me straight away?" he asked. "Or at least try to?"

"The phone calls."

"What phone calls?"

Bowman lifted one hand slowly and rubbed the side of his head. "We needed to know who'd set us up. We thought you'd know."

Cass frowned. "What do you mean?"

"The day of the Jackson and Miller shootings. I got a phone call telling me to meet Macintyre at the café. He got one too." He sighed. "Turns out neither of us had made the calls, but then the boys got shot and the film turned up. Someone wanted us caught."

"It wasn't me," Cass said. His insides churned. He had a damned good idea who it was. Silver-haired, silver-tongued, silver-teared: an architect. Someone who was always watching—someone who might want to protect Cass, and expose Solomon to him, all at the same time. Someone who everyone knew, and everyone was wary of. Some-one who had his own tests to carry out. Bowman had never stood a

chance, not against Mr. Bright. He'd simply been in the way of someone else's game plan.

"I don't know who it was," he lied.

Noise erupted around them as policemen flooded the house.

"Someone get an ambulance! We've got an injured man in here."

Cass didn't recognise the voice, but he smiled. "Oh, and just so you
know, Detective Inspector Bowman, I didn't call Paddington for back-
up. I called Chelsea."

"I thought you said it wouldn't be messy." That southern drawl
sounded familiar.

"You took your time."

"Getting detectives out of bed is hard enough for their own cases,
Cass. You should know that." He grinned. "But you seem to have it all
under control."

"Something like that."

Behind them, two officers hauled Bowman to his feet. "No one will
thank you for this, Cass!" he snarled as they pulled him outside. "No
one!"

"No one ever does," Cass said, softly. He looked around him. Blood
had filled his brother's house once more. It had all happened so quickly.
Real life was like that. Here one minute, dead the next. There were no
big car chases; it was just dirty and sordid, and over fast. Kate lay broken at his feet, her smooth stomach a ruined mess. He didn't look down
at her.

"I'm going outside."

Ramsey nodded and let him pass.

Cass didn't look back.

EPILOGUE

When Josh Eagleton finally came round, the first person he'd wanted to see was Cass, not his family or friends. Propped up in his hospital bed he looked pale and thin, and a good few years older than when one of Macintyre's boys had run him down and left him for dead. He'd have scars for life, but Cass figured that wasn't such a bad thing. Those scars would make sure he survived the next time.

It had been two weeks since Kate had died, and Cass was still nursing healing scars of his own. He'd gone back to The Bank for more answers, but surprisingly, they'd still never heard of a Mr. Bright, and no one would get him a warrant to search the building. Still, he hadn't heard from the man again. Whatever it was he wanted Cass to figure out, he'd obviously meant it when he told Cass he'd have to do it by himself. It didn't stop Cass checking over his shoulder every now and then to see if someone was watching him.

Josh opened his eyes and Cass smiled. "You did good, kid. I'm sorry I wasn't paying attention. How did you know?"

Paddington Green was in a right old mess now, with half its officers under arrest or subject to investigation. When he did finally get back to work, Josh would find the situation the same. Dr. Farmer was gone. He'd been in it up to his eyeballs with Bowman.

"I got to work first. I was eager." The kid's voice was dry. "I did a set of swabs on your brother's wife before Dr. Farmer got there. I took blood samples too." A small smile twitched on his tired face. "I wanted to impress him. When he came in, he . . . he was really agitated, and he said no one else could touch the body—he said he wanted to do it himself, out of respect for you." He swallowed. Cass waited patiently. This was Josh's story and he'd tell it in his own time.

Finally, he continued, "I didn't say anything. I didn't want to piss him off. But then when they said they found . . . what they did in your brother's wife, well, I knew it couldn't be true. The first set of swabs were clean. So I knew someone must have planted it."

Cass remembered the cheeky flash of the camera when he'd first met this young man. He'd misjudged him. Under all that youth was a clever brain. He'd go far.

"I think you're in for some fast-track training when you get out of here," Cass said. He grinned. "I've put a word in, for what that's worth, and let's face it, both your office and mine are going through a staffing crisis. If you still like the job, that is."

The young man nodded. There was still something dark in his eyes, though.

"Something else bugging you, Josh?"

A slow nod. "It's about Luke. Your nephew." His eyes were rolling slightly. He hit a button and the drip in his arm hissed as it pumped more morphine into his body. He licked his lips slightly.

"You know he's not your brother's son, don't you?" The words slurred together as the painkillers took hold.

"What did you say?" Colours in the room sharpened.

"He must have been adopted. His DNA was too different. Nothing to link him to your brother or his wife. You knew, right?" Josh's eyes closed. His breathing levelled out as he was tugged down into a drugged sleep.

Cass stared and the world shimmered. That couldn't be right. They'd been there, in the hospital, when Luke had been born. He'd been there when Jessica had given birth to Christian's son. If the boy on the slab at the morgue wasn't theirs, then where was he?

He checked that Eagleton was okay, and went back outside. The cool air did nothing to fight the burn that raged through him. Solomon, Bright, and wheels within wheels. If Luke hadn't been Christian and Jessica's son, then what had happened to their baby? His heart thumped in his throat.

Cass felt the fingers inside pulling at him again, but this time they weren't cold. They were warm and alive.

ACKNOWLEDGEMENTS

Firstly, a huge thank you to my brilliant agent, Veronique Baxter at David Higham, for clearly bringing me luck. Secondly, an equally big thank you to my editor Jo Fletcher for making my sentences so much better and my book stronger—(please edit these acknowledgements, ta!). Thanks also to both for the wine and the laughs and all the support; it's great to work with people who have become good friends. For technical advice on drugs and death, I couldn't have done without the ever-cheerful Elizabeth Hill and her veterinary expertise. The writer boys who keep me sane, MMS, Mark Morris, Tim Lebbon, Chris Golden, Graham Joyce, Guy Adams and Conrad Williams: thanks for putting up with me! My two career Yodas, Mark Chadbourn and Carole Matthews: your advice has always been invaluable, and you both rock. The Welsh Cottagers, Meloy, Neville, Greenwood, Lewis, Lockley and Volk among others—thanks for the weekends that remind me of what it's really all about: getting the stories out the best we can. Thanks to all at the British Fantasy Society for introducing me to so many writers and making me feel at home. Huge hugs to the Dastardly, to my Slutley, Julian Simpson, for his editorial suggestions and reading the first draft when I needed an opinion, and to Beth Elliott for doing the same with the final draft. And, of course, so many thanks to all the real-life non-writer friends and my family who have to put up with my weirdness from day to day; there isn't enough wine in the world, but I intend to drink it with you. I know that there are others I must have missed here—but it's the first of a trilogy, so I will amend next time round!

Sarah Pinborough
Milton Keynes, 2009